Praise for Pe

"Something truly original for fans of Jane Austen and fans of historical fiction. It's *Pride and Prejudice* meets *Gone with the Wind*—with that kind of romance and excitement."

—Sharon Lathan, bestselling author of
Miss Darcy Falls in Love

"A heart-pounding Western romance... *Pemberley Ranch* is both fresh and a great history primer."

—*Publishers Weekly*

"Caldwell successfully transplants the themes of the original to post-Civil War Texas, where the consequences and the villains are far more dangerous. Both fans of Westerns and *Pride and Prejudice* will enjoy this latest entry in the Austen craze."

—*Booklist*

"This surefire page-turner with Jack Caldwell's heart-pounding standoffs and heart-racing romantic moments is bested only by his real gift in the clever nuances and subtle references."

—*Austenprose*

"I was enthralled by this remarkable and adventurous variation... Caldwell is a skilled storyteller and his debut novel, *Pemberley Ranch*, is sure to entrance and excite lovers of history and the Old West."

—*Austenesque Reviews*

"This is a refreshing look at a Western romance with a touch of intrigue and humor mingled in. Debut author Jack Caldwell has developed some strong major characters, as well as some lovable secondary ones."

—*Thoughts in Progress*

"A successfully written Jane Austen adaptation that is just as perfectly stimulating as the original."

—*Romance Fiction on Suite101*

"Caldwell takes the basics of *Pride and Prejudice* and makes the story his own… a talented storyteller."

—*Diary of an Eccentric*

"Caldwell has taken the stuffiness of Regency England out of the story and allows Austen's characters to relax a bit and let down their hair."

—*Debbie's Book Bag*

"I loved the way Caldwell blended in the Civil War, the grievances of the North and the South, the truly evil bad guys, and of course, the wonderful romance."

—*Life in the Thumb*

"I loved this book, both as a *Pride and Prejudice* spin-off and on its own."

—*In the Hammock*

THE THREE
COLONELS

Jane Austen's

FIGHTING MEN

JACK CALDWELL

sourcebooks
landmark

Published by Sourcebooks Landmark, an imprint of Sourcebooks, Inc.
P.O. Box 4410, Naperville, Illinois 60567-4410
(630) 961-3900
FAX: (630) 961-2168
www.sourcebooks.com

Library of Congress Cataloging-in-Publication Data

Caldwell, Jack.
  The three colonels : Jane Austen's fighting men / by Jack Caldwell.
    p. cm.
  1. Austen, Jane, 1775-1817—Characters—Fiction. 2. Napoleonic Wars, 1800-1815—Fiction. I. Title.
PS3603.A4355T48 2012
813'.6—dc23
                                        2011043339

Printed and bound in the United States of America
BG 10 9 8 7 6 5 4 3 2 1

To Barbara,
who believed in me from the first.

AUTHOR'S NOTE

The Three Colonels is a sequel to the Jane Austen novels *Pride and Prejudice* and *Sense and Sensibility*. I use Austen's characters from these and her other novels in the body of this story.

Austen aficionados differ in opinion as to exactly when during the Georgian/Regency period the novels take place. For matters of continuity, I chose to date the action in the original novels based on the year of publication, rather than the years Austen originally wrote them (1795–1796). I feel justified in this, since Austen substantially edited both *Pride and Prejudice* and *Sense and Sensibility* in the years prior to publication.

Therefore, I have dated *Pride and Prejudice* (published 1813) between 1811 and 1812, while *Sense and Sensibility* (1811) is set in 1810.

By making this choice, I believe I have opened the wonderful Jane Austen universe to great possibilities. I hope you enjoy the results.

—Jack Caldwell
Faribault, Minnesota, July 2011

Dramatis Personae

Delaford Manor, Dorsetshire

Colonel Christopher Brandon, British Army (inactive)—Owner of Delaford Manor, magistrate of Delaford. A veteran of the wars of the French Revolution and the early Napoleonic conflicts, he holds an honorary position in the Life Guards. Close friend to both Colonels Fitzwilliam and Buford and a confidant of Wellington.

Marianne Dashwood Brandon—Wife of Colonel Brandon (1813), mother of Joy Brandon, and friend to Elizabeth Darcy and Jane Bingley

Joy Brandon—Daughter of Christopher and Marianne Brandon (1814)

The Rev. Edward Ferrars—Rector of Delaford Parish

Elinor Dashwood Ferrars—Wife of Edward Ferrars, sister to Marianne Brandon

Mr. McIntosh—Steward of Delaford Manor

Mayfield, Nottinghamshire

Charles Bingley—Head of the Bingley family, who until recently was in trade. Former lessee of Netherfield in Hertfordshire, which he quits in 1814 for an estate of his own in Nottinghamshire, thirty miles from Pemberley. The particular friend of Mr. Darcy.

Jane Bennet Bingley—Wife of Charles Bingley (1812), mother of Susan Frances Bingley

Susan Frances Bingley—Daughter of Charles and Jane Bingley (1813)

Caroline Bingley—Sister to Charles Bingley, friend to Annabella Adams

Louisa Bingley Hurst—Wife of Geoffrey Hurst, sister to Charles and Caroline Bingley

Longbourn, Meryton, Hertfordshire

Thomas Bennet—Owner of Longbourn, head of the Bennet family

Frances Gardiner Bennet—Wife of Thomas Bennet, mother of Jane Bingley, Elizabeth Darcy, Lydia Wickham, Mary Bennet, and Catherine Bennet

Mary Bennet—Daughter of Thomas Bennet

Kitty Bennet—Daughter of Thomas Bennet

Thomas Tucker, Esq—Clerk in Mr. Phillips's law firm

Pemberley, Lambton, Derbyshire

Fitzwilliam Darcy—Owner of Pemberley, head of the Darcy family, nephew to the Earl of Matlock and Lady Catherine de Bourgh, cousin to Colonel Fitzwilliam, friend to Colonel Brandon

Elizabeth Bennet Darcy—Wife of Fitzwilliam Darcy (1812), mother of Bennet Darcy, friend to the Dashwood sisters

Bennet Edward George Darcy—Son and heir of Fitzwilliam and Elizabeth Darcy (1814)

Georgiana Darcy—Only sister to Fitzwilliam Darcy

The Rev. Franklin Southerland—Rector of Kympton Parish

Matlock Manor, Matlock, Derbyshire

Lord Hugh Fitzwilliam, 5th Earl of Matlock—Head of the Fitzwilliam family, brother to Lady Catherine de Bourgh

Lady Alexandria Fitzwilliam, Countess Matlock—Wife of Lord Matlock

Andrew, Viscount Fitzwilliam of Matlock—Eldest son and heir of Lord and Lady Matlock

Colonel the Hon. Richard Fitzwilliam, ——rd Lt. Dragoons, British Army—Second son of Lord and Lady Matlock, veteran of the Peninsular War, comrade of Colonel Buford

Buford Manor, Wales

Mrs. Albertine Buford—Matriarch of the Buford family. Of French stock, her family fled the Revolution.

Philip Buford—Eldest son of Albertine Buford, owner of Buford Manor

Rebecca Buford—Wife of Philip Buford

Colonel Sir John Buford, CB, ——nd Lt. Dragoons, British Army—Second son of Albertine Buford, he earned the Order of the Bath due to his service during the Peninsular War. Confidant of Wellington.

Lady Suzanne Buford Douglas—Daughter of Albertine Buford, wife of Lord Douglas of Scotland

Rosings Park, Hunsford, Kent

Lady Catherine Fitzwilliam de Bourgh—Widow of Sir Lewis de Bourgh, Bart., owner of Rosings, sister to Lord Matlock

Anne de Bourgh—Daughter of Lady Catherine

Mrs. Jenkinson—Companion to Anne de Bourgh

The Rev. William Collins—Rector of Hunsford Parish, cousin to Thomas Bennet, heir to Longbourn

Charlotte Lucas Collins—Wife of William Collins, friend to Anne de Bourgh

Newcastle, Northumberland

Captain George Wickham, ——th Regiment of Foot, British Army—Husband of Lydia Bennet

Lydia Bennet Wickham—Wife of George Wickham (1812)

Major Archibald Denny, British Army—Attached to the General Staff

London

Edward Gardiner—Uncle to the Bennet sisters, brother to Frances Bennet

Madeline Gardiner—Wife of Edward Gardiner

Annabella Adams Norris—Wife of Randolph Norris, schoolmate of Caroline Bingley and Louisa Hurst

Lady Victoria Uppercross—Acquaintance of Sir John

Vienna, Austria

Field Marshall Sir Arthur Wellesley, 1st Duke of Wellington, GCB—Hero of the Peninsular War, head of His Majesty's delegation to the Congress of Vienna (1815), commander of all British forces on the Continent [*]

Lady Beatrice Wellesley—Cousin to Wellington

Countess Roxanne de Pontchartrain—Wife of the Count de Pontchartrain (member of the Royal French delegation), acquaintance of Sir John Buford

Baron Wolfgang von Odbar—Member of the Prussian delegation

Charles Maurice de Talleyrand-Périgord—Prince of Benevento, French foreign minister, and delegate to the Congress of Vienna [*]

Belgium—Waterloo, Brussels, and surrounding areas

Captain Hewitt, British Army

Prince Willem of Orange—Dutch Crown Prince, Wellington's second in command, commander of I Corps [*]

Lieutenant General Sir Henry William Paget, 2nd Earl of Uxbridge, GCB—Commander of British Horse at Waterloo [*]

Lieutenant General Sir Thomas Picton, GCB—Commander of the British 5th Division of Foot [*]

Major General Sir William Ponsonby, KCB—Commander of the Union Cavalry Brigade [*]

Major General Sir John Vandeleur—Commander of the 4th Cavalry Brigade [*]

Major General Sir Hussey Vivian, KCB—Commander of the 6th Cavalry Brigade [*]

Napoleon Bonaparte—Emperor of the French [*]

Prologue

1814. PEACE HAD COME to England.

Since 1740, George III's Great Britain had been in recurrent conflict with its ancient enemy France and all its various governments. She fought Louis XV's Kingdom of France again and again over their colonies in the New World and India. She prevented the expansion of Robespierre's homicidal French Republic and its Revolution. She had spent irreplaceable men and treasure to overthrow the menace of Napoleon Bonaparte as he tried to build an empire out of Europe.

After seventy-four years of recurring warfare, her work was done. The cost in blood and gold had been high, but the country was safe. The self-proclaimed Emperor Napoleon abdicated and was exiled to Elba, a small island in the Mediterranean Sea. A new French king, one finally friendly to Britain, was established on his throne in Paris. A grand congress of all the allies who had stood against the Tyrant was assembled in Vienna to re-draw the post-war world. Britain was master of the subcontinent. Soldiers and sailors were brought back to sweet England, paid off, and sent home.

Only the unpopular conflict with their former American colonies remained, and Prime Minister Lord Liverpool was working hard to end it. Even now, diplomats in Ghent were dancing the steps of diplomacy to fashion a peace treaty between the United States and Great Britain. It was hoped it would be signed before Christmas.

With the fall of Bonaparte and the end of the American War in sight, the people of Regency England dutifully gathered in church, sang their praises to God and king, and then turned their attention to more mundane and heartfelt concerns: the business of living happily ever after.

Dorsetshire

Colonel Christopher Brandon sat at his breakfast table in Delaford Manor, enjoying his second cup of coffee. He had become enamored of the drink while serving in India and on the Continent during the wars against France—first against the godless Jacobites and then later against the Corsican artilleryman who dared name himself emperor of the French. At first, his young, lovely wife could not reason why anyone would drink anything but tea, but she assumed it to be another of his eccentricities. Then one cold, winter afternoon, impatient for the teakettle, she seized her husband's cup and drained half of it. That impulsive act had the result of doubling the amount in the Brandon household budget for coffee.

"Look, Joy. There is your papa."

Christopher looked up, delight spreading over his rather plain features. There was his Marianne, returning his smile, holding the greatest miracle of his life—his infant daughter, Joy. Christopher got to his feet and crossed over to the pair. Holding out his hands, he received the squirming babe from his wife. Christopher kissed and cooed at the child for a few moments before handing Joy to the nurse standing nearby. The baby gurgled happily as she was carried back to the nursery. Christopher then escorted Marianne to the table, pulling out her chair and giving her a discreet peck on the cheek. Marianne returned the gesture with a caress before sitting down to her first cup of the day.

"Goodness, Colonel Brandon, I do not know what gift of yours has given me more pleasure—our daughter, Joy, or a taste for coffee," she exclaimed and not for the first time.

"Indeed, madam. I will have to increase my rents to keep you in beans." He crossed over to the sideboard to fill his wife's plate—a task he had done every morning since her confinement. Marianne declared that his kindness, while appreciated, was unnecessary since their child's birth, but the colonel would not give it up, insisting that he got much enjoyment from performing such a mundane task for her. It was Marianne's happy lot to suffer his attentions.

"Does my habit of expense threaten Joy's dowry, do you think? Heaven forbid! Well, I am afraid she will just have to marry for money."

"Like her mother, my dear?" Christopher chuckled at Marianne's glare.

"I should agree with you, sir. It would serve you right!" But the spat could not last. Marianne could never be displeased for long with those she loved. Her face finally broke out in a smile at their teasing. She shook her head and asked, "Has the paper come?"

"Yes, my dear. It awaits your pleasure," responded Christopher as he placed Marianne's breakfast before her.

Several quiet but pleasant minutes later, the two retired to the library for their morning ritual of reading the newspapers, handling the correspondence, and enjoying a last cup of coffee. The letters were handled first.

"Look, my love, a letter from the Continent," said Marianne as she handed him his share of the post. "And there is an invitation."

It was their usual practice to discuss not only their correspondence, personal and business, but also the news of the world. Since he began the improvement of Marianne Dashwood's mind three years ago, Christopher found that he had developed a valuable partner. Marianne's partner was a loving, sensible person who could keep her emotions in check, while Christopher gained an advisor whose sensibilities often gave him an insight he would not otherwise acquire.

"What news, Husband?"

"'Tis a letter from Wellington in Paris. He and Lady Beatrice send their regards."

"Lady Beatrice? I long to see her again! Did he say how long she was to remain to play hostess for her cousin?"

"Nothing in here, my dear." It was well known that Wellington was estranged from his wife and, therefore, had his cousin with him to tend to all social events.

"Any other news?" she asked as she opened the invitation.

"Besides Talleyrand being up to his old tricks? The same old frustrations—"

"My goodness!" cried Mrs. Brandon, staring at a letter in her hand.

"What? What is it, my dear? What has alarmed you?" Christopher almost shot out of his chair. He saw his wife staring at a letter.

"It cannot be! Oh, could it be true? How?"

"Marianne!" the colonel shouted. It served; he finally got her attention. Marianne waved the invitation at him.

"Do you wish to know the news? You will not believe it."

"Believe it or not, I cannot say until I am apprised of it."

"Christopher, Sir John Buford is to be married—to Miss Caroline Bingley!"

"Oh." Brandon casually returned to his chair and his mail. "Does it say when?"

Marianne was astonished at her husband's lack of reaction. "Did you not hear me? Sir John is marrying—" She gasped. "You knew! You knew and did not tell me!" This time the glare was in earnest.

Christopher smiled sheepishly. "I suspected."

"Oh!" Mrs. Brandon tossed down her letters and sat with a cross expression on her face. After several minutes, she asked, "How long have you *suspected?*"

Her husband had no choice but to answer. "Buford wrote to ask my opinion on the matter in September."

Marianne's eyes flashed dangerously. "Two months!"

"Nearer three, I am afraid."

"Christopher Brandon, I simply cannot believe you have kept this news secret from your wife for nearly three months!" she cried. There was a long pause. "Usually you relent after a week." She picked up a pillow and threw it at him.

Catching her weapon, he ventured, "When is the wedding?"

Trying not to smile, Marianne picked up the invitation. "The middle of January. She marries from Bingley House in London, at St. ——."

"Good. I would not like to travel to Nottinghamshire in winter."

"There is more." She indicated a small note enclosed with the invitation. "Mr. and Mrs. Bingley are giving a ball in the couple's honor at Bingley House on New Year's Eve."

Her husband eyed her. "Do you wish to go?"

"I am tempted, but I cannot bear to leave Joy just now, Christopher."

"But nothing could be easier! We shall bring Joy with us. We shall simply open our house in London early." He reached over and took her hands in his. "You will be fully recovered from your laying-in by then, I think. A ball would do you good."

"Oh, my dear, do you mean it? All of us—Joy's nurse and the rest of the staff? It will take two carriages at least!"

"Two or two hundred—what is that to me when I have the opportunity to dance with you, my Marianne?"

She stroked his face with her hand. "You are too good, sir."

"I am a poor fool saved by your love. You have given me joy—by giving me Joy. I shall spend the rest of my life proving myself worthy of you."

As Marianne's face beamed with affection for her husband, Christopher gathered her into his arms. There was little talking for a quarter-hour.

Elba

The emperor stood on the balcony of his palace surveying his domain, his arms behind his back in the classic at-ease position. After the customary hour-long bath he insisted on each morning, he was dressed in a uniform with the sash of the Legion of Honor peeking from under the coat. Of average height—he was four inches taller than the five feet two inches commonly believed—the casual observer would not think much of him unless he saw his eyes and the grim look on his face.

His wife, Marie-Louise, and son were *guests*—prisoners actually—of the Austrians in Parma. The Treaty of Fontainebleau had not given him much—this spit of land, a thousand soldiers, and two million francs. But it was enough—enough to start again. His lucky star would never desert him.

A servant interrupted his musings. "Your Excellency," he announced, "*déjeuner* is ready." Exactly on time—the emperor insisted on it. He had a passion for consistency and routine.

"*Merci*," he replied in the Italian-accented French that he had not been able to overcome in thirty-five years. He returned inside and sat alone before the first of the two meals he would consume that day, this one of well-done sautéed chicken, croissants, and heavily watered Chambertin wine.

Such was the change in his life. A year ago, he would have been involved in the morning *levee*, with aides, generals, and diplomats scurrying about, carrying out orders that had shaken the world. As usual, the emperor left half his meal on the plate before retiring into his office.

The Allies thought they were kind to give him this empire—one hundred thousand souls on Elba—while they placed that fool of a Bourbon onto the throne of France. A lesser man either would have accepted his fate or despaired of his condition. But he was not like lesser men. Destiny was not through with him, he knew. His preparations were almost complete.

Soon, very soon, Napoleon Bonaparte knew it would be time.

Chapter 1

London

IT WAS A NIGHT for memories.

An unsettled Caroline Bingley silently sat before her looking glass in a dress of fine ivory and peach silk while her maid finished her hair, her sisters, Louisa Hurst and Jane Bingley, smiling and observing. Tonight was the New Year's Eve ball given by her brother at Bingley House in London in honor of her upcoming marriage to Colonel Sir John Buford. She had striven all her life for such a moment, and it had finally arrived.

"Oh, Caroline!" cried Louisa. "The dress is superb! I have never seen you in better looks. Does she not look well, Jane?"

With quiet sincerity, Jane agreed. "She does, indeed. But how can she not? This is a special night for you, Sister."

"Sir John will be pleased, I am sure." Louisa actually giggled, to Caroline's mortification.

The maid halted her labors. "Are you pleased with your hair, miss?" she asked nervously.

Be kind, be kind, Caroline reminded herself. "Your efforts are to be commended, Abigail." Caroline smiled a small smile to herself. Only she would have an abigail named Abigail.

The maid sighed in relief. "Just a few more minutes, miss."

Caroline stared into her reflection. *Is this the woman Sir John sees: a dark-haired lady, elegant and refined, yet with just a touch of the bloom of youth in her cheeks? Or does he see through the disguise to behold the woman desperately escaping her roots in trade? Everything my father wanted for me—everything my mother taught me—is now in my hands. Wife to a respected, landed gentleman and knight of the realm, as well. I am happy with my choice. I am.*

But why am I uneasy?

Mixed with Caroline's joy and anxiety was a bit of weariness, for she had just undergone the most trying four and twenty months in her life.

She recalled the preparations for her last large ball.

The late Mr. Bingley, embarrassed by his position in life, worked hard so that his children would not. He succeeded in improving his situation at the cost of his relationship with those for whom he sacrificed his health. His wife, accepting his goals but resentful of his attentions to business, had pined so much during his frequent absences that a relatively mild influenza finally took her to her reward. Unprepared to raise his children himself, he sent them to the finest schools in the land where they were taught many things. Some of those lessons were useful, and some were not, but love of a parent was not among either. Any interaction Mr. Bingley did have with his progeny in his last years—before overwork drove him to his grave—consisted of exhorting them to embrace their hard-won gentility. There was nothing as wonderful as being among the highest members of the London *ton*, he told them repeatedly.

However, he taught his children ill. Old Bingley saw only the outward appearances of respectability; he had no appreciation for the hard work and duty in which a truly responsible gentleman must engage. He left a tainted legacy.

Charles Bingley, his heir, was fortunate, for among the first he met at school was a remarkable older student from Derbyshire. Fitzwilliam Darcy was attracted to the open goodness of his new, young schoolmate, and they soon became fast friends.

Louisa and Caroline were not as lucky. Quickly falling into the society of the most superior of their fellow students, they learned all that was correct and fashionable but none that was kind. They perfected the art of the cutting remark and snide aside and developed a taste for gossip. At least Caroline had taken her studies seriously. While never a great reader, she found a natural affinity for mathematics and music. Caroline took pride in this, for the mistress of a great estate must both manage and entertain.

Acquiring a great estate was the Bingley sisters' lifetime goal. The only way to bury their roots in trade forever was to marry into a family of some consequence. Louisa was able to attract the attentions of Mr. Geoffrey Hurst, a man of small estate and less sense. Caroline looked higher. If she needed a husband of respectability, who better to fill that requirement than her brother's friend, Fitzwilliam Darcy? He had everything she had been taught to look for in a match: estate, fortune, fashionable manners, good taste, and eligibility. That he was handsome was very agreeable. That love might enter into the equation never crossed Caroline's mind.

For almost three years, Caroline labored to attach herself to Mr. Darcy and his estate of Pemberley. All would end in failure on a summer's night at Pemberley when Mr. Darcy responded to her ill-judged attack on Elizabeth Bennet with the declaration that, "…it is many months since I have considered her as one of the handsomest women of my acquaintance." In her room that evening, Caroline wept in rage and frustration, her dreams shattered. She had been denied her rightful place by a mere country girl, a chit with no family or fortune to recommend her. Eliza was not even as pretty as her sister Jane, who had bewitched Charles. The unfairness of it all nearly consumed Caroline. It only grew worse a few months later when Charles married Jane, and Darcy married Elizabeth.

Caroline had no choice but to act with perfect civility if she wished to retain any connection with the Darcy family. If she could not attain Pemberley, then she had to acquire another estate. The Darcy connection was vital to that goal. Still, in her heart, Caroline cursed the upstart who had crushed her dreams. Her only satisfaction was her belief that the *ton* would see through Eliza Bennet as quickly as she had, and the dark reaches of her heart gloried in the anticipation of the chit's mortification.

The opportunity for Caroline's revenge took place on an evening a few months later at Almack's. The occasion nominally was Georgiana Darcy's debut; however, what caught society's interest was Mrs. Darcy's presentation to the first circles. As Jane was to share in the honors, Caroline was invited to attend.

Riding to Almack's that night in the Hursts' carriage wearing a gorgeous red dress, Caroline was in fine spirits sitting beside Miss Mary Bennet. That was a very strange circumstance. Caroline had developed a friendship through music with Eliza's plain, moralistic sister. Under her guidance, Mary had taken to spending more attention on her wardrobe. The girl now looked to be rather pretty. Caroline felt certain that Mary, in a beautiful gown Caroline had chosen, would embarrass no one. She looked forward to the response the *ton* would have to the new Mrs. Darcy.

Her brother and Jane arrived at the same time she did, and they shared an affectionate greeting. Caroline could not help but notice the glow Jane showed. The cause was no mystery; Jane had confided that she was with child just before they left Netherfield. Caroline was oddly pleased at this news. She supposed it was just happiness for her brother. She did not know whether she would enjoy being an aunt.

Caroline's first indication that the evening would not go as planned occurred when the Darcy party was introduced. Every eye turned to them, and the assembly was not disappointed. Georgiana was lovely, and Miss Kitty Bennet, who had become a companion of sorts to Darcy's sister, was shown to best advantage. All was as Caroline expected. However, Elizabeth Darcy was stunning. Never had Caroline seen anyone, much less Eliza, take attention from Jane Bingley, but there was no doubt about it: Mrs. Darcy was a goddess, and her debut at Almack's was a rousing success.

As Caroline endeavored to temper her disappointment at the punch table, she became aware of conversation buzzing around her. She could not put her finger on it until she—*accidentally*—overheard her friends and acquaintances among the *ton*, including her best friend from school, Annabella Adams, discussing her failure to secure Mr. Darcy. Caroline realized with horror that the *ton* was looking for its next victim, and she was their target! She turned almost as red as the dress she wore as she heard their cruel jests. She had no idea she had been so obvious.

As Caroline made her way back to her party, some of her so-called friends confronted her, attacking her with perfect civility; she knew exactly what they were doing, for she was a mistress of the art. Stunned, Caroline deflected as much of the abuse as possible before seeking the sanctuary of the library. Holding back tears, she nearly collided with a gentleman standing nearby.

Once in the library, she collapsed upon the sofa and let free her emotions. For years, she had tried so hard. She craved acceptance by the *ton*. To hide from her roots in trade, she had acted as her friends had taught her—with superior carriage, superior dress, and superior opinions. Now she saw it was all fantasy. The world she had built around her was made of smoke. She had no friends, and everything she was taught to believe to be true had turned out to assure her of nothing but pain.

She wept for loneliness and for lost opportunities. She shed tears over fears of being adrift forever between the shop and society, never fitting in with either. She was in agony, for she was certain she would never win a gentleman's admiration.

It was there she was found by Louisa and Mary, and it was into Mary's arms she cried her heart out.

That night, Caroline Bingley was reborn.

In the glass, Caroline saw Jane go to the door and ask for a maid. "Please look in the nursery and ask of Miss Susan," she requested.

"The child is fine, Jane," Caroline remarked as Jane closed the door. "You must not worry. If your servants do not know their business, perhaps you should send them away."

"Oh, our people are quite competent. I suppose I am a little silly, but I cannot help but think of Susan." Jane smiled. "When you have your children, Caroline, you will understand." Jane's beautiful face paled as she realized her *faux pas*. "Louisa! How thoughtless of me!"

Caroline saw that Louisa hid her hurt well. "Never you mind, Jane. You are quite right. Caroline will sing a different tune when it is her turn."

Caroline said nothing as she watched Jane continue to apologize to Louisa. Poor Louisa—married all these years and no children to show for it! Caroline hoped the fault lay with her brother-in-law. If Louisa were barren, Caroline considered, might she be affected as well? Caroline did not think much about having children, but she knew that society would condemn any failure of producing an heir. She did not bring much more to the marriage to Sir John than her dowry, and while it was sizable, it did little to offset her want of suitable relations. If *she* were barren—Caroline could no longer bear to think upon it.

"You must come for Easter," Jane told Louisa. "Susan would be desolate without her Aunt Hurst in attendance."

"Susan is but a babe. She hardly knows me, I am sure."

"No. She loves you to distraction, I am certain of it," Jane insisted. She turned to Caroline. "Susan will miss her godmother, too. But you will be on your honeymoon, so her other aunts must console her in recompense for her loss."

Caroline shook her head at her sister's blind goodness. Jane, sweet Jane! Who could not like Jane?

When Caroline had found herself sitting in a Meryton church on a December morning watching her brother's wedding, she at length had reconciled herself to the union. True, she did not have the connections Caroline had been taught to desire in a sister-in-law, but Jane was sure to prove to be a loving partner to Charles, a good mistress of Netherfield, and an attentive mother, and that counted for much. Caroline would be there to watch this unfold, for she could not live with the Hursts, and she was too clever to want to pay the whole of the expense of living in Bingley House in Town.

Caroline tried to be of use to her brother and sister, but the servants would not mind her commands. When she complained to Charles, she discovered to her horror that they were acting under his express orders. There would be only one mistress of Netherfield, and her name was Mrs. Bingley. Caroline learned there was a bit of steel beneath Jane's kind and soft exterior.

The relationship between Jane and Caroline grew much improved during and after Mrs. Bingley's confinement. Caroline took over many of Jane's duties prior to the birth, but took pains to act (for the most part) as she believed Jane would wish and never hesitated to ask for direction. That she disagreed with many of Jane's decisions did not stop her from holding her nose and acting correctly.

Still, Caroline was stunned that later Jane would have her join Mr. Darcy as godparents to her daughter. As astonished as Caroline was to learn that, despite all expectations, she grew to adore little Susan Frances. She took true joy in the child. Her efforts were not lost upon Mrs. Darcy,

who was visiting her sister and was in the early stages of her own confinement. The two old adversaries finally had something in common—love
for Charles and Jane's daughter.

The door opened again, and Caroline's initial look of annoyance at
yet another interruption in her preparations changed instantly upon her
recognition of the woman in maroon standing in the doorway.

"May I come in?" asked Mary Bennet Tucker.

Without hesitation, Caroline rose and moved to greet her visitor with
a smile, upsetting much of Abigail's work.

"Mary, my dear! Come in! I am so very glad to see you." She kissed
the slim, dark-haired woman on the cheek with genuine affection before
allowing Mrs. Tucker to accept the welcome of the other ladies. Reclaiming
Mary's hands, Caroline swept her critical eye over the lady's dress.

"Mary, I am sure I taught you better. The color of your gown comple-
ments your eyes, but the cut! It is positively matronly!"

"Caroline!" protested Jane. "Mary's dress is lovely."

Mary smiled. "No, Jane, Caroline is right. My dress is modest by her
standards, but as I am married, I think it suits me better." In a manner
reminiscent of Elizabeth Darcy, one of Mary's eyebrows rose as the woman
took in Caroline's décolletage. "It is certainly not as shocking as yours."

"Shocking? Mary, you must remember I am *not* yet married."

"And you wish for your intended to remain your intended?"

"Precisely!" The two laughed lightly.

Jane shook her head. "That is unnecessary, Caroline. Sir John is
violently in love with you."

Some of Caroline's smile slipped from her face. She did not doubt Sir
John's admiration, but love? No, it was too much for which to hope. Jane
had the very good fortune to marry for love, but that was as rare as hen's
teeth. Caroline only hoped for a marriage better than Louisa's. Mutual
respect was enough.

"I must go down to see to the preparations," said Jane as she kissed Caroline's cheek before leaving the room. Caroline returned to her dressing table to allow the long-suffering maid to repair her hair while Mary and Louisa conversed.

Caroline's friendship with Mary Bennet was as much of a surprise to the participants as it had been to their relations. Two more different people could scarcely be found. While neither were classic beauties like Jane, only Caroline took pains in her appearance. If left to her own devices, Mary would wear the same dark, dreary dress every day. Mary had time only for her books, particularly Fordyce's *Sermons to Young Women*, while Caroline lived for gossip.

However, the two were more alike than they knew. Both felt unequal to the world about them—Caroline for her lack of connections and Mary for her lack of attractiveness. They both took on superior airs, knowing all the time the only ones deceived were themselves. They were actors trapped in their roles, and Jane's and Elizabeth's marriages were the unanticipated agents of the two ladies' liberation.

Caroline had no occupation but to help Jane receive her daily invasion by the female contingent from Longbourn—occasionally Mary, often Kitty, but always Mrs. Bennet. Caroline's first impulse was to flee these meetings, but she thought better of it. If Jane was to be her sister, then Caroline must treat her as such, and Jane needed her support, even though Caroline felt that she did not quite trust her. For Mrs. Bennet was full of advice—rarely helpful, sometimes contradictory, often ignorant and outrageous, and always expressed in a loud, rude voice. There was nothing for it, for Mrs. Bennet would brook no request to temper her voice or opinions, and sweet Jane would not throw the baggage out. Caroline therefore attempted to find as much diversion from these performances as she might.

As the Mistress of Longbourn continued to hold court, Caroline's attention invariably would be drawn to her new sisters. At first, she found them trite and stupid, but in studying them day after day, Caroline realized there was more to Mary than met the eye. She would say little, save for some inappropriate moralistic comment or a rather obvious quotation of scripture. However, Caroline would soon see that, while uninformed, Mary meant well, but she suffered from the total neglect of her mother. She sought attention; that was why the girl would leap to perform on the pianoforte given any encouragement.

As for Kitty, the insipid girl needed better examples than her mother or her outlawed sister, Mrs. Wickham.

Caroline developed a plan: If she could be of no use to her brother and his wife, then her occupation would be to help improve her new sisters, for her own sake as well as theirs. Apparently, Elizabeth Darcy came to the same realization and quickly invited Kitty to act as companion to Miss Darcy.

With Kitty's removal to Pemberley, Caroline spent even more time with Mary. Caroline found the task more pleasant than she expected. Desperate for a companion, Mary was still leery of Lizzy's nemesis. They found their common ground in music. Before, Mary played for attention, and Caroline played because it was expected. As they discussed music and technique, they both discovered that they truly loved the sound of the pianoforte. A friendship grew as the two spent many hours in pleasant occupation.

At first, Mary resisted any attempt to broaden her choice of reading material beyond the Bible or Fordyce's *Sermons*. Finally, Caroline suggested poetry, starting with the Psalms. Mary had not considered that Holy Scripture also could be regarded as literature, and her curiosity was inflamed. A few discussions with Caroline showed that, while King David was writing of his love of God, it could also be shown that the Psalms spoke of the universality of love—including that between a man and a woman. It was as if a light had been lit inside of Mary. She began devouring any book of poetry in her father's or brothers' libraries. Caroline enjoyed poetry as well and introduced Mary to some of Shakespeare's more risqué sonnets, to the girl's embarrassed delight. This had an odd impact on Mary; she began to spend more time on her appearance and seemed to be more attentive during the other ladies' discussions of fashion.

Caroline had never before had a friend like Mary. Most of her acquaintances were people of fashion, cultivated not because of common interest and pleasant conversation but for the value of their connections. In Mary, a girl who could bring her nothing, Caroline had a protégée in whose company she found contentment. There was no need of performance. Mary was care and ease.

In the aftermath of the debacle at Almack's, Louisa offered what consolation she could, but it was Mary who saved Caroline, and in a most considerate manner. She simply left Caroline's Bible open by her bedside, a particular passage of the gospels indicated by an orange feather.

When Caroline found what Mary had done, she gasped; it was the story of Christ and the adulteress. *Is this how Mary sees me?* she had thought. Caroline held her temper, recalling how *she* taught Mary to see all of the possibilities of scripture. It was time for the teacher to learn.

Forcing herself to read and reread the familiar lines, she finally saw to what Mary had been alluding. Caroline had sinned, and her pride had made her cruel. However, the *ton*'s actions were just as extreme and hateful as the village elders' in the scripture passage. "*Let he who is without sin cast the first stone,*" said Christ, but He also said, "*Your sins are forgiven—go and sin no more.*" For the first time, Caroline had hope. She could be forgiven by those she hurt—as long as she stopped hurting them.

It was the beginning of the new Caroline Bingley, and she owed it all to Mary Bennet.

Abigail had seen to a messenger at the door and returned with a small package. "Miss Bingley, a box has been delivered from Sir John."

Caroline opened it and found inside a beautiful string of pearls with a cameo of carnelian shell, but no note. The profile was definitely her own.

"Oh, Caroline!" cried Louisa. "How lovely! It is a shame it does not complement the comb in your hair."

Never removing her eyes from the cameo, Caroline said to Abigail, "Remove the comb."

"But, Miss Bingley, your hair is done! If I remove the comb, you will be late."

"Am I speaking Italian, you foolish girl?" Caroline snapped. "Remove it! Redo my hair! Do you think I shall attend this ball without wearing my intended's gift?"

"Caroline…" said Mary in a quiet, reproachful tone.

Caroline colored. Mary was the only person in the world who could speak to her so without fear of a quarrel.

"Abigail, it is my wish to honor Sir John. Exchange my comb for another—please."

Abigail, muttering apologies, got to work, but Caroline did not attend. She had put on the pearls, and she saw how the cameo rested just above her bosom. It was lovely, slightly risqué, and definitely became her.

"Beautiful," breathed Louisa.

Not for the first time, Caroline began feeling odd flutterings in her stomach. She had no idea what it signified.

It was a hard thing indeed to admit that one's life was built around a lie, but there was nothing for it. Caroline had no choice but to realize that, while she had developed many admirers and acquaintances among the *ton*, she had few true friends. She was mortified to see how she had cut people of character—people whose friendship she should have cultivated—simply to impress people of fashion. She had sacrificed any hope of intimacy with her brother's wife because of her snobbery. She had joined in with jests and cruelties and thought little of it—until it was directed at her. For almost ten years, she had lived thus, and all she had to show at the end was a life as an old maid without friends and without a lover.

The latter was her choice. There were those who would have been willing to enter into an arrangement, offer *carte blanche*, but Caroline would not hear of it. She would be honorably married or die alone, and she knew without a doubt that she would die alone.

Caroline now had a new occupation: the rebuilding of Caroline Bingley. Mary and Louisa were her confidantes during this endeavor. They all agreed that the first person Caroline needed to approach was Mrs. Bingley. It was accomplished after all returned to Netherfield, and it achieved as much success as could be expected.

She dreaded the interview with the Darcys. Her sin there was more grievous, and to be honest, a little jealousy was still in her heart. Gathering up her courage, Caroline made her full apologies when the Darcys and Kitty stopped at Netherfield on their journey back to Pemberley with Mary in attendance. After all, surely the Darcys could not cut her completely in front of witnesses, could they?

Mr. Darcy looked to his wife. It was clear that for *her* he would do anything. Elizabeth colored and looked at her toes, considering. Then, with a smile, firmly secure in her practice of thinking only of the past as it gave her pleasure, she forgave Caroline everything and embraced her as a sister.

Restored to a level somewhere between civility and intimacy, Caroline began observing the Darcys closely. To be sure, Mrs. Darcy was unorthodox with her impertinent teasing of her husband, but Mr. Darcy seemed to relish her behavior, and Caroline was startled to hear him openly laugh. She could not recall ever hearing that sound come from him before in all the years she had known him. What jealousy remained in her died as she saw the open affection and respect each held for the other.

"There, miss. Is your hair satisfactory?" Abigail asked.

Caroline looked at her reflection. "Yes, that will do." After a pause, she remembered to add, "Thank you, Abigail."

Flustered, the girl exclaimed, "Oh, miss! Thank you, but it was just my duty."

Caroline sighed. She never realized that being good was such hard work.

"I am ready, Abigail." She stood to exit the room and go downstairs, her mind once again preoccupied by one of the most notorious rakes in society.

Chapter 2

CAROLINE DESCENDED THE STAIRS of Bingley House with Louisa and Mary. The Bingleys and Hursts were assembled and visibly relieved at her appearance. Also in attendance was a rather intense young man dressed in much less fine attire than the others.

"Ah, Mr. Tucker!" said Caroline. "Here is your wayward wife, sir. I hope you are well."

"Perfectly well, Miss Bingley. On behalf of my wife, I thank you for the invitation."

"That is quite unnecessary. How could I have such a ball without my friends? It is I who must thank you for attending."

Tucker offered his arm to Mary, who took it readily. At that moment, the Darcys, together with Georgiana and Kitty, made their appearance, and the various families spent some time in welcome.

Caroline had greeted all her guests when she noticed a figure in black with a sash of red standing in a shadowy doorway. She could almost make out his intense blue eyes staring at her. As Colonel Sir John Buford strode towards her, Caroline felt weak. She could not move if she wanted to—and she did not want to move. Within a breath, her intended was before her, ignoring all others around them.

"Good evening, Caroline," Buford said as his eyes strayed from her face to her bodice.

"Good evening, Sir John." Her voice was reasonably steady.

His hand slowly reached for and held the cameo, the back of his fingers gently caressing her skin. "I see you have worn your gift. I am pleased that it looks so well on you."

Caroline did not blush—she *flushed* from her cheeks down, due to his attentions. "I… I must thank you for such a wonderful gift. But how was it made? I sat for no commission. How did you come by my likeness?"

He placed it upon her bosom. "From memory," he stated, blue eyes boring into her. Violating all propriety, his lips descended upon hers with the lightest of kisses. Straightening up, he looked at his astonished audience with arrogant confidence as though he were challenging anyone to rebuke him for claiming what was his.

A new feeling joined the flutterings, but this time Caroline knew the name of it, for she had felt this before. *Desire.* At that moment, she cared not what other people thought; she only wanted their wedding to be the next day rather than a fortnight away.

As soon as the sentiment washed over her, she reached for her vaunted self-control. This would not do. They had guests coming, and she would not embarrass herself before their guests. She gave her intended an arch look.

"Control, sir!" she whispered. "Why, you act like a schoolboy instead of a colonel in His Majesty's army! Take your position beside me, Sir John." With that she entwined her arm in his, drawing him to stand at her side. Turning to the others, she said, "You really must forgive him. He is only a soldier, after all."

"I think I need a drink," said Hurst.

Rather than chastised, Sir John was pleased. Once again, Caroline had passed a test.

Caroline had heard of Sir John Buford, Colonel of Cavalry in His Majesty's ——nd Light Dragoons, awarded the Bath for his actions in Spain with Wellesley, now Duke of Wellington. He was celebrated as dashing, brave, well off, charming, intelligent, and exceptionally handsome. It was also whispered that he was a rake and cuckolder—a seducer of bored ladies of the *ton*. If Caroline believed half of the stories Annabella Adams, now Mrs. Norris, told about him, it would seem he bedded a quarter of the well-bred wives in London.

Caroline gave the man no notice. If she wanted a thirty-year-old soldier, there was always Mr. Darcy's cousin, Colonel Fitzwilliam. Consequently, she was completely mystified when Sir John began to seek out her company at Almack's. He asked for the supper dance and was very gallant towards her.

At first, she was amused. If Sir John thought he was going to get under her petticoat, he had another thought coming. But as the weeks went on, she continually met him at dances, at dinner parties, and in the park. It seemed the man went out of his way to put himself in her path. He was always the perfect gentleman. Never once did he attempt to take advantage of her, and their conversations were not the flirtatious ones of would-be lovers. Instead, they talked of music, family, and even current events. Their conversations seemed to be more interview than courtship.

As spring turned to summer, Caroline found that Sir John visited her several times a week. She had to admit she enjoyed his company and looked forward to their talks, but she was disturbed as well. It was true she was five-and-twenty, but her reputation was all she had. Was she endangering her future by encouraging such a man?

She could tell that Charles, Jane, and even Louisa were uneasy as well. Strangely enough, the Darcys did not seem concerned in the least that she was so often in Sir John's company. At first, Caroline thought the former animosity between the two ladies had reasserted itself, but it turned out that Eliza and Darcy had received such good reports of Sir John from both Colonel Fitzwilliam and another acquaintance of theirs, a Colonel Brandon, they seemed to promote the gentleman. Caroline thought it odd that people as upright as the Darcys would claim close acquaintance with a man of Sir John's reputation, but she was relieved, too. Yet she remained undecided.

In August, Caroline attended a ball given by an acquaintance of her friend, Annabella. She had begun to distance herself from Sir John, uncertain of her feelings or his intentions. Unfortunately, the attentions paid to Caroline by the colonel had affected her reputation in at least one person's mind. In a darkened hallway, an inebriated Sir Horace Washburn began taking liberties with Caroline's person, declaring his desire to take her as his mistress. Outraged beyond words, she had only begun to fight back when the baronet was snatched bodily from her person. Sir John, in a cool rage, looked the villain full in the face before casting the drunken man to the floor. In a clipped, emotionless voice, he informed Washburn that should he touch Miss Bingley again, he would not call him out but simply run him through. With only a word of concern for her physical state, he seized Caroline's arm and escorted her home to Bingley House in silence.

A few days later, Sir John called upon her, acting as if the incident had never happened.

Finally, as September began to fade and Caroline's time in London was coming to an end, she felt the need to settle her thoughts. When Sir John called, she suggested a walk to a nearby park, Abigail trailing behind as chaperone.

"Sir John, I apologize for not doing so before, but I must thank you for the uncommon gallantry you showed on my behalf last month with Sir Horace," she began.

"Think nothing of it. Any gentleman would do the same for a lady in distress," he replied.

Any gentleman? she thought. *Does he have no feelings for me?* "That may be, sir, but it is you who have earned my thanks." They walked on in silence for the next few minutes, Caroline's feelings in turmoil. They came to a rather private spot along the walk, and Sir John suggested a rest. Caroline was puzzled by his choice, especially when he did not join her on the bench. Instead, he held up his hand, indicating that Abigail should keep her distance, and looked up at the sky.

"I understand you are to leave London for Hertfordshire soon," he began.

"Yes, my brother is removing to a new estate recently purchased in Nottinghamshire. My family needs me to help prepare for the move."

"It is a fine thing to own one's own place," he replied rather offhandedly. "I am sure your sister will miss her relations."

"That is true, to be sure. Mrs. Bingley would be very affected were not her sister, Mrs. Darcy, residing in the next county."

"Of course, of course. Pemberley is in Derbyshire. How would you like living that far north?"

How would I like living there? How can he ask that, knowing my pursuit of Mr. Darcy? she thought. "Very well, I think, but one place is like another."

"I see." He was silent for a while. "Miss Bingley, I have a request. May I be permitted, or do I ask too much, to call upon you in Nottinghamshire?"

Surprised by the request, she blurted out, "Why?"

"Why?"

In for a penny, she thought. "Yes, why? What are your intentions, Colonel?"

"My intentions?" he cried. "They should be clear enough!"

Caroline was horrified. *It is as I feared. He wants me for his mistress.*

Sir John paced about in an agitated manner, muttering, "Too soon, too soon," then he paused and took a breath. "Please forgive my outburst. It was not my intention to speak now; you do not know me well enough.

But, madam, you force my hand! I shall speak, and then my fate shall be in your hands. But before I make my request known to you, I must ask you to indulge me this small thing. I must speak about my past. Will you allow me to speak my part in full before you respond? Afterwards I shall answer any questions you have. Please grant me this favor. I know I ask much."

Caroline silently nodded.

"My reputation has preceded me, I fear, and I must, in all good conscience, make this confession. I have not lived as I should. I know this, and I am ashamed. Some men make light of this; they are 'men of the world,' but I know better. For some time, I have failed as a gentleman." He smiled slightly. "I am sure you have heard tales."

Caroline blanched.

"Be not alarmed, madam," he quickly added, "I may have lived selfishly, but as God is my witness, I have never compromised the innocence of any maiden, low or high born. And I have never forced my attentions upon any woman. All of my... associations have been with aggressive, experienced partners from among the *ton*—"

"Other men's wives, you mean!" Caroline could not help blurting out.

"If you speak of women—I do not use the term *ladies*—who hold their marriage vows so lightly that they flirt with their lovers at Westminster Cathedral itself, then yes, that is who I mean. But know this—I was not their first, and I was certainly not their last! Do not pity their husbands. They are too busy with their own dalliances to mind their duties, as you so unfortunately discovered." At this, Caroline blushed and turned away. "Forgive me—I have distressed you."

"No, I am well, I assure you," Caroline replied.

"You are too kind," Sir John said softly. He looked out into the greenery about them. "I tell you these things not to excuse my behavior—for it cannot be excused—but that you know the whole truth of it. I sought no one out. I was always approached. But I was weak. I sought a few moments pleasure and found emptiness." He sighed and turned to her. "You, so pure, cannot know how pathetic a life I lived."

Can I not, Colonel?

"Three years ago, I suddenly saw the waste my life had become. I saw men die for friends, for their king, for a flag! I vowed to be worthy of them, of my late father—to be a gentleman again. Since my return to Britain, I have lived as I should, no matter what the gossips of society say. I have reformed. I give you my word before God as an officer in the king's army."

Caroline was silent for a while. The colonel's confession had the ring of truth. What mortification he must have suffered to make such a declaration! How was she to judge him, given *her* sins? There was one issue not resolved—for how *many* sins must he be forgiven? Did she really want to know? Yet, she could not be a woman and not ask.

In a small voice, Caroline asked, "How many women?"

Sir John struggled. "Though they do not deserve it, as a man wishing to be a gentleman, I will not name them. But I am sure it is far less than the number you have been told."

"That will not do, Colonel. Is it more than ten?"

Sir John looked away and finally said, "You can count my relationships upon one hand and not use all the fingers."

"Am I acquainted with any of them?" she had to ask, knowing his answer.

"I cannot say. Only know this—I would never insult my friends by having them or any of that set enter my house."

Caroline was silent again. She had only one question left, and she feared to voice it. Finally, she found courage. "What do you want of me, Colonel?"

"I see fear in your eyes. I do not blame you. What tales you have undoubtedly been told! I am still afraid to state my desires—yes, I am afraid! But I must. Please do not give me your answer yet. Take time to consider it carefully. I place my trust in your justice." Sir John drew breath. "I wish you to become my mistress—"

Caroline gasped.

"—the mistress of my house, the mother of my heirs, the wife of my body. I formally ask to court you with the object of matrimony."

To say that Caroline was stunned would be incorrect. She would have to be sensible to be stunned. It was the very last thing she expected Sir John to say. Frozen on the bench, questions flooded her mind.

Matrimony? He wants to marry me? Sir John Buford wishes to court me? Do I want him to? How can I marry a rake—a former rake? Was I so much better? What I did to poor Jane, who would never hurt anyone... Sir John... I would be Lady Buford—stop it! I am closer to six and twenty than not. Would a better offer ever be made? He is handsome, and he has been kind. My God, he threatened to kill for me! He wants me—has protected me. What would I give to him? On and on her thoughts flew, but in the end, she had no choice.

"Colonel Buford, you ask to court me?" she asked.

"Yes, Miss Bingley. Please take all the time you need to—"

She held up her hand. "Nottinghamshire is some distance from London or Wales. Is that a difficulty for you?"

"No distance would be too far."

"And for how long would you court me before expecting an answer?"

"You are my heart's choice, therefore, I will await your—"

"Please, Colonel." She sighed. "I see no profit in such an exercise when it would make no difference with the eventual answer. Therefore, I shall give you my answer now. Yes, I believe that you have reformed your life, and I forgive you all past transgressions. No, you may not court me. Yes, I will marry you."

"Pardon me?" Sir John asked, confused.

Caroline smiled. "Colonel Buford, I see no reason to postpone the inevitable. I would be happy and honored to become your wife."

Surprise gave way to joy, which gave way to satisfaction on Sir John's face. Regaining control, he reached out, helping Caroline to rise from the bench. He softly began kissing the back of her hands while saying, "Caroline, my own."

Caroline was almost overcome by the sight of this extraordinarily handsome man taking such liberties with her. The skin under his lips tingled, and the memory of walking into the Netherfield library while her brother and Jane were stealing a moment of affection ignited a longing of... *something*. She was unsure what that craving was, but perhaps if she imitated her relations' activity, she would discover it.

"John," said Caroline, using his Christian name, "if I must marry a man with your reputation, should not I receive some benefit from it?" At his renewed confusion, she added, "Surely you can do better than *this*," as she indicated her hands. She had forgotten all about Abigail.

Caroline never realized that blue eyes could become so dark. Sir John lowered her hands to her side and took her into his arms, a slow smile creeping over his face.

"Oh yes, Caroline, much better."

He lowered his lips to hers. The kiss started light and tender, but began to build in passion as Caroline surprised herself by kissing him back. He drew her even more firmly into his embrace, and the warmth of his closeness set a fire that threatened to engulf her body. Caroline's hands rose to his broad shoulders, hard and firm beneath his coat, when she felt his tongue brush her lips. Startled back into control, she pushed herself away slightly.

"Yes... much better, sir. But we should return to the house, I think." Caroline smiled weakly. She quickly became mortified on catching sight of a shocked Abigail.

"Of course, of course. Let me give you my arm," her newly betrothed said. As the couple began making their way back to Bingley House, Sir John asked, "To whom should I speak? Your brother, I should think. May I approach him this evening?"

Caroline shook herself and answered, "Yes, speak to Charles."

Only later would she remember that he and Jane were at Netherfield.

The Buford family of Wales was announced in the ballroom of Bingley House. The dowager Mrs. Albertine Buford came forward to greet her son and his intended. Walking beside her were Mr. and Mrs. Philip Buford, the current masters of the family estate, and her daughter, Lady Suzanne Douglas.

"Caroline!" cried Mrs. Buford in her slight French accent that thirty years in Wales had not eliminated. "How lovely you look tonight. And this is very becoming," she said, eyeing the cameo. "My son spoils you."

Caroline blushed while Sir John looked on with pleasure. "Thank you, Mrs. Buford."

"Caroline! I must insist—it is *Mother* Buford! Rebecca is Mrs. Buford now."

Caroline tried not to roll her eyes. "Yes, of course, Mother Buford." She greeted the others. "Philip, Rebecca, Lady—er, Suzanne."

Sir John frowned. "Is Lord Douglas not coming?"

Lady Douglas took Caroline's hand. "Forgive us—tenant troubles in Scotland. He promises most firmly he will be present for the wedding."

The Buford family continued to exchange pleasantries with everyone while once again Caroline wondered at the kindness shown her. For such a fine family, they were certainly informal. They were undoubtedly standoffish in the beginning. Why, Sir John, a second son, came with two thousand pounds a year! Perhaps they thought she was after his fortune. Now she wondered whether they were truly fond of her or simply happy that Sir John was settling down. If it were the latter, how long would their kindness last?

The butler approached to interrupt them. The first guests were arriving.

Chapter 3

CAROLINE, AT LAST FREE from her stint on the receiving line, walked with Jane and Louisa to the punch bowl. There she saw Eliza Darcy and Mrs. Gardiner with a young lady Caroline had not met that evening.

"Caroline, Louisa," Elizabeth said, "allow me to introduce to you a very good friend of mine, Mrs. Brandon. Marianne, Miss Bingley, Sir John's intended, and her sister, Mrs. Hurst."

Caroline smiled. "I am pleased to be able to meet you finally, Mrs. Brandon. Sir John has told me so much of Colonel Brandon and his lovely Marianne that I feel I know you already."

"You are too kind," replied Marianne as Kitty, Georgiana, and Anne de Bourgh joined them. "His friends have despaired for years that Sir John would ever settle down, but I see we had no reason for fear, for he was waiting for the right lady."

Caroline was unsure of the lady's sincerity, but she chose to ignore it. Besides, she had been dealing with people doubting her improvements for two years. "Thank you, but I am sure I deserve no such praise." She looked at the young lady, who appeared to be surely no more than one and twenty, and asked, "Tell me, to which regiment is your husband attached?"

Marianne looked askew at Caroline's odd question. "My husband is not with a regiment at the present time. He is what the War Office calls 'inactive,' but he has not resigned his commission. He holds an honorary position with the Life Guards."

"Oh…" Caroline, disappointed, looked away crossly. She had hoped that this young woman could give her some idea as to what was expected of a colonel's wife.

The silence in the room brought Caroline abruptly to her senses. She blanched at Mrs. Brandon's hurt expression. Knowing her only by reputation, the lady could only take Caroline's sigh as a snub.

"Mrs. Brandon, I am afraid I have given offense; please forgive me. I meant no disregard towards your husband. I am only disappointed. I am soon to be an officer's wife, but I do not know my duties. I had hoped you could give me guidance."

Caroline's eyes began to fill with mortification; she could not offend the wife of Sir John's particular friend! "I spoke ill. I had hoped to call upon you as my mentor, now—"

Marianne, touched by her sincere remorse, put her hand on the older woman's arm. "I am afraid you will have to look elsewhere for a mentor. We shall just be friends, shall we? Is that so bad?"

Caroline, surprised and relieved, eagerly accepted the olive branch. "Oh, thank you, Mrs. Brandon," Caroline smiled as she took Marianne's hands in hers. The other ladies present had various reactions. Jane looked on with a proud expression at Caroline's modesty, Elizabeth was pleased, and Anne seemed shocked that Caroline would apologize.

Caroline was thankful for the interruption when Mary joined the group and immediately engaged her friend in conversation. This gave Marianne a chance to speak to Kitty.

"I bear greetings from Delaford Parsonage, Kitty. Is Mr. Southerland here?"

"No, parish business kept him at Kympton. He is overseeing the enlargement of the parsonage."

Marianne smiled. "No matter—now that I consider it, I believe Mr. and Mrs. Ferrars will prefer to wish him joy in person… say at Hertfordshire in February?"

At this, Kitty turned positively red.

Caroline had been honored with the request that she assist Mrs. Darcy and Mrs. Gardiner in the debuts of Georgiana and Kitty, a commission she accepted with pleasure and only a tiny bit of self-satisfaction. Kitty's debut was short-lived; she almost immediately attracted the attention of a Mr. Southerland, son of a wealthy family from Scotland and destined for the church. Kitty was much amazed that a clergyman could be so charming and sensible—and so handsome. He deserved closer study, and so her fate was sealed, especially as he had gained the living at Kympton.

Mention of Kitty's nuptials reminded Caroline of the secret she meant to tell her and the other ladies. "Kitty, I am so happy for you and Mr. Southerland, but I am afraid that I have some news that, while delightful on the whole, may give you disappointment and regret for me."

"Oh, Caroline, what is it? Do not say you cannot come to my wedding!"

"Kitty, I am sorry, but—"

"*Caroline!*"

All turned at the source of the interruption. Walking towards them was a tall woman in a gown of the latest fashion. Caroline's expert eye took in Annabella Norris's outfit at a glance. She was certain the gown was costly, but no amount of money could buy refinement. She then noticed the hard glint in Annabella's eye, which immediately put Caroline on her guard.

"Annabella, you look lovely tonight," she greeted the woman in all false affection.

"I simply *had* to take another look at your necklace. What an unusual color for a cameo! Did you have it especially made?"

"Specially made it certainly was, but not at my request. This is a gift from Sir John."

"How thoughtful of him! Orange is certainly *your* color." Caroline hardly blinked at the attack, while the other ladies stood in silence. Annabella turned to them. "Mrs. Darcy, Mrs. Bingley, good evening. And of course, I am acquainted with Miss Bennet." She nodded at Mary.

"Mrs. Tucker," Mary retorted.

"Oh yes, you married that young man from Hertfordshire, did you not? A childhood sweetheart, I dare say. What does he do—a clerk of some sort, is he? Country romances are so charming!" Turning to Kitty, she continued, "So *you* are now Miss Bennet, unless you have run off lately?" She finished with a giggle.

Kitty showed a little hurt at the reminder of Lydia's elopement. "I still own Miss Bennet for a few months more. I am lately betrothed to Mr. Southerland."

"How wonderful! Everyone is getting married!" She ignored Mrs. Gardiner and cast her eyes upon Marianne. "But I have not been introduced to this lady."

Caroline was forced to do the honors. "Mrs. Brandon, allow me to present Mrs. Norris, wife of Mr. Norris of Park Place. Annabella, this is Mrs. Brandon, wife of Colonel Brandon of Delaford in Dorsetshire."

Annabella narrowed her eyes. "Were you not a Dashwood? Are you not related to John Dashwood of Norland?"

"John Dashwood is my brother," Marianne admitted.

"Yes! I remember you now! You had your debut three years ago." Marianne paled at this reminder of her disastrous Season. "You must know my particular friend, Sophia Willoughby!"

Marianne reeled as if struck by a blow.

"She will be *so* pleased that I made your acquaintance." Annabella nearly purred.

Of all the other ladies present, only Elizabeth knew the particulars of that terrible spring. Almost white with anger, she began to respond when she felt a touch on her arm. Turning, Elizabeth saw Caroline, who gave her a knowing glance.

No, Elizabeth—she is my prey.

Caroline did not know why Mrs. Brandon was so distressed, but she meant for this lady to be her friend and would stand for Annabella's antics no longer.

"Annabella!" she cried, interrupting her dissection of Marianne. "I cannot tell you how I admire your dress! What an unusual color! Very rare, I dare say. Very few women look becoming in it, do you not agree?" she finished with a small smirk.

Annabella's eyes grew wide, then narrowed. No one could miss the insult carelessly hidden in her words—as Caroline intended.

The others stood back—a challenge had been accepted, swords had been drawn, and the battle had now been joined.

Annabella's target that evening had been her former protégé. Attacking Caroline's friends was a way of softening her opposition. She was no fool; it would not do to insult the wife of Fitzwilliam Darcy or the wife of his particular friend. The others, however, were fair game. Now that Caroline had forced the issue, it was time to begin.

It should have been no contest. Annabella Norris was one of the most celebrated artists of the false compliment, the cutting remark, and the polite insult among the fashionable set. Having achieved nothing save marrying a rich, dull man who enjoyed billiards and brandy more than his wife's body, she lived to hurt others so that she could ignore the pain in her own empty soul. It was her one joy. Caroline had been the student, she the master, and Caroline should have been out of practice.

However, there was a grave misunderstanding regarding Caroline's transformation. Caroline Bingley never had completely destroyed what she was. She had only submerged it by exercising what she had the potential to be. Kindness had been triumphant, but darkness was there still, held under tight regulation. All Caroline required to deal with Annabella was to set her inner witch free.

"Caroline," Annabella began, "you were missed at my wedding. I am very sorry that you did not attend."

With perfect composure Caroline replied, "I *am* sorry indeed that I could not attend, but as I stated in my note to you and Mr. Norris wishing you joy, my sister had need of my presence, as your nuptials coincided with her confinement." The note had as much existence as the wedding invitation. "'Tis a joy to be engaged in employment in the service of one's family, is it not?" Caroline continued, knowing that Annabella was estranged from her only brother.

"I had not known you so maternal or so attached to your *sisters!*" replied the other, accenting on the plural. "You had not expressed such desires before, but one's views change as *years* go by, I dare say."

Caroline did not rise to the bait, but said instead, "Yes, I had expressed foolish views in the past, but one often disparages what one does not have, yet craves." Caroline glanced at Elizabeth, who did not fail to note the apology hidden in her words. "But with the years comes wisdom, I think, and my goddaughter, Susan, has been such a source of delight that I quite look forward to experiencing the same unspeakable joy my dear sister Jane enjoys with children of my own. And Sir John joins me in this desire."

Annabella giggled. "Caroline Bingley a mother? Pardon me, my *dear* friend, but you must own it to be excessively diverting! However, I am sure you would make the most excellent of mothers. Think of the expense you shall save by not employing nurses or governesses, for you shall be so attentive that no one shall touch your children save yourself."

"Indeed I deserve no praise for such talents," Caroline said gravely, purposely misconstruing the intended insult, "but"—she turned to Jane— "with guidance from my sister"—then to Elizabeth—"and my friends"— finally back to Annabella—"I shall bear the burden tolerably well."

Annabella was taken aback; the smiles on the faces of the Hertfordshire sisters gave the lie to stories of incivility between Miss Bingley and her relations, and the lady's unexpected humility set Mrs. Norris off her stride.

Caroline knew this was the moment to attack. "But I must say I am concerned for *you*, dear Annabella."

"Concerned? Whatever do you mean?"

"Why, surely you have heard the news from Vienna? It was in all the papers."

"News? What news? What does it signify what happens in foreign places?"

"Then you do not know. His Majesty's delegation has convinced the other parties at the Congress of Vienna to join Britain's ban on the trading of African slaves. Sir John has informed me that the Admiralty has sent squadrons off the African coast to suppress the slave trade. 'Tis a wonderful thing for those poor savages, to be sure—but, Annabella, how will Mr. Norris survive without sugar and slaves?" Caroline said, referring to Mr. Norris's plantations in the West Indies, the source of the bulk of his income. "But I am being foolish. Mr. Norris is a very wise and clever man; he will think of something. You have nothing to concern yourself over, my dear. Forgive me."

Annabella's alarm showed on her face. Mr. Norris had inherited the properties upon his father's untimely drowning during a hurricane. Had he not mentioned that very morning the possibility that he may have to travel to inspect his properties in the New World? She had not seen any danger; she only reflected with relief that with him gone, she would not have to submit to the wifely duties he expected every fortnight. Mr. Norris had seemed irritable and out of sorts lately, but she paid it no mind. She thought that one of his horses had lost again. She did not pay attention to her husband's business, but she knew of his income and its source; why else would she have accepted him? Could her situation be imperiled? Would Caroline invent such a thing? Her thoughts in a turmoil, but unwilling to show weakness in front of her opponent, Annabella changed the subject.

"Caroline, you speak of current events and politics with your betrothed? La, but that is a strange manner of courting!" Annabella tried to smile but failed, not realizing she had set her foot onto the very path to which Caroline had led her.

Caroline smiled indulgently. "It would certainly appear thus, but Sir John trusts me to be informed, and for a very good reason. I am glad you brought up this subject, Annabella, for it allows me to explain my unfortunate inability to attend Miss Bennet's wedding in February."

Turning to the girl, Caroline continued. "Kitty, I hope you believe that Sir John and I would be most pleased to join you and Mr. Southerland in celebrating your wedding day, but duty calls from far away." Turning back to Annabella, Caroline assumed her most haughty expression. "My wedding trip shall be on the Continent. Sir John is to join the king's delegation at the Congress of Vienna as an aide to the Duke of Wellington. I shall be assisting Lady Beatrice in entertaining the dignitaries."

This sent a shock throughout the entire party. "Lady Beatrice?" gasped Annabella. "Surely you do not mean *Lady Beatrice Wellesley?*"

"Yes," said Caroline sweetly as she sprung her trap. "We have received the kindest letter from both the Duke and her ladyship, wishing us joy and a safe journey."

The fact that Caroline had received an unsolicited letter from the Iron Duke and his cousin, who was acting as his hostess, nearly sent Mrs. Norris reeling. Jealousy and anger overcame what self-control Annabella still possessed. She could only lash out.

"Tell me, Caroline—how *did* you attach yourself to such a man?" she snarled.

The women gasped at the insinuation implied by such a question. She had gone too far—she should have retrenched—but Annabella cared not. In her pain, she wanted to hurt Caroline as much as she could, even at the risk of her own reputation.

But on Caroline's part, there was no injury. Annabella had responded just as she knew she would, and she could only regard her former friend with pity and regret. Caroline wondered how she could have been so foolish, so blind. How could she have desired the good opinion of creatures like Annabella over people of character—when she could have cultivated friendships with people like the Bennet women? With an air of sadness rather than triumph, Caroline delivered her *coup de grace.*

"You may well ask, but I have no firm answer—in fact, I do not know. Sir John is certainly above me in accomplishments and *improvements,*" she stressed the word, "and I am honored that he would choose me to be his wife and helpmate. I hope I shall make a good one for him. I know I shall labor to make myself worthy of his regard. He has pledged his belief in my abilities, and I have pledged my belief in his honor. He trusts in my mind, and I trust in his heart. I have every expectation of happiness. Few couples, I think, enter into marriage with such a good understanding of each other's character, but I am fortunate to have some examples among my acquaintance—such as you, Jane, and you, Elizabeth."

Elizabeth smiled at Caroline's use of her Christian name. It was the ultimate peace offering. "Thank you, dear Caroline," she offered in return.

Caroline smiled and nodded to her former rival. Returning to Annabella, she said, "But it is comforting to know that in *his* eyes I hold inducements to devotion other than intelligence, accomplishments, and dowry." Her hand drifted to her cameo. "But come, ladies, we are taking Jane from her duties. Shall we not return to the gentlemen? It is surely time for the dancing to commence." With that, Caroline took Jane's arm and turned to walk towards the ballroom.

Standing in front of her was Sir John, regarding her with a slight smile. He approached them and said, "Allow me," taking Caroline on one arm and Jane on the other.

As the party moved towards the ballroom, he leaned over and whispered in Caroline's ear, "Well done."

Walking behind them, Marianne whispered to Elizabeth, "I am glad I am not *her* enemy."

Chapter 4

THREE COLONELS OF CAVALRY waited in an anteroom of St. —— Church in London. One wore the red uniform coat of the Life Guards. The others were in the blue of the Light Dragoons, one with the red sash of the Bath. The man in the red coat, eldest of the three, was engaged in troubled mumbling.

"Brandon," cried one of the blue coats, "what are you about, man? You carry on as if *you* were getting married!"

"I beg your pardon, Fitzwilliam," said Colonel Brandon. "Pay me no mind—I am in a foul mood today."

"We cannot have that, can we?" replied Colonel the Hon. Richard Fitzwilliam of the ——rd Lt. Dragoons. "You will put poor Buford off, and Miss Bingley will have your head!"

Buford observed the exchange with amusement. "What troubles you, Brandon?" he asked.

"I am reflecting over a report from my steward, McIntosh. It seems one of my tenants has accused another's son of dishonoring his daughter. Mr. McIntosh refuses to do anything without my leave, but I cannot make a decision without seeing to the facts of the case myself. It will be at least a week before Mrs. Brandon and I return to Delaford, and I fear by then someone may grow inpatient and take matters into his own hands."

"Indeed, you need to speak to my cousin Darcy," advised Fitzwilliam. "He has had to deal with like situations before, thanks to a certain scoundrel whom I shall not name who has caused him great consternation in the past. Darcy has experience in settling such matters, I regret to say."

The two men continued to discuss the problem, but Buford did not attend. Today was his wedding day, and mapping out campaigns or dealing with warring tenants was none of his concern.

Sir John Buford's long campaign ended today—his campaign to find a wife.

Colonel Sir John Buford, a newly made Companion in the The Most Honorable Order of the Bath, stood against a wall in Almack's, trying to look as inconspicuous as a fine-looking man could wearing the red sash of knighthood—and failing. As a trained soldier in the service of his Britannic Majesty, he recognized a battlefield when he saw one. The first rule for surviving such a war zone was knowledge of the placement of the troops opposite, and that was best done behind concealment. As rocks and trees were in poor supply in the assembly rooms, the best Buford could hope for was to blend into the wallpaper.

It was the beginning of the Season, and all the mothers on the hunt were dragging their daughters about from event to event, trying to attach their little darlings to a worthy gentleman before all the desirable ones were snatched up. Buford had to rank among the most sought-after—a hero with a title and two thousand a year whose wealth and status were certainly acceptable for a second son. Like geese scavenging a wheat field, the colorful birds of prey glided across the room, feathered headdresses bobbing in unison, searching for the most suitable match for their offspring.

It was not that Buford disliked women—far from it. Indeed, he had the reputation of being quite the ladies' man, and it was whispered that he had dallied with some of the most illustrious young wives of the fashionable set. No, his reluctance stemmed from his character. He was a hunter and, therefore, was ill at ease being the hunted.

It was ironic. The reason Buford was at Almack's at all was that, after considering his time of life—he would not be nine-and-twenty much longer—and all the entreaties from his mother and sister, he decided the time had come to begin *thinking* about taking a wife. Coupled with the death of his honored father and the horrors he had witnessed in Spain, the colonel had come to accept the inevitability of the idea.

This was ironic for two reasons: First, the aggressive matrons of the *ton* would not have paused for an instant in their labors had they known Buford's mind. Second, those labors were just the sort of activity that would assure that their daughters would never be brought home to Wales.

"Buford!" cried his companion. "If you truly wish to be known as a respectable gentleman, there are other ways to go about it than imitating Fitzwilliam Darcy!" Colonel Richard Fitzwilliam gave his comrade-in-arms a lopsided grin.

Buford's eyes never left the crowd. "I beg your pardon, but I am certainly not as stiff as Darcy."

Fitzwilliam laughed. "Oh, Buford, you make a fireplace poker look flexible!"

Buford could not contain his smile at the jibe. He could always count on Fitzwilliam to lighten his mood or protect his flank—as had been proved many times in Spain and France. Through war, women, and song, they had become brothers of a sort.

Buford was closer to fellow soldiers like Fitzwilliam and Brandon than he was to Philip, his true brother—not that the two were estranged—not in the least. They had been very pleasant companions in his youth, and they would still do anything for one another, but now the brothers had little in common—save family. Philip could no longer understand him. No man *could* who had never taken up arms. Thomas, his younger brother, might have, had he not died a midshipman at Trafalgar.

"When such beauty is before you, how can you resist it?" his friend continued.

"Well enough. Are you not affected?"

"I?" Fitzwilliam asked with a laugh. "*I* am not on campaign!"

Yes, on campaign was a good way of putting it. Since he came to realize that he had been wasting his life, Buford sought out ways to set things right. His first step was to cut off all association with the more licentious members of the fashionable set. The next was to rebuild his reputation. His last task was to find a worthy occupation now that his fighting days were behind him.

His father had been generous in his will, but Buford could not tolerate being idle. Looking about for a calling, he closely observed his commanding officer. Field Marshall Sir Arthur Wellesley, now the Duke of Wellington, and his brother, Marquess Richard Wellesley, while of noble birth, were of Irish stock and limited in their expectations. They used their military and political talents to make themselves two of the most powerful men in the kingdom. Theirs was as good a model to follow as any other, but before he could find his destiny in Parliament or government, he needed a wife.

"'Tis rather crowded for the first night at Almack's, Fitz," remarked Buford. "What is the occasion?"

"Do you not know? The hounds of society are here for the debuts of Mrs. Bingley and Mrs. Darcy."

"So I am to finally meet the famous Hertfordshire sisters? Excellent. I am sure that Bingley's bride is just as pleasant and unassuming as he, but I am looking forward to meeting the woman who brought down Darcy.

Your cousin is an excellent fellow, Fitz," Buford assured his companion. "I like him very well, but he can be taciturn and withdrawn to an embarrassing extreme! Are you sure you are related?"

"Absolutely! You have met the Viscount." The mention of Fitzwilliam's pompous older brother caused Buford to give a snort of laughter. "Ah, I see the Bingleys are already here."

Charles Bingley had just entered with an extraordinarily beautiful woman on his arm. Buford admired Jane Bingley's grace and soft manners. *Just the sort of woman to whom Bingley would attach himself. I am happy for him.* But, in the back of his mind, unbidden, came the thought: *Better him than me. I need more.* His gaze took in the Hursts and two other women.

With the eye of a connoisseur, Buford sized up the younger one quickly. *Young, yet serious. Does not know how pretty she could become, even with spectacles. Family resemblance—could she be one of Mrs. Bingley's sisters? I heard there was a virtual tribe of them.*

The other lady held his attention longer. *Is that Caroline Bingley? My, she cleans up well. Red suits her very well. She always did look to best advantage in strong colors. Extra effort in her dress tonight. Is she still not reconciled to Darcy's marriage? How foolish of her! What a waste!*

"Mrs. Bingley is certainly the beauty," he observed to Fitzwilliam.

"Aye, she is. Had she fortune, I might have given Bingley some competition."

Not bloody likely, not the way she is gazing at her husband, considered Buford. *A love match! Well, the* ton *should forgive them that. No one expected much from Charles Bingley.*

"But still," Fitzwilliam continued, "there is something about the sister—"

"Not that mouse next to her?" Buford cried.

"No, no, I mean Elizabeth Darcy. Wait until you meet her. She has *bottom,* that one."

She had better, he thought. Aloud he said, "I am sure she is much like her sister, quiet and unassuming. I hope she is ready for what the *ton* has in store for her—Fitzwilliam, what is so funny?"

Richard Fitzwilliam could not answer him. In fact, he could barely stand for laughing. "Qui-quiet and unassuming?" Another spurt of laughter. "Oh, you have certainly taken the measure of that one quickly, Johnny Boy!"

"I am pleased you find me so amusing, Colonel Fitzwilliam," Buford observed dryly. "Perhaps a glass of punch will restore your senses."

Reduced to what sounded suspiciously like giggling, Fitzwilliam waved at his friend and staggered off to the refreshments table. Absentmindedly, Buford had begun to observe Miss Bingley again when he was accosted by a person out of his past.

"Colonel Buford! Or should I now say Sir John? What shall I say, sir?" said a female voice.

Good-bye would do nicely, Victoria, he thought. "That is up to you. Good evening, Lady Uppercross."

"So formal! And the two of us such old acquaintances!" Lady Uppercross purred. "I say, you are looking fit. War certainly agrees with you."

Scenes of carnage from his last battle in Spain appeared unbidden in Buford's mind, and it took all of his control not to scream at the baggage. Instead, in a tolerable voice he replied, "There are those who would disagree with you, madam. It is a pleasure to come home and see that few things have changed." He bowed.

"How lovely! You were always the most charming liar, Sir John. But time is no lady's friend."

"Not so. You are as you have always been," he said with false sincerity. *If you force me to compliment you, at least I shall do it my way. Your time is done. You may rely upon it.*

Lady Uppercross allowed the comment to pass. "You have been missed… by everyone in Town. Say that you are not to return so soon to Wales!"

Buford knew what her words meant. He hesitated, forming an answer that would serve to dismiss his former lover without causing a scene, when the room grew suddenly silent. Turning, he heard small gasps and whispered comments. Then his eyes took in the entrance, and he almost swore.

Fitzwilliam Darcy was walking in with three of the loveliest women he had ever seen. He thought he recognized Miss Georgiana Darcy amongst them, but it did not signify. No one could take their eyes off the glorious creature on Darcy's arm. It was not that she was classically beautiful like her sister; she was not. There was something else—a power, an intelligence, a confidence, a complete assurance of the affection she held for and received from her husband that everyone, love her or hate her, had to admire in Mrs. Darcy.

Fitz is right. She is regal yet real. Oh, Darcy, I hate you! How can you be so fortunate?

"Oh, my!"

Buford turned. He had forgotten Lady Uppercross.

"Miss Bingley will be furious," she laughed.

Seeing his opening, Buford bowed. "Lady Uppercross, a good evening to you." He then crossed to the Darcy party.

He spent a few minutes making the acquaintance of Mrs. Darcy who, upon closer inspection, was quite beautiful. Miss Kitty Bennet was judged a bit unpolished but would do for a parson's wife—some very fortunate parson. Buford was struck by the improvement to Miss Georgiana, for never had she seemed to be at such ease. He knew his reputation was not yet fully repaired, so Buford saved Darcy the concern of watching him dance with his relations by only wishing them a good evening and excusing himself.

Buford spent the next half hour strolling about, greeting a few friends here and there, but mainly observing all in the rooms. Almack's was awash in color, but the gaiety was lost on him. He only beheld the sameness in character of most of the ladies there—either mercenary or uninhibited—sometimes both.

What a waste to come here! he thought. *I only see what I do not want or cannot have.* Thinking that a spot of punch might revive his spirits, he moved to the refreshments table.

Before he could reach his goal, he was presented with the sight of Miss Bingley in conversation with two other ladies.

I say, her dress is the same color as my sash. How singular! It is certainly striking against her pale skin.

It was only then that he became aware that Miss Bingley was not only pale but also distressed. Her arms were moving in a distracted manner.

What are those vultures doing to her?

Suddenly, Miss Bingley turned in his direction and almost collided with him. His pardon died on his lips as he heard her whimper as she fled towards the library. Buford stood frozen after she entered the library, then impulsively he went in search of the lady's relations.

"Mrs. Hurst—"

"Colonel Buford! Pardon me, I meant, Sir John! Good evening, sir. Allow me to offer you congratulations on your knighthood. May I introduce you to my friend?"

"Please," Buford said politely.

"This is Miss Bennet, Mrs. Bingley's sister from Hertfordshire. Mary, this is Colonel Sir John Buford."

"Charmed, miss," he said somewhat distractedly. "Mrs. Hurst, do not be alarmed, but I must suggest that you repair to the library as soon as may be. Miss Bingley has taken ill."

Mrs. Hurst blanched. "Oh dear! Sir John, have you seen her?"

"I only observed her going into the library. She appeared ill," said Buford as kindly as he could.

Mrs. Hurst could not misunderstand the meaning of his words. "Oh, no! I knew it, I knew it," she said under her breath.

Miss Bennet looked about her, her expression becoming stern. "Beauty and goodness do not always go hand-in-hand, *especially* in Town."

Buford looked at Miss Bennet, revising his opinion of her. "Please, allow me." With that, he escorted the two ladies across the room to the library.

As they prepared to enter the room, he said to Mrs. Hurst, "If I may be of assistance to you or Miss Bingley—"

"No, thank you, sir. You have been too kind."

"It was an honor to be of service to the lady."

With that, he took his leave of them. Later he would learn that the Bingleys left Almack's through a private door very early in the evening. He could not help but overhear the sneers over that. Buford was disgusted with the whole business. He had spent the last few years with war and death and waste; the last thing he wanted to see at home was similar ugliness.

"Sir John?"

He was startled out of his thoughts. "Hmm?"

It was the vicar. "It is time, sir."

"Excellent," he said as he rose, straightening his jacket. "Well, gentlemen," he said to his friends, "shall we get to it?"

Chapter 5

IT WAS A BRIGHT January morning, and Colonel Richard Fitzwilliam was doing his best not to insult the lady seated to his left at the wedding breakfast, but he was in danger of failing. Miss Halifax was a rather comely maiden who seemed to be quite taken with him. Looks were not everything, however. What set the colonel's teeth on edge was her insipid conversation, held in a manner and tone of speech she undoubtedly considered cultured but, to Richard's ears, sounded like the squawking of chickens.

"Is not everything lovely? Everything is so charming! I do adore weddings! What is your opinion, Colonel?"

"I like it of all things."

"I do believe that our Lord was very wise to invent marriage. Such happiness—and children! Do you like children, Colonel?"

How blatant can you be, woman? "Of course."

"I should love to have children, should I marry. Two, I think. One would show a lack of feeling and three… well, I do so dislike odd numbers. Are not odd numbers so very—odd?" Miss Halifax giggled at her own jest.

"Indeed."

"And more than three—heaven forbid! I cannot see how ladies can have more than three children. It has an air of"—her voice dropped to a whisper—"*unseemliness.*" She batted her eyelashes at him.

Someone put me out of my misery. Take a sword and run me through now.

The Darcys and the Tuckers sat at the table with the pair and regarded Richard's predicament with amusement. Taking pity on him, Darcy whispered something in his wife's ear, and she turned to speak to the colonel.

"Richard!" said Elizabeth. "While you are in Town, you must come by and visit your young cousin. He has grown much since your last visit, I declare."

Richard was puzzled—*How much could he have grown in two days?*—until he recognized the rescue offered him. "Ah, I have been remiss in calling upon young Master Bennet. Forgive me, Mrs. Darcy. Regimental duties, I am afraid. I shall correct my failure at the first opportunity. Fatherhood suits you, Darcy, I think."

Mr. Darcy nodded at his cousin. "Indeed it does, as long as one has a wife of sensibility and sense to manage the household." He touched Elizabeth's hand, and she rewarded her spouse with a brilliant smile. "'Tis a requirement to deal with the Fitzwilliam Curse."

"Curse, Mr. Darcy?" asked Miss Halifax. "What can you mean?"

"Oh my, do you not know?" asked Elizabeth, eyes growing wide. "Being the wife of a Fitzwilliam or a Darcy must have such extraordinary sources of happiness necessarily attached to her situation, that a lady could, upon the whole, have no cause to repine, were it not for the curse. For centuries it has been thus. But the viscountess bears it well, and Mr. Darcy trusts that I shall do likewise."

"But, Mrs. Darcy, dare I ask the nature of this curse? Please, I do not wish to offend, but I am full curious!"

Elizabeth turned her fine eyes to her husband. "Mr. Darcy, shall I?"

"Very well, madam," replied her husband grimly. "She should be forewarned. I trust she shall not find it too distressful."

Elizabeth looked around the table and leaned forward. "Well, my dear," she continued to the girl in a low voice, "it seems that the wives of Fitzwilliams—my husband is one on his mother's side—always have at least three children, and many times more, and always an odd number of them!" Her victim's eyes grew wide, as did Mary's, but for a different reason: She knew full well that Mr. Darcy had only one sister. "Oh, the scandal, the unseemliness," Elizabeth put her hand to her eyes in a dramatic fashion, "but such is my lot in life!"

"Forgive me, my dear," consoled Darcy.

"Do not speak of it, Husband," she responded, taking his hand in hers for a moment. "I shall endeavor to persevere."

Miss Halifax colored. Whether from shock at learning such a horrible secret or the mortification of being the butt of a joke, no one could say, for she chose that moment to excuse herself.

"Forgive me, I must attend my mother. Umm... good day," she mumbled and left the table. It was well, because Richard could not contain himself much longer.

"Fitzwilliam Curse? Oh, that is rich!" he sputtered, trying to contain his laugh.

"Happy to have been of service, Colonel," said Elizabeth, an eyebrow arched. "I hope we did not offend."

"Oh, I am deeply mortified, madam," he chuckled, "that I did not conceive it first!" Richard eyed his cousin. "I am fully aware of Mrs. Darcy's talents, but I did not know you had it in *you*, sir."

"Indeed," said Mary. "It seems my sister has had an effect on you, Brother."

Darcy lifted his wife's hand to his lips. "All for the better, I can assure you." Elizabeth blushed at the gesture. "What are your plans, Richard?" he asked.

"You mean besides attending weddings? Must not neglect Miss Bennet's, you know. Thank goodness, it is the last one. I am sure Mrs. Bennet is in high spirits."

Both Bennet sisters laughed, and both of their husbands gave each other a look. "You can very well say she is beside herself, Cousin!" cried Lizzy. "It is a day to which she has long looked forward."

"'Five daughters married! Oh, Mr. Bennet, I shall go distracted!'" Mary recited in a fair approximation of her mother's voice, which sparked renewed laughter around the table.

"Will the earl and countess attend?" asked Darcy when he was able.

"Aye, if it is warmer. The old goat does not take much to traveling in the cold these days, and Hertfordshire is a bit closer to Matlock than London," said his son with fondness. "Then, after I report to headquarters, it is off to Rosings."

"In February? 'Tis very early," replied Darcy.

Since Mr. Darcy's marriage, it had fallen to Colonel Fitzwilliam to make the pilgrimage to Rosings to both pay court to Lady Catherine and to receive the annual report from the steward, as her ladyship was still not reconciled to Darcy's choice of wife.

"All is well, I take it?" Darcy continued with a trace of concern in his voice.

With only the slightest of pauses, Richard answered, "Oh yes, nothing to worry about." But the look in his eye, which his cousin did not fail to mark, gave the lie to his statement.

At that moment, there was a shuffling at the main table, and Mr. Bingley rose to give the farewell toast to the newlyweds.

"Sir John, what are you about? Put me down, sir!" cried Caroline.

The only answer she got was her husband's laugh as he carried his bride over the threshold of Buford House. The servants, accustomed to the occasionally strange behavior of their employer, gave every appearance of being made of stone.

"Lady Buford, welcome home. At least for the next five days."

"The servants! Sir John, please."

He gave her his most disarming smile. "A kiss first, lass."

"What? In front of the servants? Have you lost your senses?"

Sir John's face was very close. "No," he whispered, "just my heart."

She looked into his deep blue eyes, and the fluttering started up again. "Close the door at least. All of London can see."

He drew even closer. Just before he claimed her lips with his own, Colonel Sir John Buford said, "I care not."

Caroline stopped thinking for a while.

Buford lay quietly awake in his wedding bed, his wife sleeping sweetly, curled next to him. Usually after a night of love, he wished for nothing but to fall fast asleep and only sometimes in the same bed as his lover. This time was different; Buford was overwhelmed by a feeling he had never experienced before. *Contentment.*

In his previous encounters, no matter how jolly or pleasurable his partner, Buford would become disenchanted in the end. Most times, he would want nothing more than to leave as soon as could be, fleeing back to his own rooms and trying not to feel too disgusted with himself for bedding a willing woman of the *ton*. He knew as long as he continued in that practice, it would always be so. He finally gave up the business before his last posting to Spain. Buford did not give up *women*—he was no Papist priest—but he made a solemn vow that, the next time he enjoyed a woman's favors, it would not be with some other man's wife but his own.

It was not long after the incident at Almack's that he noticed he had begun comparing any eligible lady who was introduced, pointed out, or thrown at him with Caroline Bingley. Buford could not get Caroline out of his mind. From what he knew of her, she met many of the requirements he had for a wife: accomplishment, grace, ease in society, beauty, and a comfortable dowry.

Her disgrace at the assembly had an interesting effect on Buford. It became apparent to him that Miss Bingley was capable of great depth of feeling and that her nearest friends and family thought enough of her to protect her. Caroline's apparent break with Annabella Adams and that set relieved Buford's mind. He was aware of Miss Bingley's reputation, but her actions showed a desire for improvement, and Colonel Buford wondered if they might be fellow souls, striving for redemption.

As the summer progressed, his perception was corroborated by the actions of the Darcys—or rather the *inactions* of that august family. No matter what evils, real or imagined, that Miss Bingley had visited upon Mrs. Darcy in the past, Buford never heard a word against the lady by any member of the Darcy or Fitzwilliam family.

Buford had hoped to further his acquaintance with the lady, but he was foiled when Caroline removed to Netherfield for the remainder of the year. He did not grieve in silence. Buford continued to enjoy society, but his observations only strengthened his opinions and his resolve. He planned his strategy.

When Miss Bingley returned to Town the following spring, Buford was ready. With the precision of a military campaign, he courted her and included subtle tests throughout. Caroline passed most of them to his delight. He found that she was experienced in the management of an estate, was better read than he had been led to believe, and that her character seemed much improved. The estrangement with the Darcys was certainly past.

However, Caroline, who had seemed to enjoy his company, began to distance herself as August came, and to his chagrin, Buford realized that he was so busy trying to ascertain Miss Bingley's improvements that he had neglected to assure the lady of his desire to change. Such were his worries when Buford came upon a drunken fool pawing Miss Bingley at a ball. Without a thought, Buford sprang to Caroline's defense, and in so doing, exposed his growing regard for her. Buford declared his intentions, but the timetable for his suit was projected forward by Caroline forcing the issue in September.

Buford was pleased and contented with his choice. He felt Caroline would be an excellent manager of his house, a charming hostess for his guests, and an asset in his planned future political career. By observing her with her niece, he believed that Caroline would also be an affectionate mother. The only thing that remained was to make her a tolerable lover.

Buford was an experienced, passionate, and introspective man, and while he had every intention of honoring his marriage vows, he knew he could never be happy unless he had pleasure in *all* the activities that marriage offered. There was only one thing for it; he had to seduce his wife.

A new campaign began, culminating with their wedding night—their wedding *evening*. While Buford had never been with an innocent before, he knew how things could go wrong; one wrong move, any show of impatience or aggression on his part, and much could be lost.

Sir John sat upon Caroline's bed—their wedding bed—and held his wife's hands. "My dear," he said to her, "I do not know what you have been told about this night—how you have been prepared."

Caroline became very shy, and her cheeks grew hot. "I… I have been told enough. I know my duties."

"No. There is no duty *here*—only pleasure." He released her hands to grasp her chin lightly. "Look me in the eyes, Caroline. This night shall be given over only to *your* pleasure. Do you trust me?"

Caroline struggled with the concept and then finally surrendered. "I will try."

Sir John smiled. "An honest answer." He kissed her lightly on the lips. "I shall now call for Abigail. Will a half hour be sufficient?"

"Thank you, yes." Her husband smiled and left the room through the door that connected their suites. Caroline drew breath and made her way into her dressing room. A few moments later, Abigail joined her. Without a word, the girl helped Caroline out of her dress. *She is as nervous as I am,* thought Caroline. The maid crossed the room to Caroline's trunk.

"My lady, you wish to wear... this?" Abigail stuttered.

The maid's modesty brought a smile to Caroline's lips. "Yes."

"And the robe?"

Caroline considered it. "No. Come, girl, see to my hair."

After thirty minutes, Sir John entered his wife's room wearing a robe over his nightshirt. He beheld his bride seated at her dressing table, hair down, and her back to him. He called her name.

Slowly she rose from the chair. Sir John almost gasped. The ivory negligee she wore was almost transparent, and he could clearly see the outline of her back and buttocks. She turned and he could see that her nipples were distended, evidence of her desire.

"Beautiful—you are beautiful. Come, my dear." Sir John held out his hand.

Caroline could not believe she could blush further, but no one had ever called her beautiful before. She slowly walked towards him. To her it was a dream, and she felt somehow detached as if she were watching someone else.

Sir John slowly caressed her shoulders and arms while murmuring low tones in her ear and kissing her hair. Finally, he sensed that her reserve had been broken, and she began to relax, to respond. His lips moved to hers while his arms encircled her.

Caroline melted into the kiss, her body coming in firm contact with his. Not for the first time did she feel the evidence of his desire, but she did not flinch. She felt a need that she knew only his body could fulfill.

Sir John's hands slid downward to her hips. Caroline's eyes opened first in surprise before closing in pleasure. Her arms rose first to his shoulders, then around his neck in response. Sir John's lips moved to her chin, her cheek, her neck. Caroline felt the heat within her grow, and moaned in regret when Sir John suddenly lifted his head and cupped her face. For a moment, blue eyes bore into green. Caroline drew breath and relaxed.

Sir John stepped back and removed his robe. At first, he seemed to Caroline's eyes a bit silly in his nightshirt, and the thought acted to relax her further. The top buttons of the garment were undone, and his broad chest peeked from underneath. Unconsciously, she licked her lips. Sir John moved closer again, this time caressing her as his hands drifted down to the small points of her breasts and his fingertips made circles around them.

Caroline knew she was slim and, therefore, smaller than many ladies of her acquaintance. She had worried that Sir John might be disappointed in her. But his touch vanquished that concern. The feelings he stirred within her were all delightful, and Caroline could not help but give out a small cry of pleasure.

"Yes, Caro, let me know what pleases you," he murmured. Sir John smiled as his hands cupped her breasts, his thumbs feeling her nipples through the material.

"What... what did you call me?" she asked, trembling.

"Caro. You are my Caro—my delight—and I shall call you thus when we are together... thus."

Caroline slipped her arms around her husband again. Covering his face with kisses, she barely noticed that Sir John had dropped his hands again, this time to raise the hem of the negligee. He pulled it up, and Caroline lifted her arms to allow her husband to raise it over her head. With a flick of his wrist, he sent the flimsy nothing towards a corner. Sir John reached and lifted his bride in his arms and carried her to their marriage bed.

He placed her on the sheets. "To pleasure thee is my delight." He stood up and slowly removed his own garment. Caroline could not tear her eyes away from his manhood.

"Do not fear, my dear. 'Tis me; 'tis natural. It was made for thee."

"For me? That will fit… inside of me?"

"Oh, yes, my dear, and it will give you great pleasure." He took his place lying next to Caroline and began to kiss her, stroking her breasts again.

Currents of delight coursed through her, and she murmured repeatedly against his lips, "Yes… oh, yes."

Sir John's hand reached down to the hot, dewy core of her. Slowly, carefully, he played her as skillfully as one might play the keys of a pianoforte, but the music was Caroline's cries of pleasure as she moved against his hand.

After a time, he placed his body over hers, and her arms reached up to embrace him. "Are you ready for me, Caro?" he asked. To her nod, he added, "There will be but a bit of pain. Forgive your Johnny." She nodded again.

Slowly he eased his manhood into her. Caroline gasped as she felt for the first time the sensation of being filled. Sir John tried with all his will to be as gentle as he could, but the exquisite pleasure nearly undid him. Caroline cried out as he became fully embedded in her, but soon he felt her begin to relax.

"Caro, are you well?" he asked.

"Yes," she gasped, the pain already fading. "Oh, yes. Please do not stop." Her hands reached down to his buttocks. She grasped him and pulled him ever deeper inside.

Instinctively, he began his strokes—first slowly and then with increasing speed. Caroline's hips rose to meet each thrust. He whispered in her ear, "Caro… my Caro. I am yours… your Johnny… forever."

The fierce groan she made in reply was too much for Sir John. With a cry, he spilled his seed deep within his virgin bride.

Caroline could feel his release flooding her core, the heat radiating into her. She was overwhelmed by the sensation of being one with her husband, of completeness. She seized Sir John as tightly as she could as he continued to convulse. Finally, he collapsed upon her breast, both of them slick from the exertion of their lovemaking.

When she could catch her breath, Caroline asked, "John, are you well?"

"Ah, yes, my dear—never better. But," he stroked her face, "are you?" He saw her eyes fill with tears of joy. "I… I never dreamed. Oh John—"

"Johnny," he interrupted her. "As you are Caro, I am Johnny, when we are thus."

She held him close again. "Johnny… thank you," she said with a kiss.

The night was beyond his expectations. Caroline soon conquered any apprehension or awkwardness that had existed, and when he whispered the private name he had chosen for her—Caro—into her ear, her reaction almost overcame him. Afterwards, the look of wonder and gratification on Caroline's lovely face was the greatest reward Buford could imagine.

And now as Caroline slept, her body wrapped around him, Buford was filled with wonder and gratification as well. Another man might have basked in self-satisfaction, but Caroline's husband knew his own talents. The greatest of musicians can make an inferior instrument sound only so well and no more. He knew he was not the great lover of the world; he had not *that* much practice. To his increasing delight, Buford was coming to the realization that he had been far more fortunate in his choice of wife than he could imagine. There was something there, something hidden, that he had been able to unlock and set free. There was nowhere on earth he would rather be than next to Caroline. He could not help himself; he had to experience it again.

He leaned over and began to caress her face lightly. "Caro… my beautiful Caro."

Lovely green eyes opened and looked at him. "Hmm…" She smiled. He began to kiss her lightly on the forehead and then the eyelids. "Is it morning already?"

"No, my dear." Buford moved down to her neck.

"Oh, John," moaned Caroline.

"My name, Caro—say my name. The one I taught you for moments like this." His lips traveled further south.

"Johnny!" she purred.

Sometime later, as his labors finally exhausted him enough to join his sleeping wife, Buford's thoughts were those of caution.

I must take care. It would not do to commit that most fatal of sins against the ton*—falling in love with my own wife.*

Chapter 6

THE MORNING SUN WAS full upon Caroline's face as she awoke. At first, she was confused by the unfamiliar room until she remembered she was a married woman. She stretched like a cat, feeling aches from places before unknown to her, and recalled the events of the evening.

I am Lady Buford… Caro… Oh Lord, what a night! I had nothing to fear. John was so kind, but how wantonly I acted!

Caroline began to rise from the bed when she noticed she was not alone. Her husband was still in bed with her—not sleeping, but sitting up watching her with an amused eye—and obviously without a stitch of clothing on. That realization brought to Caroline's attention that she was as naked as he was. She scrambled back under the covers, too embarrassed to speak.

"Good morning, Lady Buford," Sir John greeted her.

"Good morning, sir," Caroline answered, too mortified to notice that her husband had used her new title. "May I ask what you are doing here?"

Sir John grinned. Caroline was reacting in just the manner he had foreseen. "I beg your pardon. I thought you were my wife."

Caroline colored. "Of course, I am your wife, but why are you still here? Do you not have your own bed?"

"Yes, and I am in it."

Caroline frowned. "Sir, it is my understanding that these are my rooms. At least that was what I was led to believe yesterday."

"Ah, I see. I am afraid there has been a misunderstanding, my dear. How unforgivable of me! I forgot to tell you something. I suppose I was preoccupied." Caroline blushed deeper. "Well, let there be a right understanding between us, madam. These are indeed your rooms. However, there shall be no talk of your bed and my bed—only our bed, Caro." Sir John's face drew very close.

"Oh! Do you mean to share my bed every night? How extraordinary! But the servants, sir! What shall they make of this?"

"The servants?" Sir John laughed. "Why, they shall think no harm of it. Only that the mistress is so enamored of the master's person that she cannot bear to be separated from him."

Caroline could not decide whether she was distressed by this observation or not. She began to rise from the bed.

"What are you doing, Caroline?"

She gave him a look. "Perhaps you can sleep the day away, but I have duties to attend—your breakfast, for example."

"Madam, please." Sir John placed his hand upon hers. "Your duties can wait for tomorrow. It is my particular wish that you enjoy your first day as Lady Buford." She paused and then, looking into those eyes, gave in. He smiled at her and then proceeded to get out of bed himself.

"But where are you going?" she asked.

He gave her a smile. "Patience, my dear. I shall return."

With that, he left the bed. Caroline could not help but look with satisfaction upon her husband as he walked across the room, naked as Adam, before he pulled on his robe and disappeared into his bedroom. A quick word to the servant and he returned, crossing over to her side of the bed.

"Well, sir?" Caroline asked with an arch look. "What shall we do now?"

Sir John grinned, then reached and took her hand. "I am sure there are matters you wish to attend to in private," Sir John said as he helped his wife out of bed and walked her to her dressing room. "I shall leave you, madam, but will return. Oh, by the way," he added offhandedly, "the staff is rather short in number; I gave most of them their liberty for the day." He bowed, kissed her hand, and left the room.

Caroline completed her morning routine by herself, somewhat irked that she would have no maid to help with her toilette. There was nothing for it—she put on her best robe and was able to do something with her hair before her husband returned. Sir John had an expectant look on his face that Caroline could not credit.

"Lovely robe," was all he said before picking her up. Caroline, crying out, thought his plan was to take her to bed, so she was surprised that they went through the open doorway into his rooms and entered his dressing room.

There she saw a bath freshly drawn, steam rising from the tub and a bucket next to it. Her bewilderment turned to surprise when Sir John put her back on her feet and lovingly removed her robe. Without a word, he gently placed her into the bath.

She gasped as she lay back. The water enveloped her body, her aches soothed by the warmth. It was exactly what Caroline needed, but to her surprise, within a moment, she felt a stream of hot water cascade over her head. Her husband, Colonel Sir John Buford, war hero and Knight of the Bath, was seated on a stool behind her, washing her hair.

Never before had the practice felt so pleasurable. Caroline was temporarily lost in indulgence. At that moment, she would do anything Sir John asked of her.

The only words Sir John spoke to her, though, was a request that she lean forward so that her hair could be rinsed. Once accomplished, he squeezed as much of the excess water from her tresses as he could before he leaned over and kissed her ear.

"A moment, my dear," he said and was gone. Disappointed with his departure, Caroline lathered the rest of her body, standing up to do her torso.

Task completed, Sir John returned to his dressing room to the spectacle of his tall, slim wife standing in the tub facing away from the door, soaping her body, her buttocks gleaming. His mouth went dry at the sight. Finally, he was able to whisper hoarsely, "Venus rises from the waves."

Caroline looked over her shoulder at him. He could see a bit of suds had clung to the tips of her nipples.

With a smirk, his wife said, "Do not stand there staring, Sir John. Help me rinse off."

Snapped out of his trance, he smiled and proceeded to do just that. Caroline reclined in the bath while Sir John reclaimed his stool. He sponged the remaining soap from her body and then held her hand while she relaxed.

Minutes passed before he said, "You will want to get dressed before the water gets cool, I think."

Caroline grasped his hand firmly, a daring thought coming to her. "Perhaps you can help dry me with a towel."

Sir John grinned. "Your wish is my command, m'lady."

Working together, they dried Caroline's body while wetting their lips with kisses. They were able to remain in some control of their passions, however, and it was not long before the pair, dressed only in their robes, returned to Caroline's rooms hand in hand.

By now, little could surprise Mrs. Buford, so it was no shock to see that breakfast had already been laid out for them on the table at the foot of the bed. Caroline noted with interest that the linens on the bed had been changed, but seeing no profit in inquiring about it, let the observation pass without comment.

While eating, Caroline asked, "What did you have in mind for today, sir? You seem to have everything planned. More tea? I assume we will leave this room at some point."

"Thank you. Why, it had passed my mind that you might wish to do a bit of shopping," Sir John replied. "Our ship leaves in four days—just long enough to have a dress or two fitted and pick up some other necessaries as well. There are shops nearby. We can be there in a trice."

There were few things Caroline enjoyed more than shopping. Sir John's suggestion brought a smile to her face, which brightened further when she realized that he meant to go with her.

"That sounds delightful, John! I would like very much to go."

She paused and then looked at him through her eyelashes. "But the shops are nearby, did you say? I can see no reason for us to hurry... *Johnny*."

She opened her robe.

There were few things that Caroline enjoyed more than shopping— but she might have found another.

Chapter 7

MARIANNE BRANDON, HOSTING MR. and Mrs. Tucker for tea the day after the wedding, sat in the parlor of Brandon House, enchanted by the sight of her husband lying face up on the floor playing with their daughter.

"Who is my love? Who is my love? Why, it is Joy! Ha, ha, ha!" Colonel Brandon cried repeatedly to the child sitting on his stomach. Joy Brandon squealed in delight.

Their guests looked on in amusement. The Tuckers had heard that the Brandons cared little about what other people thought of their attentions to their daughter. Many thought them odd, but Mary and Thomas could see no harm in it.

Finally, the babe began to yawn. "Time for a nap, my love," said Marianne, retrieving Joy from her protesting father's arms. With a sweet kiss, she gave the child to the nurse to put to bed and then returned to the guests. Already talk had turned to politics.

Mr. Tucker leaned towards the colonel in an earnest manner. "Every day, more common land falls to enclosure. It has yet to happen in Meryton, but can it be far behind? What is your opinion, Colonel?"

Brandon shifted uncomfortably. "Ah, had you asked me that question two years ago, you could be sure of my answer, but now, I see both sides. So much land has been wasted, used up. The latest arts in agriculture have not been used to their fullest extent. Those lands that have been enclosed have been the beneficiaries of suitable management. Yields are up due to proper rotation of crops. And yet—"

The young lawyer interrupted. "People are without access to land that was available for centuries. They are fleeing the villages for the cities to find employment, but on the other hand, everything you say is true as well. The population is increasing, and we need more food." Mr. Tucker shook his head. "Our world is changing, Colonel, but can you honestly say it is for the better?" They both pondered the matter for a while.

Mary broke the silence. "We must pray for the Lord's guidance to help us through these times and trust in His wisdom." She lightly touched Mr. Tucker's hand. "And we cannot forget the poor."

"Amen," said her husband, and the others nodded in agreement.

"Colonel," Mary asked, "have you given any more thought to standing for Parliament?"

Brandon glanced at Marianne. "Yes. The seat for Delaford will be vacant in a year or so. Mr. White, good man that he is, wishes to retire."

Mr. Tucker, a staunch Tory, was not as sure about Mr. White's goodness, as the man was a wicked Whig, but knowing Colonel Brandon's Tory leanings, he kept his opinion to himself. "You will be a great addition to the Commons. You have it arranged with our Friends?" Tucker referred to the only party apparatus that existed in the early nineteenth century; party politics was still in its infancy.

"Yes. They have pledged their support. I have no idea who else will stand—"

"Why should anyone?" cried Marianne. "All Delaford knows Colonel Brandon for the fair magistrate he has been. There is no more worthy man in all England!"

The fire in her voice moved Tucker. "No doubt, no doubt. The other side will not surrender the seat without a fight, Mrs. Brandon; depend upon it. But I am certain that the fair people of Delaford will come out for your husband."

Marianne began to regain control of her emotions as Christopher looked upon her with humble affection. "I would certainly expect so, Mr. Tucker." Marianne's attention was drawn to the maid entering the room.

"Ah, the tea is here. May I pour you a cup, Mary?"

Richard Fitzwilliam was no stranger to the Darcy townhouse in London. He had been in residence there so often in the past that one of the bedrooms was reserved for his use alone. Being on the best of terms with his cousins, Richard took as much advantage of the open invitation as he could. Visits were at least weekly when the Darcy family was in Town.

Now, after an excellent dinner hosted with aplomb by Mrs. Darcy, the two cousins took their ease in Darcy's magnificent study and retreat. It was a room of dark wood paneling, comfortable furniture, a fine exotic carpet before a roaring fire in the fireplace, and an excellent Chippendale desk. One wall was adorned with a small portrait of Elizabeth Darcy, another with a bookcase filled with a selection from the grand library at Pemberley. It was dignified, unpretentious, rich, and masculine, in a word—Darcy.

"Damn me! That is fine brandy," Richard exclaimed after sipping the glass Darcy poured for him. "Where on earth did you get it?"

Darcy smiled indulgently. "Such are the rewards of having an uncle in trade. I am sure Mr. Gardiner would be most disposed to setting you up."

"At the family price, I hope?"

"Uncle Gardiner is kind, but not *that* kind. Cigar?"

"Thank you," he said as he selected one.

Lighting their cigars, both men relaxed in their armchairs in Darcy's study. They silently enjoyed the evening in each other's company for a while.

"Richard," said Darcy finally, "as much as I enjoy keeping you in cigars and brandy, I had the impression yesterday you wished to discuss something with me."

Richard sighed. "I have recently received a letter from the steward of Rosings."

"Everything is well, I expect?"

"No, Darcy, everything is not at all well. In fact, it is worse than last year."

Darcy's face lost all expression. "How bad is it?"

Richard was not alarmed at his cousin's demeanor. He knew Darcy could be coldly rational when it came to business, even within the family. "The yields were off another ten percent at least."

The gears in Darcy's mind worked over the estimates. "In two years, a loss of fifteen hundred in income to Aunt Catherine. Lord knows what it was to the tenants! And yet, Mr. Bennet reported good crops last year."

"As did Sir William Lucas. 'Tis not the weather." Meryton was but fifty miles from Rosings.

Darcy leapt to his feet and began to pace. "This will not do! If the situation persists, staff will lose their positions, and tenants will have to choose between food and income." Both knew the nightmare of the English agricultural economic system was the loss of stability. "People will starve!" he predicted as he retook his seat.

The men sat silently, considering what a bread riot would do to Lady Catherine's fine garden. Richard finished his drink. "What do we do, Darcy?"

Darcy's expression was grim. "*I* can do nothing—I am still *persona non grata* for choosing Elizabeth over my cousin, Anne. This is *your* task, Richard."

Newcastle

The innkeeper of the Pig's Snout Pub carelessly poured a measure of whisky into a glass of dubious cleanliness. "'Ere you go, Gov'nor. Cash, sir, if'n you please."

The newly minted army captain tossed the money onto the bar. "Keep it filled until that runs out, my good man."

George Wickham, Captain of Infantry in the —— Regiment of Foot, took a very small sip of the drink set before him. He had to make it last. He had only a few pounds with him, and the innkeeper was under the strictest instructions not to extend him credit. In fact, the entire town of Newcastle had been told about the Wickhams—cash money and no credit.

Damn that Darcy! thought Wickham for the thousandth time.

For three years, Wickham and his loving wife, the former Lydia Bennet, had rotted in cold and cheerless Northumberland. Of course, "loving" could mean many things. In Wickham's case, it meant that, while Lydia was certainly jolly enough for a tumble more often than not, the price was high—two children already and another on the way. Wickham sighed. Within six months, there would be a third screaming child in his house—three, that is, if you did not count Mrs. Wickham.

Wickham found that as far as all other joys that supposedly came with holy wedlock, he would enjoy very few. Lydia had inherited most of Mrs. Bennet's characteristics, save that lady's famous nerves. Mrs. Wickham was vain, silly, weak-minded, selfish, quarrelsome, and foolhardy with the family money. She was also an affectionate mother, but to Wickham, that did not signify. How the family kept a roof over their heads the Good Lord only knew!

The Good Lord *and* Mr. Bartholomew, erstwhile manager of Smyth & Smyth, Wickham's bank—*damn that Darcy!* Wickham had always depended that Darcy would somehow provide his income, and when he was forced to marry Lydia, Wickham still had hopes. Those hopes increased when, for reasons undecipherable to Wickham, Darcy married Lydia's sister, Lizzy. Wickham could never fathom why Darcy did not marry Anne de Bourgh for her money and take Lizzy for his mistress. As part of the bargain they had struck, Darcy purchased Lt. Wickham's commission and the cottage in which his family now lived.

However, Darcy had something clever up his rotten Cork Street sleeve. The house was in *Darcy's* name. He arranged that *all* of Wickham's army pay, as well as Lydia's dowry and the hundred pounds a year from Mr. Bennet, went straight into a trust account at Smyth & Smyth for *Mrs.* Wickham. Accounts managed by Mr. Bartholomew were set up at the green grocer, the butcher, the bakery, and several dry goods shops in Newcastle. Food and other necessaries were provided. Whatever was left after the month's bills were paid was sent to Mrs. Wickham, minus twenty percent, which was retained for emergencies. Lydia, in turn, gave her husband an allowance of two pounds a month.

To make matters worse, Darcy had been in communication with Wickham's commanding general. All officers were warned not to gamble with Lt. Wickham or their promotions might be in jeopardy. Wickham was effectively cut out from all entertainments an officer traditionally enjoyed.

For three years, he lived thus. Then, in remembrance of the third anniversary of Lydia and Wickham's wedding, a promotion to captain was purchased by Darcy. Not only did this event bring additional income to the Wickham family, it finally gave the head of the household the chance to retaliate against his benefactor.

Wickham had befriended the paymaster. When the promotion became final, Wickham arranged for four pounds a month to be withheld from transfer to Smyth & Smyth. His friend charged one part in four for the courtesy, but Wickham gladly paid the fee, and his pockets were heavier by three pounds.

That in itself was cause to celebrate. The reason Captain Wickham was in such high spirits that night was in anticipation of his sister, Kitty's, wedding. Not that he gave two farthings for the girl, but Lydia had received passage to attend with the children. George Wickham would be a bachelor for at least a month, if not two.

Wickham moved to a table in the corner. He looked around the pub and spotted a new barmaid. He thought her a tasty morsel. She was young—and he always fancied the young ones—pert, and well padded.

Ripe for a tumble, she is, or my name is not George Wickham. The captain put down his glass and was about to call her over when he heard a voice he recognized.

"George! George Wickham, as I live and breathe!"

Wickham, startled, looked about. His eyes settled on a young major of infantry. "Denny? Is that you?"

"Ha! Yes, it is, George! Good to see you, old man," cried Major Archibald Denny, Wickham's comrade from the ——shire militia.

"Sit down, sit down! Look at you! You have come up in the world." Wickham, presuming the barmaid was lost for the evening, focused all his attention on his old friend.

"So have you," said Denny. "Captain of Infantry! Are you posted to the regiment here?"

"Yes—three years. Just got promoted."

"Then my arrival is well timed indeed. Allow me to offer you joy for your promotion, sir! Barkeep! A bottle, sir! What are you drinking?"

"Whisky. 'Tis the only tolerable drink in the house."

"Whisky, then! And be quick about it!"

The bottle of tolerable whisky was soon procured, and the two old brothers-in-arms drank and surveyed each other.

Wickham broke the silence first. "A major, Denny! You have done well for yourself."

"Thankee, George. I was lucky. I earned a competency promotion to captain, and a death vacancy promoted me to major."

Wickham, refilling his glass, studied the flashings on Denny's tunic. "You are not with the militia," he observed.

"No, staff officer with the General Staff in London." Denny nursed his drink.

Wickham, in spite of himself, was impressed. "What brings you to Newcastle?"

"I had to consult with your general here." He took a sip and placed his glass down as he said, "So how are you faring, George?"

Wickham looked away. "Same as always." He took a pull at his drink and smiled. "The new recruits cannot find their arse with both hands."

Denny laughed. For a while, they spoke of old times, and then Denny said, "You married Lydia Bennet, I remember. How is the family?"

Wickham took a long swallow of his drink. "Everyone was well, the last time I saw them." At Denny's questioning look, Wickham added, "They are to Hertfordshire for Lydia's sister's wedding next month," as he reached for the bottle.

"Everyone? You have children now, I take it?"

Wickham's hand could barely contain his belch. "Yes—two girls. Two whining, screaming girls. Three if you count their mother! Ha!" He took another drink. "Lydia's expanding again, so maybe this time a boy, eh? Drink up—let us drink to the Wickham heir!" The captain drained his glass. "I tell you, Denny, I just look at her and—boom!" He clapped his hands as he shook his head drunkenly.

Denny barely touched his drink. "There is no need to speak like that. She is your wife. She is a good woman—"

"Oh, she is *good*." Wickham suddenly stopped and looked at his companion through an alcoholic haze. "What do ya mean by that?" he slurred. "Why ya so interested in Lydia?" Wickham lurched to his unsteady feet, slamming his glass down on the table. "Just what do ya mean by your attentions to my wife?" he roared.

Denny blanched. "George, sit down," he urged. "Be still, man; you are making a spectacle of yourself." He stood to encourage the other man. "Come, sir, all is well. You know I have the greatest admiration for you and your entire family. We are friends, George! Come, have a drink." Denny poured the last of the whisky into Wickham's glass and put the drink into the other man's hand. Raising his own glass, Denny said, "Here is to you, George. To friendship!"

Mollified, Wickham returned, "Friendship!" drained the glass, and fell backwards, oversetting his chair, completely intoxicated.

Denny walked over to ascertain his companion's condition. *Feeling no pain tonight, but I cannot speak for his head in the morning.* Denny rounded up a couple of soldiers and had Captain George Wickham carried home to sleep off his carousing in his own bed. Denny stood by the bed as the servant tucked the master in.

George, George, George—shall you never change? he asked silently as he looked at his friend. Denny looked around the cottage. It was small but fairly neat. The maid did what she could but had little help.

He thought back to Wickham's outburst and colored. It was true he had admired Lydia Bennet three years ago, and he was sorry that she had chosen to go off with Wickham, but Denny thought himself resigned to their union long ago. Could his true feelings be so transparent?

In vain, Denny fought the thought that came to his mind: *Lydia deserves better than this.*

Chapter 8

Austria

It was now Lady Caroline Buford's decided opinion that sea travel was unpleasant and unrefined. It was not so much the accommodations; even Caroline knew that warships were not designed for ladies' travel. Their food was tolerable, for the short voyage assured that the passengers would not need to partake of the more common rations given to mariners, such as rotten mutton, weevil-infested biscuits, and suspect water. The passage across the Channel was uneventful, given calm seas. No, what Caroline did not like was that the beds aboard could not accommodate two.

It had been quite a change for the former Miss Bingley. Prior to her marriage, she could hardly imagine sharing her bed with a man. Now she could hardly bear not to do so. She found it a great comfort to awaken with her husband's arm holding her close, and his even breathing was pleasurable. As for the nights, she could only blush. She felt sure she enjoyed those times far more than propriety subscribed, but it did not signify, as Sir John seemed to be delighted with her.

There was a cloud over her happiness, however, and the kindness her husband paid to her person only added to her worries. She knew Sir John had not sought a love match. He wanted a partner to manage his house and entertain his guests. The time would soon come when she would have to prove her worthiness, and she was determined that she would not disappoint.

As for the quivering she felt in the pit of her stomach, Caroline began to suspect what it meant—what John meant to her—and that realization both excited and frightened her.

Once on land, things progressed in a most agreeable manner. The party left Calais in two carriages: Sir John and Lady Buford in one, the maid, Abigail, and valet, Roberts, in the other with most of the luggage. The weather was cold but not oppressively so, and the blankets provided served reasonably well. It did not stop Caroline from occasionally complaining of a chill. This would provoke Sir John to join her under her blanket, and if certain liberties were permitted and enjoyed, the curtains were drawn, so no harm was done. Otherwise, the colonel sat across from his wife, either enjoying the countryside or studying the volume of papers he had brought with him.

Caroline was astonished to learn over the course of their journey that her new husband was a bit of a linguist. Many of his papers were in languages other than English. When she inquired, Sir John admitted to being fluent in French, Italian, German, Spanish, Portuguese, and Dutch. It was for that ability that Wellington had asked for him. He allowed that his Russian and Swedish were only passable, and his Polish was terrible. Caroline, her French and Italian being merely adequate, could only gape.

During the day, the party traveled through the countryside, Sir John pointing out interesting features. At the inns where they spent the evenings, Lady Buford took charge. She had the servants see to the rooms while she handled the innkeepers and ordered their meals with her passable French. Nothing was left to chance, and Caroline saw that Sir John did nothing but rest. At night, the knight and his lady would fall into bed together, sometimes for love but always to rest intertwined for the travels ahead.

They spent little time in France; the route to Vienna was more directly through Belgium and Bavaria, and Sir John did not trust Paris overmuch. He assured his disappointed bride that they would enjoy the French capital another time. Their journey first took them to Brussels and then through the Ardennes Forest to Coblenz, where they crossed into the Saar. Caroline thought she had seen a great river before, but the sleepy Thames was nothing to the powerful Rhine.

Bavaria and the Black Forest were all delightful. Caroline had never seen such mountains before. It brought to her mind a rather silly comment Louisa had made about mountains being "unrefined." If the Peaks in the north of England had inspired such a remark, Caroline wondered what her sister would say upon beholding the Alps.

The party worked their way from Frankfurt down to the Danube River. Soon they entered Austria, and within a few days, they reached the beautiful city of Vienna. Caroline's heart was in her mouth for more than one reason. The city, on level ground with the river running through it and covered in snow, had a fairy tale air about it. At the same time, she sensed foreboding. Now Caroline's worthiness to love her husband as she feared she did—and be loved by him as she now dreamed—would be tested.

Caroline walked the rooms of their apartments in Vienna. Large French windows lined one wall, facing the street. The furniture was made of oak with colorful fabrics, unlike the dark Chippendale style favored in England. The rooms were comfortable and well appointed.

That would never do. How was Lady Buford to prove her worth if she did not leave her mark? It was all very vexing.

"Well?" asked her husband. "Does the place meet with your approval?"

Caroline said nothing, occupied with her dilemma. Finally, she pointed to a couch.

"I believe that settee should be over there and those chairs around it." Roberts and a footman complied with her instructions. Caroline contemplated the arrangement, walked over to a vase on the mantle, and moved it to a table near the pianoforte. "There," she said. "That is better. These rooms will do tolerably."

Sir John merely laughed. "Wait until spring, my dear, and you will be able to fill the place with orange tulips."

"Sir John," said his wife with just the right touch of condescension, "you may know about maneuvers and strategies and other military matters, but it is obvious you know little about decorating!"

"I bow to your superior knowledge, my lady. Allow me to introduce you to your staff."

Sir John gestured to three women standing by, two of a certain age and one a young blonde beauty.

"Helga is the cook and Frau Lippermann is the housekeeper. Roberts will serve as butler, as well as my valet. Sofia will join Abigail as your personal maid." Sofia was the blonde.

Caroline nodded to each in turn, her eyes narrowing as she beheld the lovely Sofia. In a low voice, she said to her husband, "So many for such a small household? I have no need of a second maid. Abigail is sufficient."

"Ah, but you do need another personal maid. Sofia knows German, English, and French. The other ladies speak only their native tongue."

Caroline's lips tightened. "Of course. Thank you for your foresight, sir," she said, trying but failing to hide completely her aggravation at having to rely on the girl because she had no knowledge of German. Caroline was not happy; Sofia was too attractive by half.

Raising her nose, Caroline ordered, "Sofia, please inform Frau

Lippermann and Helga that I look forward to our time together here in Vienna. They may return to their duties."

"I *vill*. Thank you, my lady," Sofia replied in heavily accented English, before speaking to the others in German. They nodded to their new mistress and left for the kitchen.

"If you will pardon me, sir, I will accompany my *maids* to my room to supervise the unpacking." Caroline gave her husband a small curtsy before leaving the room.

Sir John was puzzled. What was wrong? What had provoked her?

Buford exited his carriage in front of Ballhausplatz 2, close by the Hofburg Imperial Palace. A four-story, rectangular building, it was the seat of the Austrian Minister of State, Prince von Metternich, and where much of the work of the Congress was done.

Buford wore civilian clothes—a fine navy blue with his sash of red. He handed his topcoat, hat, and gloves to the footman and entered the vestibule. Quickly ascertaining the location of the British offices, he went up the stairs to the second floor. Halfway down the hall, he saw two men—one tall and one of medium build—conversing in French.

To respect their privacy, Buford stopped a few yards away. The taller man turned in his direction and noticed the colonel.

"Buford!" Arthur Wellesley, the Duke of Wellington, called out. "Excuse me, sir," Wellington said to his companion in English, "but I would like to introduce this gentleman. Come here, Colonel!"

Buford drew closer to the pair. "Your Excellency, may I present Colonel Sir John Buford of the British Army. Colonel, this is His Excellency Charles Maurice de Talleyrand-Périgord, head of the French delegation."

"Your servant, sir." *Talleyrand!* Buford thought as he bowed.

"Colonel, I understand you are lately married," said the foreign minister in perfect English. "Please accept my congratulations. I hope your wife did not find the journey tiresome."

Buford replied in French, "Not at all—*merci*, Excellency. She is even now calling upon Lady Beatrice." Buford tried to keep hidden his discomfort. *How much do you know, you devil? Apparently, the French Secret Service changed its allegiance as quickly as you did.*

The ambassador was notorious for changing sides: first, Louis XVI, then the Revolution, then against Robespierre, then for Napoleon, and later against the same man. Now he served as minister for Louis XVIII.

M. Talleyrand smiled. Buford's point had been made. "My lord," he said to Wellington, "duties call me away. May we continue this conversation another time?"

"Of course, of course."

"*Merci.* Colonel, welcome to Vienna."

Buford bowed again, and the ambassador, with his habitual limp, left the two Englishmen. "Well, you have met the old fox, Buford," said the Iron Duke when the Frenchman was out of earshot. "What do you think?"

Buford knew the duke wanted total candor. "He is a charming man, to be sure, but he bears watching. Lovely guest to have to dinner—just make sure that the silver is counted before he leaves."

The duke broke into a loud laugh. "Capital, sir! You shall do well here. Come into my offices. We have much to discuss."

Caroline rode in her rented coach through the streets of Vienna towards the townhouse that served as the temporary home for the Duke of Wellington and his sister, Lady Beatrice Wellesley. The anxiety she felt was not helped by the presence of her companion, Sofia.

"Lady Buford, is not Vienna *ze* most beautiful city? There is no more *vonderful* city in *ze vorld*. I am honored that I may assist you in your duties," the maid rattled on and on. "Do not *vorry*; I shall guide you."

The cheek of the girl! She presumes to advise me?

Caroline's displeasure started that morning as she discussed—or tried to discuss—the meals for the week. Caroline had particularly wanted to give her husband his first English-style dinner in some time. There was a fine joint of beef that just begged to be roasted to a turn with mashed potatoes, leaks, and dried peas; fresh peas were out of the question in winter. As usual, Sofia was needed to translate for Helga, the cook.

"What do you mean the joint is not available?" demanded the mistress.

"Helga has... how do you say... set *ze* meat aside... marinate, *ja*, marinate. She makes *sauerbraten*—a very good dish. Helga makes a *vonderful sauerbraten*," explained the blonde maid, as if to a child.

"I had hoped to serve an honest roast beef to Sir John, but never mind. Let us turn to Tuesday—"

Sofia interjected, "Lady Buford, *ve* must still decide today's meal."

"Why? I thought we were having... *sour-bratten*."

"Oh, *nein*. *Ze* marinate takes several days. *Sauerbraten* is not until Thursday."

"Well, what do you suggest? I would like to do something in the English style," Caroline asked the cook. She and Sofia jabbered in German for a minute and made several glances towards their mistress.

"Helga says she has some very nice *Würste*... sausages."

"Bangers and mash is a bit rustic, but it will have to do. I would like some mashed potatoes with that, peas—"

"No peas—is *vinter*."

Caroline raised her eyebrows. "I understand it is winter, but surely you have some dried peas."

More gibbering. "Helga has no dried peas. She *vill* make some nice beets... *rote Rüben*... along *vith Erdäpfelsalat*."

Caroline had no idea what *Erdäpfelsalat* was. "You do have bread in this"—*godforsaken*—"country, do you not?"

"*Ja!* No finer bread in *ze vorld!* As special treat, she *vill* make *Leberknödelsuppe*—*vonderful* Austrian soup—and *Meranertorte* for dessert."

Caroline surrendered with a sigh. "Very well. As for Tuesday—"

"Special treat!" cried Sofia. "*Wiener Backhendl!*"

And so the morning went on. Caroline had the distinct impression that she was an object of amusement for the staff, but she had no evidence to prove it. What was obvious was that Sofia did not think much of her mistress, or anyone else who was not Austrian. Caroline intended to speak to Sir John about it that evening.

Finally, the carriage pulled up before the Wellington townhouse. "Thank you, Sofia," said Caroline before the girl could move from her seat, "but I believe I can manage on my own. After all," she added, "we all speak English here."

"But, *vhat* shall I do?"

"I am sure there are some errands. Have the carriage back here in an hour."

Caroline took her leave of the troublesome maid and announced herself at the front door. Directly she was shown to a small antechamber near the door where she was divested of her hat, coat, and gloves.

As Caroline reentered the hall, she saw a tall, slim, elegantly dressed woman approach her. "Lady Buford? Welcome to our home. I am Lady Beatrice Wellesley." She held out her hands to the young woman.

Caroline fell into a deep curtsy, earnest to make a good impression. "I am deeply honored to make your acquaintance, my lady. I hope I am not behind my time."

A low, rich laugh escaped the older woman. "Oh, my dear, please do not stand on ceremony. There is enough of that outside this house." The two clasped hands. "May I call you Caroline? Allow me to wish you joy—this time in person—on the occasion of your marriage." Lady Beatrice's face broke into a sweet smile, and Caroline began to believe that, amazingly, Lady Beatrice was trying to befriend her. "How is dear Sir John? You both found the journey pleasant, I hope."

To her mortification, Caroline blushed. "Sir John is well. The journey was… very pleasant."

"Oh, I see." Caroline blushed deeper, which caused Lady Beatrice to laugh softly again. "Forgive me, my dear; I shall tease you no more. Come, the other ladies of the delegation are waiting to make your acquaintance. I understand you play the pianoforte; perhaps you will honor us?"

And so it begins, thought Caroline.

"…And that is the progress we have made to date." Wellington leaned back in his chair and looked at the assembled delegation about him. "Not enough—slow business this—but there it is."

"Sir, the agreement on the slavery issue is a notable achievement," said Buford.

"Thankee, Sir John. Yes, we did good work there." No politician was immune to flattery, and the duke liked it as much as the next man. "Only it is the Royal Navy that will enforce it. We cannot convince any of the other beggars to lift a finger." Wellington looked at his pocket watch. "Well, enough for now. 'Tis time to dine." The group of men rose and left the room. Buford lagged behind.

"Your lordship, I have some questions about the Polish situation."

Wellington dismissed Buford with a wave of his hand. "Enough of that, man! Get yourself home to that bride o' yours."

"How is your soup, dear?"

"Interesting." An English translation for *Leberknödelsuppe* would be liver dumpling soup. "I cannot say I have ever fancied liver, but this is good." Sir John told a small lie.

The main course was more successful. The sausages were excellent, the beets better than Caroline expected, and the dark rye bread was tasty. As for the *Erdäpfelsalat*—room temperature potatoes with onions and vinegar—it was not the mistress's idea of bangers and mash.

But Helga won over her employers with her *Meranertorte*—a piece of chocolate heaven that left the knight and his lady speechless, save for an occasional groan of pleasure. The two sat back in satisfaction as the plates were taken away.

"*Mein Fräulein, diene ich den Kaffee jetzt?*" asked Frau Lippermann.

Caroline winced. The only tea to be had in Vienna was the few boxes they had brought from England. Sofia assured them more could be acquired, but Caroline had her doubts; Sofia had recommended the *Leberknödelsuppe*, after all.

"Shall we adjourn to the library, dear?" she asked her husband. "*Kaffee*—library," she pantomimed to the housekeeper.

After they were served, the mistress waited until Sofia, finally becoming aware of her ladyship's glare in her direction, excused herself.

"Sir John, I wish to speak to you about the staff."

"What? Is something the matter?"

Now that she had begun, Caroline found it hard to continue. She did not want to lose Sir John's confidence in her abilities. "I am sorry about dinner. It was not what I was expecting—"

"Nonsense, m'dear! We are in a foreign country, you know. I will grant you the soup was a bit strange, but it does not signify. You must admit the dessert was excellent!"

"Yes, that is true, but—"

"If there is anything you do not like, just let Helga know. Sofia will translate."

Caroline put her coffee cup down. "It is about Sofia that I wish to speak to you." Sir John looked at his wife expectantly. "I have found her to be disrespectful."

"Indeed? In what way?"

"Well, nothing specific. It is her general attitude." She stopped as she heard her husband's gentle chuckle. "What do you find so amusing, sir?"

"Attitude? Oh, my dear Caroline, of course she has an attitude. She is Austrian! All these Teutonic types think they are God's gift to the world. Heaven help us if the Prussians, Bavarians, and Austrians ever get together. We would probably bring Bonaparte back to help take them on." He reached over and patted her hand. "No, you just keep the whip hand over that little girl and all will be well."

Sir John returned to his coffee, never realizing his blunder. He did have confidence in Caroline's abilities to run the household, but like so many military men before and after him, he did not understand that a household staff could not be managed like a regiment. In his experience, once an order was given, it was to be obeyed without question. This was a luxury not afforded his wife.

He also made another critical mistake. Like most men, he underestimated the young and blonde.

Caroline immediately hid behind a mask of indifference. A lifetime of training had taught her never to show how offended she might be at some careless or malicious remark. Her husband's patronizing comment had hurt her deeply, but her fear of being considered unable to do her duties—of being unworthy—stayed her tongue.

Chapter 9

Rosings Park

COLONEL FITZWILLIAM RUBBED HIS head as the carriage rocked over a rut in the road.

"Does your head hurt, Cousin?" asked Anne de Bourgh disapprovingly, sitting across the carriage from him with her companion, Mrs. Jenkinson.

"Just a slight headache. A trifle—it will pass soon enough." Actually, Richard's head was splitting, but he was not about to admit it to her.

Darcy might think nothing of fifty miles of good road in a well-sprung carriage, but Richard would wager he had never been on the road to Hunsford with a drunken headache!

Yesterday was the wedding of Kitty Bennet to Mr. Southerland, an excellent reason to make merry. That, however, was not the sole reason for Richard's current distress. His overindulgence in Mr. Bennet's excellent cellar was in anticipation of his duty today: He must journey to Rosings to set right whatever Lady Catherine had damaged. Moreover, he was to do it himself, for there would be no father or Darcy to help him.

Lord Matlock had let Netherfield for the duration of the Darcy, Bingley, and Fitzwilliam families' stay in Meryton during the Southerland wedding. For a week, Richard had been closed up in the study with his father and Darcy reviewing all contracts and other estate matters regarding Rosings. Too much wine was not the only reason Richard's head was bursting. Never again would the colonel mock his father, his brother, or his cousin, for he learned how taxing the proper management of an estate could be.

Richard eyed his cousin, who was looking out the carriage window with a sour expression on her face. He wondered why Anne seemed so cross with him. She surely knew nothing of his mission. She almost certainly thought he was taking this opportunity of returning her and Mrs. Jenkinson to Rosings to visit Aunt Catherine earlier than he usually did.

Anne's unhappy mood disturbed Richard greatly. He had always gone out of his way to pay attention to his cousin, feeling it was his duty to make up for Darcy's distance in his dealings with her. He knew that Darcy had little choice; any attention he showed Anne would have been taken by Lady Catherine as submission to her desire for a union between the two.

Simply put, Colonel Fitzwilliam did not like Anne being displeased with him.

A jarring bump in the road caused another shot of pain to race through the gentleman's head.

Lord! Four more hours of this.

"Richard! Come closer, boy. Let me have a good look at you!"

Lady Catherine was in fine form upon the travelers' arrival. She held court in her palatial sitting room, Mr. and Mrs. Collins seated on the divan next to her. Richard acknowledged the pair before addressing his aunt.

"Aunt Catherine." He bent to kiss her cheek, a jolt of pain behind his eyes. "I trust I find you well."

The old woman eyed him with a mixture of amusement and disparagement. "I was always celebrated for my strong constitution and robust health. Indeed, illness is a weakness brought on by lack of occupation and libertine behavior. I am sure that ill breeding is a cause of many of the world's maladies. One must always watch the bloodlines, be it dogs, horses, or... other things."

Will you never stop disparaging the Bennets, Aunt? Richard thought.

Mr. Collins seconded his illustrious patron's position. "Oh, yes, Lady Catherine. Why, just the other day, I was speaking to Mrs. Collins while preparing next week's sermon, pointing out a certain passage in scripture that exactly reaffirms your excellent observation of—"

"Yes, yes," Lady Catherine silenced him. The vicar deflated like a bullfrog that had ceased to croak. The mistress of Rosings must have noticed Richard's reaction to her words and hastened to correct them. "Anne is doing better now as you undoubtedly noticed during her visit in the north. Her delicate constitution is not rare among those of the highest station and must not be confused with those of low class.

"Well, Nephew, I am happy to see you. I am sure your affection for Rosings increases daily and that is what brought you to us early this year."

"How could it not?" cried her jester. "Such refinement, such—"

"Anne has gone to her room, has she? I am certain she is fatigued from the journey—coming from such a primitive part of the world." The good patroness took no notice of the flash of pain that flew over Mrs. Collins's face. "Rest is always good for the complexion."

As poorly as Richard was feeling, he could not resist responding. "Hertfordshire is a lovely place! Why, there was no snow or ice to speak of, and the roads were in good condition. Anne and Mrs. Jenkinson bore the journey very well."

Lady Catherine's face darkened. "I held the earl in higher regard than he deserves. I permitted Anne to stay with him and the countess for Christmas and depended on his judgment and sense of decorum, but he chose to involve her in this… this *circus* in Hertfordshire in the most inclement weather! Of what could he be thinking? The countess was behind it, I have no doubt! She and I have never agreed on anything. I suppose you saw your cousins while you were there?"

"Of course, Aunt. Darcy is… well, Darcy. Mrs. Darcy is as lovely as ever, and Georgiana was never in better spirits. She and the new Mrs. Southerland are particular friends. Master Bennet remained in Town, but I can assure you he is in excellent health."

"I understand Mr. Southerland has the living at Kympton," Lady Catherine stated. "It is a particularly good living—fifteen hundred per year, very likely more." Mr. Collins could not help but blanch at the considerable amount. Lady Catherine went on. "Very generous of Darcy, but I suppose he had *inducements* for benevolence."

Richard ignored the crude allegation. "Mr. Southerland is an excellent fellow and very attached to Catherine Bennet. One cannot but rejoice that the four sisters shall reside within such an easy distance of each other and that their husbands are so amenable."

The scowl on Lady Catherine's face revealed that she was displeased to have Georgiana described as Mrs. Southerland's sister, no matter how accurate it was, and Richard knew there could be no profit in the continuation of that line of conversation.

Lord Matlock had made it clear that he supported Darcy in his choice of wife, and all his family was expected to do likewise or suffer his displeasure. It clearly galled Lady Catherine to acquiesce to her brother's will—oh, how she railed against it—but *he* was the head of the family, and she depended on his "advice." There was only one thing Catherine Fitzwilliam de Bourgh feared, Richard knew, and that was her brother's anger. Therefore, the woman celebrated for her candor was reduced to making snide, somewhat obscure observations. She prided herself on being as impertinent as possible without crossing the line of impropriety—by Lady Catherine's definition of the word.

"Well," said Lady Catherine, "the hour is late. I am sure the Collinses are soon to depart." At the hint, the good reverend leapt to his feet. "You have missed dinner, Richard, but I shall have the housekeeper arrange a cold repast. Do you wish it to be sent to your room?"

Richard agreed to have his meal in his bedroom and took leave of his aunt and her guests.

"I will go down to the kitchen and have something sent up," said Mrs. Jenkinson. "You must be famished, my dear."

Anne de Bourgh sat on the edge of her bed and nodded. "Thank you, but please do not bother. You must be exhausted. I will see to it myself."

The older woman crossed to Anne, taking the young lady's hands in hers. "My dear Anne, it is no trouble, and I promise that after I eat, I will go straight to my room." She looked at her charge with affection. "I am so happy with your improved health over the last two years. It is truly a miracle. You are becoming quite the young lady. I think the time is quickly coming that you will not need old Mrs. Jenkinson to fuss over you. You will have some strapping young man for that, God willing."

Anne de Bourgh looked her old governess in the eyes with a steady composure but with glistening eyes. "No matter my fate, you shall always have a home in my house." The two women shared a quick embrace, and Mrs. Jenkinson left the room.

Later, as she prepared for bed, Mrs. Jenkinson thought over the last two years. For the twenty years since her husband's untimely death, she had been Anne's governess and companion and had despaired of ever seeing her young charge take her rightful place in the world. Anne had been a sickly child; her constant cough and runny nose prevented her from developing her talents and kept her shut up in her nursery and rooms for most of her life. It was hard to imagine the daughter of a baronet not learning to sing, or play, or dance, or draw, but at least Anne could improve her mind. Reading was her only joy—that was, reading what Lady Catherine would allow.

Mrs. Jenkinson was an obedient sort, taught never to question her betters, but her heart went out to Anne. She grew to love her like a daughter—the daughter she would never have. Therefore, she would do whatever she needed to do to help Anne survive. For twenty years, Mrs. Jenkinson followed Lady Catherine's commands to the letter, no matter how foolish or cruel. She would keep *her* girl alive, no matter how much her heart would rebel at her instructions.

Three years earlier, Fitzwilliam Darcy upset all of Lady Catherine's plans and dreams by marrying Miss Bennet. Mrs. Jenkinson by then knew her girl's mind—knew she did not love Darcy in *that* way—and that Anne was relieved of her fear of a forced, arranged marriage.

Then, two years ago, Mrs. Jenkinson's old aunt gave her some advice. Her aunt was wise in the old ways. She *knew* things—things that doctors and other men of science could not explain. Mrs. Jenkinson had thought over her advice for a long time. Then, one night, as she watched Anne's cough develop into yet another fever, she made up her mind.

That night, two years ago, she committed murder.

Richard lay on his bed, jacket off, hands behind his head, when there was a knock at the door. "Enter," he called out.

The housekeeper, Mrs. Parks, came in the room with a tray of chicken, cheeses, and bread. A bottle of Madeira was brought as well.

"Thank you. Please set it down on the table there." He rose and crossed over to the table. Popping a bit of cheese into his mouth, Richard noted that Mrs. Parks had not left. She stood in the middle of the room, looking expectantly at him.

"Mrs. Parks, I trust I find you in good health?"

The housekeeper's unreadable countenance did not change. "Well enough, I thank you."

"The… eh… staff—everyone getting along?"

"Perfectly, sir."

Richard was uncomfortable. He remembered Darcy's words: "*Trust Mrs. Parks. She can be of invaluable aid to you.*" Could Darcy have meant this stone wall? If Richard were back in his regiment, he would know how to deal with this. But he was not; this was a household and not *his* household.

Clearing his throat, Richard asked, "Mrs. Parks, is there *anything* you wish to tell me?"

In an emotionless voice, the housekeeper answered. "Everything in this household is as you see. I have no complaints to report. I very much enjoy my position here. Is that all?"

The slight air of insubordination was too much for Richard. Civilian or not, he knew of only one way to deal with this. Drawing himself up to his full height, he fixed his most severe glare on the woman—a glare that had caused not a few lieutenants concern over soiling their breeches. With the voice of a king's officer who had seen war and worse, he said, "I am glad to know of it. I will surely keep those sentiments in my mind." He allowed the pause to hang in the air before finishing. "That is all. You are dismissed."

Richard's quiet yet forceful tone lashed across the woman. It was a moment before Mrs. Parks could manage her curtsy and exit the room. No sooner had the housekeeper left, than Richard unhappily threw himself into the chair.

The interview had not gone well. Richard had learned nothing about the problems within the manor house, and that left him frustrated. He felt that he could not let down his father—or Darcy—or Anne.

Anne? He frowned. *Where did* that *come from?*

Dismissing the thought as quickly as it came, Richard returned to his meal with little appetite.

Mrs. Parks walked down the hallway towards her own quarters, fighting the small smile that threatened to come to her lips. She knew it would take a gentleman with extraordinary strength of character to stand up to the Mistress and set things right. She had quite despaired since Mr. Darcy's banishment from Rosings and had no faith in the happy-go-lucky soldier son of Lord Matlock.

But perhaps she was wrong. The young man had shown some steel beneath his genial exterior.

She could not stop herself from thinking that there might be hope for them, after all.

Anne de Bourgh snuggled deeply into her bedcovers. It was one of her favorite things to do on a cold winter's night. It was a pleasurable end to an eventful day.

Anne recalled how pretty Kitty looked—so happy, shy, and excited, all at the same time. Mr. Southerland walked around the entire time with a rather silly half-grin on his face, as if he could not believe his own good fortune. Anne wished the couple well, for she and Georgiana had become much attached to the girl.

Georgiana would be next, she imagined. How lovely a wedding at Pemberley would be! Perhaps Mr. Southerland would do the honors. Oh, how that would upset Mr. Collins! He still fretted over Elizabeth and Darcy's choice of a bishop. On and on her thoughts flew, ignoring the fact that Georgiana had no beau.

Anne loved to think of other people's weddings, for she expected none for herself. It was only in the last two years that she was healthy enough to overcome her mother's reluctance and spend time away from Rosings, but liberation from her gilded prison was limited, as was her company. Only to Matlock and finally Pemberley was Anne permitted to go.

Anne was realistic about marriage. She was not too old—yet—but she had no talents, no accomplishments, and no beauty. How was she to compete against the ever-replenishing pool of eligible young misses in society?

No, she was resigned to being the beloved, unmarried aunt to the Darcy and Fitzwilliam children. Anne's thoughts became melancholy as she began to drift off to sleep.

"I think the time is quickly coming that you will not need old Mrs. Jenkinson to fuss over you. You will have some strapping young man for that, God willing," Mrs. Jenkinson had told her.

No, dear Mrs. Jenkinson, there will be no young man for me, Anne thought to herself. *The only marriage that could have happened did not, thank heaven, because Darcy was wise enough to marry for love. And I am the same. I will only marry for love, and therefore, I will never marry, for I love in vain.*

All of her life, Anne's mother wanted her to marry Fitzwilliam Darcy. How would Lady Catherine react if she knew her daughter did love Fitzwilliam—just the wrong one?

Chapter 10

FITZWILLIAM AROSE EARLY, AS was his routine enforced by years in camp. After breakfast, he joined Rosings' steward in the library to review the condition of the estate.

Hours later, the steward left a very bewildered colonel in that room. Richard sat before a desk strewn with maps, contracts, agreements, surveys, estimates, and at least a dozen documents he could not understand. He had been prepared for work, but this was so far out of his experience that at first he felt a sense of drowning. Half of what the steward said sounded like gibberish. Finally, after giving over his pride, he began to ask what he thought were very simple questions, but the steward answered them fully, never showing in his countenance that he thought the colonel was a simpleton. No, in fact, he treated Richard with the greatest patience and respect and readily agreed to ride the property with him the next day.

As for Fitzwilliam, the lessons in estate management his father insisted he take had finally come back to him about an hour into the interview. Richard was still confused over many points, but the conclusion was clear: Rosings was failing. The realization of the true condition of the place weighed heavily on him. Richard wished that his father, his cousin, or even his brother, the viscount, were there to help him. But no, it was not to be.

For heaven's sake, man, what are you about? You have led a thousand men into the blazing guns of the French. You can do this. Richard looked at the piles. *It is simply a matter of organization. A table—that is the very thing I need.* Richard drew a blank sheet of paper from the desk drawer and began writing.

"Richard?"

Richard looked up and saw Anne peeking around the library's door, dressed in a heavy winter cloak.

"Come in, my dear." He rose, crossed to her, and took her hands. "Anne, have you just come in from outside? Your hands are like ice! Come, sit by the fire." He escorted his cousin to a chair by the fireplace, despite her protests.

"I am not chilled at all. I rather enjoy my winter walks. The air is so invigorating!"

"Really, Anne! Think of your mother. She would be distressed at this behavior."

Anne's eyes went wide, and her good cheer fled. "Oh, please do not tell Mother! She would certainly forbid me my walks!"

Richard's self-righteous concern faded at the sight of his cousin's distress. "Never fear, my girl. I will not reveal your secret. Mum's the word." He absently patted her hands.

"Thank you. Please believe me, I am not in any danger; I am so much better now. You will see." She gripped his hands firmly and then released them. Changing the subject, she asked, "What are you doing? Why are all those papers spread out over the desk?"

Richard turned to look. "Estate matters—I was quite a while with the steward."

"So, you have taken Darcy's place? Such a collection! You were shut up with the gentleman for no little time, but with this evidence of your labors, one can scarcely wonder why." Anne rose and crossed to the desk. She picked up the paper Richard had been working on. "What is this?"

"'Tis nothing." Richard was sure that Anne knew nothing of the condition of Rosings and did not want to alarm her.

"It is a chart of some sort." She peered closely at the document.

"Nothing to worry your pretty head—"

Anne's head jerked up, fire in her eyes. "Colonel Fitzwilliam, I would ask you not to patronize me in such a manner! I know I am but a poor woman, but Rosings is *my* home, and I deserve to be acquainted with all its concerns!"

Richard was taken aback. All his life he had known Anne as quiet and sickly. She had just reminded him that she was also the daughter of Lady Catherine de Bourgh.

"Forgive me. I had no intention of patronizing you." He drew closer to her. "This is a table I am drawing up. As I am new to the particulars of Rosings, and owning a preference for organization, I was compiling—"

"A chart of accounts, a listing of income and expenses. I see," she finished for him, surprising the colonel yet again. She looked up with a small smile. "'Tis not so different from running a household."

Richard had to own that it was so. His opinion of Anne rose.

She looked about at the papers. "You have quite a task before you. Tea will be served soon; that is why I came looking for you. Perhaps after we eat, I may assist you."

Startled, Richard blurted out, "You? Oh, no, I will see to it—"

"I beg your pardon?" Anne's head came up slowly and her eyes narrowed. "Do I understand you to say that I am *incapable* of helping with such a chore?" Anne demanded, her voice growing louder. "I know I am only a *poor woman*, but—"

"Peace, Cousin!" Richard cried, cutting off the lady's protests.

"Forgive me; I misspoke again. I only wished not to inconvenience you." Seeing that she still was not mollified, he added, "Think of what my aunt would say should she learn of your being involved in such a task."

Anne frowned for a moment and then brightened. "But nothing is easier! All Mother needs to know is that you returned to the library to finish your task while I choose to read this afternoon. We shall be safe. Mother never enters the library."

Unable to overcome Anne's reasonable solution, the colonel surrendered. "I would be very happy to have your assistance this afternoon, Anne." He grinned ruefully at her bright smile of thanks. She would have to learn the truth about Rosings sometime.

Four hours later, Richard sat in a wingback chair, reviewing their labors with satisfaction. The chart was not perfect; already he could see areas where it could be improved. Richard was pleased to see that Anne had anticipated some of those improvements in the notes she made in the margins.

He glanced at his cousin, still sitting at the desk. They made a good team, he thought. He could not have accomplished so much without her assistance. Anne decided that it would be best that Richard review the documents while she entered the information into the chart. Her steady penmanship and probing questions served very well, and Richard became familiar with far more details than if he had tried to do the task himself.

Of course, he was almost undone by Anne reaching into her reticule and pulling out a pair of spectacles. At his questioning look, she admitted that she needed them for close work such as reading, sewing, or writing. Anne was clearly embarrassed as she put on the spectacles, obviously under the impression that they ill suited her. Nothing could be further from the truth as far as Richard was concerned. To his eyes, she looked rather adorable, especially when she looked at him from over the rim as they hung near the end of her pert little nose.

The chart was a good beginning; already Richard could see patterns and tendencies. Various solutions already germinated in his head. The ride he planned to take in the morning would settle many things in his mind.

Anne's thoughts were different as she now gazed at her cousin, his long, fit body stretched out, feet on the ottoman. She was startled to learn how things were at Rosings. She had felt that there was something amiss, especially during her visits to the village of Hunsford, but she had not known before how badly conditions had deteriorated. She hoped that Richard could find a way of setting things right, but for her part, she was worried.

It was hard, however, to think of land and harvests and contracts when before her was such a sight of masculine beauty. Richard's ruddy complexion, grown tan by his years out-of-doors, complemented his sandy red hair and light blue eyes. He sat in the chair in complete relaxation, as only a man who had known hardship could relax. His body was lean and well formed; his years in the saddle had suited him very well. He gave every impression of a man of action, ready to defend all that he loved, yet still in possession of a kind heart. Anne sighed. There was no use in losing herself to such thoughts, so she resumed her work.

After a few minutes, Richard looked up to see Anne rearranging the many stacks of paper the two of them had spent hours on.

"Anne," he asked, "what are you doing?" His breath almost caught in his throat as she looked up at him from above those spectacles again.

Unaware of the effect she had on him, Anne replied, "I am preparing the papers to be put away."

"They are already arranged. Why change them now?"

She looked at him as though the answer was obvious. "They were arranged by type—bill, contact, letter, map. Would it not be more convenient in the future if they were filed away by name?"

All afternoon Anne had surprised Richard by her forethought, and not for the first time, he wished she were mistress of Rosings!

"Oh!" cried Anne. "It is almost time to dress for dinner. Mother will be expecting me. Richard, I will finish this task later. I expect we will see you in a few minutes in the sitting room." With that, Anne swept out of the room.

The weather the next morning had moderated, though the clouds threatened snow. Richard found the ride with the steward around Rosings holdings to be enlightening, but he was left with as many questions as answers. One parcel of land was particularly vexing: The current tenant, aged in both body and custom, was unable to grasp modern methods of farming. Richard decided to ride into Hunsford, so he bid the steward good day and rode towards the village.

On the road, Richard espied the de Bourgh carriage apparently proceeding to the same destination, so he spurred on his horse to join the vehicle. His surprise was complete to see Anne and Mrs. Collins in the carriage, and that Anne's hands held the reins.

"Good day, ladies!" he cried. "Where are you going? Shopping, I dare say."

"You may well say so, sir, but you would be mistaken," replied his well-bundled cousin with a cheeky smile. "We are to visit some of the tenant families in the neighborhood. Would you care to join us?"

"I should like it of all things. Lead on!"

The first stop was at the humble cottage of Mr. Clarke, one of the younger farmers, a man described to Richard by the steward as having ability but little land. The group was greeted at the door by Mrs. Clarke. Slightly flustered, the lady escorted her visitors into a small but neat sitting room.

"Ladies, how kind of you to visit! Colonel Fitzwilliam, Mr. Clarke will be so disappointed that he missed you, but he is attending to business in the village. May I offer you some tea? It would only take a moment."

Anne smiled. "Thank you, but do not trouble yourself." She held out the basket she had brought in. "This is from Mrs. Collins and me. It is not much—some sugar, preserves, a bit of spice." She did not mention the bread and chicken. "The children will like the cookies, I dare say."

"Oh, Miss de Bourgh, you're too kind. I cannot accept—"

"Please, Mrs. Clarke," said Mrs. Collins, "'tis but a gift." The parson's wife glanced at the children looking from around the corner. "There are *strawberry* preserves, too," she added.

The requisite protest expressed and the expected rejoinder made, Mrs. Clarke accepted the basket with good grace and not a little bit of relief. Their larder had been getting bare.

Richard watched the exchange in quiet approval. Anne was growing in his estimation with every passing day.

"I must thank you for your kind visits, Miss de Bourgh," Mrs. Clarke said. "How is your good mother? It has been so long since we have had the pleasure of seeing her Ladyship in Hunsford, save on Sundays."

This caught Richard's attention. So Lady Catherine had been neglecting her duty to Hunsford?

Anne hesitated, and Mrs. Collins began to reply, "Lady Catherine is in good health—"

"*Ah-choo!*"

All turned to the source of the sneeze. "God bless you, Miss de Bourgh. Are you well?" asked the hostess.

"I… I am—*ah-choo*!" Anne sneezed again, her eyes watering. "Just a passing fit."

Richard watched his cousin with concern. It had been some time since he had seen Anne ill. Then he saw a gray streak dart past them out of the corner of his eye. Pausing by the doorway to the kitchen was a large gray cat, its golden eyes staring back at the colonel. The animal then fled into the other room.

Mrs. Clarke saw what caught the gentleman's attention. "Oh, do not mind the cat, sir. It is no bother; the children love her and she keeps the vermin down."

Richard's reply was cut short by Anne rising to her feet. "Forgive me, Mrs. Clarke. I feel I must be going now," she said between sniffles. Everyone arose, and politely assuring Mrs. Clarke of Miss de Bourgh's health, the visitors made their good-byes and left the cottage.

"Goodness, Anne," Mrs. Collins cried after the carriage got back under way. "You are quite ill! We must return to Rosings immediately."

"No, Charlotte, I am well—'tis just a passing fit, as I said. I am feeling better already, I assure you. But I do wish to return home."

Richard, riding alongside on his horse as the snow began to fall, heard nothing of this conversation. He finally realized what was missing at Rosings.

The family, along with the Collinses, gathered for dinner. By then Anne was recovered from her sneezing attack, although her eyes were slightly red. Mrs. Jenkinson was quietly concerned. Lady Catherine, commanding the conversation from the head of the table as usual, took no notice.

"The spring planting season will be upon us very soon, Mr. Collins," she said. "It is very important to prepare the beds thoroughly for vegetables to ensure a bountiful crop. One cannot begin too soon."

"Indeed, Lady Catherine," responded her favorite, ignoring the fact that his patroness had made this speech annually at this time. "Your kind consideration to my wife and me with your excellent advice has improved my humble yet comfortable situation and has given my family far more in food and flowers than anyone could expect."

His mistress acknowledged the praise with the barest of nods. "I am glad you think so; however, I recall that your potato larder was somewhat lacking this winter. Obviously, your man did not carry out your instructions to the letter. This will not do, sir! This year you must see to the work yourself."

Mr. Collins paled at the thought, while Mrs. Collins cringed—it was evident that she knew her husband would follow Lady Catherine's advice to the letter, no matter how inconvenient or outlandish.

It was at this time Colonel Fitzwilliam decided to change the subject. "Aunt Catherine, I have been here several days and not once have you regaled us with tales of your delightful Cleopatra." Cleopatra was the latest in the line of a series of long-haired cats Lady Catherine kept as a personal pet in her private rooms. "Come, I am sure we would all like to hear about the latest mischief of that rascal."

The silence that greeted this request was deafening. The Collinses turned red, Mrs. Jenkinson kept her eyes firmly on her plate, and Anne nearly gasped. Lady Catherine, who was eating at the time, sat shock still, her fork poised in midair. Slowly the old woman lowered her fork onto her plate; only after that was accomplished did she slowly turn her eyes to her questioner. A chill went down Richard's back as he beheld the raw pain in his aunt's face.

"Cleopatra is dead," she said, her words falling heavily on the table.

"My dear aunt! I am so sorry—I had no idea! Please accept my condolences. It is an awful thing, to be sure, to lose one's pet. I take it the tragedy was a recent event?"

Anne reached over to touch Richard's hand as a warning. "No, Richard, it happened over two years ago. It is still very painful—"

"Murdered!" cried Lady Catherine. "She was murdered!"

"Mother—" began Anne.

"What did you say, Aunt?" asked Richard. "Did you say murdered?"

"Murder most foul it was, Richard." Lady Catherine became more agitated. "I went to my rooms one evening and my dear, sweet Cleopatra was missing. She never left the room! I knew something was amiss. I roused the house, looked everywhere, including outside, and then—"

Richard, ignoring Anne's tightening grip on his hand, asked, "And?"

Lady Catherine lowered her head and spoke in a dreadful voice. "She was found by a stable hand near the barn, limp and lifeless."

Now Richard was thoroughly confused. "Were there any marks on the carcass… er… body?"

Dramatically his aunt answered, "No—*none*."

"Then how is it you say that someone killed your cat?" Richard cried.

"Someone deliberately removed Cleopatra from my rooms and set her outside where some beast could attack her." Lady Catherine ranted. "Such a sweet and defenseless creature! She was frightened to death, I am sure!"

Richard was not so sure; animals had been known to seek solitude when they felt their time was near. "A tragedy, aye, there is no doubt. I am so very sorry for your loss, my dear aunt." He reached over with his free hand—Anne still held the other—and patted the old woman's hand. "Have you given any thought to getting another?"

There was a crash. "Oh, clumsy me," cried Mrs. Jenkinson. "I dropped my glass. Here," she said to the maid, "help me clean this up."

"It was water, was it not, Mrs. Jenkinson? Pray say you did not spill wine!"

"Never fear, Lady Catherine, it was only my water goblet," said Mrs. Jenkinson. "I am so sorry, madam."

"Get up all of the water, girl," Lady Catherine ordered the maid, "or the table will mark. Ah, Richard, where were we? Another cat—no, I am afraid nothing can replace my dear Cleopatra."

Richard looked upon his aunt kindly. "She was sweet and affectionate, I dare say."

"Cleo?" snorted Lady Catherine. "I should say not! She was stately and regal—"

Standoffish and cold, thought Anne.

"—very particular of whom she would tolerate—"

A hateful little beast.

"—an excellent judge of character—"

Only her mistress could approach her.

"—and the owner of the loveliest long white coat."

Cat hair all over creation.

"No, Richard, there will never be another such as my Cleopatra," the mistress of Rosings finished with a sigh.

"I quite agree," Mr. Collins injected. "Losing a pet can be the most trying of events. Why, we have sometimes thought of acquiring a small dog for the parsonage to entertain the children. But when we recall the pain our most esteemed patroness weathered with such courage when tragedy struck, I am afraid that our humble hearts are not up to the challenge."

The *grand dame* turned on the hapless clergyman. "Are you comparing my Cleopatra to a mere *dog*? Of what can you be thinking?" Before Mr. Collins could apologize, Aunt Catherine turned to her nephew and asked, "What is the reason for your inquiry, Richard? I did not know you were so fond of my cat."

"To own the truth, Aunt, I had never laid eyes on her. A small animal, I take it."

"Cleopatra was neither large nor small," Lady Catherine replied.

"Medium-sized, then—a perfect dimension for a cat."

Lady Catherine looked slightly affronted. "*I* should not describe Cleopatra as anything as ordinary as 'medium.' She was the proper size of a truly superior creature."

At Richard's puzzled expression, Mrs. Collins held up her hands indicating the size of the beast.

An officer in his majesty's army should be quick of mind, and generally, it could be said that virtue was owned by Colonel Fitzwilliam, but that day his wits failed him. "Why, that looks to be about the size of the cat we saw today in Hunsford—would not you say so, Anne?"

In that lady's panicked expression, Richard saw his error. His only hope was that Aunt Catherine did not closely follow his meaning.

A false hope.

"I beg your pardon?"

"Yes, Aunt Catherine?" returned Richard, hoping to minimize the damage.

"Am I to understand that you saw a cat in Hunsford today?" she inquired.

"Yes, Aunt Catherine."

"Anne saw the same cat?"

"Yes, Aunt."

"In Hunsford?"

"Yes."

"Where, may I ask, did you both see a cat in Hunsford?"

Before Richard could say anything else, Anne told her mother, "At the home of Mr. and Mrs. Clarke, one of Rosings' tenants."

"You saw it from your carriage."

"No, Mother—in Mrs. Clarke's sitting room. We delivered a basket."

Lady Catherine drew in her breath. "Anne, do you mean to say you, *a de Bourgh*, entered a farmer's house? One of those dirty hovels?"

Richard cut in. "Aunt Catherine, please—"

"Silence!" the woman roared. "Well, miss, what do you have to say for yourself?"

Anne leapt to her feet. "I have nothing to say, Mother, except I was doing God's work. And I would do it again!"

"God's work?" Lady Catherine sneered as she rose from her chair. "Charity promotes idleness! My daughter, risking her health, paying visits to such that should be on their knees in thanksgiving that they are allowed to reside here—it is beyond everything!" She then turned on Mrs. Jenkinson. "How could you allow this? Is this how you protect your charge?"

"Mrs. Jenkinson was not there, Mother!" cried Anne. "If there must be blame, then direct it to none but me!"

"Do not speak to me in such a manner! It is not to be borne!" At that, Anne turned and fled the room. "Anne! Come back here this instant! Ungrateful child, I am not finished with you—" She began to follow Anne when her nephew stood to bar her way.

"You *are* finished with her, Aunt," Richard said sternly but quietly.

"How dare you! Get out of my way—"

"No. Sit down, Aunt Catherine." At her glare, he leaned down close to her eyes. "Please—sit—down."

After a moment, Lady Catherine returned to her seat.

"I think quite enough has been said for one day," Richard continued. "I will attend to Anne. Do I bring with me your apologies?"

"Apologies?" she sputtered. "It is *she* who owes me her apologies for forgetting the honor due her mother! You will tell her that for me, sir!"

"She does indeed owe you deference, madam, as you are her mother, but I shall not berate her or carry any demand from you for repentance on her part. Indeed, you should be proud of her. Yes, proud!" Richard said, his voice rising as Lady Catherine made to interrupt. "She was only doing right by your tenants. She was doing *your* duty."

"Duty?" Lady Catherine cried. "What do you know of duty?"

"You forget yourself, madam!" the colonel of cavalry roared. "Remember to whom you are speaking! Do not dare speak to *me* of *duty*!" Richard allowed his glare to fall upon his wide-eyed aunt for a few moments more before leaving the room in pursuit of Anne.

Mr. Collins was shocked at the exchange he had just witnessed. "Oh, my dear Lady Catherine! What is wrong with the young people these days, to speak in such a manner—?"

"Oh, be silent," said Lady Catherine.

Richard ran out of the house pulling on his coat, having been told by a servant that Miss de Bourgh had gone into the garden. Through the lightly falling snow, he saw a figure in a hooded cloak walking slowly towards the woods. Without wasting a moment, Richard set off at a run in pursuit of the walker.

"Anne!" he called out. "Anne!"

The figure halted but did not turn. Richard caught up and turned the person around. It was indeed Anne de Bourgh, the hood pulled down over her weeping face. Richard's heart wrenched at the site of her tears running down her lovely cheeks.

"Anne… Anne, please do not cry—I cannot bear it! This is no place for you. Come, I insist that you come inside where you may warm yourself. You will not have to face your mother; you will be left in peace. I swear it."

Anne looked up at her cousin. Richard was mesmerized by the lady's lips, so soft and inviting. He could think of nothing else but to kiss those lips, that nose, those tears. The realization then hit him like a thunderbolt.

He was in love with Anne de Bourgh.

For a full minute the two stood in the lightly blowing afternoon snow, the gentleman holding the lady by the shoulders, each looking the other full in the face, not knowing how the other felt, neither saying what was in their heart.

A sudden gust of wind hit the pair, bringing them to their senses and breaking the tableaux.

"I believe you are right—we should go indoors," said the lady.

The gentleman nodded and held out his arm. Silently the pair returned to the house.

Chapter 11

RICHARD SAT IN HIS room that night, nursing a brandy and cursing himself. After he saw Anne into the house, Mrs. Jenkinson spirited his cousin to her rooms to get warm before Richard could say anything. But what could he say? How could he declare himself after insulting the lady's mother?

Instead, he retired to his room and immediately penned an offer to quit Rosings immediately and give up his office as advisor on estate matters. There was no hint of any remorse in his note for his words to his aunt; Richard felt none, and he would stand by those words for the rest of his life. He now sat and morosely waited for his aunt's response; he did not doubt that the grand lady would accept his resignation.

Richard was a competitive man. All his life, he strove to win, and it pained him to his bones to lose. His drive had kept him alive on the battle-field, but now he knew he had failed. His ungovernable temper had let down his family and cost him the woman he had unwittingly wanted all his life.

He could see that now. All the years he had been coming to Rosings, it was always to see Anne—to show her some kindness and attention, to ease her life. When had affection grown into something more? Richard could not name the date or time; it had grown slowly. He knew his feelings had blossomed in concert with Anne's own blossoming in recent years. And now, when Richard finally knew what he desired, he had thrown it all away.

Richard chuckled to himself. He could envision the scene: him standing, hat in hand, before his imperious aunt. *"Lady Catherine, I formally request your permission to court your daughter, Miss de Bourgh, for the purpose of matrimony."* He wondered if she would laugh before she had him thrown out the door.

Richard knew Anne's mind; she would never go against her mother's wishes. Of course, he was assuming the lady felt the same about him. She did not want Darcy. Why would she want poor Richard Fitzwilliam, a second son with little income aside from his pay from the crown? Perhaps it was not so much the idea of a union with Darcy that displeased Anne as it was the whole concept of marriage to a cousin. Richard's thoughts grew ever bleaker as he sipped his drink before the fire.

Finally, the expected knock came. Slowly, Richard rose, crossed to the door, and opened it to behold the butler with a note on a silver tray. Richard took the note, thanked the butler, and closed the door. He walked over to the back of his chair, looking at the name on the cover: *Colonel Richard Fitzwilliam.* As there was no profit in postponing the inevitable, he broke the seal and began to read.

Colonel Fitzwilliam,

I have received your note offering to resign your office here at Rosings. While your apology was not clearly laid out, I must assume that you meant to do so by your offer of resignation. I am pleased that you admit your fault, though it was done in such an obscure manner.

Your offer of resignation is not accepted. I expect, as a member of the Fitzwilliam family, you shall see to your duties as usual in the morning.

Yours, etc...

Richard stared at the note for some time, not quite believing the words therein. Had it not been for the haughty manner of the writing, he certainly would have suspected a forgery. Finally, he fell into the chair he had vacated, the note hanging from his fingertips.

For some reason Richard could not fathom, Aunt Catherine had chosen to view his letter as an apology so that Richard could remain to complete his task as Rosings. The colonel did not hold the belief that affection for his person had stayed the lady's hand.

No, he knew that something else was at work here. It would be a while before he could find sleep.

Anne came downstairs the next morning, not knowing whom she dreaded seeing more, her mother or her cousin. Seeing neither in the breakfast room, Anne sought out the housekeeper.

"Mrs. Parks, has either my mother or Colonel Fitzwilliam been down to breakfast?"

"No, miss," replied Mrs. Parks. "Colonel Fitzwilliam has had nothing but a cup of tea; he has been in the library with the steward this last hour. Your mother is having her breakfast upstairs. Shall I fix a plate for you, miss?"

"Just a little something—perhaps toast with jam," said a surprised yet relieved Anne. "I am to meet Mrs. Collins for a stroll very soon." As Anne ate her light breakfast, she could not prevent her eyes from straying to the door of the library down the hall. Knowing Richard was there unsettled her. She left her breakfast half eaten and prepared to go on her walk.

Anne was soon among the trees in the grove. The air, while still chilly, had moderated from yesterday's cold, and the snow was already half melted. *Spring is in the air*, Anne thought when she heard Charlotte calling her name. The two friends soon met and continued to walk amongst the trees.

"How are you today, Anne?" began Charlotte.

"Much better, I thank you. I have not sneezed once."

Charlotte eyed her companion. "Anne, as happy as I am to hear you in good health, I believe you know I was not inquiring about your sneezing." At Anne's continued hesitation, Charlotte declared, "Forgive me, Anne. It was not my intention to pry."

Anne stopped and turned to the other woman. "Oh, I do not believe that was your intention. You are concerned for me, I know. It… it is just that—oh, you will think me foolish!"

"My dear, please share your burden with me."

"Mother upset me greatly yesterday."

"Yes, we were all witness to her abominable behavior towards you." Charlotte lowered her voice. "May I tell you a secret? Even Mr. Collins was upset with Lady Catherine."

"You are joking!" Anne gasped. "Mr. Collins?"

"You could not be more astonished than I. He was troubled that his esteemed patroness would show the bad manners to publicly berate 'the district's finest flower' for doing her Christian duty." Charlotte added with a smile, "Though he only admitted it to me after we were safely in our bedroom where the servants could not overhear." Both women giggled. "But, Anne," Charlotte continued after the laughter died down, "there is more to your melancholy than your mother. Might it have something to do with a certain officer?"

Anne whirled to her friend. "How? How did you know?"

"Oh, Anne, I have known it for some time."

"Why have you not spoken of it before?" Anne then paled. "Do you think anyone else knows?"

"Mrs. Jenkinson might suspect," Charlotte considered. "Elizabeth, as well—"

"Elizabeth!"

"Georgiana… Mr. Darcy, too—they can keep nothing from him."

Anne put both hands to her face. "Oh, no!"

Charlotte took her friend's hands into her own. "Fear not, Anne. It is certain that your mother suspects nothing. No one who would inform Lady Catherine of your feelings toward Colonel Fitzwilliam has the slightest idea as to your inclinations. Your secret is safe." Anne's face could not hide her relief. "Safe even from your love."

Anne turned away. "Then everything is well—" she began to say when she heard a snort of frustration from her companion.

"Not again!" Charlotte cried to the heavens. "Three years ago only I saw what was happening between Mr. Darcy and Elizabeth. I said nothing, and look at the pain it caused!"

Anne was amazed at Charlotte's outburst. "What pain? Did something happen while they were here that spring?"

"Never mind; it is not my tale to tell. In any case, all ended well. But I shall not stand idly by again." Charlotte took Anne by the shoulders. "My dear friend, believe me when I say that Colonel Fitzwilliam is in love with you!"

"No, it cannot be," said Anne. "You are wrong—"

"Anne, I have watched the both of you. To my eyes, it is as obvious as the sun!" Charlotte tried another approach. "Anne, will you admit to feelings for the colonel?"

Anne blushed, her eyes firmly planted on the ground.

"Anne?"

"Yes," said Anne in a small voice.

"You love him?"

"Yes."

"Do you not want him to return your love, or do you believe that you are not worthy of him?" Charlotte frowned. "For it is my opinion that he is not worthy of you!"

"How can you say that?" cried Anne. "Richard is the best of men!"

"Bah! A few medals, surviving Bonaparte—what is that compared to what you have endured your entire life? If he is such a great man, why has it taken him so long to know his own mind?"

"I… I do not understand."

"Colonel Fitzwilliam has been in love with you for about as long as you have been in love with him. It is true! Only, you have admitted to the truth of your heart's desire and for a very long time, have you not? If Mr. Darcy had followed his aunt's demands and asked for your hand, you would have refused him, is that not so?"

Anne nodded.

Charlotte continued. "But the colonel has only this week realized his true feelings for you. I watched him at the Clarkes' and as he defended you against Lady Catherine. Believe me; he is violently in love with you."

Anne's mind rebelled at the words of her friend. For so long when she was ill, she felt unable to love—unworthy of being loved. Now that she was improved, why did she continue to feel that way?

Charlotte's eyes bore into hers. "Do not let your mother poison you against happiness."

Anne's head snapped up, and tears began to run down her face.

Charlotte, distressed, embraced the young woman. "Oh, Anne, forgive me!"

As Charlotte hugged Anne, a thought cut through the jumbled thoughts of the heiress: *Richard—yesterday—that look in his eyes. I thought he was going to kiss me.*

Anne broke the embrace and looked at Charlotte with a dawning smile on her face. "He wanted to kiss me."

"What?"

"He wanted to kiss me."

Charlotte was puzzled. "Who wanted to kiss you?"

"Richard, silly! It was in his eyes. I saw it. He wanted to kiss me!"

Charlotte's eyes grew wide. "When?"

"In the snow!" Anne was downright giddy now.

"When were you in the snow?"

"Yesterday! After we fought with Mother. He came after me and wanted to kiss me in the snow!" Anne broke free and did a pirouette, laughing the whole time. "Hurrah!"

Charlotte watched in open-mouthed shock at her friend's exhibition. Anne then grasped Charlotte, giggling.

"Oh, Charlotte, you are right! He does love me!" Unable to resist, Charlotte began to giggle, too. "He… he wanted to kiss me! He must want to marry me! Marry *me*! Oh, Charlotte, I have never been so happy!" The women hugged again in laughter and tears.

Suddenly, Anne pulled away and looked Charlotte in the face. "What do I do now?"

Anne's confused expression quickly sobered Charlotte. With a slight smile, she looked at her companion and said, "You must let the colonel know that his attentions are welcomed."

"But… how do I do that?"

Charlotte sighed. "You will find a way, my dear."

Upon the steward leaving the library, Richard stood and stretched to relieve the stiffness in his back. As his back was to the door, he was surprised to hear a voice.

"May I come in?"

Richard assumed a more proper pose and turned towards his visitor. "Yes, Mrs. Parks, do come in. Please, have a seat." Richard waited until the housekeeper was comfortable. "Now, madam, how may I be of service to you?"

"I understand you wish to speak to me," she replied.

"Yes, I do. I would like to speak with you about the household. As you may know, I am empowered to look into all aspects of the management of Rosings Park. Your cooperation in this endeavor is vital."

She handed him a packet of papers. "I have here the current household budget as well as the current accounts with the shopkeepers in Hunsford."

"Thank you, Mrs. Parks." Richard set the packet aside. "I shall review them in a moment. Now as for the staff here—"

"You will find a roster of all employees of the house in that packet along with their backgrounds and dates of hire."

Richard walked behind the desk to take his seat. "I have already seen the reports of the tenants and the groundskeepers here at Rosings, but I cannot find *your* employment agreement or that of the steward." He gestured at the stacks of papers.

Mrs. Parks unsuccessfully hid her slight smirk. "You will not find *them* in there, sir. The mistress had them burned, you see, but it does not signify. The solicitor has got the originals."

Richard took a moment to digest this information. Why would Aunt Catherine do that? Did she mean to sack both of them; if so, why were they still here?

"Ahem… it must be a trial, I suppose, to work here. My aunt can be rather capricious, I must admit. Your loyalty serves you well."

Mrs. Parks looked at him strangely. "As I said before—I very much enjoy my position here. Do you have any questions about that, sir?"

Richard became flustered. Dratted woman! He did not know what to make of her! "Well… I… umm… the uncertainty! I mean, there has been quite a turnover among the household staff here. I must admit I am surprised that you are still—well, to put it plainly, I am shocked that my aunt has not yet run you off!"

Mrs. Parks's expression became one of surprise. "Forgive me, sir; I had assumed you were better informed. I see now that you are operating under a mistaken understanding." Her eyes shifted to the window. "Though how you could have been sent here without being fully prepared! What a muddle—"

"Mrs. Parks," Richard cut in. "I insist you make plain your meaning."

The housekeeper returned her full attention to Richard. "Colonel Fitzwilliam, neither my situation nor that of the steward is dependent upon the goodwill of Lady Catherine de Bourgh. We are both employed by your father, the Earl of Matlock, and have been so for over fifteen years."

Chapter 12

A HALF HOUR LATER, Richard escorted Mrs. Parks through the door of the library, thanking her for her help. The housekeeper was everything Darcy claimed: intelligent, loyal, observant, and helpful. The time the two spent together was very profitable, and many questions were answered.

Richard learned that Mrs. Parks was in a constant battle with Lady Catherine over the management of Rosings Park. Mrs. Parks controlled the food budget. All else was subject to the whims of the mistress, including the hiring and firing of staff, with the exception of the butler, who answered to Mrs. Parks. The financial state was not what it should be, but it was not as dire as the rest of the estate; money had been put aside.

This coincided well with Richard's plans. He saw many places for economy, especially in his aunt's personal spending habits. He had no idea she spent as much as she did on clothes. Seeing the rather shocking figure did bring to the colonel's recollection that he had very rarely seen Aunt Catherine in the same dress twice.

As the lady took her leave to see to the dinner, Richard still wrestled with the key mystery. Mrs. Parks could not say why she and the steward were retained by his father or why Lady Catherine had agreed to such an arrangement. He made a mental note to ask the earl about this; he doubted his aunt would be forthcoming. As for Darcy, he wondered whether his cousin knew of the arrangement or whether he, too, was unaware of it.

Richard's generous heart felt a pang of concern for Lady Catherine's current state of mind. She had never been a very pleasant person, but since Darcy's marriage, his aunt seemed to grow more bitter each year. Now Richard thought he had the key to improving Lady Catherine's demeanor as well as a means to ease his way to acquiring his aunt's permission, if not approval, to seek Anne's hand. To his chagrin, he forgot to raise the matter with Mrs. Parks. He started to go after her when he espied someone who would do as well.

"Mrs. Jenkinson! Just the person I have been looking for!"

Mrs. Jenkinson curtsied. "Colonel Fitzwilliam, I am at your service."

"Thank you. I would like your opinion on a proposition. My Aunt Catherine has been out of sorts for some time. I trust we both know the reason for this." Richard did not note the alarm in the lady's eyes. "Therefore, I believe something should be done to remedy the sad circumstance that has caused her so much pain. I have in mind an idea to acquire a cat—a lovely new pet for my aunt. What color would you suggest?"

The electrifying result to this declaration was not at all what Colonel Fitzwilliam expected. Mrs. Jenkinson's eyes grew so wide that Richard thought they were in danger of popping out of her head. She began shaking, a low moan rising from her throat. Like a wild woman, Mrs. Jenkinson grasped Richard's lapel in one hand, opened the library door with the other, and dragged the stunned gentleman within.

The lady locked the door and turned on the colonel. "By all that is holy, you must not bring a cat into this house! A person's life may well depend on it!"

"Control yourself, madam!" Richard was at a complete loss to explain

Mrs. Jenkinson's behavior. "You are very ill! I must insist that you take this seat. A glass of wine—may I get you one?"

"No, no—Colonel, I insist that you pay attention to me. Please!"

"I am afraid I do not understand. Are you afraid of cats?"

"Good God!" the woman exclaimed to the heavens. "Is this my reward? I risk losing my position—even eternal damnation—to save my girl, only to be thwarted by this fool? Lord help me!"

Colonel Fitzwilliam was too astonished to be affronted.

With supreme effort, Mrs. Jenkinson gained control over her emotions. "Colonel Fitzwilliam, please. I know I have insulted you—it is insupportable—but I *know* I am right in this matter. You must know that I would do *anything* for Anne—"

"Anne? What does Anne have to do with this?"

"She has *everything* to do with it!" Once again, the lady paused to calm herself. "Sir, you are a wise man. You have a gentleman's education, and you have been to university. I deeply respect you. I believe you would make my girl—I mean, Miss de Bourgh—very happy." She saw Richard's stunned expression. "Oh, yes, I am aware of your attachment to Anne. Nothing would give me greater joy than to see you both secured in your affections and to see Anne as mistress of Rosings with you at her side."

Richard stuttered his denials, but Mrs. Jenkinson only smiled. "Forgive me, but I saw you both in the snow yesterday. No one could mistake the regard you hold for each other."

Richard's mind raced, and he tried to take in what he had just been told. *Each other? Does she think Anne feels the same way?*

Mrs. Jenkinson returned to the subject at hand. "You must believe, sir, that science cannot explain everything. It is like faith; it cannot be proved in this world. Do not ask me *how* I know—I just do. I *know* that cats are… are not good for our Anne."

Richard was still mystified. "But… but why? How can a cat hurt Anne?"

"I cannot say. But just observe! Since Lady Catherine's cat… went away, Anne's health has so improved that she believes she is strong enough to marry one day! That is proof enough for me."

In a flash of insight, Colonel Fitzwilliam realized there was much the lady knew about Cleopatra's demise that she was not disclosing.

"Mrs. Jenkinson, I must admit that I find your story… well, fantastic. It goes against everything I have been taught. But," he added as the woman attempted to interject, "I cannot deny that Anne has improved remarkably since… umm… the incident you describe. I will be guided by the evidence of my eyes. You have convinced me. I will bring no cat into Rosings."

Mrs. Jenkinson was clearly relieved. "Thank you, Colonel."

"Shall we join the others? It is nearly time to dine. We must not upset Lady Catherine by being tardy." Richard helped the lady to her feet but hesitated before going to the door.

"Let me make myself rightly understood, madam," he said in a stern voice. "I know of the affection in which you hold your charge. 'Tis a wonderful thing. However, the next time you consider taking matters into your own hands, no matter what the cause," he looked coldly into her eyes as only a Fitzwilliam could, "*do not.*"

Anne was already sitting at the table, nervously waiting for Richard's entrance. Charlotte's assurances of Colonel Fitzwilliam's affection had only changed the nature of her uncertainty. Before, Anne had been unsure of Richard's wishes. Now she was concerned over how to let him know of *her* feelings without acting in an improper manner.

Then, he was at the doorway, searching for her. The pair locked eyes for only a moment, but for her it was enough. Her entire world ceased to exist except to study Richard's face—his ruddy complexion, broken nose, funny ears, unruly sandy hair, and overly large mouth. That beautiful, ugly, darling face was graced by a small, all-knowing smile underneath his kind and lively blue eyes, twinkling with love for her.

Anne felt an overwhelming sense of clarity. She knew now that what Mrs. Jenkinson had told her was true: Her beloved loved her. She felt herself light up with joy as the nervousness fled from her body, only to be replaced by another unsettling feeling—one that could only be satisfied by Richard making his intentions known.

Lady Catherine coughed. "I am pleased you have chosen to grace us with your presence, Richard. Stop standing about in that stupid manner and take your seat or the soup will get cold."

Anne's happiness in the confirmation of her dreams was tempered; she wanted nothing more than for Richard to throw himself at her feet, in front of her mother, and beg her to make him the happiest man in the world. Of course, that could not happen. She would have to wait for a private moment soon. She hoped it would be in the same garden where they stood together in the snow.

However, her beloved could not resist giving some signal of his affection. Richard lightly brushed Anne's leg with his as he sat down beside her. His body prevented Lady Catherine from seeing the look of delighted surprise on the face of her daughter.

Conversation ended as the soup was served. Lady Catherine maintained a stream of meaningless small talk while they ate, but Anne was not deceived. Earlier in the sitting room, her mother informed her that she had magnanimously decided to forgive her daughter and nephew for their indiscretions of the day before. Anne knew that Lady Catherine's "forgiving" meant not bringing the incident up again immediately. Forgetting was not in her character, ever celebrated for its sincerity and frankness. Anne feared her mother's malice was a weapon sheathed only for the present.

As the soup was removed, Lady Catherine inquired, "I pray you have found your labors profitable today, Richard. A Fitzwilliam must always live up to his responsibilities."

"I quite agree with you, Aunt, and I have been most agreeably occupied this morning. I would like to make an appointment to speak to you about the particulars of my business—tomorrow afternoon, perhaps?"

Anne's mother was nothing if not predictable, so the heiress was astounded when Lady Catherine cried, "There is no need to stand on ceremony, sir. Speak up! We are all family here."

Richard looked up at his aunt's expectant face, shrugged his shoulders, and marched off to disaster.

"As you are aware, I have been reviewing the condition of the lands that make up the estate. It will come as no surprise to you that things are not what they ought to be. Yields and income have dropped over the last few years."

"Here, here. Have you discovered the malefactors?"

"Yes, Aunt, and I will tell you his name: Tradition."

Lady Catherine frowned. "Tradition? What do you mean by this? Come, come. Tell me the names of the indolent creatures. I will see that the constable runs them off."

Richard ignored her demand. "Aunt, there are a few older tenants who cannot properly work their lands. Their sons have fled to the cities for employment. There are also younger men who do not farm enough land to support their families. I will tell you of my plans for readjustment presently, but the real reason that yields are down is that the vast number of the tenants follow the traditional way of farming and do not embrace the new scientific methods."

"What methods?"

"Well, for one, crop rotation—allowing fields to lay fallow, to rest—"

"What! Surely you do not mean that wicked practice of neglecting one field in four!"

"'Tis a proven idea. My father uses it at Matlock—"

Lady Catherine was unimpressed. "It is a license to idleness! My income cut by a quarter so that men may sit whistling in the wind! How will my rents be paid?"

"Aunt, you must understand that yields on the remaining property will increase to such an extent that you will see no drop in income—eventually."

"Eventually?" cried Lady Catherine. "You see—you know that this method is false!"

"That is not what I meant." Richard took a breath. "The fields are in a critical condition. It will take a season or two to set things right—for new farmers to work their new fields—"

"New fields?"

"Yes, Aunt. Mr. Smith, for example, will be pensioned off. The land he worked shall be transferred to Mr. Clarke, a man small in holdings but large in abilities."

"Mr. Clarke! That babe? How will he pay the rent?"

"He will not—not for the first year," Richard admitted.

"What?"

Richard quickly explained his plan. "The harvest last season was too small to pay the rent and fill the farmers' larders. They chose to be honest men and paid their due. They have put their families at risk of hunger if not outright starvation. It is time we did right by them." Lady Catherine was too shocked to speak, so Richard continued. "I have instructed the steward to put in place my reforms and readjustments. For those who comply, there will be a rent holiday of one year, subject to review upon this fall's harvest."

Anne saw the justice in Richard's plan, but she expected her mother would prove hard to persuade. Lady Catherine did not disappoint.

"Are you saying there will be no rents this year?" Lady Catherine was finally able to squeak.

"I have reviewed your financial position. You have been frugal and have put money aside. With economy in the household and personal accounts, you will hardly notice the inconvenience, while strengthening the farming abilities of your lands. This will not go unnoticed by the people. All Hunsford will know of your generosity. By sharing their pain, you will win their hearts. Your name will be celebrated in the village square—"

"Thief!" Lady Catherine screamed. "Thief! You steal my money to give to that… that rabble! How could you do this to your family? Are you lost to all duty and honor? There is a viper in my house!"

"Mother!" cried Anne.

Richard tried to reason with her. "Madam, people will starve if we do not act."

"What do I care for that scum?" she spat. "They live in squalor, breeding their beggars, thieves, and whores! If they starve, it is God's judgment on them! And you wish to accommodate their sin!" She jabbed an accusatory finger in his direction and declared, "You are a traitor to your class!"

Anne was astonished by her mother's open vindictiveness. She looked at the others seated at the table. Richard was shocked silent, and Mrs. Jenkinson was ghostly pale.

"You will rescind your instructions at once!" Lady Catherine demanded, wagging her forefinger in the air. "Do you hear me? At once!"

Richard rose from the table. "No, Aunt, I will not."

"Do you defy me? It is not to be borne! You will not gainsay me. I shall stop your evil!"

Anne watched Richard respond to Lady Catherine's ravings with calm determination. "You may try, madam, but the steward will accept instructions only from me."

"No! I see it now! You are trying to steal Rosings from me!"

"Madam!"

"Silence! I know your twisted mind! You are in league with my brother—he is behind this! But I will stand for it no more! Out! Get out of my house this instant!"

There was a terrible stillness in the dining hall as the echo of Lady Catherine's demand faded. Without a word, a pale Richard gave his aunt a cold, polite bow and left the room.

Anne got up to follow her lover.

"Where are you going, miss?" demanded her mother.

Through her tears, Anne replied, "I care not, so long as it is away from this table. I am ashamed of you!"

With that, Anne fled the room, heedless of Lady Catherine's demands for her return.

Ten minutes later, a grim Richard stood by the door to his bedroom, watching his valet toss all his belongings unfolded into the trunk. He hated leaving Anne, but there was nothing for it. Lady Catherine had absolutely refused to see justice in his solutions to the crisis at Rosings, and he could stand her insults and wild accusations no more. At least his departure would give Anne some peace and quiet. As for himself, he would know no peace until he met with his father and devised a plan to save Rosings and protect his Anne.

His valet's task done, Richard opened the door to find Anne waiting without. He paused, searching for reproach in her fine eyes, but only found love and regret. Silently, the two unacknowledged lovers briefly embraced in the hall before heading downstairs, hand in hand, the valet carrying the trunk behind. Richard signaled that the valet continue to the coach, while he left Anne to go into the library.

Minutes later he emerged, a large packet of papers in his hand.

Richard took Anne's hand with his free hand, bowed farewell to Mrs. Parks, and exited the house with his beloved.

Richard halted before the coach. He handed the packet to the valet and turned to Anne.

"Richard!" she cried. "Take me with you!"

Slowly and sadly, the colonel shook his head. Taking both of Anne's hands in his, he looked intently at her. "Anne, I wish many things right now. I wish I could speak, but now is not the time. I cannot take you with me; you must remain. But do not despair!" He paused and then continued, slowly and deliberately, "As God is my witness, I shall return for you."

He stared at Anne until she nodded in acknowledgment.

"I do not believe you have anything to fear from your mother; her malice is reserved for me. However, should you require assistance, write to the earl, and I or another will come at once. Will you do that if the need arises? Promise me, Anne."

Anne nodded again.

His eyes softened. "Until we meet again, my dear girl."

With that, he kissed her hands and then turned them over to touch his lips softly to each of her palms. With one last, longing look into her shattered face, he leapt into the carriage and was off.

Anne stood at the foot of the steps, as still as death, watching the coach until it disappeared in the darkness.

Observing the whole scene from the parlor window behind her was Lady Catherine.

Chapter 13

Vienna

"ARE YOU ALMOST READY, my lady?" asked Sofia.

She will be ready when I am done, you Hessian hussy! thought Abigail, her annoyance with the Austrian interloper renewed at the sound of the girl's heavily accented English. Abigail was personal maid to Lady Buford and by rights should have been equal in rank with the housekeeper in the hierarchy of the Buford household. However, as Frau Lippermann only spoke German, Abigail was forced to share her position with this Teutonic troublemaker. The maid did not need a translator to know that Sofia despised both Lady Buford and her.

Abigail looked at her mistress in the mirror and saw that she too was exasperated with Sofia's superior ways. There was only one person's opinion that counted with Abigail. "My lady, is your hair satisfactory?"

"I am delighted. Thank you, Abby. The necklace, please, and then we are away." Caroline was nervous but steeled herself not to direct her anxiety to Abigail. Sofia, however, was another matter.

Abigail stood back to admire her mistress. The deep crimson dress, dyed to match Sir John's sash, showed her pale complexion to good effect, and the feathers in her hair were smaller than usual. "You look lovely, my lady, if I may say so."

Caroline smiled slightly at the maid's compliment. "Thank you, Abby." The two of them had developed a friendship of sorts in the last weeks, brought together by their mutual loathing of Sofia. "Come, Sofia; we must not keep Sir John waiting."

The Austrian maid mumbled something in German; to Caroline's ears, it sounded slightly insulting. If only she could speak German, she would put the impertinent baggage in her place!

Caroline discovered Sir John in the parlor, splendid in his full-dress, blue Dragoon uniform, sabre at his side, cape rakishly thrown over one shoulder. Caroline tried to remember to breathe as a chill went down her back. The look in Sir John's piercing blue eyes screamed that he wanted Caroline in their bed—*now*. For her part, Caroline was very agreeable to the unspoken suggestion. All the irritation she had felt over her husband's inattention to her domestic difficulties vanished for the time being. The two looked at each other with pure desire until Roberts cleared his throat.

"Uh… sir, my lady, it is time to leave."

The Embassy Ball, hosted by Lady Beatrice, would begin within the hour, and Lady Buford was to assist the hostess. Without a word, Sir John offered his wife his arm, and they sailed out to the waiting coach with Sofia trailing behind.

Sofia babbled in the coach as the party moved through the late afternoon streets of Vienna. "It is *vise* for you to take me along *with* you, Sir John. I know my *vay* around Vienna very *vell* as I *vas* raised here."

Caroline barely heard the girl; she was too concerned over her duties that evening. Soon, the carriage drew before the Schönbrunn Palace, and the Buford party made their way inside.

"Sofia," Lady Buford said after they entered the building, "report to Lady Beatrice's secretary. She will assign you your duties." She did not notice that Sofia had mumbled something under her breath.

Caroline and Sir John continued into the main ballroom, where they were greeted by the duke and his cousin as well as the other members of the British delegation.

Caroline's tension had eased somewhat, for the other ladies of the delegation had, on the whole, proved to be pleasant and gracious. There were at least two with whom Caroline was desirous of becoming better acquainted, and they seemed to welcome the newcomer into their sphere. The ladies went off to see to the final preparations in good spirits.

Within an hour, the ballroom was filled with the height of Viennese society. Never had Caroline seen such finery and jewels, having never been presented at court. Not that it would have mattered; European fashion made the London scene look dowdy by comparison. She and Sir John were making the rounds when she heard someone calling her husband.

"Colonel Buford! What a wonderful surprise!" A beautiful young woman of medium height approached them. She wore a silver gown with a shocking décolletage, her blue sash of rank tucked beneath her ample bosom. She drew close to the colonel and, in a very familiar way, touched his red sash. "What is this?" she asked with a faint French accent. "Are you now Sir John? Have you been elevated?"

"Yes, Countess, as have you."

"Ah, but you earned your knighthood by your labors for your king, *n'est-ce pas?* I have done so by the usual method afforded to women." She finally turned to Caroline. "Will you introduce me to your companion?"

Buford ground his teeth. He knew Roxanne could see their wedding rings. "Countess, I present to you my wife, Lady Buford. Lady Buford, Countess de Pontchartrain-Villières. Her husband, the Count de Pontchartrain, is a member of the French delegation."

"Countess." Caroline curtsied.

"Charmed. So, you are married, Sir John? But how could you not with such a lovely creature." She nodded at Caroline. "I had not heard; is it a recent event?"

"Our wedding was in January, Countess," Caroline answered.

"And a honeymoon in Vienna! What could be more delightful! Sir John, you must not keep this charming lady to yourself. You simply must excuse us. Come with me, Lady Buford." The countess gave each of them a smile, took Caroline's arm, and walked off with her.

Sir John could only look on with a shade of concern on his face.

Caroline could not like the Countess de Pontchartrain. Her familiarity with Sir John set her teeth on edge. She wondered at her pointed attentions, but she tried to submerge her doubts. The countess was French, she reasoned, and the French have strange ways. Besides, Caroline was a veteran of the games of the London *ton*, so surely she could handle a French vixen. Still, she found herself striving valiantly not to feel completely underdressed next to the countess.

For the next few minutes, Caroline was introduced to several other grand ladies and was quizzed politely about herself. Finally, Countess de Pontchartrain pointed out a handsome gentleman standing a little ways from them, wearing a black suit with a red-and-white sash.

"Have you been introduced to that gentleman, Lady Buford?" When answered in the negative, the Countess called the man over. "Baron, allow me to introduce Lady Buford of Wales. Lady Buford, this is Baron Wolfgang von Odbart of Prussia."

A roar of laughter rolled across the room, and the countess glanced away. "Oh! I must leave you now; my husband calls, I think. The baron is capable of ensuring your entertainment, Lady Buford. À *bientôt*." The countess then left the two together.

The dashing baron turned to Caroline. "Are you available for a set, Lady Buford?"

"The second set is available, sir."

"*Wunderbar. Bis dann*—until then, my lady." He clicked his heels, bowed, and left her.

Soon, other august noblemen were introduced to Lady Buford, and it was not long before her dance card was filled, two sets reserved for her husband. Caroline tried her best not to appear as intimidated as she felt, but it was a relief when Sir John came to claim the opening set with her. Sir John was an excellent dancer, and Caroline was able to lose herself in the movements of the dance, watching her husband.

Soon the dance was over and Sir John surrendered his happy bride to her new friends. She was in conversation with the ladies when the baron reappeared.

"Lady Buford? It is time for our set," he informed her as he held out his arm.

Caroline accepted the gesture and allowed herself to be glided to the dance floor. She did not see the looks of concern on the other ladies' faces.

Buford stood by himself, taking in the crowd and enjoying the dancers, when the Countess de Pontchartrain approached him.

"I finally have you to myself, *Jean*," she said in French.

His contentment evaporated, the colonel responded in the same language. "What can you mean, *Comtesse?*"

The lady laughed lightly. "*Jean*, have I not always been Roxanne to you? Surely, you have not forgotten."

Fighting his feelings, Buford remained gallant. "Of course not. But those days have passed, *milady*."

"Surely, you do not refer to our… recent acquisitions?" The countess looked upon him with dancing eyes. "Have you met my husband, *chéri*? *Non?*" She glanced over her shoulder and smiled. "Well, he is over there, across the room."

Buford looked to the gentleman she indicated. He beheld a rather dandified older man wearing not only a wig but also what looked suspiciously like rouge on his cheeks. The look was a bit excessive, even for a French noble.

"You spy him, *oui*? Well, observe the man to his left. Watch!"

Buford saw a young footman, who could not be older than one-and-twenty, crossing over to the *comte* with a glass of wine. His clothes were very fine and fit like a glove. Count de Pontchartrain accepted the wine, taking the glass with a slight caress of the young man's hand. It was very brief, and only one who had been observing very closely would have caught it.

The countess chuckled. "Yes, Pierre is a particular favorite. What say you?"

Despite his deep revulsion, Buford could not help himself. "A ballet dancer's breeches should fit so well." They were so tight as to be almost indecent.

"Ah, how did you know? My husband pays better than *ballet de l'Académie impériale de musique*." She laughed. "Of course, we know he is also a spy for the government, sent to keep an eye on us—an amusing game."

In a very low voice, Buford demanded, "Why do you tell me these things, Roxanne?"

"We have an understanding, he and I, as pertains to *les affaires d'amour*. We are discreet. I do not embarrass him, and he does not embarrass me. I have no reason to complain. Have you a similar agreement in your house, *chéri*?"

"Absolutely not," he replied with some force.

"You may need to—observe!" She gestured to the dancers with her fan. Buford saw Caroline dancing with Baron Wolfgang von Odbart.

Buford's throat tightened; he had learned via his research into the other members of the Congress that Baron von Odbart was a notorious seducer and womanizer. Buford saw no parallel to his own previous behavior; his past conquests had all been voluntary, but the baron's had not.

"They look lovely, *oui*? I think she will thank me for the introduction," the countess purred. "What time shall I expect you tonight, *Jean*?"

Deep anger flushed Buford's face. He turned to her, and it took all of the colonel's discipline not to slap the woman.

"Madam," he spoke in English through clenched teeth, "I am afraid you are under a mistaken impression of our acquaintance. I shall say no more. If you would excuse me, I shall return to my wife."

The countess's jaw dropped slightly. "Have you made *un mariage d'amour*—the love match?" She laughed again. "Oh, that is too amusing; that cannot be. Not *you*, *chéri*."

Buford pursed his lips but said nothing. He certainly would not reveal his feelings for his wife to *her*.

A grin touched by malice was on the countess's face. "You had better hurry, *chéri*. The dance is finished."

Buford whirled around. Sure enough, the music had ended, and most of the couples had already left the dance floor. Caroline was nowhere in sight.

After two sets of dancing, Caroline was in need of refreshment, and she noticed that others were like-minded.

"Lady Buford, these tables are so crowded," said the baron. "Come, there is another near the library."

Wishing to slake her thirst as soon as possible, she allowed herself to be escorted out of the ballroom. Once they reached the table, the baron gave Caroline a glass of punch. She drank as quickly as a gentlewoman could and shyly requested another.

"*Ja*, dancing is hot work, is it not?" remarked the baron with polite humor. He handed Caroline her replenished glass. "Here you are, my lady. I am at your command."

"Thank you, Baron."

"*Sie sind herzlich willkommen*—you are most welcome."

Caroline thought it would be best to make some polite conversation with her companion before she was claimed for the next set. "Have you always lived in Vienna, sir?"

"I was raised in a small village outside Berlin. My estate has been in my family for eight generations."

"It is very beautiful, I am sure."

"*Ja, es ist ein schöner Ort*—a most beautiful place." He grew very close to Caroline as he eyed the library door. "I will take you there soon, *mein schönes Mädchen.*"

"Baron von Odbart, what are you saying?" Caroline asked.

Buford tried not to appear anxious as he walked through the crowd looking for Caroline. Unconsciously, he looked for feathers—Caroline was one of the few ladies wearing them. He had searched the ballroom twice without success, when he noticed M. Talleyrand looking at him. While he was anxious to find his wife, Buford could not ignore the French ambassador.

"*Bonsoir*, Excellency," he greeted him in French.

"Good evening, Sir John," he returned in English. "Are you enjoying yourself?"

"Very much. Do you join the dance?"

"*Non*, such pastimes are beyond me. I take pleasure in observing the festivities." The minister owned a pronounced limp.

"Yes, the ladies are lovely."

"*Oui, tout à fait*—yes, indeed. But there is more; one can learn much from watching." Talleyrand eyed Buford closely.

Buford knew he was trying to alert him. "Absolutely, *monsieur.*"

Talleyrand sighed. "There is much beauty to be found by a dashing knight. It is everywhere—the ballroom, the dining room, the library…" The sentence hung in the air.

It took Buford a moment to understand the ambassador. "I—excuse me, Excellency. I have enjoyed this enlightening conversation. *Merci beaucoup. Bonne nuit.*"

"You are very welcome, Sir John. Good night." Buford headed towards the library. The ambassador watched him go with a glint in his eye.

"Baron von Odbart, what are you saying?" Caroline asked.

"Lady Buford—"

"Ah, there you are, my dear!" said Sir John as he entered the hallway before the library. "Baron, good evening!"

"Sir John!" Caroline exclaimed in surprise and relief. The Prussian glared at the interloper.

"Have you been keeping *Seine Exzellenz* company? *Wunderbar!*" Sir John turned to the baron. He let the Prussian know that he had heard their last exchange and that he spoke German. "Lady Buford takes her duties as my wife seriously—*all* of them," he said with a mouth that smiled and eyes that did not.

Baron von Odbart did not reply. The two men locked eyes.

"My dear," Sir John said, half turning to Caroline but not breaking eye contact with his adversary, "Lady Beatrice was looking for you. She is near the dining room, I believe." His smile never left his face.

Caroline was confused. She had at last realized that she had been propositioned, but Sir John did not seem to be angry at all. The last time a man did thus, John had threatened to kill him, but now her husband just smiled at the baron.

"I… thank you, dear. Baron, excuse me," she offered with the barest of civility, before she turned and left for the ballroom.

The two men were left alone. Finally, the baron spoke. "If you will excuse me, I shall return to the ball."

He is an ambassador—you can do nothing, Buford reminded himself. *I cannot challenge him; I cannot!* But Buford could not let things lie and remain a man.

"A question first, sir. Do you hunt?"

The baron looked into his eyes. "*Ja.* Grouse and deer."

"Musket?"

"*Ja.*"

"Perhaps we should go shooting together once the spring comes. I am proficient with the musket, rifle, pistol, and bow. I particularly enjoy hunting at dawn. Very productive, you know. I have had many success-ful... *hunts* at dawn."

The baron replied with a grunt.

Buford lowered his voice. "Have you ever hunted with a blade? There is nothing like killing a wild boar with a sabre. The sound it makes when the blade strikes home... ah!" There was a wild look in his eye.

The baron shuddered; the message had been delivered. "I shall remem-ber that. But, excuse me please; I do not think I shall have time to... hunt while in Vienna. The Congress..." he shrugged. "My apologies—*bitte entschuldigen Sie. Gute Nacht.*"

"Lady Beatrice, you were looking for me?" greeted Lady Buford.

The older lady smiled at her friend. "Why no, but I am glad to see you. Did someone say that I was?"

Caroline's confusion returned. "Sir John did. I was just with Baron von Odbart—"

Lady Beatrice started. "Baron von Odbart!" She collected herself. "Caroline, is Sir John still with the baron?"

"Yes, I just left him—oh!" Caroline finally made sense of her hus-band's odd behavior. *He was trying to get me out of the room before he...* She began to turn back to the library when she felt Lady Beatrice's hand on her arm.

"Caroline," she said in a low voice, "we shall go together... slowly."

The two ladies had only taken a dozen steps before they saw, to their immense relief, Sir John strolling from the direction of the library. "Ladies!" he called out gaily.

Caroline was mortified, and true to her sex, exorcised her embarrass-ment by scolding her husband. "Sir John! What are you about, sir?"

Lady Beatrice asked, "Where is the baron?"

"The baron?" the colonel said nonchalantly. "Oh, he is about somewhere. Wretched man—turned down the opportunity to go hunting with me."

"Hunting, sir?" cried his wife. "You wished to go sporting with that man after he—"

"Lady Buford!" hissed the hostess. To Sir John she asked, "Would this... hunting have anything to do with pistols or swords?"

"The very thing! I cannot see why he declined, but one can never tell with these foreigners."

"Yes," said Lady Beatrice dryly, "an *ambassador* is usually too busy for that sort of thing, especially with a mere advisor. I would not ask again, sir. I do not believe my brother would approve."

Buford understood Lady Beatrice's warning. "Yes, my lady."

Caroline did not quite follow the conversation, but she knew that Sir John had been warned off some improper behavior. She began to defend him when another gentleman approached the group.

"Lady Beatrice, Sir John, excuse me please," said one of the senior British diplomats. "Lady Buford, it is time for the supper dance." He smiled as he held out his arm.

"Oh! Of course, my lord."

Sir John smiled. "Enjoy your dinner, my dear. I shall see you for the final set."

"Lady Buford," said Lady Beatrice as Caroline was led away, "if you would be so kind as to call on me day after tomorrow, I would be most obliged."

Caroline was taken aback by the formal tone. "Of... of course, my lady."

"Wonderful. Let us say three o'clock? I shall send my card around."

After Caroline left, Sir John asked, "Lady Beatrice, do you dance tonight?"

"Oh, no, my dear colonel. A hostess's job is never done. However, I would not object if you would lend me your arm to the dining room."

By the time the Bufords were riding back home in the carriage, all discord between them was once again gone. Caroline was tired and happy. In the back of her mind, she was still a bit disappointed that Sir John did not defend her more vigorously before the baron. Go sporting with him, indeed! However, the dinner was delightful, and she loved to dance with her husband. And Sofia's gossip from the servants' quarters was interesting.

"*Ja*! I *vould* not believe it had I not seen it *vith* mine own eyes! Baron von Odbart *vas* chased out of the back door by a Russian count! There will be some merry talk around Vienna tomorrow, I can assure you!"

Caroline was so sleepy and relaxed that she broke with propriety, placed her head on Sir John's shoulder, and closed her eyes, a contented smile on her lips. Sir John simply held his wife's hand as the carriage rocked through the nearly empty streets.

In the darkness of the carriage, they could not see the frown on Sofia's face.

Chapter 14

ONCE AGAIN, CAROLINE FOUND herself in a coach heading for Lady
Beatrice's townhouse, but this time she was alone. She insisted that
Sofia stay at home because Caroline planned to do a bit of shopping
afterwards. Strangely, the girl did not object overmuch.

It was now two days since the embassy ball, and Caroline was keeping
her engagement to join Lady Beatrice for tea. She almost sent her regrets;
for some reason Caroline awoke that morning feeling unwell, but fortunately, the spell passed. Soon the carriage reached its destination, and she
was shown to the parlor.

Caroline was surprised to find Lady Beatrice quite alone. She was not
pleased by this; she at once feared that she had committed some unknown
blunder during the ball and was now to account for it. Still, hiding behind
her mask of civility, Caroline calmly took the seat offered her.

"Cook has assured me that tea is almost ready, Caroline. That is a
lovely dress. Fuchsia, is it not?"

"I suppose, my lady. The dressmaker called it dark rose." Mortification
joined anxiety, even though Lady Beatrice had reverted to the informality
of using her given name.

"It is a lovely color, whatever its name." The tea tray now made its appearance, and soon cups were poured and served. "Are you enjoying your time in Vienna, Caroline?" asked Lady Beatrice as she stirred her tea.

Caroline began shaking. *Now it begins. What in heaven have I done?* "Yes, madam."

"I am glad. You have certainly made friends here."

"Thank you, my lady, I hope I have. The ladies of the delegation are all delightful and kind."

Lady Beatrice leaned forward and touched Caroline's hand. "I hope that you count me among your friends—" She stopped. "Why, my dear, you are shivering!"

"'Tis nothing, my lady." Caroline was near tears.

"Are you cold? Should I have the fire lit?"

"No, please, I am f… fine." Caroline burst into sobs.

"My dear, whatever is the matter?"

"Please!" Caroline cried in return. "Keep me in suspense no longer. Tell me what I have done—whom I have offended. To whom must I apologize? Let me make amends."

"You poor dear!" The older woman joined Caroline on the couch and held her hand. "Dear child, you have offended no one! You have nothing for which to apologize."

Caroline sniffed through her tears. "No one? Truly?"

Lady Beatrice gave her a kind smile. "You are well liked among the ladies. You have received many compliments for your efforts at the embassy ball." She handed Caroline a handkerchief.

Caroline dabbed at her eyes. "Please forgive me. Goodness, but I do not know what came over me. I am not so much of a ninny, I assure you."

"Think nothing of it. But what gave you the idea that I was displeased with you?"

"I could think of no other reason for the invitation here today, especially with no one else attending," Caroline admitted.

"I am sorry to have given you distress, my dear." She paused. "I did, however, want to speak to you privately—about a certain matter."

Caroline steeled herself. "Yes, my lady."

Lady Beatrice sighed. "Caroline, forgive me. The diplomatic world is new to you, as I think you would agree. It is far different from the world of London society or even the Court of St. James. Here empires may rise or fall. Wars may break out or be ended. This world attracts a certain type of individual—hard, clever people who are used to having their own way and know how to get it."

"Yes, madam. But is it so different from the *ton*?"

"Oh my, yes! The *ton* are but children compared to what is outside these doors. London society plays their games for sport. Diplomats play with life and death. The games are far more dangerous here."

"Forgive me, but I do not take your meaning. You say I have offended no one. Then what have I done wrong?"

Lady Beatrice took Caroline's hand again. "You have not harmed anyone yet, but you are in danger of harming yourself. You must take care when choosing with whom you associate."

Caroline recalled the incident with Baron von Odbart. "Oh, I see. But all ended well. The baron withdrew. There was no harm done."

"But harm *could* have been done."

"Never!" Caroline gained control of her emotions. "Forgive my outburst, my lady, but you must understand. I would never so dishonor myself or my husband."

She patted her hand. "Of course not! That is not my meaning."

"Then I do not understand."

Lady Beatrice looked into Caroline's eyes. "What of your husband? What of danger to him?"

"Sir John? Ha! He was in no danger. In fact, he invited the scoundrel hunting. You were there; you heard."

"Yes, I was there and heard his real words." Lady Beatrice decided that friendly tact was no longer useful. "Think, Lady Buford! You know your husband's character. Would he actually seek out the company of a man who sought to cuckold him?" Caroline flinched. "Forgive my direct language, my child."

"I… I do not know! I thought Sir John was going to call him out; I was sure of it, but he did not—"

Lady Beatrice cried, "I know I have called you my child, but it was a term of endearment. Are you really so naïve? Did you truly think this hunting scheme was anything but a challenge? Be glad he was unsuccessful!"

"Be glad? My husband is no coward!"

"Would you prefer him dead or in disgrace? This is no game." Lady Beatrice turned cold. "I was under the impression you were fond of Sir John."

Caroline paled at the verbal slap.

"Had his challenge been accepted by Baron von Odbart, and had Sir John survived, your husband would have been sent home in disgrace, dismissed from the delegation. I do not believe you would wish this for him."

Caroline was dismayed at her childishness. *Heavens, she is right—and John knew all the time and still challenged the oaf!* "Oh no, my lady," Caroline cried. She reached out to the other woman. "I have been unforgivably foolish. I thank you for showing me how stupidly I have behaved. Is it any wonder Baron von Odbart thought me a woman of easy virtue? I have risked my husband's life and career!"

"I must disagree with you! The baron, and the baron alone, is responsible for his sins. You have done nothing to warrant censure in that matter." Lady Beatrice smiled. "As for the other issue, is there a woman alive who has not acted foolishly from time to time for a man? All is well now, Caroline, and we have all learned a lesson."

The visit would continue for another half hour. It was barely enough time for Caroline to gain control of her emotions. Yet she was still uneasy. She had unwittingly placed her darling husband in danger. How was she to make amends to him when she had yet to tell him that she loved him?

Buford was glad that the Congress was not in session that day, for it gave him the time to catch up with his correspondence. He sat quietly in his library for some time, reading and answering letters. He was so occupied that he did not hear the door open.

"Sir John?"

The colonel looked up. Sofia had closed the door behind her and was halfway across the room.

"Yes, Sofia. May I help you?"

"I hope you *vill*, sir." She crossed over to the desk.

As she got closer, Buford noticed that the bodice of her dress was pulled unusually low. "Uhh… yes?" he said stupidly, as the hairs on the back of his neck started to rise.

The girl said nothing at first—she just stood by the desk, looking him up and down through her eyelashes.

"I have *vaited* for a chance to speak to you alone. I have been patient a very long time. Your work takes up so much of your time. You must be tired."

"I beg your pardon?"

"You are so handsome—*ansehnlich*—*mein Liebling*. I know how to make you happy. Everyone in the house is busy. No one will bother us." Sofia smiled and began to move. "You must know I *vant* you. *Ich liebe dich von ganzem Herzen!*"

Before he knew what was happening, Sofia had come around the side of Buford's desk and thrown herself on his lap. With one hand, she grabbed the back of his neck as she kissed him furiously; with the other, she seized his hand and thrust it on her breast.

"*Liebe machen—*"

Buford finally recovered from his surprise. He pulled his hand free and, taking hold of Sofia by her shoulders, forced her away from him and held the girl at arm's length. "What are you doing, woman?"

There was a crash.

Buford's head snapped to the door. There stood a shocked Lady Buford, her reticule on the floor.

"Caroline!" he cried.

"*Nutte! Dieser Mann gehört mir!*" screamed the girl.

With a sob, Caroline dashed through the door, revealing Roberts and Frau Lippermann staring into the room. Buford leapt to his feet, and with a thud, Sofia fell to the floor, her skirt up around her knees.

Buford cared not. He moved quickly to the door and shouted a command to Roberts. "Take that whore"—he pointed to Sofia— "and toss her out this instant!" Buford left the library to the sound of Sofia's curses.

Up the staircase he dashed to find a wide-eyed maid outside Caroline's room. "Abigail, I need you to go downstairs. There is some rubbish that needs tossing out."

She looked at her master. "Is it Sofia?" Her face broke into a savage grin as Sir John nodded. "It would be my pleasure!" With that, the maid hurried down the stairs.

Buford tried the door only to find it locked. The only answers he received to his entreaties were heart-wrenching sobs. Finally, Buford took a step back and, with all his might, kicked the door in.

Buford was a good student at university, but he forgot Newton's Law, which states that for every action there is an equal reaction. The door swung open with such force from the kick that it rebounded off the wall and came back to its original position. Unfortunately, Sir John's head was in the way, and he was struck with enough force to knock him off his feet. He lay stunned outside his wife's door.

"*John!*" cried Caroline. She flew to his side, all else forgotten. "John, John, speak to me! Oh, you are injured! Do not move, I pray! Help! Help!" she screamed through her tears. "Sir John is hurt!"

Buford, lying on the floor, could not decide what hurt his head most—his injury or the screams in his ears.

"Caro—"

"Oh, my dear, do not move! Help is coming!" A moment later, Roberts arrived and helped his mistress carry the master to her bed. "Oh, you must send for a physician this instant!"

Buford was able to take his wife's hand. "No, my dear... not necessary... I will be fine."

"Sir, the person in question has been removed from the house," reported Roberts. "Was there anything further?"

Through his throbbing pain, Buford managed, "No, that is all." Roberts closed the door as he left. "Caroline—" her husband began.

With Sir John's life no longer in danger, Caroline was free to remember her own hurt. "Oh, do not speak to me!" Her tears of fear were replaced by tears of grief. She left the bedside and sat at her dressing table, away from him.

Colonel Buford struggled to his feet and staggered to his wife. "My love, listen to me—"

"How could you?"

His strength gone, Buford fell to his knees before his wife. "You must believe me," he urged through his pain. "I have been faithful to you. I love you so." He fell forward on her lap. "I have kept my vow."

Sir John's words finally reached Caroline's tortured mind. She looked at him wide-eyed, spent tears running down her face. "What… what did you say?"

He looked up. "I have kept my word to you." He winced as a shot of pain coursed through his head.

Caroline took his face in her hands. "No, before that."

Buford, defenseless, laid his soul naked before his wife. "I love you, and only you, with all my heart."

Caroline took a moment to comprehend what her husband admitted and then fell on his face with kisses.

"Oww… ow… oh, my dear… please," begged Buford.

Caroline helped him rise from the floor and walk back to the bed. Helping him onto it, she then climbed in after him and lay by his side, taking him into her arms and putting his aching head on her breast. There they rested in silence for a time.

Finally, she began. "What happened? Did she attack you?"

"I suppose it could be called thus. It was certainly uninvited."

"When I saw the state of her dress! Oh, forgive my lack of faith in you."

"No, my dear, you have no need to apologize. What were you to think with the girl wrapped around my person?"

Caroline began to chuckle. "As I look back at it, it was rather silly."

"Silly?" Buford rolled onto his back.

She began to laugh heartily. "Yes, it was something out of a Shakespearean comedy." She dissolved in laughter. "You… her… the door—"

"Stop! It… it was not that funny." He began to laugh with her. This continued for a time until finally, their laughter sated, Sir John caressed Caroline's chin with his finger.

"I meant what I said."

Caroline closed her eyes. Could she dare to open her heart as well? All her life she was trained never to leave herself vulnerable, open to hurt. Sir

John deserved an answer, but the words caught in her throat. She had to find another way.

"I believe I need your assistance, Husband." She rose on one arm to look at him.

"Anything."

"I need to work on my knowledge of languages, if I am ever to match yours."

Buford closed his eyes, frowning. "How so?"

"Well, for example, I believe the correct phrase in French is *je t'aime*, is it not?" She looked down into his eyes.

Wordlessly, Sir John searched her face. "Yes, that is correct, but I believe the formal version is *je vous aime*."

Caroline repeated, "*Je vous aime. Oui.*"

Sir John swallowed. "I must say, however, that I prefer *je t'adore*. 'Tis used between lovers."

She smiled. "*Je t'adore*—it is far more agreeable, I must admit." She kissed him tenderly. Sir John reached up and ran his fingers through her hair, deepening the kiss.

Caroline moved away slightly. "My Italian is not what it should be, I confess. *Ti amo* I believe is right?"

"Oh no—*ti voglio* is much better."

Caroline's eyes widened. "Indeed? Very well then—*ti voglio*." This time the kiss was passionate and long. "And, of course, Spanish is *te amo*."

Sir John liked this game. "*Te amo, te adoro, te deseo.*"

"But I have no German. You must help me. Did your... *friend* teach you the phrase?" she said with a grin.

"Wench! It was that baggage that was taught a lesson."

Her laughter rained down on him like a summer shower. "This will never do! Teach me, Husband!"

"Let me see. *Ich liebe dich* is perfectly acceptable."

"*Ich liebe dich*. Do you know Russian?"

"*Ya tyebya lyublyu*, I believe."

Caroline started to giggle. "Surely your talents know no bounds! Do you know any others?"

"*Eu adoro-te* is Portuguese. The Dutch say *ik hou van je*. For the Irish it is *ta gra agam ort* or *taim i' ngra leat*. Do not ask me to say it in Polish—there is no telling how badly I would butcher it. I would probably say, 'I like your stomach.'" Caroline was laughing now. "But the way I like best is the Welsh way."

"And what do the Welsh say, Johnny?"

"They say *rwy'n dy gari di*."

Caroline's eyes sparkled. "Yes—*rwy'n dy gari di*."

Sir John smiled back. "*Rwy'n dy gari di*."

The sounds of the lovers would continue throughout most of the evening.

It was the middle of the night when Caroline awoke. The knock on her door and her husband arising to answer it had broken her slumber. She opened one eye slightly to see Sir John in a robe reading a letter by the fireplace. The stiffness in his posture caught her attention. Completely awake, she sat up in bed, the sheet falling away from her naked torso.

"John, what is it?"

He turned to her, backlit by the fire, his expression unreadable.

"Bonaparte has escaped from Elba."

Grenoble

The men of the 5th Regiment stood nervously across the road to Grenoble. Before them were over a thousand people, many of them armed. Their orders were to arrest the tyrant who dared leave his exile on Elba. The officers moved about the soldiers, reminding them of their duty to the king.

Suddenly, a man approached on horseback. He wore a simple military greatcoat and a cocked hat with a tricolor cockerel at the peak. He stopped and observed the forces before him. He then dismounted and approached the soldiers alone, on foot. When the man was within earshot of the men, he threw open his coat, the Legion of Honor clearly visible.

"Soldiers of the Fifth, you recognize me! If any man would shoot his emperor, he may do so now!"

Following a brief silence, the soldiers and officers erupted into shouts of "*Vive L'Empereur!*"

The emperor basked in the adulation for a few moments before returning to his horse. He had been called many things in his lifetime: genius, monster, lawgiver, tyrant, Defender of the Revolution, Destroyer of Mankind, but no one doubted his personal courage or underestimated his knowledge of men's hearts. Today he had reminded the world of those talents.

The soldiers sent to stop the tyrant instead joined the ranks behind the emperor to march on Paris.

Chapter 15

Matlock Manor

"AND THEN AUNT CATHERINE ordered me out of the house." Colonel Fitzwilliam took a large swig of his father's port and looked around at each of the other men in the study, searching their faces for any hint of censure. His cousin, Fitzwilliam Darcy, was his usual impenetrable self, keeping his opinions hidden behind his oft-used mask of indifference. His brother, Viscount Andrew Fitzwilliam, stared intently into his own glass of port, and his father, Lord Matlock, looked deeply disturbed.

"Well, you could not expect me to remain after that performance, could you? I packed up my belongings, gathered the documents there—" he pointed to the opened packet on the desk—"and left for my lodgings in London. The rest you know. What would you have me do? Father?" Richard turned to his cousin. "Darcy—come, man, support me!"

"You did no wrong, Richard," Darcy replied.

"Could you have done better?"

Darcy hesitated.

"You see?" Richard cried. "You *do* think I failed!"

"Richard, that is quite enough!" Lord Matlock's voice boomed across the room, his tone indicating disappointment in Richard's childish display.

After all these years, his son should have known that Darcy would always believe that he would do better in everything. "You did the best you could, son. 'Tis not your fault but Catherine's. I do wish you had not left Anne there, though."

Richard colored, which was not lost on his brother. "Richard, is there something you have not told us?" asked Lord Andrew.

"No! It would have been improper had she come away with me. I could not jeopardize Anne's reputation."

"Balderdash! A woman riding to her family's townhouse with her cousin and companion? Do not be ridiculous! You are leaving something out." He eyed his brother. "Good Lord, you are smitten with our fair cousin!"

Richard did not answer.

"Richard," demanded his father, "is this true?"

Richard shook his head. "We are not engaged. I have not compromised her, and I have made no promises—"

"Out with it! Do you wish to marry the girl?"

Richard sighed. "Yes, sir."

Andrew snorted. "Fool! You will be a poor man if you do. Auntie Cathy will cut her off without a penny."

"No, she will not," declared Lord Matlock.

Richard was uncomfortable with this discussion. "That is neither here nor there. Anne and I are not engaged. Whether or not we do become so in the future is not relevant now. We are talking about Rosings. If we do not save the place, the questions as to inheritance for Anne will be irrelevant."

Darcy turned from his usual place near the mantle. "Richard is correct. Rosings is the reason we are all called here today. We must discuss Richard's actions. Do you have any concerns over Richard's orders to the steward?"

The earl picked up one of the papers on the desk and closely studied it. Richard was suddenly struck by how elderly his father now appeared.

For the first time in his life, Richard contemplated a world without Hugh Fitzwilliam, Earl of Matlock. The concept frightened him.

"Are these figures accurate? The harvest was this bad?"

"Yes, sir."

"And all of the tenants are paid up in full?"

"Some were late, but yes, all are paid up now."

Lord Matlock handed the paper to Darcy, who scanned it for a moment. "Good Lord," Darcy muttered and gave the form to Lord Andrew. "I believe Richard was correct to order the rent holiday."

"I only wonder why it was not done two years ago," Andrew mumbled after a moment. Richard turned to his brother in surprise. "What? Do you not think I can add figures in my head?" said an irritated Andrew at the colonel's wonderment.

Andrew had changed, thought Richard. Viscount Andrew Fitzwilliam was the eldest son of an earl, and for most of his life acted so. Assured at an early age that he would inherit a title and a grand estate, Andrew went through life demanding respect he had yet to earn. When younger, he showed little concern for those beneath him and little deference for those above. The Fitzwilliams were taught to be self-reliant, but Andrew reacted badly to his lessons, believing his opinions were all that mattered. His self-confidence in his judgment and abilities became over-confidence.

Now Richard beheld his brother with new respect. Since taking over the day-to-day management of Matlock, Lord Andrew had shown not only greater responsibility but a bit of decency as well. Perhaps the viscountess had been a good influence after all.

"Father," asked Richard, "do you approve?"

"Yes, you did the right thing—the only thing, rather. I do not like setting the precedent—damned inconvenient—but there is nothing for it. I am sorry you had to endure your aunt's wrath. You did not deserve such treatment, I assure you."

"Will it be enough, do you think?"

"You did all that could be expected. Darcy?"

"I agree. The holiday, along with a good harvest, will make things right again."

"It is not like the old girl will be too pinched." Andrew was studying the personal financial documents. "She has certainly put enough aside."

"Richard, what you have done may well be the saving of Rosings."

"Yes, sir," Richard answered his father. "Assuming Aunt Catherine does not undo everything I have done."

"She cannot," declared his lordship and Darcy in unison.

Richard frowned. "Why not? I have been meaning to ask you. Why are Mrs. Parks and the steward employed by you, Father? Why it is that Aunt Catherine cannot countermand my instructions? It is her land."

"We have been given authority—" began Darcy.

"Hold, Darcy," interrupted the earl. "It is more than that. I am afraid that you and Richard have not been told the whole story. It is my fault; I apologize." The others in the room were taken aback at this admission. The earl never apologized for anything. "In short, Lady Catherine cannot countermand any instruction you give as my representative, Richard. She has not the authority."

"But Rosings belongs to her," cried Lord Andrew.

"No, Lady Catherine does not own Rosings."

Astonishment filled the study. "What?" cried Richard. "Why… then who does?"

"Legally, Anne does."

"Sir Lewis left Rosings to *Anne?*" sputtered the colonel.

"Yes, he did."

"Why on earth did you not tell us?" cried Darcy.

Lord Matlock sighed. "Fill your glasses. 'Tis a long tale and better told over good port."

After the glasses were filled and cigars lit, the earl continued. "Forgive me, gentlemen, but I must start at the beginning. My father was a man ahead of his time when it came to the education of his children. I, of course, received all that was expected of a gentleman and more, but my father also saw to my sisters' education. The best tutors and instructors were found; nothing was lacking. Father was particular that his daughters master mathematics as well as languages and the arts."

He turned to Darcy. "Your mother, Anne, was an excellent student. George Darcy often told me that he had married more than a wife; he married the best helpmate and advisor he had ever had. I do not think he ever recovered from losing her."

Darcy bowed his head in acknowledgment.

"Catherine, on the other hand, was a poor student. Nothing wrong with her head, you understand. Sometimes we all thought of Cathy as—potentially—the most gifted of all of us, but she never seemed to apply herself. She always seemed distracted… agitated. Oh, how Father and Mother labored to get Cathy to mind, but nothing worked. The only study that seemed to hold her attention was that of current society and manners. She was a severe disappointment to my father.

"When it came time for my sisters to marry, Father was happy to unite Anne with George Darcy. He knew that they would get along very well. With Cathy, Father was more cautious. He arranged for her introduction to Sir Lewis de Bourgh, a baronet he considered to be of good sense. Cathy saw Rosings and a title, and she was satisfied. Sir Lewis was a man who saw to everything himself and, therefore, was content with a good-looking bride. Catherine was considered quite a beauty in her day, you know, though she was nothing to Anne. Rosings was well run, so it had no need of a good mistress.

"But Sir Lewis was no fool. He and Father had long discussions, and many things were considered. I was party to the marriage negotiations, and after the marriage, George Darcy became an advisor as well. In the wedding agreement and afterward in his will, Sir Lewis made sure that Catherine could do little to damage his family estate. Rosings and the title would go, of course, to the eldest son upon Sir Lewis's death.

"Where Sir Lewis was clever was in the circumstance of his heir being a daughter. Sir Lewis wanted Rosings to go to his offspring and not to be entailed to some distant male relative. He also did not trust his wife to be a good manager of his estates. He knew she did not have the necessary ability to govern or to be advised. So he set up, in case of his demise, a system called *usufruct*. Lady Catherine would get the income of Rosings, but the ownership would be held in trust until his male heir reached the age of majority or, in case no son survived him, until his eldest surviving daughter married. When either of those conditions was met, Lady Catherine would receive the right of dowager, including the dowager house. He also named George Darcy and me, and our heirs, as trustees.

"When Sir Lewis died unexpectedly, George Darcy and I acted quickly. We made sure the solicitors understood the peculiar aspects of Sir Lewis's will and gained complete control of the grounds, farms, and household as trustees for Anne. The housekeeper at that time was considered too close to Lady Catherine, and the old steward was ready to retire, so old Darcy and I placed our own people there. We allowed Cathy to have power over the rest of the household staff as a peace offering.

"To say the least, Cathy was displeased by our actions. Our gesture was nothing to her. Oh, how she railed! She tried everything to overturn her husband's wishes and our efforts. She even had Mrs. Parks and the new steward's contracts burned. Eventually, she gave way, especially after we threatened to force her into the dowager house immediately as a matter of economy.

"For many years thereafter, George Darcy and I were responsible for the supervision of the management of Rosings. When your good father died, Darcy, you were placed in his stead."

Darcy looked hard at the earl. "I thought that such an honor was given me in expectation of my marriage to Anne. You should have told me, Uncle."

"Aye, I should have. I offer no excuse. I suppose I was afraid of stirring things up again with your aunt."

Richard grunted to himself. *You are being dishonest, Father. We both know Darcy. He never would have tolerated Aunt Catherine's behavior had he known of his true power over her. War between her and the family would have been ignited long ago. The inevitable has only been delayed.*

"Father," asked Lord Andrew, "what would happen if Anne never married?"

"The *usufruct* would remain in effect until Lady Catherine's death. It would be up to the trustees whether to transfer control to Anne or continue to act on her behalf."

"Ha!"

"What do you mean by that, Andrew?"

"Do you not see? *This* is the genesis of Aunt Catherine's plan to marry Anne to Darcy!" He turned to his cousin. "There never was an agreement between my aunts for you to marry our cousin, was there?"

"No," answered Darcy. "My mother wanted me to make my own choice."

"But had you found Anne agreeable, would you have quit Pemberley?" Richard flinched at Andrew's words.

"Never!"

"Ah, the perfect solution to her problem! With Anne married to you and removed to Pemberley, Auntie Cathy would remain Mistress of Rosings rather than occupant of the dowager house. The income would probably continue to flow to her for Rosings's expenses. You always were softhearted, Darcy. It was never about blood—only money!"

The other men were stunned silent. The answer was so obvious they all questioned their wits that they had not realized it sooner. Lady Catherine's character was certainly capable of fabricating such a scheme.

Lord Andrew was in his element now. "It was rather clever, you must admit. That is why she never turned to you to take Darcy's place, Richard. You would have taken over Rosings in a heartbeat. No, either the old lady would find some other well-landed suitor for Anne, or our cousin would never marry!"

A blade twisted in Richard's stomach.

"I disagree, Andrew," said Darcy. "Anne is of legal age; she can marry without permission."

Richard hid a smile. Anne's declaration upon his leaving Rosings had given rise to a new hope. Perhaps Anne would marry without her mother's consent. If Rosings were indeed Anne's, she would be able to marry him without sacrificing her situation. Richard would not have to depend on a colonel's pay and could support Anne in the style to which she had been accustomed. Anne was of age; she wanted him—ha! He did not like the idea of making Lady Catherine his implacable enemy, but he would not let that stop him. If Anne would have him, let the old woman rage. It was her choice. There was nothing she could do to stop their happiness!

"Well," Lord Matlock rumbled as he puffed his cigar, "I believe that Catherine will storm for a bit, but no harm will come of it. The important thing is that Rosings Park is safe."

Andrew turned to Richard. "What is next for you now that Bonaparte is loose?"

Richard was pulled from his very agreeable musings. "The regiment is on alert, watching events in France."

At that moment, the butler entered. "Begging your pardon, you lord-ship, but there is an express rider at the door."

"Ah, yes." The earl got to his feet. "I have been expecting something from my banker in London. Please excuse me." Lord Matlock followed the butler out of the room.

"Well, I expect we will be hearing next of that damned Corsican's head on a pike. The Frogs cannot be stupid enough to want him back!" Lord Andrew declared.

Darcy turned from the mantle. "I must disagree with you again, Andrew. King Louis's government is very unpopular. There may well be civil war."

"Here is something new—you disagreeing with me, Darcy! All is right in the world as long as Fitzwilliam Darcy finds fault with Andrew Fitzwilliam! Tell me, is there anyone you totally agree with except that wife of yours?" At Darcy's glare, Lord Andrew continued with a smile, "Oh, come now! Do not take offense, old man! You know we approve of Elizabeth."

"It took you long enough to come around."

"Again with that? Very well—yes, we have come to see that she is not the uncultured country girl we feared. She has not hurt our standing in society, and she has done wonders with Georgiana. In short, she is too good for the likes of you. How you managed to win her I will never comprehend."

Before Richard could express his opinion, all conversation ended with Lord Matlock's reentrance, a grim look on his face. Without a word, he handed a letter to Richard. Richard immediately noted that it was from the War Office addressed to him. With a sinking feeling, he murmured an apology, opened the letter, and read in silence.

Finally, Lord Andrew could bear no more. "What is the news?"

Richard looked up slowly, all his hopes dashed. "I am recalled to London. King Louis has fled the country. Bonaparte has entered Paris and declared himself again Emperor of the French Republic. It is war."

Delaford

Richard Fitzwilliam was not the only one receiving express letters.

"Do not worry, my love," Christopher Brandon told his wife as his valet packed his trunk. "I shall only be gone for a little while—less than a fortnight, I should not wonder."

"But, Christopher, you are requested so urgently!" Marianne observed. "Why would they want you? You have been inactive for so very long."

Because Wellington wants me, he replied to himself. The country was not ready—it had too many troops on the other side of the Atlantic because of that insane war with the Americans. "Perhaps they need a new staff officer in London during the crisis. If so, I will send for you and Joy to join me at Brandon House in Town." Brandon turned to his valet. "All done there, my man? Excellent." He opened his arms. "My love, I must leave."

Tearfully his wife embraced him. "I am so worried."

"Never fear, my Marianne. Nothing will keep me from returning to you."

Newcastle

Captain George Wickham entered his commanding general's office along with the other officers.

"Gentlemen," the general began without any other preamble, "it seems our old enemy is back. Yet another coalition is being formed to contain Bonaparte. All training regimens are hereby doubled. We leave for Belgium in a month."

Wickham looked about stupidly. "Begging your pardon, sir. Did you say we were leaving?"

"Yes. Any questions, Captain?"

Wickham could not restrain himself. "Why, sir?"

The general gave the assembled a crooked grin. "It seems we are invited to the party this time. The War Office has ordered this regiment to join Wellington on the Continent."

A stunned murmur arose from the attending officers. Wickham did not join in; he was too shocked. Finally, thoughts began to form in his head. War? He was going to war! He did not join the army to fight a war! He thought he was in a safe regiment!

He suddenly remembered that he did not "join" voluntarily, and he did not choose his regiment—someone else did.

Damn that Darcy!

Chapter 16

Vienna

ON THE DAY BEFORE Easter, the ambassadors of Austria-Hungary, Prussia, Russia, and Great Britain gathered around the table, documents scattered before them. The other members of the delegations—diplomats, advisors, secretaries, and others—stood watching against the walls of the room, while staffers moved about the great men, papers and pens in hand. Some representatives of the lesser powers were also in attendance.

The French Delegation was nowhere to be seen. It was understandable; the authority of the ambassador of the Court of Louis XVIII of France was dissolved with the king's flight from Paris.

This was the largest gathering of the Congress, and its task was grim. The treaty before them was based on the declaration of 13 March 1815. It stated that Napoleon Bonaparte, self-appointed Emperor of the French, had placed himself outside civil and social relations and handed himself over to public justice as the enemy and disturber of the peace of the world. The signatories agreed to establish a coalition—the seventh of its kind—to oppose the Tyrant, and they pledged to raise armies of at least 150,000 each to enforce the peace and security of Europe and restore the lawful government of France.

One member of the audience turned to another. "Does the duke realize what he is doing? He is committing the government to war—and at such a scale," the British diplomat whispered to his companion.

"I believe his lordship knows exactly what he is about," answered Buford. "He is forcing the government's hand—not that it matters. He has already been named commander-in-chief of all British and Hanoverian forces on the Continent. We simply await the official commission."

The situation was grave. Marshal Ney had promised King Louis XVIII that he would bring Bonaparte back to Paris in an iron cage. Instead, Ney defected to his old commander along with the six thousand men under his command. Marshal Murat, the Bonaparte-installed king of Naples who had joined with the Coalition the year before when France's defeat seemed certain, now betrayed his new allies and declared for Napoleon and a united Italy. He was already attacking the Austrians.

"Do you join the duke in Brussels?" Buford was asked.

"We leave directly. I am to serve as advance staff until my regiment is shipped from England."

"And Lady Buford? Does she remain in Vienna?"

"No," said Buford firmly. "She journeys with us to take a boat for England. I would have her safe with my family."

A bustle at the table drew the gentlemen's attention. The signing done, the ambassadors shook hands and began leaving the room. Wellington walked over to where the British delegation had gathered.

"Well, that is that. Come, gentlemen—there is work to be done."

After attending Easter morning services, Caroline rushed about the apartments, overseeing the last of the preparations for their departure. Roberts and Abigail saw to the clothes and personal items, while Caroline worked with Frau Lippermann and Helga to arrange for the packing of the few vases and *objets d'art* that the Bufords had purchased during their stay and the shutting down of the household.

It was a bit of a challenge. Abigail was all atwitter; she feared that the Tyrant's armies might march down the street at any moment. The housekeeper and cook had no English, and Caroline had no German—except for three words, and *they* were not applicable to the situation—but through patience and pantomime, progress had been made.

Finally, all was accomplished: trunks were packed, debts were discharged, and arrangements were made. Sir John and several footmen strode into a forest of packing rather than the chaos that produced it.

Sir John looked about the mass of trunks and boxes with a knowledgeable eye. He had a fair idea of logistics and knew what his wife had accomplished. It was no less than he had expected, yet he was wise enough to praise Caroline.

"My dear, you have done wonders," Sir John said as he kissed her hand. "Give these men but a moment, and we shall be off."

A moment turned into the better part of an hour, but it did not signify. It gave Caroline a chance to bid farewell to her remaining staff.

"Frau Lipperman, Helga, I wish to thank you for your services—*Ich bedanke mich*," she read from a card. "You have done good work—*gut gemacht*. Here is my recommendation—*Dienstzeugnis*—for each of you. I hope you find employment very soon. I wish you Happy Easter—*Frohe Ostern. Auf Wiedersehen.*"

The two women looked at her for a moment before rushing to hug their former mistress. "*Danke sehr! Wir werden Sie vermissen! Leben Sie wohl! Gott segne Sie—Frohe Ostern! Auf Wiedersehen!* Goot bye, my lady!" Helga was actually in tears. It took no little time for the departing mistress to extract herself from the tearful farewells.

Soon, two carriages were making their way out of the Austrian capital. Caroline looked back at the city as they left. So much had happened there in just a month, she thought as she grasped her husband's hand.

Shall I ever look upon Vienna again?

The trip to Vienna in early February had been a delight. The trip from Vienna in late March was a nightmare. Time was of the essence, and the horses were pushed to their limits. The carriages rocked the occupants cruelly. The spring rains threatened to wash out the roads on more than one occasion, and ever-present was the fear that Napoleon would strike before the Allies were ready.

What was beautiful before was no longer. Mountains that were awe-inspiring became obstacles to overcome. Deep forests now seemed closed-in and menacing. Any castle or town, no matter how stately or charming, could contain an enemy, and the rivers were living things that sought to destroy the little group.

Each day the party rose before sunrise. They would seldom stop before dusk, except for changes in the teams, when they would consume a hurried meal. The travelers could not be particular as to the choice of lodging—any inn with relatively clean beds would do. The food, for the most part, was revolting.

The only pleasure the couple enjoyed was sought at night. No matter how exhausted the lovers were, Sir John and his lady would lose themselves in each other's arms. Their lovemaking was intense and urgent, as if the pair felt they needed to consume a lifetime of love within this single journey. They never spoke of it or of the future; it was understood. The only words that passed between them were those of love and devotion and need. They basked in their newfound understanding of the other's feelings. In the coach during the day, they never left each other's side.

The trip was harder on Caroline than on her husband. More mornings than not, she awoke sick to her stomach, but she would not complain, request a moderation of the pace of the journey, or even speak of her discomfort, for she refused to be a burden to Sir John.

Finally, in early April, they crossed the Rhine into Belgium.

Antwerp

"Damnation! There is no passage to be had!" cried Buford as he entered his rooms. He ran a hand through his hair. "I have asked everywhere, but I can get no proper passage for you and our servants back to England, at least anytime soon. In a month, *perhaps*, they say. Damn them!"

Caroline left off writing to her sister and rose to see to her husband. "Sir John, please," she gently scolded him. "Would it be so bad if we remained? Other officers have brought their wives."

Sir John looked torn. "My love, the selfish side of me would wish you by my side, but that is impossible! The others are fools! I will not have you here in danger. Perhaps I can arrange for a fishing boat—"

"No, sir! As I said before, I will not go without Abby and Roberts or our belongings!"

For at least the fourth time in as many days, the couple argued the point, and the colonel found that he still could not budge his wife. Assured in her husband's esteem and affections, Caroline's old assertiveness had returned, and her time in Vienna had instilled in her a fierce attachment to their servants.

"Woman, you shall do as I say!"

"Is this how I should expect a king's officer to speak to his wife? I was led to believe that there were gentlemen in the army!"

"Caroline, please—"

"I shall not be moved, no matter how much you beg!" On and on it went, with the same result. "My love, do you not see? I cannot—I will not—abandon our people or our belongings. I do not wish to be a burden upon you, but there it is."

"But dear, I would have you safe with our family in England."
She touched his cheek. "I know."

Buford needed to find another way. Consequently, he did what many people would do who possessed his connections. He wrote to Darcy.

London

"Fitzwilliam! What a pleasant surprise!" cried Mr. Gardiner as the tall, finely dressed husband of his niece was announced. "Come in. May we get you something? Allow me to alert Madeline that you are here."

"No, Edward, please do not," answered Darcy. "May we retire to your library? There is a matter of business I should like to discuss with you."

Edward Gardiner knew something was wrong. "Of course, my boy. Right this way." In the years since Elizabeth's marriage to the Master of Pemberley, the Darcy and Gardiner families had grown so close that Christian names had become *de rigueur*, and Mr. and Mrs. Gardiner considered Fitzwilliam and Georgiana as a nephew and niece.

After seeing his guest into the library and closing the door, Mr. Gardiner asked, "May I get you something?" To his eyes, something rare happened: Darcy started to fidget. "Fitzwilliam, is something amiss? Out with it, my boy."

"I am afraid I must ask a favor."

"Is that all?" the older man exclaimed in relief. "Why, by your countenance, I thought someone died!"

Darcy continued to squirm.

"Come, tell me, man. Whatever it is, you shall have it."

Darcy gritted his teeth. "It sits ill with me to ask this of you—"

"I know—you would sooner do it yourself. But think nothing of it, my boy," he said with affection. "We are family."

Darcy nodded at the truth of this. He reached into his coat pocket, extracted a letter, and handed it to Mr. Gardiner. Falling back into cold politeness, as he always did when he was uncomfortable, he said, "Pray, do me the kindness of reading that letter."

Mr. Gardiner opened it.

April ——, 1815
Darcy House, London

My dear Darcy,

Lady Buford, our servants, and I arrived safely in Antwerp four days ago. Such a journey from Vienna! One day I shall relate it to you as I consume your best port. Please let Mrs. Darcy and Miss Darcy know that Lady B is in good health and good spirits. She bore the ordeal without a word of complaint. What a woman! Surely, my friend, we have both been more fortunate than we deserve in our marriages.

Darcy, I have a request of you. It is my wish that Lady B and our people be safely transported back to England. However, passage may not be secured until May at the earliest. With events on the Continent as they are, I am certain you will agree that this situation is intolerable. My wife would stay, but I shall not rest easy until she is under my family's protection.

I have no contacts that may be of service; but you, with your wide range of investments and interests, might know of some manner of relief. I would not ask this of you were not the situation dire and the safety of those dearest to me at risk. Please be assured that whatever the result, I shall be eternally in your debt, should you make some small inquiries into this matter.

Your obt. servant,
BUFORD
Antwerp

"I see," said Mr. Gardiner.

"Poor Buford," said Darcy. "What it must have cost him to write such a letter!"

Mr. Gardiner thought for a minute. "I can have a ship at Antwerp by week's end—ten days at the most."

"Edward, I do not know what to say."

"Fitzwilliam," said Mr. Gardiner softly, "would you do any less for me, were it in your power? Come, give me your answer to Sir John. I shall dispatch it with the ship. It shall wait at dock until our friends are aboard."

Antwerp

Darcy's note had arrived in mid-afternoon. The sailor who delivered it said the ship would sail upon the morning tide the next day. The shipmates he had brought along were to move the baggage and other possessions aboard that night. Sir John assured the messenger that the passengers would arrive in good time in the morning.

Caroline was distressed, knowing she had but one last night with her husband. She reached deep into herself for her control; it would not do to take leave of Sir John crying like a blubbering idiot. By pure strength of will, she was able to face her husband with at least the appearance of composure after the last of the trunks were on their way to the ship.

Buford was not deceived. He addressed his small household staff: "Tonight is your last in Belgium. We shall not require you this evening. Here is some money. Roberts, take Miss Abigail out to the finest restaurant in town. 'Tis my farewell gift to you both."

Roberts and Abigail understood. "Good night, sir," his man said. "We shall see you in the morning."

After the servants left, Sir John took Caroline by the hand and led her downstairs. To the owner of the inn, he stated, "Your public rooms are closed for the evening. Name your price."

The innkeeper struggled between his greed and his fear—Sir John was wearing his sword. Finally, he gave an amount. Buford handed him the money but added, "There will be dinner out of that and your best wine." The innkeeper sighed—his profit not as great as he hoped—and left to fetch the first bottle.

Sir John turned to his wife. "Play for me?" he asked as he gestured to the pianoforte in the corner.

Caroline nodded and walked over to the instrument. She had no music, so she played from memory. When the wine arrived, Sir John poured two glasses and placed Caroline's on the pianoforte within her reach. He then retreated to a table and chairs close by and listened attentively.

For an hour, Caroline played and sang for her audience of one—every piece she knew and loved. Never had she performed with such emotion. The instrument was poorly tuned and would have affected the pleasure of the casual listener, but to Sir John it was the most beautiful music he had ever heard. The innkeeper had to fight tears as he served the supper.

Finally, Caroline sounded the final chord. She took a sip of her wine and gracefully moved over to share the meal provided them. For the next half hour, the two ate in contented silence, sometimes holding hands.

Finally, after an after-dinner brandy, Caroline rose, took her husband by the hand, and returned upstairs to their rooms. "Tonight is my gift to you, beloved," she said to him once the door was closed. "You have given your Caro so much love and pleasure."

She gave him a gentle kiss, then took two steps backwards and unfastened her gown. After a bit of reaching, she slipped it from her body. Looking Sir John in the eye, she removed the remainder of her garments. Nude, save for the carnelian cameo he had given her, she stepped close to him and began to remove his jacket. Slipping it off, Caroline placed it upon a chair near the window. She then turned her attentions to his neck cloth and shirt.

Once Sir John was bare-chested, Caroline gently pushed him towards the bed until he was forced to sit upon it, and at once, she removed her husband's shoes and stockings. Caroline then rose and kissed Sir John as her hands unfastened his breeches. The lovers kissed more passionately as Caroline worked the remaining garment down Sir John's legs, and then urged her husband to recline on the bed. She climbed up on the bed and knelt at his feet.

Caroline slid up his body, kissing the skin as she went, before snuggling into his arms. The pair lay together for a time, resting and caressing each other. Finally, Caroline rose up on her elbow and looked her husband in the eye as she stroked him.

His need as great as hers, he complied eagerly. No preliminaries—he drove himself into her, filling her as she expelled a satisfied gasp. Caroline's green eyes bore into her husband's, urging him on. Their coupling was mad, rushed—hands, lips everywhere—until her muscles convulsed around him, her flood triggering his, both crying out in mutual delight.

As they lay spent, Caroline ran her fingertips along his chin while looking into his blue eyes with adoration.

"*Rwy'n dy gari di*, Johnny."

"*Rwy'n dy gari di*, Caro."

Sir John awoke before the sunrise to find his wife not in the bed beside him. He turned to see her form near the window, facing out, waiting for the dawn. Wordlessly he left the bed and crossed over to Caroline, embracing her from behind. She leaned against his strong body and softly sighed. Adam and Eve then watched the cruel sun steal the last of the night from them.

The captain of the merchantman eyed the hourglass as the last of the morning watch drained away. He planned to set sail by two bells in the forenoon watch—nine in the morning, about an hour away—assuming that the special passengers had arrived, of course. By then, the tide should be running.

Mr. Gardiner would lose a bit on this run, he thought to himself. The little bit of cargo would in no way cover the expense of the trip, a loss that would only increase if the ship missed the morning tide. He turned and looked over the harbor. Warships and merchantmen, mostly Dutch and British, filled the port and the ways while boats scurried about between them and the docks. Men and matériel were flooding into Antwerp in preparation for war.

A master's mate cried out, "Eight bells!" and turned the glass. As the last of the bells rang out, a coach pulled alongside. The carriage door opened, and a tall cavalry officer in Dragoon blue stepped out; he turned first to assist a maid and then a lady of consequence. From the other side of the carriage emerged a servant. He and the maid gathered up some carpetbags and stepped towards the gangplank. They were stopped by a mate, who turned to look at the quarterdeck.

The captain called out, "Colonel Buford's party, sir?"

"Aye," came the reply from the officer. "Permission to come aboard, sir."

The captain nodded and called to the boatswain, "See to the passengers, Jones," pleased that the customs of the sea had been followed by such a landlubber. The boatswain directed a few men to relieve the servants of their burdens as he escorted the maid and valet below decks.

The last to board the ship were the army officer and his wife. The colonel walked up to the ship's captain, his lady on his arm.

"I am Colonel Sir John Buford. This is my wife, Lady Buford. My man, Roberts, and my wife's maid, Abigail, have just gone below. I thank you and your employer, Mr. Gardiner, for your kind assistance to my family."

The captain gave a nod. He may have reached no higher than lieutenant while he was in the Royal Navy, but as captain of a merchant vessel, he bowed to no man whilst on his own quarterdeck. "Very happy to be of service, Sir John, Lady Buford."

"I deliver into your hands all that is precious to me."

The captain blinked at the raw emotion in the colonel's words. "Never fear, sir. I'll watch over 'em as if they were me own."

Sir John mumbled his thanks and turned to his wife. Instinctively, the captain turned away to grant the couple what little privacy could be had on a ship's deck. To his irritation, he saw one of the ship's boys gawking at the couple.

"Avast there! Get along with ye, or you'll see the end of the boson's starter!"

The colonel began to raise his lady's hand to his lips when she tore loose from his grasp, flung her arms around his neck, and kissed him quite openly. The captain was quite embarrassed to witness such a private moment. He felt like an intruder on his own deck. The couple murmured words to each other that sounded to the captain's ears like Welsh, and then the officer turned and walked down the gangplank to the dock.

"Jones!" called the captain. "Get the ship under way!" The crew leapt to the work of warping the ship out of dock, while the lady moved instinctively to the stern, watching the colonel, who stood by the carriage. Soon the morning air began to fill the sails. At the command, topsails and gallants were dropped and the ship picked up speed.

The lady remained at the ship's stern until land was out of sight.

Caroline searched through her carpetbag in the cabin she shared with Abigail, a cabin that had previously belonged to the sailing master. The wind had turned against them, and it would take at least a night of tacking before the ship could pass by the cliffs of Dover.

As she looked for something to sleep in, Caroline came across the items that were used during her monthly courses. She held up the items, a strange thought suddenly occurring to her.

I have not used these for some time. When was the last time? Just before the wedding?

Other thoughts came to her—her sickness in the mornings, her clothes feeling tighter, her breasts becoming tender. Things she had dismissed before as resulting from anxiety, rich food, and intense lovemaking.

Can it be? Am I with child? Could I be carrying John's child?

All of her life, Caroline dreamed of marrying an important, titled man. Childbirth had never occurred to her. Motherhood, yes, in an obscure manner, but not the actual process of pregnancy and childbirth. Fear and uncertainty flooded her mind, along with a single thought: *I must let John know!*

But first, she must be certain. She must seek out a physician straight away once she reached London.

London

Lady Buford was escorted down the gangplank by the captain himself, Roberts and Abigail trailing behind. No sooner had her foot touched land than she heard her name called. Caroline turned and saw Philip and Rebecca Buford waving, standing next to a coach. As her in-laws approached, Caroline thanked the captain for his kindness and took her leave of him. Roberts began to see to the collection of their trunks as Caroline greeted her family.

"Philip, Rebecca, I am so happy to see you! Thank you for coming."

"Thank us?" cried her brother. "What sort of foolishness is that? Of course we are here. You are a Buford, you know." After kissing her on both cheeks in the French style, he excused himself to help Roberts. There was that informality again, thought Caroline.

"Caroline," said Rebecca, "are you well? You look a bit flushed."

Caroline reminded herself that she would have to become accustomed to the Bufords' abruptness. She prevaricated. "I am well, Rebecca, I thank you—only desirous to get home."

"Very well, my dear." Mrs. Buford then called out to her husband. "Philip, Caroline is tired and wishes to go to the house!"

Caroline was taken aback. *What? But I said—*

"Very well, my dear. Take the coach—bring the maid with you. Roberts and I shall see to all this baggage. I shall meet you at Buford House. Farewell!"

"Caroline, my dear," said Mrs. Albertine Buford as she embraced her daughter-in-law and kissed her on both cheeks.

"Mrs. Buford—I mean, Mother Buford, I am glad to be here," answered Caroline. She then looked beyond the old woman and gasped.

"I see you have noticed our little surprise, yes?" Mother Buford said with a smile. Standing in the sitting room were Louisa Hurst and Jane Bingley. Caroline dashed to embrace her sisters with tears in her eyes.

After exchanging kisses and tears, Caroline asked about her brothers. "They will join us at dinner, will they not, Louisa?" answered Jane as she wiped her eyes with a handkerchief. "They wanted us to have a bit of time to ourselves. But there is someone who wishes very much to see you." She turned to a maid who was holding Susan Bingley. Caroline's tears were redoubled as she took her goddaughter in her arms.

The physician was requested two days later, and Caroline received him in her bedroom. "Congratulations, my lady," said Mr. Wexley as he finished his examination. "You are indeed with child and everything seems to be progressing well."

Caroline could not decide whether or not she was happy. "When will the baby come, Mr. Wexley?"

"Oh, I believe we should look for the happy event somewhere around the first week of November. Nothing to worry about now. Do not tire yourself, and eat well. That is my usual recommendation. Your confinement will not be for some time yet." He paused and looked hard at her. "I must say, after everything you say you went through on your journey home, well... if there was any danger, it is passed already."

An hour later, Caroline shared the news with the Buford ladies. Both were delighted with Caroline's report and showered the expectant mother with kind words and affection. Though she found it hard to believe, Caroline was coming to the opinion that the two ladies actually liked her.

The response of Louisa and Jane was as joyful as expected. Charles was silly, and even Hurst said something kind. The Buford, Bingley, and Hurst families were sitting down to tea when the Darcys were announced.

Is this a tea party or a ball at Almack's? thought Caroline with a bit of impatience.

Mother Buford noticed Caroline's mood. She leaned over and whispered, "Good friends are like good wine—they should be enjoyed at every occasion. Life is too short to stand upon propriety, my dear, especially in times like these."

Lady Buford considered her mother-in-law thoughtfully.

Col. Sir John Buford
——nd Lt. Dragoons, Antwerp, Belgium

My dearest love,

Forgive the delay of this letter. Our party arrived safely in London four days ago. We were met by Philip and Rebecca, who took us home to Buford House.

This morning, two soldiers from your regiment came with written instructions to gather up your uniforms, necessities, sword, and equipment—your "kit," I believe one of them called it. No sooner had I escorted them to your rooms than Colonel Fitzwilliam was announced. He was kind enough to assist me to supervise the packing. He told me that he has already been in contact with your second-in-command, and he shall see to it personally that your saddle and other equipment arrive safely in Belgium. I am happy you will have the company of such an amusing and thoughtful friend as the colonel while you are away from your home and those who dearly love you.

My dearest, I send news of the greatest joy. Come November, there shall be another Buford in the world. Please do not be concerned. The physician was quite satisfied, and I am in excellent health and spirits. Our family is delighted at the news—Mother Buford, I think, most of all.

When I look into a mirror, I almost weep knowing that the evidence of our love is even now growing within me. That is, until I recall what this will do to my figure—then I do weep!

I shall close now, but I promise faithfully to write you as often as may be.

Rwy'n dy gari di,
CAROLINE
Buford House, London

Chapter 17

Rosings Park

A MISERABLE COLONEL RICHARD Fitzwilliam rode slowly through the town of Hunsford towards Rosings Park. As he passed the Clarke household, he barely acknowledged the wave of welcome from the inhabitants.

Such a greeting is not surprising. Thanks to me, your income just doubled, he thought with uncharitable bitterness.

Richard's uncharacteristic bitterness sprung from his expectations for his short visit. Whitehall had been most desirous of his return to duty, and it had taken much of Lord Matlock's influence to secure this short leave. Richard was exceedingly thankful for his father's efforts, for he could not bear to sail to the Continent with his regiment without first taking his leave of Anne. That meant admitting his feelings for his cousin, but the earl and the viscount had chosen to be kind rather than caustic. Richard knew well his hypocrisy; he loved nothing more than to tease, but he had little tolerance for it being aimed in his direction.

Richard was melancholy enough at leaving Anne now, just as he finally knew his heart, but to face her gatekeeper again—his harridan of an aunt—after their last interview was a price painful to pay. But pay he must if he meant to say good-bye to his beloved.

Within a few minutes, he passed the parsonage and saw the Reverend Mr. Collins attending his garden.

"Colonel Fitzwilliam!" he cried, "how good to see you again so soon. What a pleasure it is to have the company of such an august gentleman as yourself, unselfishly serving our king…"

Richard allowed the man to prattle on. The vicar meant well, and Mrs. Collins was a good friend to Anne. Within a few minutes, the lady of the house came out to join them. "Colonel, you are welcome indeed! Please take a few moments to step inside and take your ease."

Something in Mrs. Collins's demeanor encouraged Richard to agree to her suggestion. Richard knew he had chosen well when Mrs. Collins declared to her husband, "Mr. Collins, what are you about? The meeting of the church lay council starts within the half hour!" She effectively shooed the man upstairs to make himself presentable before returning to their guest.

"I am glad we have these few moments to talk in private," Mrs. Collins began. "Things have been very strained at Rosings since you left. Your orders have improved things in the village, I dare say. Even Mr. Collins will agree—in private—but Lady Catherine has been… very unhappy since your departure in February. I am afraid Miss Anne has taken the brunt of her abuse."

Richard turned white with anger. "Is that so? Why has my father not been informed?"

"Because Miss Anne would not permit it," came a voice from the hallway.

The two turned at the sound. Mr. Collins, wearing an unreadable expression, stood at the foot of the stairs, his cravat in his hand to be tied.

"Mr. Collins!" exclaimed his wife. "I—"

"Charlotte, you do not need to explain. I know why you sent me away." He crossed over to her and laid his hand on her shoulder. "It is I who need forgiveness. I have given far too much of my attention to our unworthy patroness and not enough to the mother of my children. I have not lived up to my own sermons. It is no wonder that you do not confide in me. I shall labor to earn your trust."

Mrs. Collins looked upon him in absolute shock.

The tall vicar turned to Richard, clearly in shame and regret. "As I said before, I am very glad you are here. Miss Anne, who had shown such Christian condescension as to befriend my dear Charlotte, has been most unhappy. Lady Catherine, I am not pleased to report, has been very unkind to her—indeed to the whole household. Why, she even had cross words for Mrs. Collins just last week! I know I owe my situation to Lady Catherine's benevolence, but it is dearly bought. We must pay deference to those of high rank, but... but to treat my wife no better than a servant? The daughter of a knight? It is becoming intolerable!

"I throw myself at your feet, begging for deliverance. I have attempted as Lady Catherine's pastor, in the most respectful manner, to advise her to better behavior. I have tried to make her see the errors of her ways but to no avail. I would do more, but... you see, my family..." Mr. Collins threw up his hands in defeat. "She has made threats."

Richard's heart was touched. "Fear not, sir. I pledge to you that your family is in no danger. I speak for my father, the Earl of Matlock, and my cousin, Mr. Darcy, in this matter."

To Richard's embarrassment, tears came to the man's eyes. "Oh, Colonel, you cannot know what a burden has been lifted from my shoulders. That you would turn your attention to such an unworthy man as myself is beyond any reward I could hope for. Speak! Ask any question; my wife and I are at your disposal." Mr. Collins had clearly switched his allegiance to the family of Matlock.

"But your meeting, sir?" asked Richard. "I fear I am delaying you—"

Mrs. Collins rose to her feet. "I shall advise them that you are in a most important meeting with Colonel Fitzwilliam, my dear," she told her husband. She turned to Richard. "They shall understand. Your name is upon everyone's lips as the savior of Hunsford."

A half hour later, a better advised Richard Fitzwilliam rode to the doors of Rosings. Handing the reins to the stable hand, he ascended the steps and announced himself at the door. The butler was clearly nervous. He begged the colonel to wait upon his ladyship's pleasure.

"Nonsense, you know who I am!" Richard declared in false good humor. "I will just let myself in. No need to bother Lady Catherine, my good man." Richard slipped past the butler and went in search of Mrs. Parks. He found her in the empty breakfast parlor.

"Colonel Fitzwilliam!" she cried. "When did you arrive, sir? Are you staying long?"

"No, madam—just to have a word or two with Lady Catherine and Miss Anne, but first I would speak with you. I understand things have been difficult lately. What may I do?"

"Oh, sir, do not worry yourself on my behalf! I am well, and I will do what I can for the staff. Please, you must save your efforts for Miss Anne."

"The Collinses have said the same. What has happened?"

"Nothing yet, but I believe Lady Catherine is planning to take Miss Anne away—to Bath."

"That is my understanding. Why is this a concern?"

"Lady Catherine has been after her to improve herself in order to attract a suitor."

Richard paused before the great doors of the sitting room, steeling himself for the interview to come. "You may announce me," he said to the butler.

A moment later, he heard a voice. "You may come in, Richard."

The colonel entered the elaborate sitting room and saw his aunt sitting in her usual chair at the far end. She gave the impression of a spider in the center of her web. A slight smile seemed to dance upon her lips.

"Ah, the savior of Hunsford returns! To what do I owe this visit, Nephew?"

"Do I need a reason to visit?"

"Do not play games with me, boy. Always I have been celebrated for my frankness of character. I expect nothing less from any of my family. Why have you returned?"

"To bid you farewell. I am off to the Continent to face Bonaparte."

This declaration seemed to take Lady Catherine by surprise. After a silence of a few moments, she said, "I am afraid I do not understand your meaning. Is not the tyrant held captive on some small island—in the Mediterranean, perhaps? Why would you need to face him? Does he need to be arrested?"

Richard was stunned that his aunt did not know what had happened. "Bonaparte has escaped Elba. He is back in Paris, and the French king has fled. The tyrant is raising an army. Britain goes to fight him yet again."

Lady Catherine was affronted. "Escaped? Surely someone has not done their duty. I assume it was one of those foreign types that was responsible. Such a thing would not happen if an Englishman was in charge."

"I am sure you are correct. In any case, it falls upon those who wear the king's uniform to set things right."

"When do you leave?"

"The regiment sails in May."

"Then you go with my blessing. Was there anything else?"

"I would like to speak to Anne before I go."

"Yes," she looked at him narrowly, "I suppose you do."

Richard became wary. "Is she about? My time is short. I must leave soon."

"What business do you have with my daughter?" Lady Catherine demanded.

"To take my leave of her, as I have done with you."

"And is that all?"

"I am afraid I do not take your meaning, Aunt."

"I am sure that you *do*, sir. Oh, yes—I know much more than you think."

"I do not think I like what you are insinuating. Are you accusing me of improper behavior?"

"Is it proper to make love to my daughter under my very nose?"

"Madam!" Richard fought hard not to lose his temper. "I do not know what lies you have been told, nor do I wish to hear such vile accusations made against your daughter. Let me simply assure you that I hold Anne in the highest regard and respect, and would let nothing damage her reputation while I have breath in this body."

"A very pretty speech. Yes, very pretty. Do you think me blind? I watched you 'take your leave' of Anne in February. What other liberties have you been permitted? Answer me, boy!"

"Lady Catherine, I shall not dignify that question with an answer. By God, if you were a man—" Again Richard struggled to retain control. "I have nothing to say to you about Anne at this time, except this: My intentions in matters of this kind have always been honorable. Is it your belief that I have compromised your daughter? If so, than I am prepared to do the right thing by her." *Come, Aunt, make my dreams come true.*

"Oh no, you shall not have your way that easily. I know that it is Rosings Park, not Anne, that is your desire, and *that* you shall never have!" Lady Catherine's temper grew into a passion.

"I care nothing for Rosings. Besides, Rosings belongs to Anne, not you—as you well know."

"Only because of the legal chicanery of your father and uncle! But Anne is *my* daughter; she needs my permission to marry."

"Anne is of legal age."

"Anne shall do as she is told! I have already made preparations—begun inquiries. Anne will be united to a proper family, one that is worthy of a de Bourgh!"

Richard narrowed his eyes. "One that can be manipulated, as well. Such a compliant man shall be hard to find. Do you believe you will find such a person in Bath?"

His aunt sneered. "Bath—London—it matters not. I know Anne shall not travel to Derbyshire again!"

Richard looked at his aunt with as much composure as he could manage. "You would condemn your daughter to a loveless marriage just so you can hold on to Rosings?"

"Love?" Lady Catherine raged. "You speak the same foolishness as your cousin! Pemberley has been polluted forever by that… that creature Darcy married. Anne will have an estate of her own, and I shall prevent you and my hateful brother from stealing Rosings from me!"

"And if Anne refuses to cooperate?"

"She would not dare! However, if none of my candidates are suitable, Anne and I will live here comfortably for the rest of our lives."

Richard stood in awe of his aunt's selfish, ignorant maliciousness. One word from Anne would destroy her whole world. She was of legal age; Anne could marry anyone she chose. He wondered if his aunt was quite sane.

"I think there is nothing more we can say about this or any other matter. I will leave you now. Farewell, Aunt." Richard turned to leave.

Lady Catherine called out, "I have not forgotten how you mistreated me when last you were here. You dare to speak to me without first offering me your apology? I am most severely displeased!"

Richard halted before the door. With one hand on the knob he said, "Do not be unhappy, my lady. With any luck, the French may solve your problem with me forever." At that, Richard left the sitting room, closing the door behind him.

Richard stormed through the halls, trying to control his emotions, when he came upon Mrs. Parks again. She looked at him with compassion and simply said, "She is in the gardens, sir."

With a smile, he thanked the housekeeper and dashed out the doors. Anne stood in the very same spot as in February, looking at the new buds.

"Anne!" he called as he ran to her. She, in turn, waved to him, her smile heartbreaking in its beauty. He reached her and took her hands in his. "Ah, the pretty buds of April, and here is the prettiest!"

"Oh, Richard, it is so good to see you—even if you do say such lies," she said with joy.

To Richard's concern, he found that he did exaggerate Anne's looks. There were circles under her eyes, and she looked as if she had eaten ill for some time. Richard wondered just how horrible it had been for her at Rosings while he was gone.

Anne's eyes took in her cousin. "Richard? Why do you wear your sword?"

"Do not worry about that, my dear. Let me look at you." Quietly, he asked, "Why did you not send for me?"

"There is nothing she can do to hurt me. Are you here long?"

"No, I must leave for London soon—"

"Did you bring the coach? I did not see it." She looked around him and saw only his horse. Anne turned back to him. "You rode?" Suddenly there was a forlorn expression in her eyes. "Richard, why are you here?"

"Anne, I—"

Realization came to her. "It is the crisis, is it not? You are going back… back to fight Bonaparte!" Unlike her mother, she had been reading the newspapers.

Gravely, Richard answered, "Yes, Anne."

"Oh, God." She lay her head on his chest. "When?" she whispered.

"We sail in May. I came to—I had to see you before—"

In a small breaking voice, she said, "I thought you had come back for me."

Richard was in anguish. He took Anne's face in his hands and stared into her eyes, memorizing every lovely feature. "Anne, there is so much I wish to say… but now is not the time. Oh, my dearest!"

Anne shook her head, her eyes swimming in tears. As her small fists began beating on him, she cried, "No, no… not now! How can you say these things to me now? Now that you are leaving me, perhaps never to return. How cruel! I cannot stand it! Leave me—let me go! Please!" She broke away from Richard and fled into the house.

Richard stood like a statue, watching her flee. Then slowly he sat on the bench behind him, removing his hat and holding his face in his hands.

Anne rushed past the housekeeper and up the stairs. She had her choice of her rooms to which to run. By very good fortune, she chose her sitting room. There she found Mrs. Jenkinson.

"My goodness!" the woman cried as she rose from her chair. "Whatever is the matter?"

Anne, her face swimming in tears, hesitated and then embraced her companion. "It… it is Richard. He is going away to France!"

"To France? Whatever for?"

"The war—Bonaparte—he goes to fight Bonaparte. He did not come for me. Good-bye—he came to say good-bye. Oh, I cannot bear it!"

Mrs. Jenkinson was distraught, but she kept her wits about her. "Oh my dear, how distressing! What you must be feeling!" She allowed Anne to weep for a few moments more before asking, "How did you leave it with the colonel?"

"W… what? Leave it?"

Mrs. Jenkinson asked sharply, "Anne, what did you do?"

"Do? I did nothing. I… I fled."

"Oh, my girl, what are you thinking? Colonel Fitzwilliam comes here to bid you farewell—forgive me, but perhaps for the last time—and you just ran away?"

Anne's tears stopped as she realized the extent of her blunder. Her eyes grew wide and panic-stricken.

"He goes to war, my dear," Mrs. Jenkinson continued. "Have you any idea what he shall be going through in the weeks to come? Perhaps the only comfort he shall have will be the knowledge that those he cares for at home are thinking of him. Oh, my love, you cannot be this cruel." She held her charge at arm's length. "Anne—no secrets now—do you love him?"

Eyes downcast, Anne said, "With all my heart. Oh, Mrs. Jenkinson, what shall I do?"

Mrs. Jenkinson raised Anne's head with her hand under the girl's chin and looked into her eyes. "You must let him know."

"Oh, where is paper?" Anne dashed for her desk.

Mrs. Jenkinson moved towards the door. "Quickly as ever you can, my dear. We will delay him."

Colonel Fitzwilliam knew not how long he sat dejected in the garden. Finally, the sound of hooves against cobblestones brought him back to himself. He slowly rose to his feet, took one last look at the door Anne had rushed into, and turned to leave.

As he approached the front of the house, Richard saw that most of the household staff had gathered on the front steps, Mrs. Parks and Mrs. Jenkinson among them. The housekeeper approached him.

"Colonel Fitzwilliam, the staff wanted to see you off as you go to serve the king in defense of the country. We wanted you to know that you have done good service here at Rosings and Hunsford and that we all shall be praying for your safe return."

A murmur of "Hear, hear" rose among the throng. First the butler, and then others came forward to offer their hands. After accepting good wishes with as much composure as he could manage with a broken heart, Richard noted that the crowd began to part.

There at the open front door stood Anne, looking regal and beautiful—every inch a de Bourgh. Richard's heart turned over. She walked down the steps and stopped a few feet from Richard. After giving him an imperious look, she turned to the servants.

"It is well that we do homage to Colonel Fitzwilliam. While we stay here safely at home, involved in our daily tasks, he goes across the seas to join our troops to face the tyrant of France—the monster who endangers freedom everywhere." She turned back to Richard. "Colonel, you go to battle with our thanks and prayers. Do honor to our gracious majesty, George III, and return home safely to us. God save the King!"

"God save the King!" repeated the crowd.

"Colonel, here is an additional report from the steward. He entrusted it to me to be delivered to you personally." Anne handed Richard an envelope. "Good-bye, Cousin, and Godspeed!" She held out her hand.

A very confused Richard gave Anne's hand the most perfunctory of kisses before turning to mount his horse. As he did so, a shout arose from the gathered servants.

"Three cheers for Colonel Fitzwilliam!"

"HIP, HIP, HURRAH! HIP, HIP, HURRAH! HIP, HIP, HURRAH!" All cheered lustily, including Anne.

Richard awkwardly tipped his hat at the recognition and rode off, the people of Rosings waving until he was out of sight.

Richard spent the first half of his journey to London in quiet misery. He repeatedly thought about what had happened and what he might have done differently. Anne's contrariness confounded him; one moment she embraced him, the next she ran away. Her farewell was particularly confusing. She acted as he might expect Lady Catherine to behave. Had he misjudged her feelings? No other answer occurred to him.

After about an hour while walking his horse, Richard recalled the letter from the steward. Deciding to occupy his mind with estate issues rather than romantic ones, the colonel took the letter from his inside coat pocket and opened it. To his surprise, the note had only three words written on it:

I love you.

Richard stopped his horse and stared at the note for what seemed an eternity, his mind working to believe what he saw. Finally, reality was triumphant, joy overspread his features, and a shout of glee escaped his lips. There was no doubt who had written the beautiful words; Richard knew Anne's hand very well. All of his doubt erased, the colonel looked about him in happy confusion.

To his horse he said, "Look! You see? Ha, ha! She loves me—Anne loves me! Hurrah! Oh, the world is wonderful! Oh, I think I shall go mad with happiness!" He began to dance in front of his mount. "What shall I do? Shall I return to Rosings? Yes, I shall see my sweet Annie again, speak to my aunt—"

Richard stopped short; reality reigned. He knew he could not successfully face Lady Catherine again. What should he do? He could not return to Rosings; Lady Catherine would never give her consent. Anne would come away with him regardless, Richard was sure of it, but that would assuredly ignite war within the family now, just as he was going to France. No, that would be selfish.

But Richard knew he must respond. Anne must be told that he returned her feelings. Oh, what a brave, wonderful woman she was! To take such a chance—to risk the exposure! She must be protected. But how would he communicate with her?

He could not write to anyone at Rosings, save Lady Catherine, and there was no solution there! He thought about contacting Mrs. Parks or the steward or Mrs. Jenkinson, but that would not serve. Richard could not ask them to be part of such a conspiracy.

Another moment's thought and Richard leapt upon his horse. He spurred his mount towards London and the one person who could help him.

The Darcy family was gathered in the sitting room when the butler announced Colonel Fitzwilliam.

"Richard!" said Elizabeth. "Welcome to Darcy House. We were just sitting down to tea. Would you care to join us?"

Richard bowed to his cousins. "That would be most agreeable."

Darcy eyed him. "You have ridden hard, I think. Perhaps something stronger than tea?"

"No, Cousin, perhaps later. Tea is just the thing to set me up."

"I am so glad to see you again," said Georgiana. "I thought when you took your leave of us last week we should not meet again until you returned from… well—"

"I must report to my regiment tomorrow, but tonight I have business here." Richard smiled at his ward.

Darcy became alert. "I see. Shall we adjourn to the library then?"

"Darcy, Darcy, I did not say my business was with *you*. I must speak with Georgiana." He turned to the girl. "My dear, I need your help."

"Richard, I cannot say I like this scheme of yours," complained Darcy.

"Why not, Brother?" asked Georgiana. "I think it is perfectly sensible. Besides, he asked me, not you."

Darcy frowned. When he married, he had hoped that Elizabeth and her sisters would have a lively effect upon Georgiana, but not this lively. "Georgiana, I am still your guardian—"

"Yes, Husband," injected Elizabeth, who handed Anne's note back to Richard, "and a most reasonable one you have been," she added with a raised eyebrow—an unmistakable signal that told him to trust her in this matter. Darcy knew there was no winning this battle, as he had learned upon previous occasions.

In any case, he thought, *she is usually right.*

"I will allow this… slightly improper plot," Darcy said magnanimously, "as long it is under Mrs. Darcy's supervision." *There—it is your fault should things go badly.*

"My husband is most wise," Elizabeth said with only the smallest twinkle in her eye. "Richard, you will give your sealed note to me. Georgiana, I am afraid I must approve of your letter to Anne prior to it being sent with Richard's note enclosed." Both Richard and Georgiana agreed to the conditions.

Elizabeth's twinkle did not escape Darcy's notice.

You shall pay for that, my love—he promised with a slight smile—*tonight.*

Elizabeth smiled in return, acknowledging that she guessed her husband's plans and heartily approved of them.

Mrs. Jenkinson looked upon Anne with a sense of helplessness as her charge paced her rooms like a caged wildcat. Anne could not go out of doors—the April rains had come with a vengeance—and there was no relief downstairs with her mother's incessant plans for Bath.

She knew her advice to Anne to reveal everything to her beloved was sound. She had half-expected Colonel Fitzwilliam to have returned by now; surely, he had read Anne's note. Since the girl's impulsive act of giving the colonel such a blatant, unladylike declaration of her feelings, Anne's emotions had swung between mortification and anxiety. Anne had told her that she longed to hear from her colonel, but at the same time was frightened to know what he thought of her rash action. Everything now depended on the colonel to act in such a way as to give comfort.

It had now been three days and there was no sign of the man. Mrs. Jenkinson worried. Had they misjudged the young man?

Her ruminations ended with a knock at the door. Mrs. Jenkinson opened it to find Mrs. Parks with a letter for Anne from Georgiana Darcy. From the look on the housekeeper's face, it was certain that Mrs. Parks felt that the only way to prevent Lady Catherine from intercepting Anne's mail was to deliver it herself.

"Anne," said her companion, "here is a letter for you. 'Tis from Miss Georgiana."

"Thank you, Mrs. Jenkinson. Please excuse me. I shall read it in my bedroom."

"Go on, my dear," Mrs. Jenkinson replied. To Mrs. Parks she said after Anne had left them, "Thank you, Mrs. Parks. It was good of you to bring the post directly to Miss Anne. She has been quite low these last two days."

"'Tis no trouble. I am glad to be of service to dear Miss Anne." She lowered her voice. "I only hope that we have not placed our trust in an unworthy gentleman."

"I cannot believe him to be so—" Mrs. Jenkinson began.

"Hurrah!"

The two women looked in surprise at the giggling shout that came out of Anne de Bourgh's bedroom. A few minutes later the occupant emerged, relatively composed, save for the heightened color on her cheeks.

"Mrs. Parks, there will be a letter of reply for Miss Darcy. Please see that it is posted directly."

"Yes, miss," responded a puzzled housekeeper.

"Mrs. Jenkinson, please excuse me, but I must see to this letter at once."

"Of course. I will just see to dinner, shall I?" The two older women gave each other a knowing look.

As Anne reached her writing desk, she added, "Oh, by the way, Mrs. Jenkinson, please be so kind as to inform my mother that I shall not be accompanying her to Bath—not next month, nor any time in the future. Thank you, that is all."

Mrs. Parks and Mrs. Jenkinson walked down the hall, each fighting an urge to cheer as well.

Chapter 18

London—April, 1815

Buford House, London

My dearest wife,

Can it be that you have been gone for only a fortnight? It has been an age, I am sure. I rattle about my empty rooms, expecting to find you reading in some out-of-the-way corner. If I listen closely, I can hear you playing on the pianoforte. Ah, but I am a pitiful fool!

Most of the staff officers have arrived from London, so I am released to prepare for the arrival of my regiment. I have met the young Prince of Orange. I wish you were here to meet him yourself, my own Queen of Orange—ha! You would find him amusing, I dare say. As for the prince being a military man, I have my doubts.

Darling, I must close now. I shall write as often as I can, but do not be alarmed if you do not hear from me as often as you could desire. My duties take up almost twenty hours of the day.

Longing to kiss you good night, I remain

Yours,
JB

PS—Pray ask Colonel Fitzwilliam to see to my equipment. I have good officers in my regiment, but their heads will be filled with their own concerns.

Caroline frowned—Sir John had not received her letter. She reached for ink and paper.

Delaford

Marianne Brandon was seeing to the last of the packing of her husband's trunks, the family dog, a greyhound named Princess, about her feet. The family owned several greyhounds, but Princess was a particular favorite. Marianne tried desperately to anticipate Colonel Brandon's needs when he got to Belgium: shirts, breeches, and trousers, flannel waistcoat, coats, uniform coats, stockings, small clothes, neckcloths, and—handkerchiefs!

Marianne raced to the dressing room, searching for Christopher's handkerchiefs. "Where are they?" she mumbled to herself before opening the correct drawer. How many would her husband need? Would six be enough? He might catch cold in the rain. Would Christopher have to sleep in a tent?

Finally, the absurdity of the situation struck her.

You silly goose. Christopher is going to war. He cannot be bothered with handkerchiefs.

Dropping them, Marianne slid to the floor of Colonel Brandon's dressing room, completely overcome with tears.

"Christopher, you are joking. Please tell me you are joking!" Marianne had cried the day before.

Colonel Brandon was as miserable as he had ever been in his life. He had just told his wife that he was not reporting for duty in London. He was called to Belgium instead to serve on Wellington's staff, as requested by the duke himself.

"My Marianne—"

"But you are so old! You have not served for years!"

Christopher winced at the blow. He tried not to resent the comment. It was true, after all.

"What do you know of wars and fighting and cannons and—"

"Marianne," he interrupted her ranting. "I am a colonel—"

"You *were* a colonel! Why you? *Why?*"

"Because there is no one else."

Marianne resumed the packing after a little while. She neatly folded the handkerchiefs she had embroidered with his initials before placing them into the trunk. Nightshirts, robe, shaving kit, soap, tooth powder, and coffee were put in next. The last item brought a small smile to her lips when she remembered their fondness for sharing it. Salt, pepper, sugar, tea, polish for his boots…

The bedroom door opened as Sergeant Masters, Colonel Brandon's aide, valet, and right-hand man, came in carrying a long, wrapped bundle.

"Please excuse me, missus," he said as he placed the bundle inside the last trunk. "All done 'ere yet, ma'am?"

"I believe so, Sergeant," Marianne answered.

"It looks ta me like you 'ave done a fine job. Beggin' your pardon, though, but I think I will just double-check."

"Of course, Sergeant. I would not dream of objecting. I will be downstairs with the colonel. Come along, Princess."

The soldier eyed Marianne kindly as he gave the dog a pat. "A right good idea, ma'am. It would mean a lot to 'im, it would. And you should not worry. Me an' the colonel been through a lot together. I will be watchin' out for 'im. You got me word on it."

"Thank you, Sergeant. I shall hold you to that, sir!"

"Yes, missus." Masters began digging into the chests.

Marianne meant to leave, but she found she was rooted to the spot. The bundle Masters had brought was slightly unraveled due to the sergeant's efforts. There, gleaming in the sunlight, was the hilt of Christopher's sabre.

Arriving at the foot of the stairs, Marianne was about to ask a maid where the master was when she heard Joy giggling to a familiar chant.

"Who is my love? Who is my love? Why, it is Joy! Ha, ha, ha!"

Marianne closed her eyes for a moment as she grasped the banister for support. *I must bear it for him*, she told herself. Back in control of her feelings, Marianne entered the parlor. There on the floor was her husband in the campaign uniform of a colonel of cavalry, playing with their daughter. She leaned against the door frame and watched, allowing Joy this special time with her father.

After a few more minutes, the child began to yawn. Christopher pulled Joy close to his chest as he sat up. Propping himself against a couch, the colonel rocked his daughter to sleep, singing a lullaby. Princess had gone to lie next to her master on the floor, her head on his lap. The only reason Marianne did not weep was that she had no more tears to give.

Finally, Joy was fast asleep. Christopher looked up at his wife as she walked over to him and relieved him of their daughter.

"I will be just a moment, love," she said to him before returning Joy to the nursery.

By the time she returned, Christopher was back on his feet, pouring a cup of coffee from the pot the maid had just delivered. Before she could ask, he handed her the cup and poured another one.

"Shall we retire to the library, dear?" he asked. She nodded, and the pair left the parlor.

Once in the library, Christopher placed his cup down on his desk and held out a chair in front of it, indicating that he wished Marianne to sit there. After seating his wife, Christopher reclaimed his cup and sat behind the desk, facing his wife.

"My love, here is all the information you need to manage Delaford in my absence—ledger, chart of accounts, book of contracts, an address book with the names of the solicitor, banker, agent, contacts at the War Department—everything. The steward, Mr. McIntosh, has been in my service for a dozen years. He is hardworking and honest."

He held up an envelope. "Here is my will, and here,"—he handed Marianne another envelope—"are my instructions naming you as my agent, giving you full power of attorney. This means you speak with my voice, and all decisions you make are final."

Marianne could hardly mark what her husband was saying—her attention was riveted on those evil papers he referred to as his will. Christopher caught what had attracted his wife's notice. He held up the will again.

"This states that I leave everything to Joy, that you are trustee of Delaford lands and mistress of Delaford Manor for the rest of your life, and you shall receive half the income. The house in London is yours, free and clear. There is also a bequest to my ward, Eliza." At Marianne's distressed look he continued. "We must speak of such things, my dear. To know that you, Joy, and Eliza are well provided for is a comfort to me.

"Now here is a letter explaining all to Mr. McIntosh—oh, blast! I meant to add something," he mumbled. "I forgot to leave instructions for McIntosh to reverse the ratio of barley to wheat this year. Oh, where is paper—"

"Christopher, I want to have another baby!" cried out Marianne.

Christopher looked up. "Pardon me?"

"These legal and business matters give you comfort. But I wish for something, too. I want to have another baby—a son," she said to him seriously.

"But... but these things are unpredictable—"

"I know that, you silly man, but I wish to try before you leave in the morning."

Christopher looked into the earnest eyes of his wife. Leaving her pregnant was not comforting to *him*, yet he could see the justice in her words. To be in her arms was his greatest delight, and the odds were tremendously in his favor.

"Are you certain, my Marianne?" he said in the love code only the two of them understood.

She nodded.

Christopher reached out a hand to his now beaming wife. Hand in hand, they left the library just as Sergeant Masters came downstairs.

"Beggin' the colonel's pardon. All the cases are checked and locked tight." His eyes drifted to the couple's clenched hands.

"Very good, Masters. I shall see you in the morning," said Colonel Brandon.

To Marianne's amusement, the sergeant flushed profusely as he turned and left them. Marianne then left instructions with the housekeeper that the master and mistress would take their evening meal upstairs in the mistress's rooms. The old woman did not blink but simply nodded.

Marianne and Christopher then ascended the stairs, still hand in hand.

A crowd had gathered about the coach that was to take Colonel Brandon to Portsmouth. All the staff from Delaford was there, as well as Mr. and Mrs. Ferrars, Mrs. and Miss Dashwood, and Sir John and Lady Middleton from Barton Park. It was kindly suggested to the baronet that since the colonel wanted no ceremony for his departure, Sir John and Lady Middleton might take their leave of their friend as he passed on the road.

Sir John Middleton responded to the suggestion with an amused snort. "Nonsense, nonsense! Lady Middleton shall be very pleased to see the colonel off properly, as should I. It is no bother. Why, Delaford is no distance at all from Barton Park—no distance at all!"

Colonel Brandon was taken aback by the size of his audience, but he bore it in good humor, taking time personally to take his leave of everyone there. He spent no little time with his extended family.

Edward Ferrars said, "I shall keep an eye on Marianne and Joy for you, never fear."

"I shall depend upon that," Christopher answered, before turning to his sister. "And you keep an eye on him, Elinor!"

"Take care, my son," cried Mrs. Dashwood as she hugged him.

Christopher saluted Margaret. "I take my leave of you, Captain!" Margaret Dashwood, now a lovely young lady nearing eighteen, old enough for a sweetheart in the navy, blushed and hugged him as well.

Christopher took his ward, Eliza, into his arms and kissed her on the forehead. "No tears, my dear, no tears. Marianne is depending on you." Eliza only cried harder.

Finally, he turned to Marianne, who was holding a squirming Joy in her arms. He simply embraced them; with all that had passed in the night, there were no words left. To Joy he whispered, "Who is my love?" He then looked Marianne in the eye.

"As God is my witness, I shall come back to you, though Hell itself bars the door," he said in a voice just for her ears.

"Go, my Odysseus," she said, eyes gleaming, "and like Penelope, I shall faithfully await your return."

Colonel Brandon turned to Sergeant Masters. "Come, it is time we were off."

As he climbed into the carriage, he said to Marianne, "My dear, I forgot! Tell McIntosh to switch the ratio between the barley and the wheat."

Marianne nodded. "Switch the ratio between the barley and the wheat. I shall tell Mr. McIntosh."

A quick kiss. "Good-bye, my Marianne." The door shut and the carriage jerked into motion.

"Give Boney what-for, Colonel!" shouted Sir John Middleton.

Christopher leaned out the carriage window, holding up his hat. The crowd waved until the coach was no longer in sight. Princess, restrained by the butler, barked for a very long time.

Chapter 19

Delaford Manor

SEVERAL DAYS LATER, MR. McIntosh knocked on the door to Delaford Manor. "The missus sent for me," he announced to the footman in a thick Scottish burr. The footman showed the steward in and left to alert the butler.

Marianne awaited her first interview with the steward. She had intended to receive him in the library but thought better of it. She believed that meeting with the man might be less formal in the bright and sunny parlor. Besides, she found it difficult to enter Christopher's favorite room.

"Mr. McIntosh," the butler announced. A slight man of about five and forty came into the room nervously, holding his hat in his hands, mustache twitching.

Marianne had to restrain a giggle. "Mr. McIntosh, come in. Please take a seat."

The steward's expression clearly indicated he doubted the fine thing would hold his weight. It was with reluctance and trepidation he carefully sat down upon it. No disaster occurred, and the man looked expectantly at the mistress of Delaford.

"Thank you very much for coming. As you know, Colonel Brandon has been called away on military business. We do not know when he will be back. I know you will join me in praying for his swift return."

"God willin'," was all the man said.

Apparently, Mr. McIntosh was a man of few words; Marianne found that infuriating. "Colonel Brandon left this for you." She handed him his letter. "I know we shall muddle through in his absence, but I shall rely on you to advise me."

The steward looked at her curiously as he opened the letter. He began to read it.

"As you can see, Colonel Brandon left the management of Delaford to my care. He has full faith in you, as do I. The only instructions he gave me that are not in that letter were to change around the barley and the wheat—"

"No."

"I beg your pardon?"

Mr. McIntosh put down the letter. "No."

"No?" Marianne was confused. "I am afraid I do not understand your meaning. No to what, may I ask?"

"No—I *canna* take orders from ye, ma'am."

"Excuse me?" Marianne cried.

"With all due respect, I *canna* take orders from ye."

"But… but you have Colonel Brandon's instructions right there in your hand!"

McIntosh nodded. "Aye, ma'am, and I means to follow them as far as the law o' God allows."

"What are you talking about?" demanded Marianne.

"God made woman to be man's helpmate. 'Tis against holy scripture for a man to take orders from a woman." He held up Brandon's letter. "I'll follow any instructions written by Colonel Brandon, so long's it *dinna* violate God's Law."

Marianne was astonished. "Mr. McIntosh, I am the Mistress of Delaford. Colonel Brandon has given me legal power to act on his behalf." McIntosh shook his head. "I am deadly earnest, sir!"

"Mrs. Brandon, I am terribly sorry, but I *canna* do it. You are a good lady; you have been generous to th' poor, but I *canna* put my soul at risk."

Marianne stared at the Scot. "We are at an impasse, I see."

"Aye."

"I can dismiss you, you know."

"Aye."

Marianne was absolutely stymied.

"Maybe it would be best if I give ye my notice now, ma'am," McIntosh offered.

Marianne paled. She was deeply offended at the man's stubbornness, but she needed a steward to manage the farms. She could not afford to have him resign. "Mr. McIntosh," Marianne drew breath. "I hope it does not come to that. There must be some way around this." She thought for a moment. "What are your plans for the next month?"

"'Tis the plantin' season, ma'am."

It was exactly as she feared. She could not lose the Delaford steward right before planting season! "Yes, that was the last instruction given to me by Colonel Brandon. He wanted to change the ratio of barley and wheat."

"What's that, missus?"

Marianne thought hard. "His exact words were, 'Switch the ratio between the barley and the wheat.'"

McIntosh looked down at the letter. "Beggin' your pardon, missus, but that *inna* in here."

"Yes, yes, I know that. He told me just as he was leaving." McIntosh shook his head. "Is that not good enough?" Marianne cried.

McIntosh's eyes were filled with worry. "Mrs. Brandon, that *inna* in here."

"Are you implying that I am lying?" The mistress of Delaford rose in anger.

Mr. McIntosh rose in sorrow. "Mrs. Brandon, I enjoy my position here. The colonel's been as fine a master as any could wish." His eyes filled with a fanatical light. "But it *inna* worth losin' my eternal reward. Would ye be wantin' my notice?"

Marianne knew there was no moving the man. She needed to think. "No, not at this time. I think there is nothing left to say about this subject at this time. Perhaps we need to postpone this interview until a later date. We will have time to reflect on what we have discussed. Thank you for your time, Mr. McIntosh. You may return to your duties."

"Thankee, ma'am," he touched his forelock. "God bless ye an' the colonel." He turned and made for the door of the parlor. As he opened it he said, "I'll not go against God, missus. I will not."

Marianne sat back down in complete and utter frustration.

"Mr. McIntosh belongs to a rather evangelical church, Marianne," reported Edward Ferrars that night at dinner. "I have no influence with the man."

"What about the rector at the Scottish Reformed Church?" asked Elinor.

Edward rose from his chair and began to pace the dining room in the parsonage. "No, my dear, that would not help. The members of McIntosh's church left the Reform congregation because they felt it was not... reformed enough." He turned to their guest. "They take a rather literal view of scripture."

"So I gathered," remarked Marianne with an edge of irony.

"So, what is to be done?" asked Elinor. "The planting season is upon us."

"Perhaps you could write to the colonel—" Edward began.

"God's blood, I will not!" cried Marianne. "Christopher left me in charge. This is my home—my land. I will not bother my husband with matters such as this while he faces…" She could not finish.

Husband and wife looked at each other. Never had they heard such language from Mrs. Brandon before. "Marianne," Edward began carefully, "I quite understand your feelings—"

"I will not write Christopher, and I forbid you to do so!"

Edward sighed. "As you wish, but I think I may say without fear of contradiction that you do need help."

Marianne glared at her brother, mainly because she knew he was right.

"Perhaps your solicitor?" suggested Elinor.

"No," snapped Marianne. "He would just storm about talking law and contracts and writs, and end up driving Mr. McIntosh away. I need someone who can find a way of managing Mr. McIntosh so that the planting takes place as Christopher wanted—without surrendering my authority. I need someone exceedingly clever."

"Who? A magistrate, perhaps?" asked Edward.

Marianne looked at them both with determination. "Elizabeth's husband, Mr. Darcy, is the cleverest man I know. I met his solicitor in London. If Darcy trusts *him*, then so will I. I need Mr. Tucker."

"Friends," called the preacher, "let us refer to the words of our Lord in Matthew, chapter five, beginning with verse seventeen.

"'Think not that I have come to abolish the law and the prophets; I have come not to abolish them but to fulfill them. For truly, I say to you, till heaven and earth pass away, not an iota, not a dot, will pass from the law until all is accomplished. Whoever then relaxes one of the least of these commandments and teaches men so, shall be called least in the kingdom of heaven; but he who does them and teaches them shall be called great in the kingdom of heaven. For I tell you, unless your righteousness exceeds that of the scribes and Pharisees, you will never enter the kingdom of heaven.'

"What could be clearer, friends? Our Lord Jesus Christ calls upon us to follow God's law—the law that is here in this book! The law Moses brought down from Sinai, the law of the prophets..."

Mr. McIntosh sat with his eyes closed, nodding in his usual pew, the third from the front, next to his wife and his remaining son and his growing family. McIntosh had been raised in the Scottish Reformed Church and attended services regularly, but he was always uneasy; he felt there was something missing. The day his eldest son died was one of the worst of his life, and the patronizing platitudes of his minister only made things worse. The tragedy forced McIntosh onto a spiritual journey for fulfillment, one that ended in the very church pew in which he now sat.

For it was only a few months after joining this congregation that his wife fell ill with the same malady that had carried away his beloved son. The doctors shook their learned heads, despairing of his wife's recovery. McIntosh could still see in his mind's eye the long vigil in his small parlor, members of his new church holding hands with his family, led in prayer by the preacher. All night they prayed. McIntosh made a promise to his Creator that if he would spare his wife, he would become his instrument here on earth. With the sunrise came a cry from the bedroom—the fever had broken; his wife would live.

On his knees, McIntosh thanked the preacher, who refused credit, telling him that all glory belonged to God. From that moment on, McIntosh pledged his devotion to his new church. He gave up drink and all manner of vice—oh, how he missed his wee touch of whisky in the evenings! But there was nothing for it; God had answered his prayer, and so he would now follow his new preacher. He had become an elder and one of the most respected members of the church council. He would follow God's teachings, no matter what it cost—even his position at Delaford.

"We all must bear witness to the glory of God!" the preacher said. "For it is written: 'You are the light of the world. Let your light so shine before men that they may see your good works and give glory to your Father who is in heaven.' This is not an easy path."

McIntosh nodded again.

"But Our Lord did not have an easy path on the road to Calvary! He warned us: 'Blessed are those who are persecuted for righteousness' sake, for theirs is the kingdom of heaven. Blessed are you when men revile you and persecute you and utter all kinds of evil against you falsely on my account. Rejoice and be glad, for your reward is great in heaven, for so men persecuted the prophets who were before you.'"

"Amen," said Mr. McIntosh.

"Mr. Tucker, Mary, thank you so much for answering my invitation so quickly," gushed Marianne after her guests were shown into the parlor. She realized that it was not so much an invitation that she issued but a summons.

"We thank you for the opportunity to visit Dorsetshire, Mrs. Brandon. Delaford is lovely, do you not think so, dear?"

Mary smiled. "It is my happy task to add Delaford to the list of beautiful homes I have had the honor of visiting. You are very kind to ask us here, especially on such slight acquaintance." At Marianne's look, Mary smiled again. "Forgive me, Marianne, but you know my sisters Jane and Elizabeth much better than you know me."

"Mary! I have known you for years!"

"Yes, as Elizabeth's sister. And you know my husband hardly at all." She gave Marianne a knowing look. "Mr. Tucker and I discussed this on the way here. As much as you and I have enjoyed each other's company, I do not think this invitation was issued for *my* company." She glanced at her husband. "Do not be embarrassed, dear Marianne. I am not offended."

Mr. Tucker looked seriously at Marianne. "How may I be of service to you, Mrs. Brandon?"

Marianne sighed. "Well, since I did have you come here under a false premise, the least I can do is to request that you call me Marianne as your wife does." He agreed and asked that she call him by his Christian name, as well.

That settled, she continued. "I have a problem with my steward."

Several days later, Mr. McIntosh knocked on the door to Delaford Manor. "Mrs. Brandon sent for me," he announced to the footman, who left to alert the butler.

This time, McIntosh was showed into the library. There, waiting for him was not Mrs. Brandon, as he expected, but two gentlemen—one a stranger and one he knew.

"Mr. McIntosh, come in, sir!" cried one of the gentlemen. "It is good to see you. And how is your family?"

"My family is well, Mr. White, thanks be to God," McIntosh told the MP.

"Wonderful!" said the politician. "Allow me to introduce to you Mr. Tucker, solicitor for Colonel Brandon." It was not a falsehood— Mrs. Brandon acted as Colonel Brandon's agent in securing Mr. Tucker's services.

"Sir," said Tucker formally.

"Come, sit down, sit down," requested Mr. White.

McIntosh carefully took his seat in the same frail chair, clearly expecting the worst.

Mr. White smiled at the Scot. "There have been some changes at Delaford, and Mr. Tucker and I thought to have you in for a chat, to let you know how things are now." Mr. White leaned over the desk. "I have been retained by the colonel to oversee all operations of Delaford lands." Tucker handed a document to McIntosh for his perusal. "As you can see, all work on the farms must be approved by me. Do you have any questions, sir?"

McIntosh looked up from the document, a bit of relief coming to his features. "No, sir."

"Excellent! We thought it best to have our first meeting here, but in the future, we shall meet at my office in the village—every Tuesday morning. Is that agreeable to you, sir?"

"Aye."

"Fine. One last thing, McIntosh." Tucker handed the steward a second piece of paper. "This is my written instruction to you, now that spring planting is upon us, to switch the ratio between the barley and the wheat. Is that clear, sir?" Mr. White looked hard at him.

"Aye, Mr. White." Tucker thought he saw a smile begin to dance about the steward's mustache, but he could not be sure.

"Very good. I suppose you wish to get back to your work."

"Aye. Good day to ye, Mr. White, Mr. Tucker." Thus dismissed, McIntosh quit the library and Delaford Manor in far better spirits than when he entered.

The two gentlemen made their way into the parlor to join the ladies.

"Well," asked the mistress of Delaford, "did Mr. Tucker's plan work?"

Mr. White beamed. "Perfectly, Mrs. Brandon. You shall have no further trouble from Mr. McIntosh."

"And the crops?"

"The change shall be accomplished."

"Thank you, Mr. White. May I offer you some tea?"

"Thank you, no. I must be off. Ladies, Mr. Tucker." Mr. White bowed as he was escorted out by the butler.

"Well, that is that," began Tucker as he picked up his cup of tea. "Mr. White is not a bad chap—for a Whig."

"It may be over until Mr. McIntosh finds out who hired Mr. White," grumbled Marianne, who was drinking coffee instead.

Tucker smiled. "Oh, I think he knows, Marianne. He seemed quite relieved, actually."

Mary sat on the couch with Princess. "Devotion to God is a wonderful thing—as long as it does not go too far."

"It still sits ill with me—the cheek of the man! And I had to find *another* man to solve my problem!" cried Marianne. "It is all very vexing!"

"All is well that ends well, Marianne," said Mary.

Paris

The emperor was back in his palace, but he was not content. Many of his countrymen had flocked to his banner—but not all. Many of the common folk were taking a wait-and-see attitude. As for the military, his success was not universal. Most of his marshals had returned, but he had been abandoned by many in the navy.

The emperor did not have a free hand this time. The deputies actually wanted a voice in policy. He would have to keep his promises of reform, at least for a while.

All these troubles were as nothing compared to the reaction by the rest of Europe. He had sent out pledges of peace, vowing to live up to the treaties that ended the war, but the great powers rejected his overtures. Led by the hated English, they called him an outlaw and set up another Coalition to attack him.

The emperor would have to move quickly. He wanted an army of six hundred thousand to take the field, but that would take the summer to raise, and he knew he did not have that much time. He could not use conscription again, and he had to have a victory. He needed to break the Coalition first.

He began by recalling all undischarged troops and mobilized the National Guard. That would give him nearly 125,000 men. Equipment would be a challenge, but he could not wait.

He had to decide where to attack. The Austrians would not be ready for some time—and the Russians even longer. The immediate threat was from the British and Prussian armies gathering in Belgium.

That was where he had to strike. Hit one or the other before they could link up, and he would destroy them. The other Coalition partners would be shaken, which would give him time. They might actually sue for peace.

Besides, the emperor considered this English duke a bad general and the English bad troops. Given surprise and the emperor's lucky star, it would be a picnic.

He would begin at the morning *levee*.

Chapter 20

Brussels

COLONEL CHRISTOPHER BRANDON LOOKED about the staff room, and despite the riot of colors of the uniforms and the brightness of the medals adorning the tunics, he could not say he was overly impressed. True, there were some veterans of the Peninsula—the popular Lord Hill and the foul-mouthed Sir Thomas Picton, both extremely talented—but Christopher did not know most of the others. Young Prince Willem of Orange was certainly brave enough; he had proven that in Spain. However, was that enough for a corps command? At least the prince's chief of staff, Rebecque, seemed to know his business. The other officers would do, but Brandon was shocked at the duke's choice of cavalry commander—Uxbridge, of all people!

"Gentlemen," the Duke of Wellington said after giving a report of his May 3 meeting in Tirlemont with the Prussian commander, Field Marshal Prince Gebhard von Blücher, "we believe that Bonaparte will not attempt anything until July at the earliest. By then, our troops will have linked up with Blücher and his 80,000 Prussians. Keep your eyes on the west; undoubtedly, Bonaparte will try to cut us off from the coast and our line of supply. The town of Hal is the key. Prince Fredrick and General Colville will be responsible for its protection. Are there any questions?"

"Fear not, my lord!" cried the Prince of Orange. "Let Napoleon try to invade! We shall crush him!"

Brandon rolled his eyes.

"Thank you, Your Highness," responded Wellington, as if the young man had just given a report of the weather. "That is all, gentlemen."

Brandon saw Major Denny leave with Canning, Gordon, Stanhope, and the other *aides-de-camp*, all young, spirited, and talented. He dawdled, however, until the room was nearly empty and he was able to catch Wellington's eye.

"Yes, Brandon—something on your mind?"

"Yes, sir," replied the colonel. "It has been years since I have last served, and... uh... I was wondering—"

Wellington gave him a hard stare. "And you were wondering why I chose a broken-down, old man like you?"

Brandon kept his face impassive though his insides roiled at the insult. "Yes, sir."

"I am starting to wonder myself."

"I beg your pardon, my lord."

"Have you no eyes, Brandon?"

Christopher's lips tightened. "There is nothing wrong with my eyesight, sir."

"Then tell me what you saw today!" Wellington demanded.

Brandon hesitated before he spoke, trusting in the duke's penchant for frankness. "I saw a room full of officers who are unknown to me. I have no idea how they will act under fire."

Wellington sighed. "Very succinct, Brandon, and I agree with you." At Brandon's intake of breath, the duke continued, "Most of the fellows who were with us in India and Spain are now in Canada—that is, the ones who are not dead in Louisiana."

"Indeed." Brandon was well aware that two thousand British soldiers had fallen during the disastrous attack on New Orleans. In January, a ragtag band of locals, frontiersmen, and American regulars had held off the finest of the king's infantry. Two generals were dead, including Major General Sir Edward Pakenham, brother-in-law to Wellington. Several regiments were shattered, including the Highlanders—and for naught. The ill-begotten war had been over for weeks—the treaty signed in December—but word could not get to Louisiana quickly enough to stop the bloodbath. "I am sorry about Pakenham, sir."

"I am, too. I could use him. Green troops, green cavalry, green officers—that is what we have here, Colonel! An infamous army, what?"

Diplomatically, Brandon replied, "If you say so, sir."

Wellington laughed. "Ha! There is my Brandon—always wary, always careful. I need you, Brandon. I need men I both know and trust."

"Is that why—?" Brandon blurted before he could catch himself.

Wellington nodded. "Yes, that is why I asked for Paget, the man who cuckolded my brother."

It was common knowledge that Henry Paget, the Earl of Uxbridge, friend and comrade-in-arms to Sir Arthur, had run off with the wife of Henry Wellesley, British ambassador to Spain, while both were still married. Brandon was aware that both had been granted divorces, and Charlotte Wellesley and Uxbridge married, but for five years, there was bad blood between the Wellesley and Paget families.

"I cannot speak to Paget's private affairs, but I need a man who will keep those hotheaded cavalry lads in line. Uxbridge can do the job." Wellington's voice dropped. "As for his highness, the prince, he is second-in-command in name only. I retain control of all British troops. He should not do too much harm."

Brandon hoped the duke was right.

"Once Blücher arrives, we will have over 150,000 in the field, so I expect we should give a good account, even of Bonaparte. He may not want to attack such strength, you know, and that will give the Austrians and the Russians time to reach the French frontier from the east." The duke paused.

"Before I left Vienna, Tsar Alexander came to me and placed his hand upon my shoulder. Do you know what he said, Brandon? 'It is again up to you to save the world.'

"That is our task, Colonel."

"All right, you men," called out Captain George Wickham to his company. "Two salvos, then five rounds of volley platoon fire. Sergeants, take over."

Wickham walked over to the shade of a nearby tree and discreetly retrieved a flask of brandy from his pocket. Taking a small sip of the fiery liquid, he surveyed his company. The sergeants were making sure that the company took up the proper four-row line—one low, three standing—that made up the square, the heart of the British method of infantry fighting. The months of training were evident; only a few men were out of place.

"All ready, sir!" called out a lieutenant.

Wickham strode to the line and took his proper place. Drawing his sabre—just as he would in battle—he pointed at the target thirty paces downfield.

"COMPANY, MAKE READY!"

A hundred muskets were cocked. Normally, the fourth line would not shoot—they served as reserves, but this was an exercise.

"TAKE AIM—STEADY!" The muskets came up pointing at the dozen hay bales that served as targets.

"FIRE!" The line disappeared in a cloud of smoke as the muskets went off as one. Hurriedly, the men reloaded. Wickham waited until most of the muskets had come back up, his watch in one hand.

"FIRE!" A hundred muskets crashed again. In the smoke, Wickham cried, "VOLLEY FIRE! VOLLEY FIRE!"

Beginning with the kneeling line, each line fired a volley in turn. The effect was a wall of constant fire, as the other lines reloaded as their comrades shot.

Finally, the fourth line fired its fifth shot, and the smoke dissipated. The haystacks were the worse for wear, an effect the army knew would boost the soldiers' morale.

Wickham looked at his watch and shook his head. "Well shot, my lads, but too slow! Barely two volleys in a minute—should be closer to three! Sergeants, take your men for some extra drill," he said as he dismissed the company. He was then approached by a Dutch officer who had observed the exercise.

"Your men did well, Captain," he said.

"Thank you, Captain, they did," Wickham replied. It was all well and good to say so to some Dutchman, but Wickham would not compliment the men to their faces; he needed to maintain discipline.

"But the waste in powder and balls!" The Dutch officer shook his head. "How can you English afford it?"

Wickham said nothing. While he had no personal experience of war, those who did claimed the live-fire exercises improved the infantrymen's marksmanship, which had proven invaluable in the Peninsular campaign. Wickham was simply following orders.

The Dutch officer changed the subject. "Are you attending tomorrow night's ball, Captain?" Many of London society had followed the army to Brussels, and entertainments were necessary to break the monotony.

"No, I shall not be able to make it, old boy."

In reality, Wickham's commanding colonel, put on his guard about Wickham by a well-timed letter received from Pemberley before embarking to the Continent, had made Captain Wickham Officer of the Day on the day of the ball. In fact, Captain Wickham was to have the honor of being Officer of the Day *any* day there was a ball.

Damn that Darcy!

Buford sat moodily in the public rooms of his lodgings, nursing a before-dinner glass of wine. He was feeling very sorry for himself.

A month, he railed, *a month with no letter from Caroline! You would think, with all we said, all we shared… damn!* Buford took another drink. *Careful, man! Best not to get drunk. There might be a good reason why you have not heard from her.*

The front door opened to reveal Colonel Fitzwilliam walking in, obviously after a tiresome day. "Buford, my good man, pour me a glass—quick!" Buford did so and Richard took a sip. "Ah… at least there is something to be said for this misbegotten place!"

"Rough time of it, Fitz?"

"Argh, ever seen to the unloading of a bloody horse regiment?" He paused for a moment as Buford gave him a knowing look. "Oh, yes, of course you have. Well then, how can you ask how my day went?" he cried.

Buford smiled. Richard's antics took his mind off his troubles. "Thank you for seeing that my equipment made it over."

"No trouble, old man. Glad to have been of service. Your wife was very keen that I should give the matter my utmost consideration."

Buford then realized that his wife had received his letter. But that still did not explain why there had been no answer. He changed the subject.

"Brandon should be here any moment."

"Excellent—what is for dinner?"

"Beef stew in red wine with onions and mushrooms, *pommes de terre sautées*, and peas."

"Any beer to go with that?" asked Colonel Brandon as he strode to the table. "I am famished!"

"Sit down, Brandon, and welcome!" cried Fitzwilliam. "I am glad you could accept our invitation. I have not seen any trace of you since I got here. Staff work keeping you occupied?"

"Yes." Brandon lifted his newly arrived beer. "To us, gentlemen—three colonels of His Majesty's cavalry! To hell with glory, let us go home!"

"To home!" the others replied.

"Colonel Brandon?" asked a voice from behind.

Brandon turned to see who had addressed him. "Ah, Denny! Will you not have a seat?"

"Oh no, sir, I am just delivering a packet from headquarters." The major handed him the papers.

"Have a seat, Major," said Buford. He had gotten to know Denny during his short time on the staff.

Denny eyed Fitzwilliam, who had turned his face away from him. Finally, after another entreaty from Buford, Denny sat across from Fitzwilliam.

Brandon poured him a glass. "To your health."

"Thank you, Colonel," Denny said as he sipped his wine.

"Beau's been keeping you busy, Denny?" Buford used another nick-name for their commander-in-chief. Wellington was well known for his sartorial splendor.

"Yes, sir—the ——th Regiment just came in. I must see that—"

"The ——th Regiment from Newcastle?" Richard cut the major off.

"Yes, Colonel." Major Denny looked warily at Fitzwilliam. "Assigned to the reserve corps."

"I see."

Brandon began again. "I hope you like the stew—"

"Seen Wickham lately, Denny?" demanded Richard.

"No, sir. I have not seen Captain Wickham since he disembarked at Antwerp."

"I am surprised, Major—you being such good friends," Richard said savagely. The other two officers looked on in bewilderment.

Denny set down his glass. "Excuse me, gentlemen, uh… I just recalled a previous engagement. Perhaps another time." He rose to leave.

"Denny, I—" cried Buford, but he was interrupted by Brandon.

"Of course, Major. Do not let us detain you. I will see you tomorrow." Brandon rose and pointedly shook Denny's hand. Buford rose and did likewise. Fitzwilliam simply sat and glared at the major. Finally, Denny left the boardinghouse.

"What the devil was that about, Fitz?" demanded Buford. "Denny is a very good fellow. There is no need to treat him like that."

"If you really knew him, you would treat him no other way, Buford," he said as he sipped his wine. Richard Fitzwilliam was not a vindictive man. It was not usually in his nature to hold grudges. But the happy-go-lucky visage he presented to the world hid the deep feelings of devotion he held to those few he loved. He would allow no one to harm his family or his closest friends. Chief among those he would protect with his life were Anne de Bourgh and Georgiana Darcy. George Wickham's failed seduction of Georgiana and her subsequent melancholy had affected him more than anyone knew, including himself. He would never forgive Wickham—or anyone he suspected of helping him.

Buford was preparing to respond when Brandon restrained him with a touch of his arm. "It is something personal, I take it, Fitz. We would not dream of inquiring. Let us just drop the matter and enjoy our fellowship and our meal."

Fitzwilliam nodded but did not closely attend. He was too busy thinking over the information he had just received.

Wickham is here. How interesting! I half expected him to run. I should keep an eye out for that bastard.

Rosings Park

Anne de Bourgh sat at her writing table in her suite of rooms, penning her latest secret dispatch to Richard via their co-conspirator, Georgiana Darcy. She hummed happily as she wrote; thoughts of Richard were a welcome distraction from the situation at Rosings.

For the last month since Anne received her life-altering letter from Colonel Fitzwilliam, the household was in a state of undeclared war. Anne had categorically refused to travel with her mother to Bath or to leave her suite of rooms to greet any visitor to Rosings other than family or the Collinses.

Lady Catherine, for her part, refused to talk to Anne or even acknowledge Anne's existence when they were in company together. Messages were sent in writing through Mrs. Parks, the housekeeper, who had continued to take possession of and responsibility for the post, much to Lady Catherine's displeasure. Lady Catherine also refused to allow Anne use of any of Rosings's carriages under threat of dismissal for any groom who might come to the aid of Miss de Bourgh. Anne was reduced to walking the gardens or woods with Charlotte Collins.

Anne had just finished her letter. Only happy subjects were mentioned; Mrs. Jenkinson had been quite insistent upon that. "*A soldier only wants good news from home. It keeps his spirits up. Bad news... well, it does him no good, with him being so far away,*" she had told Anne.

"Come in," Anne called to the knock upon her door. Mrs. Parks entered with a grave expression on her face. "Good heavens, what is the matter?" Anne cried.

Mrs. Parks gave her young mistress a significant look. "It is Mrs. Jenkinson, miss." She motioned towards the lady's room with her head.

Anne thanked the housekeeper and walked quickly to her companion's door. "Mrs. Jenkinson, it's Anne," she said as she knocked on the door.

"Come in, my dear," answered a voice that unsuccessfully hid sobs.

Anne opened the door to behold her longtime companion sitting at her desk, holding a piece of paper in one hand and wiping tears from her face with the other. Anne rushed to her side. Taking the older woman's hand in hers, she asked, "What pains you? Can I be of any service, any comfort?"

Mrs. Jenkinson only shook her head and handed the letter to her former charge. A glance was enough. It was a signed notice from her mother dismissing Mrs. Jenkinson from her employ at Rosings. Anne flushed with anger but not surprise; she had expected this move by Lady Catherine.

She took the older woman's face in her hands and said, "I have told you before, Mrs. Jenkinson, you shall *always* have a home with me."

"But not at Rosings—not now," she said softly. "Where am I to go? I have no children, and my family is all gone."

Anne's face had gone stony. "Do not despair. Leave this to me." She rose and turned towards the door.

Mrs. Jenkinson rose in alarm. "Oh, Anne, what are you going to do? Please, do nothing rash. I shall manage—"

Anne de Bourgh turned back to her former governess, fire in her eyes. "This has gone on for far too long. It ends today." She then left the room.

Mrs. Jenkinson gasped, for her former charge sounded just like her mother.

Anne swept down the hallway towards the staircase. At the head of it, she intercepted Mrs. Parks.

"Where is Mother?" she barked.

"In the parlor, miss."

Acknowledging the reply with the smallest of nods, Anne marched down the stairs and to the doors of the parlor. Without preamble, Anne opened the doors and moved resolutely towards Lady Catherine. Her mother was at her writing table, reviewing her correspondence.

"Mother," Anne greeted Lady Catherine with an icy voice, "it has come to my attention that you have dismissed Mrs. Jenkinson. Is this indeed your intention?"

"Well, miss! You now presume to speak to me! I should thank you, I am sure. Yes, I have let your governess go. It was my impression you had no need of one," Lady Catherine sneered. "Besides, we need to economize now that we should expect no rents this year."

Anne ignored the jab. "Do not play games with me, Mother. You do nothing without cause. What do you want?"

"Watch your tone, miss."

"What do you want?"

Lady Catherine glared at her. "Your obedience and your deference, Anne."

"So—I am to go to Bath, is it?"

Anne saw her mother's eyes gleam. "Yes, Bath. I know what is best for you. You must be with society worthy of you. It is all arranged. I have been in correspondence with a General Tilney..."

Anne watched her mother rant on in silence. Why was she doing this? What was the reason for her determination? She was almost desperate. Was it just her feelings of betrayal at the hands of her uncle?

"...and a house of your own, a great estate, that is what you are destined for, Anne! Just follow my lead—"

Anne interrupted. "Are you saying that if I do this—go with you to Bath—you will reinstate Mrs. Jenkinson?"

"Of course, my dear."

Anne started to laugh.

"What do you find so amusing?" Lady Catherine asked in a dangerous voice.

"You, Mother! Do you believe this is the Dark Ages? You would blackmail me, your only daughter, into marriage to some rich, landed fool? You think the only price you will pay is the wages for my companion? How did you grow so corrupted?"

"How dare you—"

"Silence, Mother! Your schemes are not to be borne! Let us have a right understanding between us, madam. I will *never* go to Bath with you. The day Mrs. Jenkinson leaves this house is the day I do. You have a choice before you—suffer my companion or lose both of us."

"Where would you go, child?" shouted Lady Catherine. "To the streets, I suppose?"

"No, to my uncle," Anne said, as if explaining to a child.

The result was unexpected; Lady Catherine went pale. "N… no, that will not be necessary!" She halted and worked to get control of her emotions. "I had not realized how… how attached you have become to your companion. Far be it from me to cause you any pain. Please let Mrs. Jenkinson know that her services shall be welcomed here for as long as you wish."

She paused and then, incredibly, began to beg. "Do not turn your back upon me, dear Anne. I could not bear it. I do know what is proper for you, but we shall not speak of it now. Let us consider each other's view and talk again another day. Come, give your mother a kiss."

Anne looked wide-eyed at her mother. As she bent to kiss Lady Catherine's cheek, she could only wonder if her mother had finally gone mad.

"Thank you, my dear. Shall I see you for dinner, then?" Lady Catherine turned back to her letters.

Anne only wanted to leave the room at that instant to sort her own raging thoughts. "Yes, Mother—until then." Anne left the room with as much composure as she could muster.

Within a few minutes, she was sitting in Mrs. Jenkinson's room again. Her friend was overjoyed at news of her reprieve.

"Oh, thank you, my dear. That was such a brave thing for you to do. But I do not wish to be a source of disagreement between you and your mother," the older lady said. "But it is so strange! That her ladyship would give in so quickly! I do not see the cause of it."

"Neither do I, but I think I may know someone who does."

London

Caroline was finishing her weekly letter to her husband. She wrote of family doings, news from society, and the latest events caused by her changing physique. Three months along now, her morning sickness had finally stopped—that was the good news. The strange cravings for odd foods puzzled Caroline intensely. She was assured by all her female relations that it was perfectly normal, but it still made no sense to *her*. She wrote of it anyway, thinking Sir John would find her predicament amusing.

Caroline had received no other letters from her husband after the one in late April. She told herself not to worry; he was undoubtedly busy with all the things that soldiers do—whatever that might be. He had warned her, after all. Besides, it was her duty to write—to brighten his day and lighten his cares. Caroline was surprised at the contentment she felt at giving rather than taking.

It had been decided that Caroline would remain in London for the duration of her confinement. She had no wish to go to a Welsh physician she did not know for this first child of hers. Also, London was closer to Belgium; surely her letters would get there faster.

Godspeed you to Antwerp, she thought as she kissed the letter.

Brussels

"Good ride, gentlemen!" cried Colonel Fitzwilliam to his regiment as he dismounted. "Enjoy your evening. We shall ride tomorrow at nine."

Richard gave the reins to a private, patted his horse, and began walking into his guesthouse. He had not gone but a few yards before he beheld Major General Sir John Vandeleur and the Earl of Uxbridge, his commanding officers, arriving on horseback. Coming to attention, Richard fired off a salute.

"Your regiment looks very good, Fitzwilliam," Uxbridge congratulated him as he lazily returned the gesture.

"They will do, sir." Fitzwilliam knew it had been some time since they last saw action in Spain.

"Veterans—wish we had more, eh, your lordship?" said Vandeleur.

"The heavies will do their job, never fear," replied Uxbridge. "Carry on, Fitzwilliam."

"Good work, Colonel. I will inspect your regiment the day after tomorrow," said Vandeleur as he and Uxbridge rode away. Richard continued his walk towards the guesthouse. There he found Buford waiting in the dining room.

"How was today, Buford?" Richard asked as he took his seat.

"No troubles—the regiment is a bit rusty, but they are coming along. You?"

"The same. Oh, thank you," Richard told the innkeeper, who had just handed him a letter.

"Go ahead, open your letter," said Buford as casually as he could.

Richard slipped Georgiana's letter into his coat pocket. "No, I will just read this later," he said with a cat-got-the-cream grin.

Buford sipped his wine to hide his agitation. *Why does Caroline not write?*

Chapter 21

Rosings Park

LADY CATHERINE CAME DOWN the stairs in mid-morning feeling very sure of herself. Since her confrontation with Anne a fortnight ago, she had been busy with correspondence to General Tilney in Bath and to her friends in London, Lady Metcalfe and Mrs. Ferrars. She had also been careful not to upset Anne. The plan was to take Anne to London, ostensibly to support Georgiana during the Season; society would have its way, war or no war.

In secret, Lady Catherine was trying to arrange that General Tilney and his son would "accidentally" meet with her and Anne during a ball. Surely, Tilney's son could take matters from there. If not, Mrs. Ferrars and Lady Metcalfe knew of other good, titled families. It was all a matter of opportunity—Anne was here and Richard was across the sea. Lady Catherine would have her way—and Rosings—in the end.

As she reached the bottom of the stairs, she noticed that the footmen were acting strangely. They were talking behind their hands to one another.

"Here, what is this?" she cried. "Do you have nothing to do but stand in idleness? Be off with you! See to your duties, or you shall be looking for a new situation!"

As the men scampered away, Lady Catherine allowed herself a slight smile; it always felt good to put the help in its place. It never occurred to her to inquire about the subject of the conversation—surely a servant could say nothing worth hearing.

She moved towards the parlor when she noted Mrs. Parks and the butler standing next to the library. They also were having a whispered conversation. The pair noticed Lady Catherine's presence and ended their tête-à-tête, yet made no effort to leave. It grated on Lady Catherine's soul to put up with those two, but there was nothing for it; they were employed by her traitorous brother, the earl. She still considered giving them a piece of her mind, but the grand lady thought better of it and entered the parlor.

As she walked to her writing table—there was another letter to General Tilney to write—she noticed some movement outside the window. Lady Catherine was as curious as the next person—in fact, more so. She could be considered downright nosy. True to her character, she looked out the window and beheld her destruction—the carriage of the Earl of Matlock.

For a moment, she stared dumbfounded at the evil vehicle, as though the harder she looked, the more likely the image before her would evaporate. Stubbornly, the carriage refused to disintegrate, and Lady Catherine was forced to come to the awful realization that her brother, Hugh, was here—at Rosings—*with Anne.*

Fear gripped her heart, but not strongly enough to choke the cry that escaped from her lips. Blindly, Lady Catherine dashed from the room into the main hall—right into Mrs. Parks. Gasping like a fish, she was able to manage, "Where are they?"

Mrs. Parks did not have to ask to whom Lady Catherine was referring. She had been waiting fifteen years to tell her.

"They are in the library."

Lady Catherine turned to the door, already opened by the butler, and dashed inside. There she found the earl at Sir Lewis's old desk with Anne sitting in a chair beside him. Standing next to both of them were her nephew, Darcy, and another man. All were reviewing a stack of papers. Lady Catherine gasped, which caught the attention of those assembled, as well as a fifth person she failed to notice.

"Your ladyship!" cried her toady, Mr. Collins. "Are you quite well? Please, you must take care of yourself. One with your august constitution should not be gasping out of breath! Come, I will help you to a chair—"

"Do not touch me, worm!" she cried. "What are you two doing here?" She pointed at her brother and nephew.

"Setting right what I have allowed to fester for too many years, Catherine," the Earl of Matlock replied. "May I introduce my new solicitor, Mr. Tucker?"

"Very glad to make your acquaint—" began Tucker.

"Silence!" Lady Catherine shouted. "Anne, I do not know what lies they have told you, but do not believe them, I beg you!" Anne turned her head. "Anne, I am your mother! You will obey me! I am mistress of this house!"

Anne faced her mother with a look of steel. "No, you are not, Mother. I am!"

"That is not so! Brother, tell her!"

The earl turned to Anne. "As we have been explaining to you, Anne, your father left Rosings to you, with your Uncle Darcy and me as trustees—"

"No!" Lady Catherine interrupted. "Rosings is mine until she marries or I die!"

The earl turned to Mr. Tucker. "If you would be good enough to explain again, Mr. Tucker."

"Of course, my lord. Lady Catherine, you are correct in stating the intent of Sir Lewis's will. He did leave Rosings to your daughter, with you holding a *usufruct* on her inheritance, until either Miss de Bourgh marries or inherits from you, whichever occurs first."

"Yes, yes, that is correct. What nonsense is all this? I am certainly not dead, and Anne is not married—" Horror came over Lady Catherine's face. "Are you, Anne?"

"Aunt, please be so good as to allow Mr. Tucker to finish," requested Darcy.

For his part, the earl almost felt guilty over the pleasure he was receiving from this experience—almost.

"Thank you, Mr. Darcy," said Tucker. "Lady Catherine, as your daughter is of legal age and of sound mind and good character, I do not think it would be particularly difficult for a court to set aside this completely ridiculous will, especially as the management of the estate has been in the hands of others for years."

"You can try, sir!" Lady Catherine cried. "I have my own resources!"

"Yes, I am sure you do. However, that matter is moot, as Miss de Bourgh has fulfilled the requirements of the will."

"But she is not married!"

"No, but she is betrothed."

"*What*? To Richard? She cannot be! I have not given my consent!"

Mr. Tucker looked hard at Lady Catherine. "Miss de Bourgh is of the age of consent; therefore, your permission is moot." He turned to Anne. "Miss de Bourgh, have you been writing letters to Colonel Richard Fitzwilliam?"

Anne looked Mr. Tucker full in the face. "Yes, I have."

Gravely, he continued, "And has Colonel Fitzwilliam replied to you?"

"Yes, he has." Anne smiled.

"I can categorically affirm that they have exchanged letters," declared Darcy.

"Such behavior sounds very much like a betrothal to me!" piped in Matlock. "What do you say, Mr. Collins?"

The vicar rose, and in a very solemn voice intoned, "It is a great indiscretion for persons who are not engaged to correspond privately with each other. I fear that Colonel Fitzwilliam has compromised Miss de Bourgh's reputation. If they are not betrothed, steps must be taken to preserve the good name of de Bourgh—"

"Sit down, you traitor!" screamed Lady Catherine. "I will have you out of Hunsford parsonage before nightfall—you and that horrid wife and loathsome children of yours!"

Anne leapt to her feet. "You will not threaten *my* parson! Mr. Collins is correct—Richard and I have been indiscreet. Since we have defied society and acted as an engaged couple, I will accept the fact that I have indeed entered into such a promise. I consider myself betrothed to Colonel Fitzwilliam."

"I speak for my family," intoned the earl. "I declare that Richard is indeed betrothed to Anne."

Lady Catherine looked down and then tried one last tack. "I am still mistress of Rosings. Anne is not yet married—"

"Ah, true," began Tucker, "but if the families involved publicly state that the couple is engaged, and Colonel Fitzwilliam does not deny it, they are indeed betrothed. In this case, Colonel Fitzwilliam is away at war. If anything should happen to Colonel Fitzwilliam, the law would look at Miss de Bourgh as if she were already married to him. They are betrothed, and the law treats this very seriously. As this is the case, it could be argued that the law would recognize that Miss de Bourgh has met the require-ments of this unorthodox will and is now owner of Rosings Park, as it recognizes her as married over other matters.

"You could, of course, contest all this—"

"I certainly shall! I will never agree that Anne is betrothed to anyone!"

Tucker was unruffled. "That is certainly your right, Lady Catherine, but I must advise you to think better of it. If you do bring this to court, Lord Matlock and Mr. Darcy have pledged to act on Miss de Bourgh's behalf. Every detail of this business will become public in the trial: Sir Lewis's will, the trusteeship, and Miss de Bourgh's... actions."

Lady Catherine blanched at the thought of all their private affairs being published in the London papers. She turned to her daughter.

"You do not have to do this! This can be repaired!" begged her mother.

"Mother," said Anne, "I want to marry Richard."

"But he has nothing!"

"He has my heart; that is enough."

"Love—you love him? Oh, do not be a fool! Love is not enough to live on!"

"What more is there?" Anne shot back. "What joy has wealth and position ever brought you? Has Rosings brought you happiness? You have barricaded yourself in your great house, estranged from your own family. You go nowhere; you see no one. Well, Mother, how is this existence different from being dead?

"And *this* is the life you planned for me. Well, I choose differently. I shall marry the man I love and fill this dank place with the laughter of my children. Is that so foolish?"

Lady Catherine had no answer.

"Gentlemen," said Anne to the others, "thank you for your counsel. However, I would ask for a few moments alone with my mother." The gentlemen rose and left the room.

"We have a few decisions to make—first, where you wish to live."

Lady Catherine gasped, but she was allowed no chance to respond.

"The dowager house is not ready, so my uncle has kindly offered his house in London for the duration. However," she overrode an angry retort, "I have no objection to your remaining here at Rosings until Richard and I marry. Then you may decide whether to move into the dowager house or into your own residence in Town, which I would be happy to provide.

"Let me make myself perfectly clear, Mother: Should you choose to remain at Rosings, you must accept my supremacy. The choice is yours: live in *my* house or your brother's."

Lady Catherine gave a slight grimace. "Would I be allowed my own servants?"

"Of course." She knelt beside the older woman and took her hands. "Mother, surely you understand why this is necessary. It was Father's wish, and Richard and I need to start our marriage alone. Do not be concerned. You shall want for nothing." She kissed her mother's cheek. "I do love you, Mama."

Tears sprang to Lady Catherine's face. "Y… you have not called me that since—"

"Since you told me it was unladylike for a young woman to refer to her mother as Mama." Anne had a wry smile.

"Well, it is. Oh, Anne, I love this house so!"

"It is just a house. Richard and I shall make it a home." She thought to ask Lady Catherine whether she loved Sir Lewis, but she decided not to broach that subject today; they both had been through enough. "You like Richard; admit it, Mama. He was always your favorite nephew."

"Your favorite cousin, too, I warrant. How long have you felt this way, Anne?"

"I do not know. It seems forever—years at least."

Lady Catherine sighed bitterly. "It seems I have been trying to foist the wrong Fitzwilliam on you." The grand dame collected herself and continued in her more familiar manner. "Well, you may have your wish. You may have Rosings. I will not challenge this *ridiculous* claim. I know I would eventually triumph, but not at the cost of bringing disgrace upon the de Bourgh name. You have obtained your inheritance, but it shall be recorded that it is done by *my* will, and not due to the chicanery of your uncle and his lawyers," she sneered. "What else did you wish to *discuss* with me?"

Anne thought her mother capitulated far too easily, but as there was nothing she could do to upset the plans of her uncle and Mr. Tucker, she set that concern aside. "I shall be leaving for London. I have accepted an invitation to call upon Lady Buford, and I shall be staying at Fitzwilliam House. Are you to accompany me?"

Brussels

"Come, Buford," urged Richard, "you must come to the First of June ball. Every officer has been invited to —— Château in Brussels for the celebration. It will improve your spirits!" Richard was worried about his friend. He knew that Buford had not received any letters from home.

"No, you go without me. I do not wish to socialize with empty-headed British expatriates who have come over to the Continent to see the fun of war."

"Such bitterness! Buford, I *know* Caroline has written. Something has happened to the post. This is not the first time; you know how the army is." Richard hoped rather than believed that Lady Buford had written her husband. He recalled his last interview with the lady; surely, there was some feeling there.

Buford looked up, trying to hide the hurt he felt in his heart. "Yes, you are right."

"Of course, I am! So, you will come on Thursday?"

Buford sighed. "Very well."

Chapter 22

Delaford

MARIANNE LOVED DELAFORD MANOR almost as much as she loved Christopher. One of her favorite places was the extensive gardens. Many hours' pleasure was found walking its fragrant paths, the eye resting agreeably upon the colorful blooms and lush foliage. The gardens were hers, her husband had decreed upon their marriage, and Marianne spared no expense for their care.

It was there this fine May morning that Marianne fled in an attempt to distract herself from missing her husband. Her excursion was not solitary; Mrs. Ferrars had answered her sister's invitation and come up from Delaford Parsonage to join in the meanderings. Marianne kept her eyes away from those things that would remind her of her Christopher, such as the stable and the house, and focused solely on the sweet scent of the roses, sweet pea, and peonies.

She allowed the fineness of the weather and company to transport her back to those halcyon days of her youth at Norland Park. She returned to that magical decade when she and Elinor passed their childhood as young ladies of property should in peace and serenity, when only lessons, dancing, and reading dreadful novels concerned her—before death stole from her first an honored uncle and then a beloved father. She and Elinor were girls again, laughing and traipsing through the flowers of their mother's garden.

Elinor's surprised gasp broke Marianne's daydream. Her eyes flew to hers, and she meant to ask what had alarmed her, but Elinor's expression held her. She was looking at something to the right, behind Marianne, and when she looked, Marianne saw a gentleman and gasped herself.

He had obviously come from the stable, his riding clothes sure evidence of that. She knew him at once, of course. Only death could remove the image of *that man* from her mind, even after years of bliss with her husband. Marianne was human, and she could not stop the involuntary lurch in her heart.

Time had been kind to him. In height, he had not diminished; in dress he was as he always had been—trim and striking, broad of shoulder and long of leg. In looks, he seemed open, spirited, and affectionate. As always, he was the very model of a young lady's hero right from the pages of a favorite story.

John Willoughby remained a handsome devil.

Willoughby removed his hat, bowing slightly. "Good morning, ladies. I trust you are enjoying the day." He said this as if he had been expected. He had not lost one iota of his charm and arrogance.

Marianne could not put two words together, so it fell to Elinor to speak, and she did so in a rather sharp manner. "Mr. Willoughby, what brings you to Delaford?"

He replaced his hat, smiling easily. "I had business at Allenham and thought I would come and pay my respects."

The word *respect* brought another person to Marianne's mind—Eliza Williams, her husband's ward and former victim of Willoughby. She quickly pulled Elinor aside.

"Eliza is expected to join us," she whispered. "Please go to the house this instant and keep her away."

Elinor glanced at Willoughby. "But, Marianne—"

"The gardener is nearby. I shall be safe. Eliza must be protected. Please go." She paused as a thought occurred to her. "And return with Joy."

"What? Bring Joy? Why?"

"Please do as I ask."

Indecision warred in Elinor's face, but she bowed to her sister's request. To Willoughby, she said in a loud voice, "You must excuse me, sir. I am needed in the house. Good day to you." With one last warning glance at Marianne, she swiftly walked back to the manor.

"I am still not her favorite person." Willoughby grinned as he approached closer. "You look very well, Marianne."

That lovely, smooth, slightly teasing voice still sent shivers down Marianne's back. Memories of the hours they spent together at Barton Cottage returned to her—the perfection of his opinions, so attuned to her own at the time, and his laughter at her observations, the feeling he displayed while reading aloud prose and poetry. How could a young, romantic, foolish girl of seventeen *not* fall in love with Willoughby?

But *that* girl was no more. Pain, anger, and anguish had crushed that child, leaving in its place a battered yet wiser soul, ready to be filled like an empty glass from a wine bottle. Fortunately for Marianne Dashwood, her vintage was Christopher Brandon.

The totality of her past history with Willoughby flashed through Marianne's mind in an instant. *Oh, Willoughby! You led me on only to abandon me, just like Eliza. How foolish I was! In my despair over you, I nearly died. Thank heaven for Christopher! He gave me the gift of love and faith, not just in others but also in myself!*

A calming sensation flowed over her. She was not afraid of him. She knew herself; she was no longer anyone's victim.

"Marianne?" Willoughby asked again, a rather smug grin never leaving his lips.

She assumed a haughty appearance. "I would answer you, sir, should you choose to call me by my name—*Mrs. Brandon*," she said coolly.

Willoughby, dumbfounded, flinched as if she had struck him. "What do you mean? We have been such good friends, Mari—"

"Sir," she said sharply, "you no longer have the right to use my Christian name. Be so good as to remember that."

"Forgive me," Willoughby returned, clearly taken aback. "I meant no disrespect, truly."

"Of course not." Marianne did not believe a word of what he said.

As she gazed at her one-time love, Marianne realized there were many things she no longer believed about John Willoughby. She had come to see there was a great difference between *acting* with feeling and *owning* those feelings. Willoughby seemingly wore his heart on his sleeve. He talked as a man filled with sentiment and passion should. The way he used his voice and body in conversation and in reciting poetry and prose had at one time been enchanting, but now seemed but playacting. For when it came to action, Willoughby was woefully inadequate.

Colonel Brandon, however, said little but did much. He was a man who not only felt deeply but also acted upon his impulses. Christopher did not fill the air with empty words. He did not need to charm the world to earn friends and favor. His deeds spoke volumes. He was the true romantic.

"How is Mrs. Smith?" she asked.

Willoughby chuckled. "My aunt is in revoltingly good health. She will be with us for many more years to come and will have many opportunities to upbraid me. I am, of course, pleased that she is well."

Marianne was pleased, too. Willoughby's current seat was at Combe Magna in Somerset. Allenham Court was in Devonshire and closer to Delaford, far too close for Marianne's comfort. She certainly did not want him to inherit Mrs. Smith's estate anytime soon.

Still, Marianne was disturbed by Willoughby's answer. He had made a jest of his relation's health, but she did not mistake the undertone of his desire to inherit sooner, rather than later. No, there was still very little love lost between Willoughby and Mrs. Smith. There was a selfishness, a cruelty in Willoughby she had not perceived before.

Which led to another question. Willoughby had made his peace with his demanding and honorable aunt. He had resumed his yearly visits to Allenham, but this was the man's first foray into Dorsetshire since that ill-fated party to Whitwell, the day Christopher received the express about Eliza. Why had Willoughby returned to Delaford now? And with Christopher out of the country? Marianne did not believe in coincidences.

She decided to probe. "Is Mrs. Willoughby at Allenham?"

"No, she remains in Somerset."

"That is a shame, as we are enjoying the most beautiful weather."

"Mari—Mrs. Brandon, why ask about her?" Willoughby flashed his most winning smile and began to move closer, picking a rose. "This is a stilted conversation for old friends. I am very happy to see you."

Marianne stepped back. Her suspicions confirmed, she dropped the empty civilities. "That is as may be, but I cannot return the sentiment."

Willoughby stopped dead in his tracks. "What? Marianne!"

"Sir, recall your manners! Why are you here?"

It was plain to see that the man expected a different outcome. He gestured with his arms. "To see you! Is that a crime?"

"That remains to be seen." Fighting her outrage, Marianne spoke as calmly as she could, relieved that the gardener was near and eager for Elinor's return. "You presume much, sir, knowing my husband is out of the country. But understand this—I have my protectors. You shall leave Delaford."

"What do you mean? Ah, I see it now—I see you are still angry with me over those unfortunate events in London," Willoughby cried. "Would that I had the chance to do them over again! But you must remember that I was not at fault."

"Not at fault!"

"Surely your sister told you all? That letter, that terrible letter, was all my wife's doing! She, in her jealous insensibility, could not bear that I possessed even the smallest remembrance of you. The ball, where I was unfortunate to meet you under her observation, was to her character intolerable. She demanded of me that letter.

"I had no choice! My finances were in a wretched state, and I had been dismissed from my aunt's favor. Had any other opportunity offered itself, I swear to you I would have grasped it like a drowning man. But to live, I had to give you up." Willoughby wore his most pitiful expression. "No, Mrs. Brandon, you need no protection from me!"

Marianne did not care if he was in earnest or not. "I am glad to hear it. However, there are those under our protection who have suffered at your hands, and your presence here is a hardship to them."

"What? Who do you mean?" His eyebrows shot up. "You speak of Brandon's chit?"

"Willoughby! That innocent you ridicule is my husband's ward and the mother of *your child*! You have no right to speak ill of her or anyone in my household!"

The gardener started to move closer, obviously alarmed at the tone of the conversation, but Marianne gestured that he stay where he was.

Meanwhile, Willoughby attempted to defend himself. "Innocent! You declare she had nothing to do with her situation. I assure you, madam, that was certainly not the case."

Marianne grew livid. "For shame, Willoughby! You took advantage of a mere child! I believe my husband schooled you better in manners than that?"

Willoughby's color rose. "He told you of the duel, did he? I should have known!"

"Of course, he did. There are no secrets between us."

"Oh, yes, I am sure he told you everything! Tell me, were you impressed with his skill with a blade? Did that make you see him in a more favorable light? For there was a time when you thought as little of him as did I."

Willoughby is jealous of Christopher! That fact reassured her; she knew how to revenge herself upon him. "Thank you for reminding me of my foolish youth. As you see, I have learned better. As for matters of my heart, they are none of your concern. But I will say this—I am ashamed of the girl you knew, and I thank our Lord every day that Colonel Brandon took pity on me and gave me an undeserved chance to truly know him. I am a better woman for loving him."

Willoughby blanched, and for a moment, Marianne thought he was going to be ill. Just then they were joined by Elinor, who held a small bundle in her arms. Right behind her was an irate, cudgel-bearing Mr. McIntosh.

With a thankful smile, Marianne took her daughter Joy from Elinor. "Have you met Miss Joy Brandon, Willoughby?" She stroked the child lovingly about the head, cooing at her for a moment before turning her disdainful eyes to her former suitor. "Look, my love. This is Mr. Willoughby. Mark him well. He is just the sort of man with whom your dear papa and mama do *not* want you to associate." She smiled at the mortified and angry gentleman, and moved Joy so he could better see her. "Do you not think she has the look of Colonel Brandon about her, sir?"

"I see I have wasted my time here," growled a humiliated Willoughby. "I had thought, I had hoped… but it is no use. Is it possible I might see my child before I leave?"

"Why? You have never requested it before."

"She is mine, as you say."

Marianne shook her head. "Only if you formally acknowledge her as your daughter, sir."

"You know I cannot do that. Mrs. Willoughby would never allow—" Willoughby bit his lip. "Forgive me for taking up so much of your time, Mrs. Brandon, Mrs. Ferrars. I meant no harm, no infamy, I assure you."

"Why *did* you come, Willoughby?"

Gone from Willoughby's face was the façade of *bonhomie*. Instead, it was replaced by longing and regret. "To see you, to renew our acquaintance. I have always regretted you, you know. Ask your sister."

Marianne sighed sadly. "Oh, Willoughby, you only came because Brandon was not here. You are such a coward. Truly, I do not wish you ill. Look to your own marriage for happiness; you shall find none here.

"Good-bye, Willoughby. I trust we shall not meet again." With that, she turned and walked towards the house with Joy in her arms and Elinor by her side.

Mr. McIntosh stepped closer to the visitor, his club twisting in his large and rough hands. The gardener joined him, brandishing his trowel. Neither looked the least friendly.

A nervous Willoughby took a reflexive step back. "Here now, none of that."

McIntosh's eyebrows twitched. "My mistress bade ye leave, sir. We're makin' sure ye do."

"No need for that," he said, eyeing the club. "I am leaving directly."

The steward pointed towards the stable with the cudgel. "You'll find your horse right where ye left 'im. But a wee bit of a word first. My master, Colonel Brandon, charged me to watch out for th' missus, an' that's my sworn duty, afore God. I've marked ye, sir, an' I mean to let th' whole of Delaford know of ye. You're not welcome here, and ye best remember that. Be on your way an' don't come back."

London

Mrs. Rebecca Buford was walking from the parlor to the music room when she heard a cry come from the library. Rebecca did not hesitate to open the door to see to the matter. She discovered Caroline, staring at a letter in obvious distress.

"What on earth is the matter?"

Caroline looked up wide-eyed at her sister-in-law. For a moment, she struggled with the thought of fleeing to her room without a word. Instead, she did the bravest thing she had yet done in her young life—she handed the letter to Rebecca.

May ——, 1815
Buford House, London

Caroline,

Every evening I return to this small boardinghouse outside of Brussels, exhausted from my labors for the king. The food and fellowship are tolerable, but they cannot replace what I desire most in this world. Every day I look and wait, and yet no word comes.

Why do you not write? Since you went away, I have heard nothing from you.

If you are unwell, tell me so at once. Do not withhold word to protect me—my imagination is so great that nothing save your being in dire straits can be any worse. Let me share your burden.

Have I hurt you in any way? Please tell me. How else may I make amends? Please, just a few lines would salve my soul.

Your faithful husband,
JB

"I do not understand!" cried Rebecca. "This cannot be! You write constantly!" She saw that her sister's distress had increased. Rebecca instantly realized that she must do what she could to help Caroline, lest the babe be endangered. She tossed the offending letter upon the table and pulled a chair near Caroline to take her hands in hers. "There has been some sort of misunderstanding."

"He… he thinks I have forgotten him!" Caroline cried. "He feels so betrayed! What shall I do? What has happened to my letters?" She grew even more agitated. "Someone is stealing them! I know it! Who would do such a monstrous thing?"

"No one is stealing them." Rebecca strove to soothe her sister. "There has been a mistake, that is all." She picked up the letter again.

"Perhaps the French are sinking our ships on the way to Antwerp!"

"I do not think so. It would have been in the papers—did you say Antwerp?"

"Yes, that is where he is."

Rebecca indicated the letter. "But this is from Brussels."

"Brussels? No, he is in Antwerp. He must be!"

"My dear, look!" Rebecca pointed to a line in the letter. "And here he says that his lodgings are outside of Brussels."

"I have been sending my letters to the wrong place!" Caroline wailed. "Oh, what have I done!?"

"Caroline! There is no time for that. The army has failed to forward the post. You must write to him as quickly as may be! The letter must leave this half hour!"

"Yes, yes, you are right." Caroline began focusing on the problem at hand. "But, Rebecca, can one send an express to Brussels?"

"We can try, my dear."

Delaford

Marianne sought the solitude of a long walk through the Delaford woods. She had much upon which to reflect, given the events of the day before.

Her confrontation with Willoughby had finally closed the book on that chapter of her life. She had not known how she would respond to him, had she ever come across him, and her forcefulness took her by surprise. She blushed to think how she could ever compare that man to her darling Christopher. At that moment, she doubted they were even of the same species.

John Willoughby had admired her but just for her exterior—her looks, her voice, her open manners. Christopher saw more; he loved her for who she was. He adored her body, mind, and soul. He shared everything with her, everything he loved and cared for. He trusted her opinions and sought them out.

Marianne's improvements were not the result of a project taken on by the colonel to satisfy his vanity. By sharing his love of books and learning, her husband unintentionally ignited a passion for learning in his wife. She grew in talents and confidence, so much that, when he was called away to war, Christopher placed her in charge of Delaford Manor. He placed his unwavering trust in her abilities. If she had not already loved him, she would have fallen hard at that point.

Marianne berated herself. It had taken so long for her to realize her feelings. After her recovery, Christopher began his two-year courtship. By the time he did propose, his attentions were obvious to everyone, including his intended. She remembered wondering what took him so long to come to the point, because by that time, she had resolved to accept her great friend, and she had every expectation of marital felicity. However, when she did not feel the burning passion she had felt for Willoughby, she thought she did not love him.

Living with Christopher taught her there was more than one kind of passion, not just for the act of love but also for thinking well of another— caring about another's comfort before one's own and knowing that your partner in life considered your needs first as well. Yet it was not until

Joy was in this world that brave, wise Marianne could admit to herself what Elinor saw on her wedding day: She was violently in love with Christopher Brandon. There were three days forever etched in Marianne's consciousness—her wedding night, the day of Joy's birth, and the afternoon she told her husband of her feelings for him.

Since embracing her love of her husband, she feared that she could not live without him. The last few months had proved otherwise. A thought that had been in the back of her mind flooded her awareness: She might have to do so for the rest of her life. A searing pain coursed through Marianne's heart, but there was no panic in her mind. Should the unthinkable happen, she would grieve for her beloved for the remainder of her days, but she would not fall down and die. There was too much to live for: Joy and Delaford. They depended upon her, and she would have to be strong for them.

John Willoughby had dallied with a mere girl. Colonel Christopher Brandon had left Delaford Manor to the administration of a woman, full-grown and tested. Her soft heart might break, but her steel backbone could bear any burden.

With this resolve, the mistress of Delaford returned home to her duties.

Brussels

Colonel Brandon was at his desk concentrating on paperwork when he noticed Major Denny leaving Wellington's office. "Is that the schedule for the southern patrols, Denny?" he asked.

Denny assured him that it was and handed over the paper for Brandon's perusal. A quick glance told him everything.

"This is it?"

"Yes, sir," said Denny in an emotionless voice.

"And the duke *approved* this?" Brandon looked at the younger man.

Denny looked over his colonel's head at the wall behind him. "Yes, sir."

Brandon thought for a moment before rising to his feet. "Wait right here."

He strode to Wellington's door, and with only the briefest of knocks, he entered the commander-in-chief's domain. He found the duke in consultation with the Quartermaster General, Colonel Sir William de Lancey, who was acting chief of staff.

"Sir," Brandon began, "pray, forgive the intrusion, but I must speak to you."

Colonel de Lancey's eyebrows rose, but Wellington's imperial visage remained impassive. "Yes, Brandon, what is it?"

He closed the door behind him. "I hold here the schedule for the southern patrols—"

"His lordship has already dealt with that, Brandon," interrupted the chief of staff, but the duke cut him off.

"You have some question about this?"

"Sir, the number of men assigned to this duty is completely inadequate for the task. You must increase the patrols."

Wellington pursed his lips. "I disagree. Bonaparte will do nothing for at least six weeks, if not longer. We do not need to waste men touring the Belgium frontier."

"Sir," said Brandon sharply, "I beg you to reconsider. Has Bonaparte ever done the expected? We know troops are massing in the north. The earlier he strikes the better for him. It would be well to err on the side of caution."

"Colonel, are you implying that I am wrong?" asked Wellington dangerously.

Brandon swallowed. "I believe you are acting under incomplete intelligence, your lordship." Brandon knew he was risking his career. He did not want to be sent to Belgium, but now that he was here, he would do everything in his power to assure the success of their mission, including taking the risk of being sent home in disgrace. His sense of professionalism would allow nothing less.

Wellington gazed at the colonel down his long nose—quite a feat, as the Iron Duke was still sitting. "Double the patrols. Was there anything else, Colonel?"

Brandon came to an even more rigid attention. "No, sir," and fired off his salute.

"Return to your duties, Brandon," ordered the duke as he turned again to a bewildered de Lancey.

A minute later Brandon handed the schedule back to Denny. "Double the patrols, as per orders I have just received from his lordship."

Denny looked upon his senior officer with near awe before responding. "Yes, sir—thank you, sir." He hurried out of the office.

Brandon looked about the office to see Major General Sir Hussey Vivian, commander of the 6th Cavalry Brigade, looking at him. One hand was injured and in a sling.

"Not bad, Brandon. I wonder if you have anything on the old man."

"No, sir," replied the colonel in embarrassment.

"Do not be so modest. It is not just any man who can get the Iron Duke to change his mind. I congratulate you."

Brandon nodded at the compliment and returned to his work. He was still uneasy. He felt they had far too many men at Hal, but he was not willing to beard the lion in his own den twice in one day.

London

"Do not be silly, Caroline," Rebecca said. "Do not change your plans. Of course, you should have your friends visit. You cannot disappoint them."

"I will be poor company, I am afraid," Caroline replied, still distressed over the letter fiasco.

Rebecca took her sister's hand. "Sir John will receive his letter in a few days. All will be well. He would want you to be happy—especially at this time."

Caroline considered as she caressed the very slight bulge in her midsection. She did want to see Anne de Bourgh, as well as renew her acquaintance with Marianne Brandon.

"Oh, very well."

Delaford

Mrs. Dashwood and Margaret had come up from Barton for an overnight visit, and Mr. and Mrs. Ferrars had joined Marianne in attending them. The ladies sat in the parlor, speaking of many subjects, save one—the impending war. Their conversation was broken by delivery of the mail. One letter caught Marianne's eye, and she begged leave to open it.

"It is from Lady Buford," she said, "and she invites me to a week's stay in London at her relations."

"Oh, how wonderful," cried her mother. "Such diversions to be found! Marianne, you should go before Town grows too warm."

Marianne was tempted, not only by the diversions London offered but also by the company. She wanted to know Caroline Buford better. However, she had responsibilities. "Nothing could be more delightful, but I should not leave Joy."

"Nonsense, Marianne," said Mr. Ferrars. "We should be happy to have our niece stay at the parsonage."

"Indeed, Sister," confirmed Elinor. "Enjoy yourself in Town."

Marianne smiled. "Thank you. I believe I shall!"

Chapter 23

Brussels

THREE COLONELS OF CAVALRY strolled into the palace where expatriate British civilians were holding yet another ball. Brandon and Richard were in full-dress uniform, while Buford wore a suit of black with white stockings and his sash. Already the hall was filled with Dutch royalty, exiled Frenchmen, traveling members of the London *ton*, and officers from many different nations, in and out of uniform.

"Quite a crowd here tonight, eh, Buford?" offered Richard. Buford's reply was noncommittal.

"I find it hard to believe that so many have come here from England," observed Brandon.

"Bored, useless vultures—the lot of them," grumbled Buford. "The *ton*, looking for excitement, journey across the sea to see a war. What fun! Bastards," he added *sotto voce*.

"Well, I am glad you are enjoying yourself, Buford!" cried Richard.

"The two of you, be quiet! We have to pay our compliments," warned Brandon as the group walked towards the receiving line.

Having been presented and received, the three officers entered the main ballroom—right into the path of one who was very familiar to Buford.

"*Bonsoir*, Sir John! Pray, introduce me to your charming companions," purred Countess Roxanne de Pontchartrain.

Captain George Wickham could hardly believe his luck. Somehow, the colonel of his regiment had not realized there was a ball that night, and poor Hewitt was scheduled to serve as Officer of the Day. Wickham was finally out from underneath the colonel's, and by extension Darcy's, thumb and was free as a bird. He was under no illusion that this freedom would last or that it ever would be repeated. Therefore, Wickham was determined to enjoy himself as much as possible.

Helping himself to the first glass of wine he could secure, Wickham stood in his infantry-red best, looking for opportunities for diversion—if not more. Noticing one of his fellow officers conversing with a couple of ladies, he strolled over. There he was introduced to a Mrs. Norris, and he applied his considerable charm to the lady.

He was making progress when he noticed a familiar face out of the corner of his eye. He looked to make sure, and his countenance paled. Wickham beheld one of the two men in the world he least wanted to meet at a ball, or anywhere else for that matter—and this one was not Darcy.

After being accosted by Countess de Pontchartrain, the three colonels had separated. Richard walked about, taking in the dancing, when he almost walked into Major Denny. Turning away abruptly, cutting the man, Richard was surprised to see George Wickham not twenty feet away.

Richard stood rooted to the spot, staring a hole through his nemesis. His eyes narrowed and his fists clenched as he observed the creature—he could never call Wickham a man, much less a gentleman—who had labored so to ruin Georgiana, chatting with someone else's wife. He unconsciously reached for the sabre that was safely in his trunk back at the boardinghouse.

The corners of Richard's mouth twitched as he saw Wickham's face go white when he became aware of his presence. Richard began to move in the blackguard's direction. He had no plan; his legs moved of their own accord. Before he could take more than a few steps, he felt a hand restrain him. To his shock, it was Major Denny.

"Release me, sir!" Richard demanded.

"With all due respect—no, sir. You must come away. Wickham is not worth it."

"I should have known *you* would defend him!" Richard's voice rose.

"Remember who you are and *where* you are, sir!"

Eyes blazing with rage, Richard looked about the room. Recalling he was in a packed ballroom with officers, diplomats, and ladies, he went still, his arms no longer twitching. His gaze returned to Denny. "Yes, you are correct."

Denny looked past Richard. "He is gone now. You had better come with me."

Richard was taken aback. "For what reason?"

The major looked back at him. "For a drink, sir—why else?"

"An excellent idea," said Colonel Brandon from behind Richard.

The game room was determined to be the best location, and five minutes later the three men were sipping brandy.

"Well, a toast to Denny," offered Brandon.

Richard snorted. "Defender of Wickham."

Brandon gave him a withering look. "Actually, he is the rescuer of Richard Fitzwilliam's career."

"What do you mean?"

"Were you not going to challenge Wickham?" asked Denny.

Richard snorted. "No! Believe me, I have had plenty of opportunities to do that and chose not to. Your precious friend was safe from me."

Brandon frowned. "Are you certain, Fitz? I saw your face. I had the same fears as Denny. What were you going to say to him?"

Richard took a drink. "Honestly, I do not know, but I must admit that I would not mind ridding the world of that useless piece of garbage, given half a chance. Wickham's too much the coward to give me an excuse, more's the pity."

"Deuce take it, Fitz!" Brandon shouted as he slammed down his glass; by some miracle, it did not break. "The duke has made it quite clear—*no duels!* We need every last mother's son out there, whether his name is Wickham or not! You would be lucky if the only thing they did was cashier you!"

Richard was incredulous. "Put me in prison for facing Wickham on a field of honor? I cannot believe it!"

"I would listen to him, sir," said Denny quietly. "The duke is serious."

Brandon continued his dressing-down of Richard. "We are to fight a *war* against the greatest threat to face England since the Armada. Get that through your thick skull. We are not here to satisfy your personal notions of honor." He was merciless. "Save it for the French, Colonel."

The last cut hit Richard hard, but he tried to stare down Brandon without success. The older man did not waver. Finally, Richard looked down, acknowledging defeat.

"Forgive me, Brandon, you are correct. I let that bastard rile me."

Brandon let out a breath. "It is all right, old boy; I understand."

Richard rolled his eyes, said, "Forgive me, but I do not think so," and took a swig of his brandy.

Brandon simply said, "Ramsgate."

It was amazing that neither he nor Denny were hit by Richard spitting out all of his brandy.

"How… how is it you know about *that?*"

Brandon explained, "Marianne is very good friends with Mrs. Darcy and Miss Darcy. My wife and your cousin compared cads some time ago."

Richard whirled upon Denny, concerned that he had heard too much about Georgiana, but found him unsurprised at the revelation. "You, too?"

Denny looked down. "Wickham boasts when he is in his cups."

Richard raged. "He *boasted* of—enough! I should have called him out years ago!"

Brandon crossed his arms. "Well, you shall have to wait a while longer, Fitz. You shall not challenge Wickham while you are both in Belgium. Do I have your word?"

Fuming, Richard relented.

Denny was thoughtful for a moment. "Colonel Brandon, I would like to discuss a private matter with Colonel Fitzwilliam. Would you please excuse us?"

Brandon gave each of them a look. "As you wish. I will see you gentlemen later." He left the room.

The two remaining officers eyed each other warily. Richard was the first to speak.

"What do you want, Major?"

"Permission to speak frankly, sir?"

"Granted." Richard sipped his brandy.

Denny looked at Richard. "I was hoping you could tell me what you have against me."

"I do not like your friends, Denny."

Denny raised an eyebrow. "All of my friends or just one in particular?"

Richard put down his glass. "Any man who could be friends with the likes of George Wickham—"

"Forgive me for interrupting," said Denny softly, "but there might be some who say the same about you, sir."

Richard was taken aback. "Just what do you mean by *that?*" He quickly swallowed his indignation. "No—go on, Major."

Denny paused. "I have the greatest respect for Sir John—"

"*Sir John?* Now, just wait one minute!"

Denny stared Richard right in the eye. "Sir, can you deny what he was?"

Richard looked down, stymied. "There is all the difference in the world! While his behavior was questionable, the gentleman never harmed anyone. And besides, he has ended his dubious behavior."

Denny shook his head. "There are those in London who would disagree with your opinion of that gentleman's 'harmless' behavior—husbands, brothers, fathers."

"I suppose you are correct," Richard allowed.

"Yet, you stood by him. Why? Because you saw goodness in him; you saw what he had the potential to be. And the gentleman has proven that your faith in him was not unwarranted."

Richard looked at Denny unbelievably. "And you see the same in *George Wickham?*"

Denny was pained. "I can hope. I changed; at one time, I was not so different from George. Might he change as well someday?"

Richard shook his head in wonderment.

Denny sighed. "Yes, sir, I might be a fool, but I do hope for my friend. In the meantime, I try to see that no one is harmed." He smiled without mirth. "I know what George is capable of doing. I am a fool but not an idiot."

Richard looked at the younger man for a long time. The two drank in silence for a time.

"So, you were protecting more than Wickham, eh? You are protecting me?"

Denny nodded. "Yes, sir."

Richard frowned. "One last question—what do you know about the events in Ramsgate and Brighton?"

Denny sighed. "I first met George when he joined the ——shire militia, so I only know what he told me about Ramsgate. Subsequent events have led me to believe that George was not truthful *there*. As to Brighton, I knew of Miss Lydia's partiality for George, but I thought nothing of it at the time; she being quite attentive to… many there."

There was a flash of pain again, and Richard could only wonder as to the cause.

Denny continued, "George showed no particular interest in Miss Lydia, and he did not acquaint me with his plans, so I was as surprised as anyone when they departed." He looked at Richard. "I have the greatest respect for Mrs. Wickham and wish both of them long life and happiness."

Richard thought the man protested too much. He suspected that Denny's acquaintance with Wickham—and Mrs. Wickham—was far more complicated than the major let on. Deciding not to push the issue, Richard gave Denny a lopsided grin.

"Well, I guess I can shake the hand of the man who kept me out of the guardhouse." He offered Denny his hand; he took it readily. "Every last mother's son, is that it, Major?"

Denny smiled. "Of course, Colonel—why else?"

Richard laughed. "Come on, Denny, let us rejoin the party."

"Will you not stay to finish your brandy?"

Richard laughed. "That swill? No, that will kill you, my man. Now, let us see if we can find some really good claret, eh?"

Wickham finally poked his head out of the kitchen, where he had fled after the near-encounter with Colonel Fitzwilliam. Wickham disliked Darcy, but he truly feared Fitzwilliam. Both were better than he was with the sword, and Fitzwilliam was more likely to use it.

Wickham still managed to enjoy the ball; he ate his fill in the kitchen and dallied a bit with a comely housemaid. His mission now was to "liberate" a bottle of cognac. Looking around, he saw people preparing for the final dances of the evening—and no Fitzwilliam in sight. Luck was with him, he was sure, and he strode directly towards the library, where he was certain the liquid treasure was stored. He reached for the doorknob.

"Boo!"

Instantly, Wickham's mind flashed back to an incident when he was but a mere lad. He had challenged Darcy to enter a dark cave near Pemberley, claiming that there was pirate treasure within. Darcy did so, and a few minutes later, he cried out for Wickham to come and see the treasure. Wickham dashed in—to find near total darkness. Feeling his way around, he was startled by the selfsame noise—uttered by…

"Good evening, George," said Colonel Fitzwilliam. "Looking for something?"

Wickham gasped and leapt back. Fitzwilliam did not look as if he possessed a sword, but there was no reason to take chances.

Fitzwilliam grinned. "I have been looking forward to this."

"You… you would not dare… here?" stuttered the captain, back against the wall.

Fitzwilliam approached him, hands behind his back, Wickham's eyes growing larger with every step he took. When he was mere inches from his trembling quarry, he leaned in and said, "Go."

Wickham was not one to miss an opportunity when it was presented. Without a sound, he squeezed past his tormentor and ran unsteadily down the hall. Not completely trusting his old childhood companion, he kept looking over his shoulder for the expected pursuit. A mistake—for the next moment he collided with someone.

"Watch it, you damn fool!" snarled Wickham as he picked himself off the floor.

"Wickham?" cried his commanding colonel as he sat upright on the floor. "What are you doing here?"

"Sir!" Wickham was able to cry before his mouth went completely dry. "I... I... excuse me, sir. I regret—"

"What are you doing here?"

"I... I was at liberty. Hewitt has the post tonight. Oh, let me help you, sir."

After being assisted to his feet, the colonel rudely showed no sense of appreciation. "An oversight, I assure you! Get back to camp, Wickham—now!"

Wickham blinked twice and ran out the door.

Fitzwilliam leaned against the door of the library and laughed his head off.

Chapter 24

Sir John raged as he sipped his brandy. Roxanne—of all the people to see here tonight!

He thought of Roxanne's beauty and allurements, so wasted on him, for his thoughts kept returning to Caroline. Never did he long for her as now. He needed her laugh, her sharp, biting humor, and her sweet attentions. Why was it that he could not have what he wanted? He should never have sent Caroline away.

Just then, he noticed that Annabella Norris was in attendance. The faint hope that she might have some news of Caroline overcame his revulsion of the woman. He crossed the floor and bowed. He found her with two other former acquaintances from the old days—Lord Braxton and his latest paramour, Lady Daphne Glevering.

"Are you enjoying Brussels?" Buford asked Braxton after they exchanged the usual greetings.

"It has pleasures enough, Buford. A change of scenery is always welcome in the summer," replied Braxton carelessly.

"We in the army are always hungry for news from home. No matter how many letters one receives, it is never enough. How did you leave London?"

"The same—blasted hot this year."

"Yes," simpered Annabella. "Town is so boring! I am so glad we took this opportunity to come to the Continent. It is so exciting!"

"Come, Daphne—the music's started," said Braxton, tugging at her arm. "Another time, Buford." The two made their way to the dance floor.

Annabella and Sir John watched them depart. Sir John was temporarily trapped—it would not be good form to abandon the lady before another of her acquaintances arrived.

Annabella asked, "Are you not dancing, sir?"

Sir John looked nonplused at her. Finding no polite reason to excuse himself, he held out his hand. "As you wish."

"Oh, no. Do not think I am looking for a partner. I should be content to share some conversation if you would indulge me. I much prefer talking to dancing."

Buford nodded his acquiescence, wondering what the woman was about. "I hope I am not detaining you. Is Lady Caroline here?"

"No. She is in London."

"How sad! Her grand adventure is over. I feel for her, poor dear—to miss such parties and lively, elevated company." She glanced at Buford with a smile.

Buford stiffened. He supposed that she was trying to tempt him into an assignation, but the officer vowed that no matter what arts and allurements Mrs. Norris might employ, the woman would not succeed. "We thought it best that she return to England with hostilities imminent."

Annabella looked about the room with amusement. "Really? Are the French here? Which one is Napoleon?"

"Mrs. Norris, war is not a joke."

"Of course not, but to abandon you to your own devices while still on your honeymoon—how sad. But that is my dear Caroline; she must have her own way. I am sure she is well occupied. You must be very lonely."

"I manage, madam." Annabella's implication of Caroline's possible activities in London both angered and frightened Buford. Such thoughts had begun to take root in his mind, no matter how hard he fought it. He lashed out. "By the way, where is your husband?"

"In the West Indies, inspecting his plantations. So, you see, I too have been abandoned. Cold and lonely." The unspoken offer floated in the charged air.

"How unfortunate for you. As for me, I find thoughts of home keep me warm enough at night." He had had a bellyful of her insinuations. "If you would excuse me."

"Sir John, you would leave me?"

Buford hissed, "Mrs. Norris, do not think that my wife and I have not talked about our former acquaintances in Town! Oh, yes, I know exactly what you are about. I was a fool to waste my time speaking to you. You are no friend to my wife and can have no knowledge of her. Your behavior is infamous. Find someone else to share your bed, madam. You disgust me."

Annabella Norris turned purple in her outrage and dismissal. Grimly satisfied, Buford turned on his heel and went in search of another brandy.

Buford nursed his drink, glowering, when he was interrupted again.

"Come, *chéri*, things cannot be all that bad," said Countess de Pontchartrain from behind his left shoulder.

Buford expected her. "Enjoying yourself, Roxanne?"

"Tremendously. Are you still angry with me?"

He turned to her. "That ball in Vienna. Why did you introduce Lady Buford to Baron von Odbart, of all people? What game were you playing? Surely you could not expect an assignation on my honeymoon."

She chuckled. "Oh, *Jean*, you are as clever as I remember."

"I knew you were trying to entrap my wife! But why? Surely you do not think I would divorce her, do you?"

"*Jean, Jean,* I was not trying to entrap your *wife*..." She let the sentence linger as she eyed him closely.

"*Me*—you were after me? You knew how I would respond!"

"Almost—you showed amazing restraint. We thought surely you would challenge the baron."

Buford knew he almost had. "What purpose would that serve? I would have either lived or died. What difference would that make? I am not that important."

"You are not important—but the Congress was."

With a sinking feeling, Buford realized he had been played for a fool. Such a scandal as a duel between delegates would disrupt the Congress and hurt negotiations, particularly between England and Prussia. It had been a trap, and he almost fell into it, nearly causing immeasurable damage to his country.

"Who are you working for, *Comtesse?*" he demanded.

A haughty laugh escaped her lovely lips. "You think only those who wear a uniform are patriots, Colonel? I serve France!"

Buford's mind raced through the possibilities, but only one name remained. Only M. Talleyrand could have approved such an operation. The ambassador had been so helpful at the ball just so Buford could find his wife and the baron together. The French must have hoped, he now suspected, that the two would have been caught *in flagrante delicto.*

"Was this operation your idea or the ambassador's?"

"Actually, it was my husband who came up with it. He has a delightfully wicked turn of mind, do you not think? Besides, I knew you would win any duel."

"And you just do what you are told."

Countess de Pontchartrain stroked his face, causing him to flinch.

"*Jean*, you are a dear friend, but not so dear as you think. I see the need to protect France from your so-called Big Four as surely as His Excellency does." Her eyes grew hard. "France is alone; we cannot allow you English to divide up Europe with the Austrians, Prussians, and Russians. France will be great again!"

"Whether under a king or emperor?"

"Bonaparte—that upstart? Bah. No, Colonel, too many of my country-men have died under that monster." She grinned. "So, let the grand Seventh Coalition crush him for us. My kind will reclaim what is ours again when you are through."

"The First Estate again the first among equals?"

The countess pursed her lips. "Do not mock us so. You English with your class structure are not so very different! Or are you a Republican now?"

"Do not be ridiculous." Buford glared at her. "I can forgive you for your actions against me, but you should not have used my wife."

The countess sighed. "*Un mariage d'amour*—I never would have thought it of you, *Jean*."

"Looks can be deceiving." Buford could not keep the bitterness out of his voice as he took another gulp of his brandy. He could feel the alcohol racing through his veins, but he cared not.

Roxanne's eyebrows went up. "Really? *Un serpent au Paradis?* It happens to the best of us." She looked around. "Ah, my escort to supper is awaiting me, *chéri. À plus tard.*"

Buford watched her depart, feeling betrayed, disgusted, and very stupid.

It was nearly midnight when Richard went in search of Buford. He found him speaking with Sir John Vandeleur, their commanding officer. It was a few minutes before the general begged his excuses and wandered off, allowing the two comrades to talk.

Richard frowned, for Buford seemed to be in his cups. "Buford, shall we leave now? I will get a hackney, if you like."

Buford slapped his friend on the back. "No, no, you go without me, Fitz. I will be only a little while longer."

"Buford, I think you should come with me." When Buford refused him again, he would not relent until Buford grew angry.

"Blast it all, Fitzwilliam, you are not my nursemaid. Let me be!"

Richard knew there was no good in trying to convince Buford when he was so determined. "Forgive me. I shall see you at breakfast, then."

Buford nodded, and Richard could do nothing but return to their inn.

The library was dark at this early hour in the morning, lit only by a solitary candle and the occasional flash of lightning from the thunderstorm raging outside. A lone figure, which had remained behind after the ball ended, sat in a chair and watched the illumination, sipping a cognac. His host had suggested that, due to the inclement weather, Colonel Buford take refuge at the castle and had ordered a room prepared for him, and Buford was waiting for his accommodations. The storm did not bother him; rather, he thought the weather mirrored his own feelings.

When he married Caroline Bingley, he knew her reputation as she knew his. He had labored to make himself a better man, and he was led to the conclusion that his wife had done the same. They were kindred souls, so he thought. During the time of their courtship and their marriage, he had grown to admire and finally love her.

A mistake. He feared it could be, and he was right. Apparently, Caroline's devotion could not be relied upon once he was no longer in residence. They had shared passion but not true love. He had been deceived.

There was a reason that fashionable society frowned on love matches.

It was because love matches rarely last. He knew the risk, but he never dreamed that her affections would not last a trip across the Channel.

Buford put down his glass and shook his head; he had felt tears coming on. No! He would not weep for her or for what might have been! He had made his bed; now he must lie in it.

"Sir John, your room is ready," said the butler in French as he opened the door.

"*Merci beaucoup*," he replied as he got to his feet. With steps only slightly impaired from the alcohol he had consumed, he made his way to the bedroom. There, with no valet to attend him, he stripped off his clothes and threw himself onto the bed. As he pulled the covers over him, he hoped that he would not again dream of Caroline as he did most every night.

An hour later, he felt a soft warm body slip under the covers with him. Moist lips caressed his cheek and neck as practiced hands touched him. Groaning, half asleep, he responded to the attentions, returning the kisses and caresses.

He moaned aloud, "Caro."

"Whatever pleases you, *chéri*."

Chapter 25

BUFORD AWOKE WITH A start early the next morning. Looking about the unfamiliar bedroom, he tried to recall where he was. He moved again and groaned in pain; his throbbing temples reminded him of the amount of alcohol he had consumed the night before, and his state of undress spoke volumes about his activities afterwards.

Buford got out of the bed and padded to the dressing room. He found it empty as expected; Roxanne had the good sense to return to her rooms during the night. He completed an abbreviated toilette and dressed in the same black suit he had worn to the ball. He knew he would not be conspicuous; many gentlemen would sleep off a great ball at the host's home.

Within a few minutes, he was on the street, walking to his board-inghouse. It was early, and there were few coaches for hire available, but there was nothing for it. The last thing he wanted to do was encounter the countess.

Fortunately, the distance was not too great and the morning not too warm. The walk might have been pleasant had not his head and con-science tormented him. Buford had been shocked to learn that the naked woman in his arms the night before was not his wife but Roxanne. By the time he was fully aware of what was happening, his resentful desires got the better of him. He told himself it was not of his doing. Roxanne had seduced him while he was unable to resist. Why not take advantage of the situation? Caroline apparently did not care; the damn woman could not be bothered to post a single line to her own husband.

Buford tried to drive Caroline out of his mind with Roxanne, but once he had finished with her, his discontent remained, now augmented with regret. He passed out trying to tell himself that he had not betrayed the woman he loved. Caroline was the betrayer; she neglected him. However, Buford could not dismiss the fact that he had broken his vow of faithfulness.

It was not long before he reached the outskirts of Brussels and his boardinghouse. His empty stomach reminded him that he had yet to have breakfast, so he hurried his steps, hoping that he was not too late. Upon entering the common room, he saw Richard sitting at a table with a huge grin on his face. Before him was a tall stack of letters, all in the same stationery, tied with a string.

"They were just delivered last night after we left for the ball, old man!" Richard said with a self-satisfied grin. "Some blunder at the port. I always suspected the people at the post cannot read!"

Buford hardly heard what his comrade said. He approached the pile carefully, as if the mass of correspondence would leap up and attack him. Sure enough, the words he most desired and ultimately feared were written on the envelopes in a fine, female hand: *Colonel Sir John Buford*.

London

Marianne made good time to Town and was warmly greeted by Caroline and Rebecca Buford. The three ladies sat in the parlor, and the topic immediately turned to Caroline's pregnancy.

"The illness in the morning has passed, much to my relief," Caroline reported, "but I have such cravings now! Pickles—anything pickled, and I must have it. Is that so very strange? I do not recall my sister Jane having such desires."

Marianne laughed. "For me it was sweets."

Rebecca said, "I cannot remember any unusual foods every time I was with child, but I did want to consume my portion of my dinner and my husband's too."

"How many children do you have, Mrs. Buford?" asked Marianne.

"I have three, and if you are to stay in this house, I must be Rebecca to you."

Marianne thought that a rather strange request, as the two ladies had just made each other's acquaintance. Caroline had warned her that her new family was unorthodox, and Marianne had to agree. Rebecca Buford was the most informal person she had ever met. At least it was a pleasant form of peculiarity. "Very well, please call me Marianne, Rebecca."

Caroline smiled at the interaction. It was amusing to watch others react to her relations.

"Well, if you would excuse me, I must prepare for our visit," announced Rebecca.

"Really?" inquired Marianne to both ladies. "Are we going somewhere?"

"Oh, I am sorry, I forgot to tell you. We dine at the Matlocks' today. Miss de Bourgh invited us."

"Good!" cried Marianne. "I long to see Anne again."

"I am looking forward to it," Caroline replied, anticipating how diverting the earl's response to the unorthodox Bufords might prove.

Brussels

Buford wandered the afternoon streets of the Dutch capital in despair. As he walked up grand boulevards and down small lanes, the magnificent historic buildings and small modern shops passed by his eyes without recognition.

In the last four and twenty hours, he had read and re-read each of Caroline's letters at least three times. His guilt and remorse battled with his delight at the news of Caroline's pregnancy, but after reading the initial news, Buford's self-disgust grew.

Weekly! She had been writing to him weekly while he had closed himself up in his rooms feeling ill-used. He was not worthy of her love and devotion! Damn the army! Why could they not forward the letters before now—before Thursday—before that deuced ball? Roxanne had seduced him, the whore, but he could have—should have—resisted her. How could he be so weak?

His thoughts flew in a thousand directions, mainly focused on recriminations against the army, postal clerks, and Roxanne—but eventually his reproaches returned to the one most at fault—himself. He had failed his wife, his unborn child, his uniform, and his own promise to himself. He hated Roxanne de Pontchartrain, but he hated himself more.

Just past the *Grand-Place*, along the *Rue au Beurre*, Buford came across a small Catholic church. Something made him stop before the ancient structure. The name above the door proclaimed it to be in honor of St. Nicholas. He stared at the door for a long time, trying to decide before opening it and walking inside.

It was early afternoon, well before Vigil Mass, so the sanctuary was empty, dark, and unwelcoming. The only light was from a few candles burning before the statue of the Virgin Mother. The structure was unusual. The three aisles of the nave were built at an angle to the chancel. Buford looked up and spied a cannonball, of all things, embedded high up in the third pillar on the left of the nave. Obviously, the parishioners had kept the gruesome memento of some long-ago bombardment as a badge of honor.

While he was looking at the odd ornament, a priest entered the sanctuary and genuflected before the large crucifix above the altar. As he turned, he noticed the British officer standing in the middle of the church and cautiously approached Buford.

"Good afternoon, my son," he said in English. "I am Father Amadie. May I help you?"

"*Bon après-midi, Père*," Buford responded in French. "Your English is very good."

"*Merci*, Colonel. What brings you to the Church of St. Nicholas?"

"I do not know. I should not be here. Certainly, I am keeping you from your work."

Father Amadie, no admirer of the tyrant or of the revolution that he represented—the revolution that had sent so many of his brothers to the guillotine—warmed to the young defender of his country. "Forgive me, but I can tell you are troubled. Please, share your worries with me."

"Surely I am keeping you from your duties."

"I am only preparing to hear Confession."

A sudden idea came to Buford. "Father, would it be possible? Would you hear my confession?"

Father Amadie frowned. "My son, are you Catholic?"

Buford shook his head. "I am no Papist. I mean, no, I am not Catholic."

"Do you understand what you ask of me?"

"Father, my mother was a French Catholic. My aunt was of your faith, and she would take me to Mass when I was young. I know your sacraments; I know what they mean."

"Then you know that I cannot give you absolution," Father Amadie explained gently.

"I know, but… but my heart is heavy with regret. It would be a comfort. Please, I know I ask much of you."

The priest reflected for a moment. He knew he should ask the English Protestant to leave, for to his bishop, the soldier was no better than a heretic. He knew countless Catholics had died at the hands of the Church of England during the Reformation and that Catholics still did not have full rights in Britain.

Father Amadie believed in God and His Holy Church with all his heart, yet he knew that both sides had engaged in religious warfare. The Inquisition in Germany was matched by the Inquisition in Spain. Catholics and Protestants had heaped unspeakable acts upon one another in the name of salvation. Did being right justify such behavior?

Amadie had joined the Church to serve God and the people—and serve he would. Besides, what his bishop did not know would not hurt him.

"Come with me, my son." He gestured to a side wall of the church where a small door was flanked by two curtains. The priest opened the door and sat in his familiar chair, where he heard so much of the pain of this world. By the time he slid open the window, the English colonel had already taken his position on the kneeler.

Buford bowed his head. "Forgive me, Father, for I have sinned."

Buford returned to his room to write a letter.

My dearest Caroline,

I take up pen to write to you, deeply mortified at the pain my unjust and unworthy letter must have caused you. Destroy it at once, I beg you, my dear wife! If I could reach across the seas, I would snatch up that evil document and consign it to hell! What a wretch you have married!

Too good, too excellent wife, how could I write such lines to you?

Before me are the results of your most faithful labors. I feel unworthy to touch them. But read them I must, for thoughts of you are in my every sleeping hour—and waking hour, too.

I know you wish news of me, your most undeserving husband. I am well in body but ill in spirit. If I were a selfish man, I would beg you to fly to my arms and comfort me. But I cannot—I will not. I am happy you are safe in England, and I am pleased to know you have found a home with my most excellent family. Your letters are a godsend to my soul.

My equipment safely arrived. Thank you for your kind attention to that. The men, all veterans, were ill-prepared for battle when they disembarked, but constant drill has sharpened them like the edges of their sabres. They will be ready for whatever Providence brings.

My love, you write that our family is increasing. What happy news! That God would so smile upon us! I wish I could be there to share this time with you, my dearest one. You write that your belly is growing; nothing in this world sounds so beautiful! Know that I send kisses to that wonderful roundness, that evidence of our love, and its mother too. You say you wish it to be a boy. I would be as proud as a prince to have a son by you, but I cannot help but wish that it be a lovely girl instead with her mother's looks. That way I might have two Carolines to spoil.

I think your idea to remain in London is a good one, for nowhere else in the kingdom boasts better physicians. I beg you to take care of yourself—but who am I to tell you your duty? You have proven yourself to me a hundredfold.

I must admit something to you, dear Caroline. When I first met you, while I was pleased with your outward appearance, I was only looking for a mistress for my house. I never thought I would fall in love with my future wife. But God in heaven is merciful and has given me a great gift—the sweetest, wisest, kindest, loveliest woman any man could ever wish for.

I love you, Caroline. I love your loving soul. I love your excellent mind, so wise and sharp. I love your form and figure. Oh, how my dreams of you keep me up at night! I love your eyes—so full of expression. And I love your lips—for your sharp, amusing words and for your sweet kisses.

I do not deserve you, my wife. You should have married better than I. I know my faults, and I will strive for the rest of my days to improve myself, to make myself worthy of calling you my beloved wife and lover and mother of my child.

Adieu, my dearest love. I shall write again as soon as time permits. I shall sign this as you have done so consistently,

Rwy'n dy gari di,
JOHN

Letter finished, Buford needed it to arrive in England as quickly as may be.

"You want me to do *what?*" cried Major Denny.

"Come, man, I am not asking you to do anything illegal," pleaded Buford. "A small thing—what is that between friends?"

Denny looked at the colonel. "You want me to enclose a personal letter in the official pouch to London, and you call it a small thing? Forgive me, Colonel, but I would like to know what you would refer to as a great favor!"

"You can do it, can you not? You have a friend on the staff who will either post it or deliver it?" Buford begged.

Denny thought. "Yes, Castlebaum would do it, especially if there was something in it for him. It will cost you a half-crown, sir."

"Done and done, sir!" cried Buford as he shook the man's hand. "Here is the money. I call it a bargain!"

Colonel Fitzwilliam watched his men practice, and it did not make him happy.

"What do you call that, gentlemen?" he bellowed. "You ride in that lackadaisical manner against the French, and they will cut you to pieces. Show some spirit! Do the drill again!"

Four at a time, the forty riders of the third squadron took off down the training course, while the other nine squadrons watched. The course laid was a fifty-yard dash to a straw bundle, then halting at a post wrapped in cotton and burlap, then a final gallop past another post, this one uncovered. All the time the troopers were to slash at the targets with their swords. Most did the drill correctly, if cautiously. None did it quickly.

"Hell's fire! Must I do everything myself?" Fitzwilliam cried. "Stand clear!" He drew his sabre and readied his mount. With a drive of his spurs, the horse shot forward.

"ARRRGGHH!" he screamed as he headed down the left-hand side of the course, leaning over the horse's neck and pointing the sword forward. At full speed, he cut at the haystack with all his might, straw flying everywhere. Pulling back at the reins, he expertly pivoted and dashed to the second target. His mount danced about the post as Richard slashed at it repeatedly. Then in a blink, he was off again, his blade this time held at an angle to his body. It made a satisfying *thunk* as it struck the last post. Reaching the end of the course at top speed, he halted in a cloud of dust.

"Time!" he called.

His aide checked his pocket watch and informed the rapt audience that the colonel had bested their top performance by ten seconds.

"There!" Richard called out, breathing heavily. "If an old man can do that, you can certainly do better. Do the drill again, and a pint of ale to any man who bests my time by twenty seconds!"

A cheer went up from the troopers. "I will be drinking your beer soon, Red Fitz!" cried one unnamed rider as he took off down the course.

Richard could not help grinning at the use of the nickname by which his men referred to him, usually when he was out of earshot. By the time the exercise was over, Colonel Fitzwilliam was poorer by a gallon and a half.

Happy to have found something to motivate his men, he turned to his aide. "A barrel of Belgium beer to the squadron with the best average time." The aide grinned and left to deliver the message.

Richard was satisfied. His troopers would be ready.

London

While Caroline performed at the pianoforte, Marianne hid her disquiet as she had tea with Anne, Mrs. Albertine Buford, and Rebecca. Marianne knew that Caroline was unhappy, for while she played with great skill and technique, there was a want of feeling. Her friend was mechanically going through the motions.

Caroline finished and turned to her guest. "Do you play today, Marianne?"

"I thought you were my friend," Marianne exclaimed.

Caroline was taken aback. "Whatever do you mean?"

Marianne smiled at Mrs. Buford and Rebecca. "She would have me, with my meager talents, follow such a lovely performance. For shame! I shall be thought as the most rank beginner in comparison, I am sure."

For the first time that day, Caroline allowed a smile to adorn her face. "Meager talents, indeed! Come, Marianne, you leave tomorrow. I would love to hear you play once more."

The guest sighed dramatically. "Oh, very well, if you insist." Privately, Marianne was very pleased with her efforts to lighten Caroline's mood.

She sat before the instrument and started into a light country air while Caroline took a seat next to Anne.

Anne looked at Marianne and sighed. "If only I had learned to play." She turned to the group. "You know, my mother always said if I had ever learnt, I should have been a great proficient if my health had allowed me to apply. She is confident that I would have performed delightfully," she said with a straight face.

Caroline's face had turned the brightest red as she screwed up her mouth, holding back the laugh that threatened to erupt. She had heard that comment countless times from Lady Catherine de Bourgh—in fact, every time she played before the old biddy. The other Mrs. Bufords could only look on in puzzlement as first Caroline then Anne began to giggle, but the ladies could resist no longer and the sounds of laughter began to drown out Marianne's performance.

Mrs. Brandon stopped her piece and turned. "I say, what is so funny?" she demanded with all injured eloquence. With that, she started to play again, which only redoubled the two ladies' mirth.

"Dear," asked Mother Buford to Rebecca, "do you know what they are about?"

"No, but it seems to have a proper effect." They, too, had noticed Caroline's melancholy, but unlike the other ladies, they knew the reason.

The ladies sat back to enjoy the concert when it was again interrupted. This time the offender was Roberts, the acting assistant butler.

"Lady Buford, there is an army officer to see you."

Silence descended upon the room. The five ladies knew that the visit of an officer was often to deliver the worst sort of news.

Caroline's face became a stone mask as she rose and slowly followed Roberts out of the room. First Rebecca then the others followed. They beheld a short captain in a red coat conversing with Caroline in the vestibule.

"Lady Buford? Captain Castlebaum at your service. I am charged with delivering this letter to you." He held out an envelope.

Caroline saw at once that the writing upon it was in her husband's hand. Taking it with trembling hands, she willed herself not to tear it open on the spot. "Thank you, Captain. We are at tea. Would you care to join us?"

"Thank you, no, madam. I must be off. Happy to have been of service to you." The half-crown in Denny's envelope with the directions would be reward enough.

Caroline grasped his arm. "God bless you, Captain."

"It was an honor, my lady." He bowed and left.

Caroline turned and mumbled, "Pray excuse me," as she made her way directly into the library. The other ladies followed at a discreet distance and stood silently outside the closed door. A few moments later, they were distressed to hear the sound of weeping from within. Ignoring propriety, the four entered the library to find Caroline softly crying on a sofa, the letter in one hand.

Mother Buford reached her first and embraced her daughter. "Oh my dear, oh my love!" She could think of nothing else to say.

Caroline hugged her tightly. "Oh, Mother! All is well, all is well." She smiled through her tears.

Rosings Park

Anne and Mrs. Jenkinson alighted from the de Bourgh carriage that had carried them back to Rosings from their short trip to Town. Anne walked up the front steps of her ancestral home with a new assurance. Rosings had always been the place she grew up; now it felt like home— *her* home.

"Mrs. Parks," Anne greeted the housekeeper. "How fares the house? Any mishaps during my absence?" She handed her traveling cloak to a footman as Mrs. Jenkinson saw to the luggage.

"No, ma'am," reported the housekeeper with a touch of pride. The tone of her voice betrayed the fact that to her mind, it was well worth fifteen years of dealing with Lady Catherine to see this confident young lady assuming her rightful place.

Anne smiled as she handed her hat to the butler. "No trouble at all? Not even from my mother?" She began to remove her gloves.

Mrs. Parks smiled in return. "No, ma'am. *That* would be difficult from where she is."

Anne turned slowly. "I beg your pardon?"

"Why, you know—Bath."

Anne blinked. "I am afraid I do not comprehend your meaning. Am I to understand that Lady Catherine is not in residence?"

Mrs. Parks was confused. "No, ma'am, but—"

"Did you say she was in *Bath?*"

"Miss de Bourgh, your mother said you were aware of her plans! She was very insistent—"

"I know nothing of this!"

Mrs. Parks's hand went to her face. "Oh, dear!"

Anne thought for a moment and then walked quickly to the parlor. Throwing open the door, she went directly to Lady Catherine's writing desk. Sure enough, there was a letter for her.

Dear Anne,

I congratulate you on your ascension to the management of Rosings Park. I am sure you shall do your duty to your heritage, both as a Fitzwilliam and a de Bourgh.

I have removed myself from a household that no longer needs nor desires my company. As Rosings Park is now forever taken from me, I shall secure myself a proper household as befits my station.

Do not concern yourself on my behalf. Lady Metcalfe has provided lodgings for me and shall act as my companion in Bath. Already, General Tilney has agreed to call, and Lady Metcalfe is desirous to introduce a Sir Walter Elliot to my acquaintance. It may be that I shall quit the name de Bourgh in no short time after you do so.

I insist that you write soon to acquaint me with your plans for your wedding so that I may guide you.

Your loving mother,

LADY CATHERINE de BOURGH

Mrs. Jenkinson and Mrs. Parks watched in amazement as Anne doubled over in laughter. Instead of answering their entreaties, she handed them the letter. Mrs. Jenkinson started giggling as she read, but the housekeeper was aghast.

"Ma'am, should I have a new team assembled for the carriage?"

Anne looked up. "What—whatever for?"

"So that you may go to Bath to collect Lady Catherine."

Anne could not stop laughing but put her hand out. "No, I do not think so. I think Mother can handle this on her own."

Brussels

"You want me to send *another* letter?" Denny cried.

"Yes, if you would be so kind," Sir John replied. He had just received Caroline's express and had to respond quickly.

Denny was conflicted; he wanted to say no, and he had the right to do so, but the look in Colonel Buford's eyes convinced him. "All right—but this is the last time, sir."

"I understand, thankee," he said as he handed over the envelope and the required half-crown.

Paris

After a farewell dinner with his family, the emperor walked down the steps of the *Palais des Tuileries* to his waiting carriage at half past three in the afternoon. Unlike the events that had occurred earlier in the month when he tried to raise morale and faith in his leadership with the people, this leave-taking was without imperial pomp. He wore the blue infantry coat with red epaulettes of a grenadier, adding only his Legion sash. After saying good-bye to his brother Joseph who had been left in command of the city, he set off to join his *Armée du Nord* with his *aides-de-camp*, ordnance officers, and four hundred imperial guardsmen.

He had also secreted over one million francs' worth of diamonds in the coach, just in case.

And so, with protection, wealth, and his lucky star, the emperor set out to secure his throne with one last mighty victory.

Rosings Park

Anne helped her extremely subdued mother out of the hired coach that had brought her from Bath. She offered the use of her arm and helped Lady Catherine up the front steps into the house. With no greeting to or from the staff, the two women walked slowly up the stairs to the older woman's suite of rooms. Once there, Anne instructed that Lady

Catherine's luggage not be brought upstairs until requested and then entered the sitting area behind her mother.

Lady Catherine sat down with a huff. "Well, I suppose you should be saying, 'I told you so.'"

Anne pulled a chair close to her and sat down. "No, Mama."

"Sir Walter Elliot, indeed! Of what could Lady Metcalfe have been thinking? The man is a dolt! Never have I seen a man so vain! And the way he looked at me; you would think I had grown two heads! I have always been celebrated for my youthful appearance." She looked at her daughter. "It is certain that you inherited your lovely complexion from me, my dear," she said as she caressed her face. "Yes, you have turned out very well indeed."

"Thank you, Mama."

"And General Tilney—why the way he looked at me! It is certain what *he* desired." She leaned close. "My *money*."

Anne patted her hand. "You have had a narrow escape."

"I have indeed. Thank goodness for my unerring judgment of character." Lady Catherine sighed.

"Are you tired, Mama?"

"A little. Bath is no easy distance. Perhaps we may talk later… about improvements to the dowager house?"

Anne kissed her mother. "As you wish."

Brussels

Buford and Fitzwilliam were sharing dinner together at the boarding-house, perhaps for the last time. Rumors of the French crossing into Belgium had been circulating around the camp for days. It did not help that Wellington had placed the army under a form of alert; certain units were moving as they ate.

"Brandon says nothing?" asked Buford.

"No, and Denny, neither. What good is it to have friends at head-quarters if they will tell you nothing?"

Buford grunted. "You and Denny have reconciled, I take it?"

"Yes, he is a good sort of fellow, in his way," Fitzwilliam allowed.

"Even though he is friends with Wickham?" Buford goaded him.

Richard's eyes were on his plate. "I suppose I cannot hold that against him. After all, I eat with you."

It took a full glass of wine to relieve Sir John after he choked on his food.

Later over port, Fitzwilliam asked, "Are you going to the Duchess of Richmond's ball?"

Buford looked down. "I think I have attended all the balls I am going to during this campaign, Fitz. You?"

"No, I have a feeling I need to be close to my regiment."

"Yes, I feel it too."

The next afternoon, Colonel Brandon and Major Denny were conferring with the other ADCs regarding the rumors of a French invasion of the United Netherlands, as the polyglot Holland and Belgium were known, when the door burst open at about three o'clock. A sweaty and dusty Prussian officer, who had obviously ridden hard, walked in the room.

"Where is the duke?" he cried in German. *"Die Französisch sind hier! Der Französisch haben Charleroi genommen!"*

Wellington walked out of his office. "What was that, sir?"

The officer repeated in English, "The French are here! The French have taken Charleroi!"

The office was deadly silent. Charleroi was only thirty miles away.

Over the next hours, the staff worked to verify the information.

Soon information from riders sent by Blücher and the Prince of Orange corroborated the intelligence. By five, the duke began ordering his troops into position south and west of Brussels, but the staff still did not know whether the thrust at Charleroi was a feint or the main axis of Napoleon's attack. Until the picture was clearer, the duke could not advance.

"Sir," asked an aide, "what about the Duchess of Richmond's ball?"

Brandon looked at his chief.

Wellington looked up. "Until we know for certain, there is no reason to panic. I do not feel that Bonaparte can advance so fast. Morale is important. Let the ball go ahead as planned."

The Duchess of Richmond's ball was the social event of the season. Held in an impromptu ballroom in what used to be a coach maker's depot, the over two hundred invited guests included the Prince of Orange, the Duke of Brunswick, the Prince of Nassau, four earls, twenty-two colonels, and a total of fifty-five women, only about a dozen of whom were unmarried. The hall was done up in crimson, black, and gold with flowers every-where. The music was gay, but the attendants were not, as concern over the rumors of a French advance were everywhere.

At about midnight, Wellington and his staff arrived. A young woman, Lady Georgiana Lennox, dashed to meet the duke.

"Sir," she cried, "are the rumors true? Are the French here?"

Wellington's face was grave. "Yes, they are true. We are off tomor-row." The room buzzed with alarm. Wellington walked over to a sofa to sit with Lady Dalrymple-Hamilton. Between chats with the woman, the duke would give the odd order to some senior officer.

"Come, Denny," said Brandon, "let us get something to eat while we can." Apparently, the Iron Duke felt the same, as he left the sofa for his meal.

As the men ate with all the room watching, a pale Prince of Orange approached the commander-in-chief. His whispered message had an extraordinary effect on the duke. A look of utter disbelief flashed across his aristocratic face and then faded.

For the next twenty minutes, Wellington ate and conversed with his fellows, showing no alarm. Finally, the duke rose and informed his host of his intention to retire for the night. As good-byes were exchanged, Brandon overheard his commander whisper in Lord Richmond's ear, "Do you have a good map in the house?"

Brandon and Denny followed their chief into the study, and the requested map was spread open before Wellington. He studied it hard, looking at the distance between the French border, Charleroi, Quatre Bras, and Brussels. Brandon knew he was using his extraordinary memory of the physical features of the countryside. Wellington looked up, shocked.

"Napoleon has *humbugged* me, by God! He has gained twenty-four hours' march on me!"

"But what are you going to do?" asked an incredulous Richmond.

Wellington looked at the map again. "I have ordered my army to concentrate at Quatre Bras, but we shall not stop him there. And if so, I must fight him *here*."

His finger moved over the map and stabbed down just south of a small village called Waterloo.

Chapter 26

Waterloo

AT EIGHT O'CLOCK IN the morning, the emperor met with his marshals at the La Caillou farmhouse south of the village of Waterloo that he used as his headquarters to plan the final destruction of the Allied army. The plan he outlined was simple.

He would bombard the Allied line at Mont St. Jean with cannon fire while making a demonstration—a diversionary attack—against the strong point at Château de Hougoumont. Then a few hours later, there would be a major thrust led by Marshal d'Erlon's corps from the right. If all went well, the French would roll up Wellington's army while dividing it from the Prussians. To prevent any interference from the Prussians, the emperor ordered Marshal Grouchy and his 33,000 men to find Field Marshal Blücher's army and finish the pounding the French had delivered two days before at Ligny.

The emperor needed a simple plan. Time was not on his side. Yes, his Army of the North had won a great victory at Ligny—so great, in fact, that he expected Blücher to fall back, perhaps into Prussia. However, in case the field marshal proved stubborn, the emperor had to destroy the English. The battle at Quatre Bras, also on the sixteenth, had been inconclusive. Marshal Michel Ney, his "bravest of the brave," had lost a great opportunity to smash Wellington. The Anglo-Dutch had retreated to Mont St. Jean between the French and Waterloo.

The emperor was pleased that Wellington chose to make a stand here. He needed to crush his enemies now and did not want to burn weeks chasing his prey. The longer this campaign took, the greater the chance that either the Prussians would recover or the other Coalition members— the Austrians and the Russians—would become involved.

Heavy rains the night before had made the battlefield wet, soggy, and therefore difficult to move artillery and horses about. He would need time for the field to dry before he attacked and crushed the combined English and Dutch forces opposite. The cannons would open fire at 11:30 a.m., which was the signal to attack the English right. D'Erlon would be unleashed ninety minutes later to strike at the left under the command of Ney.

The emperor was unhappy with Ney over his failure on the sixteenth, but while his thinking might be questionable, Ney's courage was not, and the men loved him. The emperor would have to keep an eye on his cavalry commander.

The Defender of the Revolution asked for comments.

Some of his marshals looked uneasy. General Honoré Reille spoke up. "I must tell you, Sire, that I consider the English infantry to be impregnable."

Marshal Soult added, "Sire, in a straight fight, the English infantry are the very devil!"

Where did this defeatist talk come from? The emperor shot back, "Soult, because *you* have been beaten by Wellington, you consider him a great general. And now I tell you that Wellington is a bad general, the English are bad troops, and this will be a picnic!"

There was silence in the room.

The emperor dismissed his generals. "Return to your troops. I will review them directly. We open fire at 11:30."

Colonel Brandon could not understand it. Bonaparte was wasting daylight reviewing his troops! He could hear the cries of *"Vive l'Empereur!"* drifting from the French lines at La Belle Alliance, a mile south of Mont St. Jean. Wellington and the entire staff had thought the French would strike at dawn, but they had not.

It was not much of a dawn, he reflected, as he gazed at the cloudy and misty morn. There was the small comfort that it was not storming as it had throughout the night.

Denny rode up. Such was the suffering endured by the staff at Quatre Bras that Denny had received a brevet promotion to lieutenant colonel, but there was no time for a change of flashings.

"The Frenchies are making quite a noise, Colonel."

"Yes." Brandon lowered his voice. "How are the troops taking it?"

"Mixed. The veterans are shrugging it off. Our green troops and the Dutch are far more nervous. As for the King's German Legion, they are so stoic, I cannot tell." Denny looked out at the enemy again through the light mist. "There are a bloody lot of them—that is for certain."

"Yes, but they cannot see us."

Wellington had made his stand here for two reasons: first, because Mont St. Jean was the Iron Duke's type of battlefield. He had scouted it a year ago, but every detail had been ingrained in his astonishing memory for terrain. The ridge along the Mont St. Jean road offered the reverse slope he had used to such great effect in the Peninsular War. Because the majority of his men were placed downhill of the summit, only a few of the troops were visible to the enemy—and the enemy's cannon fire. The troops would be brought forward only at the last instant. Enemy infantry and cavalry would be forced to march uphill against a withering fire. Of course, it only worked in defense and if the enemy did not flank the position. Iron discipline would be required of the troops to wait in place while the enemy marched toward them, cannonballs falling about.

The second reason was that Field Marshal Blücher had pledged to march three whole corps today to join up with Wellington if the Duke would offer battle to the French, giving the Allies overwhelming power.

The question on all the staff's lips was when would the Prussians arrive?

"The Prince is eager and ready for battle," offered Denny.

Brandon glanced over at the young Prince of Orange. The hotheaded royal had almost led the Allied troops to disaster on Friday at Quatre Bras. Only the timely intervention of Wellington had preserved the stalemate. Too many of the Belgium-Dutch troops had already quit the field, and the remainders were suspect. That was the reason the majority of the 17,000 troops far to the west at the town of Hal were not British. Wellington needed all the dependable troops he could get his hands on. Still, only a third of the 67,000 men he had were British—and only half of those had seen Peninsular service.

Brandon was nervous about leaving so many men at Hal. If Bonaparte attacked in force, they could never get here in time. Yet "Beau" was convinced that the French would try to turn his right flank and cut the Allies off from Antwerp and the Channel. The duke brushed off complaints, reminding the staff that 80,000 Prussians were supposed to be coming in from the east.

Too much depends upon the Prussians, thought Brandon, as he reviewed their defensive position. The Anglo-Dutch line stretched three miles, from Château de Hougoumont on the right, eastward along the road towards Wavre. The center was anchored by a strong point, a farmhouse at La Haye Sainte, entrusted to crack KGL troops. The left flank was left weak because it was expected that the Prussians would soon come. The heavy cavalry was stationed in the center, and the light dragoons were on the left. The French were thirteen hundred yards to the south on the ridge before La Belle Alliance.

It was a small battlefield, which gave Bonaparte little room to maneuver.

Suddenly there were gunshots from several groups of soldiers, startling Denny.

"Never mind them," advised Brandon. "Some lads find it easier to clean their muskets by firing them off. Come, let us rejoin the duke."

George Wickham was in the middle of a barrage of soldiers "cleaning" their muskets, and his ears rang because of it. "Hewitt, tell those fools at least to point their muskets towards the French!"

The last seventy-two hours had been very demanding on Wickham. Quatre Bras had been a fiasco. By the time his force-marched company had arrived, the battle was over. His colonel, curious to see the enemy, had ridden too far ahead and had gotten his fool head shot off. Wickham at first rejoiced, delighted that he was finally free of Darcy's tormenting agent, before remembering that, when it came to making life difficult for him, Darcy was incredibly resourceful.

A quick rearrangement of officers had made George Wickham a brevet major of infantry in charge of a battalion. Captain Hewitt was now in charge of his old company and was not doing a bad job of it. The rank of major suited Wickham just fine. His job was to order the captains about. It was his subordinates' responsibility to deal with the rank and file.

The newly promoted Major Wickham and his new battalion marched back towards Brussels in the pouring rain. They made camp at Mont St. Jean during the worst of it, half his men without tents. Wickham hated thunderstorms, and last night's had been a terror. The only thing that seemed to escape soaking was the gunpowder.

That was a very good thing, he considered, as his eye scanned the opposite ridge.

"Breakfast, sir?" asked Hewitt as he held out a bowl of questionable mush. At Wickham's look, he added, "Sorry, but it might be the only meal we get for some time."

Wickham took the proffered plate and choked the gruel down. As he ate, he caught sight of his commanding officer, Lt. General Sir Thomas Picton, riding by, still wearing his civilian clothes from the Duchess of Richmond's ball. The officer's appearance made Wickham recall another incident from Friday.

As his men were preparing to leave Quatre Bras, Wickham had nearly bumbled into General Picton. To his amazement, he saw that the general was trying to hide the fact that he was bleeding.

"Sir," he had cried, "you are—"

"Shut your goddamned mouth, Major!" growled Picton in his usual course, profane manner. "Say nothing about this! You fucking understand me, sir?" He had stared Wickham right in the eye.

Wickham had nodded. Far be it from him to disobey such an order.

Major Wickham stirred himself from his recollections, for the enemy was opposite, and there was work to be done. Handing the bowl to an aide, he stood.

"Hewitt, prepare the men for inspection."

Colonels Fitzwilliam and Buford prepared their regiments for battle. Their position was on the extreme left wing, a mile and a half from the center of the line. They would be the first to see the approach of their Prussian allies from the east—if they ever got there.

As they saw to their preparations, the two veterans could not help but glance from time to time at the heavy regiments nearby. Unlike the sober and experienced Light Dragoons, the Union and Household Brigades seemed lighthearted and anxious for action. The men in those units came from the heights of British society—and acted like it. Major General Sir William Ponsonby was riding among them, speaking to his men and keeping up their spirits.

Major General Sir John Vandeleur rode up. "How are preparations going, gentlemen?"

"We will be ready, sir," replied Buford.

"Well, hopefully they will not need us for some time." The Light Dragoons were held in reserve.

Fitzwilliam lowered his voice. "General…" He gestured with his head at the heavy cavalry.

Vandeleur dismissed his concerns with a shrug. "That is Uxbridge's problem, Fitz. Let us keep our mind on our duty. Keep a sharp lookout on the flank. Until later!" He spurred his horse into a trot towards the rest of the 4th Cavalry Brigade.

At that moment, the French cannons opened up, and the troops manning the Allied guns dashed to respond in kind. It was 11:30 a.m.

Dorsetshire

Although the grass was damp, Elinor insisted that the planned picnic on the grounds of the parsonage proceed as scheduled, for Mrs. Dashwood and Margaret had made the short trip from Barton Cottage; she would not disappoint them, and Edward would not disappoint *her*. The blanket spread and Joy merrily occupied by her grandmother, uncle, and aunt, Marianne took the opportunity to take a turn in Elinor's garden with Margaret. The youngest of the Dashwood sisters had grown into a lovely woman of eighteen, old enough for a serious conversation—one that was sorely needed if what Marianne had learned recently about her sister was true.

Marianne began directly, once they were out of earshot amongst the blooms. "Margaret, do you have an understanding with Lt. Price?" Lieutenant William Price was a naval officer Mrs. Dashwood and Margaret had met while visiting friends. The officer had now returned to his ship.

Margaret colored. "What? I do not know what you mean."

"Oh, stop it!" Marianne demanded. "Do not play childish games with me! I know he is exchanging letters with Mama, but I believe his interest in Barton lies elsewhere. I asked you, adult to adult, of your attachment to Lt. Price if one exists. This is serious, Sister."

She looked down. "We have no understanding between us except friendship."

Marianne breathed out in relief. "That is well. Would I be wrong in deducing that you wish for something more?"

In a small voice, her sister said, "No, you would not be wrong."

Marianne looked kindly on her sister. "Do you know what you are about, Meg?"

"I do not take your meaning."

A pained expression came over Marianne's face. "My love, I am a soldier's wife. My dear husband is even now in Europe, preparing to face battle." She stopped and seized her sister's hand. "Christopher may not return. Do you understand this?"

Margaret's eyes grew wide. "I... yes, I do."

"Good. The wife of a man in the king's service must be ready to lose him to that service. I have learned this the hard way. If you encourage Lt. Price's attentions, you must face that reality as well. He is a sailor; the sea is his home, upon a man-o'-war. He can only win fortune and advancement through action." Her eyes became hard. "By action I mean fighting and killing. He may suffer grievous wounds—or worse. A hurricane could sink his ship—"

"Stop it!" Margaret cried. "Say no more!"

Marianne was relentless. "I shall not stop! You are choosing a hard road, Margaret. Lt. Price is a fine man. He would make some woman a fine husband, but she must be one who will support him in his profession. Are you that woman? Are you willing to take the chance that you might lose him to the sea? Think!"

Margaret looked miserable. "I do not know." She began to cry.

Marianne embraced the girl. "Hush, my love. Shed no tears over an honest answer. Truth can be hard and ugly sometimes, but it is the only path to happiness. Lt. Price deserves nothing less." She tilted her sister's head up. "Please think about what you want. I love Christopher enough to risk losing him, for I would never ask him to be anything but what he is. I will support you whatever your choice is. But, if you wish to travel my road, you must do it with a full heart and open eyes."

Margaret looked at her through her tears. "You mean, you do not object?"

"No, my love, just as long as you are aware of what you are doing."

The French fired their cannons for nearly two hours, but the damage done was minimal. First, the soft, muddy ground plugged the cannonballs, containing the explosion and preventing them from skipping. Second, the reversed slope had protected the vast majority of the troops—all but a few Dutch regiments that the prince had placed too far forward. *Those* units were taking a terrible beating.

Denny was puzzled as he observed the action around Hougoumont. The French had attacked the outpost, but they seemed to go about all wrong. The enemy was using far too many troops for a demonstration but far too few troops to take the château. It would take the whole of Napoleon's army to raze Hougoumont, especially as the veteran Coldstream Guards made up the bulk of the defense. It would be madness to try to take the château with Wellington ready to smash his flanks.

The French movements made no military sense, but Denny knew Bonaparte's reputation as a genius. Did the tyrant know something that had escaped the duke's attention? Was the Corsican preparing to spring some unforeseen trap? Where was the immediate threat?

Suddenly, Denny's attention was drawn to the enemy ridge thirteen hundred yards away. An entire corps of infantry, 18,000 men strong, began to appear at the crest. To the sound of horns and the fluttering of battle standards, the host moved downhill in columns two hundred men wide. It was obviously the main attack.

It was now 1:30 in the afternoon.

"Prepare to receive infantry!" the duke cried repeatedly in his plain black uniform as he spurred his warhorse, Copenhagen, along the line.

The troops had about twenty minutes to form into two lines—one kneeling—and await the horde. The Allied artillery redoubled their efforts, their merciless barrage of ball and canister tearing great holes in the French formations.

Denny, watching with horrified fascination, noticed two things. First, the wide columns, while impressive, gave the Allies easy targets at which to shoot. Second, there seemed to be a lack of French artillery and cavalry support. Denny could not complain about this state of affairs.

Now the Dutch and British muskets opened up. The French, slogging uphill, were being murdered, yet on and on they came.

Unexpectedly, there was disaster—a Dutch brigade suddenly broke and fled their position. Trying to maintain control, officers rode among the troops, reminding them of their duty before general panic took hold. The prince himself was screaming after his fleeing men, exposing himself to enemy fire. Denny felt some pity for the Dutch, for they had suffered greatly at Quatre Bras due to bad leadership from their generals.

Closer and closer drew the French, now firing their muskets. English, Dutch, Belgian, and German troops fell.

However, at the moment the huge force reached the summit of the hill, General Picton, still in his civilian clothes, stood up, sword in the air. The 5th Division rose from their hidden positions, muskets aimed.

"FIRE!" the general screamed. The line disappeared in a cloud of gunpowder. In an instant, the smoke cleared and Denny could see hundreds of French soldiers lying dead or wounded.

"Now charge!" Picton ran forward at the head of his entire division, continuing to yell, "Charge! Charge! Hurrah!"

Denny had never seen anything like it. A great cheer went up from the line. Officers and men dashed at the enemy with swords and bayonets, screaming.

"Charge—!"

At that moment, General Picton was shot through the head.

As he fell, his men swept over him, engaging the French with bayonets. For long minutes—a lifetime it seemed to the participants— the soldiers grappled with each other in a macabre dance of death. The French assault wavered.

Lord Uxbridge saw his moment. "Cavalry, charge!"

Denny could not call it much of a charge. The heavy Household and Union brigades simply entered the fray at a walk through the Allied lines. Sabres flashing, they plunged in and cut and killed hundreds of French soldiers while other cavalrymen swept away the French cuirassiers guarding the enemy flank. The redoubtable Scots Greys were able to seize an eagle standard, the mark of a French regiment. As closely engaged as they were, the men did not fear French cannon fire, as the enemy could not shoot without killing their own.

Denny watched the enemy fall back in disorder.

Buford and Fitzwilliam watched the action with their telescopes. To their professional eyes, Uxbridge had attacked at exactly the right moment.

The shock of being hit by twenty-five hundred sabres had completely undone the French. The endless assault by the heavy cavalry broke the enemy's spirit. Now it was time for the cavalry troops to withdraw.

"Buford," said Richard, his eye glued to his telescope, "something is wrong. They are not withdrawing. Are they not sounding Recall?"

"Aye, but the troopers are not listening."

"But they will be cut to pieces!" Richard lowered his glass. "Turn back, you fools!"

The commanders of the heavy cavalry well understood the danger. Uxbridge and Ponsonby rode desperately to recall their troopers, but it was for naught. Blood was in the men's nostrils. Were they not the greatest cavalry on Earth? To a man, they cried, "To Paris! Death to Bonaparte!" They would win this battle on their own!

Free of the French soldiers, both living and dead, the cavalry troops galloped towards the French cannons, led by the Scots Greys. Soon they were upon the guns.

Colonel Brandon, at the center, turned from observing the line of what would prove to be three thousand prisoners being taken to the rear to watch the cavalry attack, the sound of Recall floating over the din. One glance at the tactical situation and all his years of experience came back to him in a flash. He saw what was going to happen and acted without another thought.

With a "By your leave!" shouted at the duke, Brandon dashed forward and downhill. He rode to and fore, screaming Recall at the members of the Household Brigade.

The Union Brigade was already far uphill on the opposite slope.

Richard and Buford watched in horror as the enemy cavalry counterattacked. The French cuirassiers with their swords and the lancers with their lances fell upon the exhausted British dragoons. The British tried to maneuver, they tried to fight, but numbers and fresh animals told the tale. It was a slaughter. By the time the remainder of the Household and Union brigades returned demounted in rage and regret to the Allied line, over a thousand of their comrades, including the valiant Ponsonby, were lost. For all intents and purposes, the Allies had no heavy cavalry left.

It was now 3:00.

London

Roberts gave the Sunday afternoon newspaper to Abigail with a worried look. She took one glance at the headline and dashed upstairs in search of her mistress. She found her in her rooms, looking wistfully out the window, a letter from Sir John in her hand.

"Lady Buford!" Abigail cried. "There has been a battle on Friday. Look!" She thrust the paper at her.

Caroline snatched the newspaper from the maid, the letter dropping to the floor.

"John! Oh, John!"

Major Wickham moved his troops forward as Wellington committed his reserves. Taking up a position in the line, he was shocked at the carnage before him. Everywhere there were dead and wounded soldiers—French, Dutch, and English alike. Downhill about five hundred yards away, he saw the La Haye Sainte farmhouse under heavy attack; however, no one was shooting at Wickham, and for that he was grateful.

Wickham watched a group of men respectfully carry the body of General Picton to the rear and fought the lump that grew in his throat.

An aide to Wellington rode up, interrupting his thoughts. "Major," he called out, "get those wounded men to the rear!"

"Yes, sir. Hewitt, form a party and recover the wounded." It was understood by all that no one spoke of recovering *French* wounded; they would have to fend for themselves until the fighting was over.

For the next half hour, various parties labored to carry the broken bodies to the dubious comfort of the surgeons' tents. Teams swarmed over the ridge of the hill, hoping the odd cannonball would miss. At about 3:30, the cannon fire seemed to intensify. Wickham, while a novice at war, understood what that was about.

"Recall the recovery teams—hurry!" he ordered.

At the signal, the men began returning to the line in some haste. Wickham noticed renewed fighting at the farmhouse. He thanked his lucky stars he was not down there.

Some minutes later, the French battle horns sounded again, but the tone this time was different. Wickham looked up and saw an awesome sight—five thousand cavalry charging down the French slope, right at Wickham's position.

"Form square!" he screamed. "Prepare to receive cavalry!"

The men dashed to get into position, and as they did so, Wickham reflected that, if the Prussians were to come and help, now would be an excellent time for them to do so.

It was now 4:00 p.m.

Chapter 27

IT WAS HELL. THERE was no other word for it. George Wickham had died and gone to hell.

Horns blaring and flags flying, the French cavalry charged the center of the Allied line. Avoiding the fire from Hougoumont on the left and La Haye Sainte on the right, they rode in narrow columns up the muddy slope towards Mont St. Jean. The Allied artillerymen, especially the British and KGL, resolutely stood by their guns and poured shot and canister at the approaching horses until the last moment. Then they dashed to the safety of the nearby squares, protected by the muskets and bayonets of the infantry.

Like the waters of an incoming wave against a rocky shore, the cavalry poured over and around the line, the squares resisting the onslaught. Volley after volley issued from the Allied positions while French cuirassiers and lancers slashed at their tormentors. Finally, the human surge receded, leaving dead men and animals in its wake—and fewer and fewer redcoats standing each time. What heavy Allied cavalry remained harassed their counterparts during the withdrawal.

The artillerymen hastened to their guns. For some reason, the French failed to either spike them or carry them away. Reloading and reforming, the Allies prepared for the next assault, and then the same terrible sequence repeated itself.

Wellington and his staff rode constantly up and down the line, exhorting the men and filling in what gaps they could. When the enemy approached, they would join the artillerymen in the relative safety of the squares. Once, Wickham found himself standing next to Colonel Brandon during an attack.

For two hours, the attacks came and came. Wickham lost count after ten. The crack of muskets and the roar of cannon fire had deafened him. It was good fortune, for he could hardly make out the screams and moans of wounded men and horses. All about him were dead and dying British soldiers; they had no time to evacuate them to the rear. Every time Wickham caught his breath, the French charged again.

"Charge" was a relative term. As the battle wore on, the assaults were made at no more than a trot, as man and animal were pushed beyond the breaking point. On and on, the gallant enemy came. Again and again, the steadfast defenders sent them to their eternal reward. It was no longer war; it was suicide.

About an hour after the attacks commenced, the order was given to "Well-direct your fire." In other words, *shoot low at the horses*. It amazed Wickham how difficult it was to carry out such an order. There seemed to be no hesitation in shooting the riders; why was it harder to kill animals than men?

Wickham recalled killing his first man—a charging officer of cuirassiers who was knocked off his horse by the ball from his pistol. By the time two hours passed, he had lost count of the number of men he dispatched by gun or sword. It could be twenty or twenty thousand.

After yet another assault began to fall back, an exhausted Wickham looked about him and saw there were more men down inside the square than not. He turned to speak to Hewitt just as a French trooper spurred his horse, leapt over the dead men before him, and got inside the square.

The next moments were a lifetime to Wickham, as he and the cavalry-man fought desperately, but neither was able to land a telling blow. Then, Wickham suddenly found himself twisted around, vulnerable to the man's sabre. Wickham could not turn in time. Terror seized him. The Frenchman's sword raised high, and Wickham awaited the inevitable strike—and Hewitt fired his reloaded pistol into the back of the French trooper's head. The cuirassier fell dead at Wickham's feet. The terrified horse, now free of his burden, leapt back out of the square and raced headlong downhill.

Wickham enjoyed an instant of elation. He turned to thank Hewitt—and the captain received a musket ball in the belly. Hewitt's blood spattered on Wickham's uniform. He caught his wounded subordinate as Hewitt fell screaming.

"Peace, Hewitt, peace! I shall get you to a surgeon," he lied through his teeth. It was impossible to leave the square.

After a few minutes, Hewitt quieted down, an unworldly calm coming over the captain. It gave Wickham the chance to look up to see if the French were coming again.

They were not. They were retreating.

"Major," gasped Hewitt, still in Wickham's arms, "I am all right. It… it does not hurt any more. That is g… good, is it not?"

Wickham somehow knew it was not. "That is good, Hewitt. Hewitt? Hewitt? Oh, God! Hewitt! God damn it!"

Major Wickham carefully laid Captain Hewitt's inert body on the ground, reached down to the pale face, and closed the unseeing eyes. Wickham took one deep, shuddering breath and looked up. He beheld dead and dying men all around him. There was an overpowering stench of powder and blood and excrement. Beyond was a sea of dead men and animals. Smoke and mist obscured the French lines.

But it was over. He could just make out the retreat of the cavalry towards La Haye Sainte.

A broken Wickham moved a few staggering steps and sat upon an upturned, empty ammunition box, his head in his hands. He was weary, bone-tired from fear and exertion. His ears deafened, and his mind was in a fog. His belly was empty, and his lips ached for water. Caked with mud, blood, and worse, he looked an unholy terror. His heart grieved for Hewitt, the loyal subordinate who had saved his life. He also felt relief—for he had survived and the battle was over. It had to be over.

It was nearly 6:00 in the evening.

Buford and Fitzwilliam watched the whole of the French cavalry assault upon the Allied line, aching to do something to relieve the strain upon the infantry, but it was not to be. Their mission was to protect the left flank and to watch for reinforcements.

"Sir!" cried one of the troopers. "There are men coming out of the woods there!"

The two colonels turned their telescopes to the east; they had been so preoccupied in observing the battle that they had forgotten their responsibility.

"I see them," exclaimed Richard. "Can you make out the uniform, Buford?"

"No." It was still light on this late June afternoon, but low clouds and smoke had washed the colors out of the world. "They look gray."

"They are!" said his companion. "They are here—the Prussians are here!"

Buford swung his 'scope to the right. "We are not the only ones who have seen them." Masses of French soldiers were marching across the ridge to engage their new enemy.

Wellington continued to ride along the Allied line, escorted by what was left of his staff. To a man, they were distraught at the carnage. The duke was well known to lament losses deeply. As they continued to assess the condition of their defenses, the Prussian liaison informed the duke that the Prussians were engaged with the right wing of the French army. Before the staff could celebrate the good news, disaster stared them in the face.

The squares in the middle of the line had suffered so badly that the proud companies had ceased to exist. Worse, the KGL, badly mauled and out of ammunition after a heroic four-hour stand at La Haye Sainte, had no choice but to quit the farmhouse and fall back to the Allied ridge. The center of the Allied line was wide open. Defeat was at hand, should Napoleon become aware of their weakness.

Wellington was quick to recognize the danger. "Denny! Ride to Lord Hill and have him reposition Second Corps to join up with our right wing! The rest of you—see to the condition of the squares and get all the German troops of the division that you can to the spot, and all the guns, too! I shall order the Brunswick troops to the spot and other troops besides. Ride!"

It was 6:30.

A hated sound floated across the battlefield one last time, forcing Wickham to look up again. He saw that on this occasion the trumpets heralded not cavalry but something far, far worse. Masses of French infantry began forming on the far ridge.

The spotless uniforms on these men were different from any seen on the battlefield this day. The soldiers seemed gigantic, especially with their tall bearskin hats. The *esprit de corps* of these men was higher than any other French soldiers Wickham had engaged.

Horror seeped into Wickham's barely functioning brain. He realized that there was only one unit in the French army to which those men could belong. They had to be the Emperor's undefeated Imperial Guard. His crack division, they were only used when Napoleon was assured of victory; they always delivered the *coup de grâce* at the end of the battle. They were invincible—they were fearless—because they always won. No army had ever stood before them.

And they were forming before the center of the Allied line.

Slowly Wickham rose to his feet. What was left of his senses fled him. He was utterly broken by the hours of combat he had undergone. Thoughts of honor, glory, and duty were as dust to him. Even fear of the punishment for desertion could not register in his mind. Wickham's only thoughts were for flight and survival.

Wickham fell back to a horse standing by. Only the grime on his face hid the paleness of his features. To the sergeant holding the reins he shouted, "I am going back for some reinforcements and more ammunition! Stand by your position!" He leapt upon the horse and headed to the rear.

The sergeant was confused, for they had just received a delivery of gunpowder.

"Brandon," ordered Wellington, "ride to Vandeleur's position! He is to reposition the majority of his horse to the center! Quickly!"

Brandon rode to the east and soon came upon General Vandeleur and his men riding towards him. Clearly, the general had anticipated the duke's command.

"Brandon, well met!" called out the general as his brigades continued onward.

"I see you have read the duke's mind, sir!"

"Yes." The general gave Brandon an appraising look. "Do you ride, Brandon?"

"I would be honored, sir."

"Good—take Buford's and Fitzwilliam's regiments and protect our left flank! And watch out for our Prussian allies!" With that, the general rode after his men. By this order, Vandeleur had just placed Brandon in command of an ad-hoc brigade.

Brandon was soon among his friends and informed them of their mission. "Fitz, you and I shall attack the French flank. Buford, you shall have the left and engage the enemy cavalry. Form the men!"

"Aye, Brigadier!" responded Richard. As Brandon was now senior colonel in charge of a brigade, Richard acknowledged his new role. The two regiments began to get into position.

His message to Lord Hill delivered, Denny dashed back to Wellington's position when he saw a lone rider heading to the rear. Suspecting a deserter, he flicked his reins and moved to intercept the man.

"Halt!" he ordered as he pulled in front of the rider, his hand upon his pistol grip. "What... Wickham?"

"Denny!" cried a wide-eyed Wickham. "I... I was looking for reinforcements! We have been terribly cut up and—"

"Yes, we know, George!" said Denny, releasing his pistol. "Second Corps is moving to fill in the gaps! And, George, the Prussians are here! They are engaging from the east!"

"But do you know who is coming?"

Denny could well hear the terror in his friend's voice and attempted to calm him. "Yes, it is the Imperial Guard." He moved closer to Wickham. "George, if we can hold Bonaparte here by the nose, the Prussians will kick him in the arse. We will defeat him in detail, but only if the line holds—it must! *Everything* depends upon it. We are concentrating all of our forces *here*. Wellington is moving in not only Second Corps but the Light Cavalry as well. We will be right here with you, George. We can do it!"

Just then, the sound of horses caught their attention. Vandeleur and Vivian's men began appearing behind the Allied line. Their mission was twofold: to reinforce the center and to prevent any desertions.

At the sight of the horsemen, all the life seemed to go out of Wickham's countenance. He stared at nothing for a moment, bowed his head, and then in a flat voice he replied, "I must return to my men, Denny." He turned his horse and started slowly back up the ridge.

"Of course, of course. Keep your spirits up, George! Until later— *bonne chance!*" cried Denny.

Wickham stopped and turned his face to his friend. His visage caused Denny to start.

"Good-bye, Denny."

Wickham spurred his horse forward and loped up the ridge.

Denny could not move for several moments, for the expression on Wickham's face had shaken him to his core. It was as if he had beheld a man already dead.

The emperor rode his gray horse forward, escorting his five-thousand-man-strong Imperial Guard towards the Allied line. He stopped before the ruined farmhouse at La Haye Sainte and took the salute of his most faithful soldiers. "*Vive l'Empereur*" rang out repeatedly as they filed by. With a grim look on his face, he waved at his troops.

His confident carriage belied his inner turmoil. He had risked everything to defeat the English before the Prussians entered the battle, but Grouchy, d'Erlon, and Ney had failed him—Ney most of all. He recalled his response to Ney's demand for reinforcements during his stupid cavalry attacks: "Troops? Where do you want me to get them from? Do you want me to make them?"

Now the Prussians had arrived. Grouchy, whom he had just raised to marshal, had failed to engage Blücher and keep him occupied. Failure and incompetence were all about him.

Yet the emperor still believed in his lucky star. With the fall of La Haye Sainte, the center of the English line was wide open. He could see no troops opposite. Once he split the Allied line, he would force Wellington off the field. He would then turn his attention fully upon the Prussians, a force he had already beaten two days before.

The emperor looked again at the English lines, not five hundred meters away. He saw some enemy troops moving about, but nowhere near enough to stop his Invincibles. With a nod to his still marching men, he turned his horse and rode back towards his headquarters at La Belle Alliance, already planning his assault on Blücher. Victory would be his.

It was 7:00 p.m.

The sergeant looked over as Major Wickham returned to the front lines. "Sir, are there any reinforcements coming?"

Wickham slowly dismounted and entered the pit of death that was supposed to be a square of British infantry. "I understand that Second Corps is moving to link up with the line," he started in a flat voice. He looked about at the men, lying prone. They were no longer in square; they had again formed lines, as to prepare to receive infantry. "I see we have a few Germans amongst us."

"Yes, sir. The duke himself brought them. He has ordered the men to lie down. We should only fire at the last moment."

"Good idea. I suppose we should join them." They moved a few bodies out of the way and sat on boxes.

"Major, those Frenchies. Are they—?"

"The Imperial Guard? Yes."

"Sir, are the Prussians here yet? The duke said—"

"Only God knows, sergeant," replied Wickham. The two grew silent; there was nothing left to say.

The French trumpets reverberated again, along with the strange sound of fife and drums; the marching band was advancing as well. More and more cannonballs fell around the lines. Wickham and his men turned to watch Armageddon approach slowly up the hill.

Brevet Brigadier Brandon and his brigade watched the Imperial Guard move slowly up the rise toward the center of the Allied line about a mile distant from their position. The little bit of woods protected the cavalry from French artillery fire, for the French could not hit what they could not see.

The three colonels of cavalry watched the climax of the battle, waiting the order to engage, immersed in their own thoughts:

Buford: *Too often in my life, I have thought only of myself. Now this is my chance to redeem myself—to prove myself worthy of my king, my uniform, my men, my friends—and especially my Caroline. God help me, but this is the only way to wash myself clean of my sins—through the blood of my enemies. I shall earn my place by your side, my beloved!*

Fitzwilliam: *The French are moving in a rather narrow column. Must take care, but there is an opportunity here. If we can hit them at just the right time, we can cause no little disruption to their plans. Hit and run and circle back behind them. That is the idea. Must keep the men focused.*

Brandon: *What am I doing here? Marianne was right—I am too old for these sorts of games. Oh my love, what I would give to be at Delaford now with you and Joy! But there is only one road home, and it is before me, through those men there—through Paris. I swore to you, my Marianne, that I should return to you—and I shall. God help any Frenchman who dares to stand between me and home!*

Suddenly British troops, hidden from sight along the path, seemed to appear from nowhere. The cloud of musket fire was as good a signal as any for Brandon. Wearing a borrowed Light Dragoon blue coat—something Fitzwilliam had good-naturedly insisted upon—the brigadier placed his hand upon the hilt of his sabre.

"Draw swords!" he called out as he pulled his sabre free. Immediately, eight hundred hands drew eight hundred sabres from their scabbards. The metal flashed in the fading daylight as the swords were first held up, as if to salute the enemy, before coming to rest upon the troopers' shoulders.

Brandon spurred his horse forward at a walk, not looking to see if the brigade would follow. As a man they all did so, moving slowly out of the woods in a wedge formation.

Down and across the ridge the brigade advanced, the three colonels with but one last thought in their minds: *Redemption! Victory! Home!*

First at a trot, then a canter, the brigade moved towards the battle, dodging fallen men and animals, cannonballs splashing mud about the field. Finally, Brandon lowered his sword, pointed it towards the enemy, and shouted, "SOUND THE CHARGE!"

Trumpets blaring and regimental flags flapping, a roar arose from eight hundred throats as the men rose in their saddles and leaned over their galloping mounts' necks, sabres gleaming in the sunset. Mud flying everywhere, Brandon's Brigade rode towards destiny.

Chapter 28

PAIN.

His whole existence was confusion. He was blisteringly hot and then bitingly cold. He was wet with sweat and then dry and feverish. The sky was startlingly bright and then inky darkness. There were horrific screams, there were quiet murmurings, and there was deathly silence. But always there was pain—waves of pain of varying intensity.

The last thing he could remember clearly was the charge. It was a riot of noise and images and smells. The brilliant colors of the uniforms slashed against the gray mist as his horse slammed into the enemy. He struck one cuirassier down, the man's shiny breastplate offering little protection against his sabre. He ducked just as another fired a pistol, and in the next instant, his sword made quick work of him. Again and again, he struck at men and horses, his arm rising up and slashing down a thousand times, his charger firmly beneath him as he worked like a machine.

And then—everything changed. The left side of his body exploded in pain. After that—blackness.

The rest was a dream—nay, a nightmare. A crushing weight held him down, and wet mud coated his face for what seemed an eternity. Night became day. Shadowy figures moved about him. Loud shouts and gentle arms lifted him. Lifted him—every movement blazing agony. He wondered whether it was his own voice screaming—then blessed blackness again.

The nightmare was complete when he awoke to find a stub where his left arm used to be.

He drifted in a dream world where he could escape the hot, painful fog for the mist of gentle memory. Father, mother, brothers—*his lady*! An angel with dark hair and kind eyes, smiling at him, touching him, loving him, comforting him, whispering again and again that all would be well. He lived for that dream world. He fought hard not to leave it, because all that awaited him in the other world was unending pain.

He wondered—was he dead? Was this heaven?

The pain would return, and he cried out for the angel—again and again and again.

A rough shaking of his cot woke him. He opened his eyes, and above him was the orderly who attended him—a man he had come to hate—grasping the end of the cot.

"'Ere we go," the man said to his companion, who had a similar hold on the foot of the cot. They lifted the patient and his cot and began to make their way through the hospital ward.

Sudden fear lanced through the patient. "What is happening? Where are you taking me?"

"Don't ya worry none, Colonel," said the orderly carelessly. His tone was flat, affected only by the efforts of his current task. It held no concern for the man on the cot. He might as well have been meat. "You're not fur the surgeon today, no. Ya got visitors, like. Got ta pretty ya up fur th' quality."

The sun outside was painfully glaring, so he draped his good arm over his eyes and bore the painful transit without a word of protest. Not only was it beneath an officer to complain, it would not have done a bit of good. His damn orderly had not a drop of human kindness in his black heart, he was sure of it. They were soon inside a building near the field of tents that made up the hospital outside of Brussels, and after maneuvering down a hallway, his bearers deposited him in a small room.

His orderly began to wipe his face with a wet cloth while the other tucked a fresh blanket about his body. Such were the degradations he suffered during his month in this place that he considered a clean blanket a luxury.

The orderly cursed. "Them bandages need changin'." He turned to his partner. "Nate, step over ta th' dispensary and fetch some new cloths. I've got ta clean this one up." Nate went out the door, leaving it ajar. Meanwhile, the man returned to his chore and not at all mildly. "Damn, you're a dirty one, ain't ya?"

"Here now, man—gently, if you please!" cried a voice that was somewhat familiar—proud and deep, a voice used to instant obedience. The patient *knew* that voice, but from where?

For the first time in weeks, Colonel Sir John Buford opened his eyes willingly. At the door were three people—two gentlemen and a lady. The men were instantly dismissed from Buford's attention; he focused only on the lady. She was dressed in traveling clothes, black hair peeking from under a bonnet. Her eyes were green and wet. Tender lips half-hidden by one small, gloved hand moved wordlessly. Tears ran down her cheek along skin he knew was as soft as velvet. The most dear, the most beautiful face in the world.

He gasped and croaked, "Ca… Caroline?"

Lady Caroline Buford made a sound like a hiccup. She smiled—a very teary smile—before her countenance crumbled. With a groan, she dashed to his side, pushed away the orderly, knelt, and buried her face in his chest.

"Oh, John!" she cried. "Oh, thank heaven, my John, my John."

Weakly, Buford raised his good arm and ran the fingers of his hand over her bonnet. "Caro, Caro… what are you doing here? How?" He forced his eyes from his wife to look at the gentlemen standing by. "By God!"

They were Philip Buford and Fitzwilliam Darcy.

"By God," he said again. "How came you to be here? Am I not still in Brussels?"

Philip knelt beside Caroline, and Buford reluctantly gave up his attentions to his wife to grasp his brother's hand. "It is Darcy we must thank for our transport here. Yes, this is Brussels, but you shall not be here much longer. We have come to take you home."

"Home? Home to England?"

"As soon as we get you to Antwerp and aboard the boat—yes."

Buford turned his attention to the weeping woman on his chest. "Caro, my love, this is a miracle." His hand left Philip's and slid under Caroline's bonnet. "A miracle—the babe!" Buford's eyes shot wide open. "The babe! You must leave this instant! There is disease here!" Panicked, he turned to the others. "You must get her out of here!"

She tightened her grip on her husband. "No, I will not leave you!"

"Caroline, you must!" He looked to the others. "Help me!"

"Do not concern yourself, John," said Philip. "We leave this very day. All will be well."

Meanwhile, Darcy spoke to the orderly. "We have papers that allow us to leave with Sir John. You will gather his things and bring them to our carriage."

The orderly frowned. "See 'ere, I ain't his servant!"

Darcy's voice was cold and sharp. "I have your orders. You will be paid for your services. *However*, if anything is found missing from the colonel's belongings, it will go badly for you."

"I can't be held responsible fur that!" the orderly complained.

Darcy raised his chin. "Then I would be thorough if I were you." Darcy jerked his head towards the door. The orderly, completely cowed, quickly left.

Caroline turned, sniffed, and said with a small smile, "Bravo, Darcy. I could not have done better myself."

Two spots of color graced Darcy's cheeks, but he only nodded his head. "Mr. Buford and I will see to the arrangements for our departure. We will return shortly." Philip gave his brother's shoulder a squeeze and left with Darcy.

Buford stared deeply into his wife's pale face. He could read the revulsion clearly written upon it. "Caroline, you should not have come."

"Why not? I bore the voyage well, and the babe is in no danger."

It cost him some hurt, but Buford turned his head away anyway. "You should not see me… like this."

"John, I had to come."

All the fears that had built up inside him since the battle now burst out. "What kind of husband can I be to you? I am but half a man!" He held up his left arm, the sleeve pinned back over the stump the surgeon left. "Look at me! Look at the wreck I have become! Left arm gone, face scarred, hip slashed wide open. I do not know if I will even stand again!" He did not grieve for himself; he accepted his wounds as payment for his mistrust of and infidelity to his wife. He had committed great sins against his marriage, and he earned every iota of pain he now suffered. The tears that ran unheeded down his battered face were for everything that *Caroline* had lost—a strong, faithful, useful husband who could provide for and protect his family. "You deserve better than me."

His wife's wet eyes went wide with hurt. "What madness is this?"

"Caroline, you cannot even look at me without crying."

Understanding flowed over her countenance. With fierce determination, Caroline grasped her husband's good arm. "Now you see here,

Colonel Buford!" she managed through her weeping. "I do not weep for *me*! I am pained beyond measure for *you*! I am in agony for what you have endured! Could I but bear this burden for you, I would! But since I cannot, I will have to bear it *with* you."

"But you should not have to—"

"Is that not what I promised to you and God when we married? Do you think I will shirk my duty now? What a low opinion you have of me, sir!"

"You twist my words—"

"Do you really think I will abandon you now? God's teeth, you are my very life. I will never leave you, my love—never!"

Buford wept without moderation. "Oh, Caro, my love!"

Caroline tried to kiss him, but he flinched. "Does it hurt?"

"No, but my face…"

She gently touched the undamaged right cheek. "Johnny, I kiss not your face—but *you*."

Buford painfully tried to embrace her, but he could not. His left arm had been taken off at the elbow. "Damn it! I cannot take you into my arms!"

"Oh, Johnny," she said, "do not concern yourself. I have arms enough for both of us."

When Darcy and Philip returned, they found Lady Buford half lying over Sir John in a tender embrace. The two stepped back into the hallway and gave the couple a minute's privacy before Philip coughed loudly.

"Is the carriage packed and ready, Philip?" came Caroline's voice from within.

"No," said Philip, "but it will be very soon."

"Then come back when it is. And close the door."

The two gentlemen looked at each other in embarrassment. Darcy reached out and pulled the door shut. He cleared his throat. "It is the least we can do."

"Umm... yes," agreed his companion. "Did I see some chairs on the porch?"

"I believe you did," said Darcy. "I do not think it too warm to sit outside. Do you?"

"Not at all. Very pleasant today."

"Yes. Well..." Darcy gestured towards the outside door.

The two made their way outside, took their seats, and watched the coachman load the carriage.

Chapter 29

THREE COLONELS—ONE IN red, two in blue—rode with the owner of the Darcy carriage through the streets of London on an uncommonly mild August afternoon. The four gentlemen were silent as the carriage made its way from the docks to the more fashionable part of town. Finally, the coachman brought it to a stop before the Buford townhouse. The gentlemen disembarked and climbed the few steps to the door. They were met in the foyer by the butler and Mrs. Albertine Buford.

Moments later, the group was shown into the sitting room. Awaiting them were two people: a lady in light blue and a gentleman wearing a black coat and breeches. The gentleman's struggles to rise from the sofa caused his wife some distress. She made to help, but she was gently brushed aside.

"Now, leave off, Caroline," grumbled Colonel Sir John Buford. "I will meet *these* guests on my two feet. I need no assistance."

The four men watched as Buford slowly, shakily rose, his right hand tightly gripping a cane, while the sleeve of his left arm was pinned at his elbow. He clearly favored his right leg, and his once-handsome face was scarred and bandaged. Still, his bright blue eyes were clear and only slightly pained, and once on his feet, he looped the cane about his outstretched arm and made to shake each of his guests' hands.

"Brandon, Fitzwilliam—well met! And Denny, too! By thunder, it is good to see you all again. Darcy, thank you for bringing them."

While her husband greeted his friends, Caroline watched over him with pride. "Would you gentlemen please be seated?" she asked. "Colonel Brandon, how well you look in a Dragoon uniform! Blue becomes you, I think." She then helped her husband retake his own seat.

"Caroline, may I introduce—" Buford looked again to be certain, "*Colonel* Denny? Congratulations, my friend!"

"Thank you, sir."

Buford turned to Fitzwilliam and grinned. "I understand you are to get the Bath, Fitz. It could not happen to a better fellow!"

"Shall we call you Sir Richard, now?" asked Caroline.

Sir Richard laughed. "From you, I would prefer Richard or Fitz. I know I will never get anything else out of Buford!"

Sir John chuckled as his wife continued. "And you, Colonel Brandon—I thought you a brigadier."

Brandon smiled. "It was my temporary rank during the occupation, my lady. I shall retire at my permanent rank, but with the Light Dragoons rather than the Life Guards." He looked at Buford. "I will never wear any uniform except Dragoon blue from now on."

Buford nodded in understanding. "So, tell me of your occupation duty in Paris. Was there any trouble?"

Caroline watched as Sir John conversed easily with his former comrades, now as dear to her as they were to her husband. In Brussels, she had learned that these three men searched the Waterloo battlefield relentlessly for hours for a sign of Sir John. They were the ones who carried his battered body back to the surgeons. If not for Brandon, Denny, and Fitzwilliam, Caroline knew she would be wearing black instead of light blue this night. These men saved her husband's life. Tears pricked at her eyes.

The same thought must have occupied Mrs. Albertine Buford, as a sob escaped her lips as she rose slightly unsteadily to her feet. "If you gentlemen would excuse me," she apologized, "I should see to the tea." Lifting a hand, she forestalled her daughter. "No, my dear, stay and entertain your guests."

The gentlemen were uneasy, and Sir John was concerned, but Caroline explained, "All is well, gentlemen. My mother is... very thankful for all you have done. She has lost so much already."

The atmosphere sobered, and Sir Richard looked hard at Sir John. "Buford, I want you to know—we all want you to know that... well if you need anything, any assistance, you have but to ask."

Brandon quieted Richard with a hand on his shoulder. "What Fitzwilliam means is that, as well as our friend, you are our comrade. Whatever you need done, we shall do it, if it be in our power. We swear it." Colonel Denny nodded in agreement.

Buford's face darkened, Darcy shifted uncomfortably in his chair, and Caroline remembered her husband's response to a similar offer from Darcy only a fortnight before. She prayed his reaction would not be as abrupt.

Buford spoke sharply. "I thank you for your kind offer, gentlemen, but I am not the useless cripple I appear, I assure you!"

Caroline took Buford's hand. "John," she whispered.

The two locked eyes, a message only the two of them could decipher flowed between them, and Buford's countenance softened. "Forgive me, my friends." He looked down, his eyes blinking. "I know you mean well, and I thank you for your kindness, but it is unnecessary." He raised his face, his emotions back under control. "My days of soldiering are done, and I must find my own way in the world. It is not so bad; a man can do much with a bad leg and one arm. Besides, I have my rock with me." With that, he kissed his blushing wife's hand. "No better nurse ever lived, by

God. She took care to understand every instruction from the physician. She made certain I exercised every day without fail and stood by my side the whole time, badgering me when I wanted to quit and making me rest if I pushed too hard. The only reason I can stand today is because of her. A fine drillmaster she would make."

Caroline was beet-red. "John, please!"

His response was to kiss her hand again, sigh, and smile at the others. "We shall return to Wales. Caroline and I will be with Mother in the dowager house. Buford Manor is being enlarged as we speak, and we shall remove there in the spring."

He glanced at Caroline, who touched the six-month-along bulge in her midsection that her shawl had failed to conceal. "My child shall be raised as a Buford should—in Wales," he vowed. "We shall be very comfortable. You must come and see us once we are established at Buford Manor."

"Are you going to farm, sir?" asked Denny.

"No, I leave that to Philip. I have a fancy to stand for office once I recover my strength. I suppose one can give as good a speech in the Commons with one arm as two, eh, Darcy?"

"Do not bring me into this," cried Darcy. "Politics has no attraction for me." Darcy intended to leave that to his brother Tucker.

While the others shared a hearty laugh, Darcy's eye fell upon Lady Buford. He could only marvel at the strange twists life could take. It was finally obvious to him that this woman was no longer the Caroline Bingley he had once known. *That* person was cold, grasping, and rude—a selfish member of the *ton*. But this lady was everything that person was not. During the whole of this terrible month, to his surprise, she had carried herself with dignity and grace, thinking only of others. Buford did not lie when he named Caroline as the most attentive of nurses. Darcy had been a witness to it, and he had to admit that he had underestimated the lady.

What was the difference? Had her soul been forged for the better in the fires of pain and anguish like the saints of old? He did not know. All he knew was that Elizabeth and he could not be fond of Miss Caroline Bingley, but that, for the rest of their lives, they would name Lady Caroline Buford among their dearest friends.

Caroline looked over at the door. "*Frau* Lippermann, *ist der Tee bereit?*"

"*Ja, Frau* Caroline. Here is *de Kaffee.*"

The new assistant housekeeper brought in a pot of coffee while Helga carried a dessert behind her. "Tea—just *vone* minute, *thankyou verymuch.*"

"*Danke.*" Caroline received the plate from Helga; meanwhile Mrs. Albertine Buford, now composed, rejoined the party. "Mother Buford, will you pour the coffee?" She smiled at her guests. "Philip arranged for *Frau* Lippermann and Helga to emigrate from Austria. Was that not considerate of him? We have been practicing; I speak German to them, and they speak English to me. With two Mrs. Bufords in the dowager house, we are *Frau* Albertine and *Frau* Caroline."

Sir John laughed. "It is well I speak German, else I would be forever wondering what mischief was about!"

Caroline gave a loving look to her husband, a gesture whose meaning escaped the others' understanding.

She then said, "Richard, may I offer you some of this *Meranertorte?* I must insist you have some. It is simply divine."

An hour and a half later, the same carriage made its way to Darcy House. The gentlemen inside were just as solemn as before, if not as quiet.

"So, you still plan to leave for Delaford in the morning, Brandon?" Darcy asked.

"Yes—thank you for inviting me for the night. It saves me the cost of an inn." Christopher never would open Brandon House just for one night.

Darcy turned to his cousin. "And you, Richard, are you still for Longbourn with us?"

"Yes, I will pay my respects to Mrs. Wickham, then I am off to Kent."

"Going to beard the lioness in her own den?" teased his cousin.

Sir Richard patted his coat where he kept two letters next to his heart—one he received in April, the other in June. "I have all the armor I need right here, Cuz. I have faced Napoleon's hordes. What is an elderly aunt to me?"

Before more could be said, the carriage reached its destination. As the party approached the door, it was flung open by the mistress of the house herself. She greeted her husband passionately, her cousin affectionately, and the others very cordially. Darcy escorted the group into the front hall, Elizabeth on his arm.

"Oh, Richard, I neglected to tell you that family business has come up," said Darcy. "Would you join me in the library?"

"Now?" cried Sir Richard. "I have just arrived! Can it not wait?"

"Richard, it is *family business*," repeated his cousin gravely.

"Oh, for heaven's sake! Are you ever on holiday from business? I wanted to spend some time with Elizabeth and Georgiana, but apparently, there is nothing for it! Come on, then—let us get to it!" Disappointed and aggravated, Sir Richard stormed into Darcy's library. There he found a lady waiting for him.

Sir Richard was frozen for a moment, trying to believe his eyes. Anne de Bourgh, in a beautiful blue gown, stood smiling at him. Then, with three quick steps, Richard seized his beloved's face between his hands, and, for the first time, thoroughly kissed her. Anne's arms went quickly around his neck and pulled him even closer.

Darcy discreetly backed out of the room and closed the door.

Colonel Brandon, who had seen all, chuckled in the hall. "Now, *that* is a proper greeting for a returning soldier," he remarked to Elizabeth as she led him into the parlor. There he found his own surprise.

"Christopher!" cried Marianne Brandon as she leapt into his arms.

Brandon tried to speak, but he found that he could not for all his wife's kisses.

As Elizabeth turned to Colonel Denny after closing the parlor door, she saw the officer looking about with wide, nervous eyes. "May I help you, Colonel?" she asked.

"I do not know, Mrs. Darcy. You do not have Miss Augusta Liverpool lurking about anywhere, do you?"

"No. Pray, who is Miss Liverpool?"

A relieved Denny said, "Someone I hope is *not* waiting for me."

Elizabeth laughed gaily while Darcy patted the officer on the back. "You are safe from Miss Liverpool. Come into the sitting room. I promise that all that awaits you are my sister and cucumber sandwiches."

Sir Richard and Anne finally came up for air. "I have so much to tell you," they cried in unison.

"You first, Anne."

"No, you first."

Richard kissed Anne again. "Your last letter—is it true? We are engaged?"

"Well, what do you expect for compromising me?"

Sir Richard's face broke into a wide grin. "Anne de Bourgh, I love you."

Anne smiled cheekily in return. "That is well, for I adore you!"

"You know, I have not kissed you before today."

"Egad, we have been engaged for over two months! We have some catching up to do."

"Marianne, my Marianne, I cannot believe it." Christopher stroked her face.

"I am no dream, m'love."

"Why did you not tell me you would be in London?"

"I wanted to surprise you."

"You did that. Wait, whose idea was this?"

"Mine, why do you ask?"

"It sounds like something Mrs. Darcy would plan."

"Well, she helped."

Christopher kissed her forehead. "My love, where is Joy? Back at Delaford?"

"As if your daughter would permit that!"

"What do you mean? She is here?"

"If by here you mean Darcy House, no. She awaits her papa at Brandon House." At his look she added, "Oh no, Christopher! We must remain for some little time—for form's sake, at least. Joy is napping now, in any case. Let us rejoin the Darcys."

The party sat comfortably around the sitting room. The Brandons took up most of one couch, Marianne practically draped over her husband. Denny was embarrassed, and Georgiana was slightly shocked, but the Darcys looked upon their friends with a lenient eye. Sir Richard and Anne had yet to make their appearance.

Elizabeth addressed Colonel Denny. "Thank you for volunteering to come to Longbourn with us. I trust Mrs. Wickham will appreciate your kindness. I am instructed to tell you that she personally thanks you for your compassionate letter to my family."

The colonel colored slightly. "It is the least I can do, Mrs. Darcy. It is I who must thank you—for lodgings here tonight and for transport tomorrow." Denny was traveling with the Darcys to Meryton to offer his personal condolences to Lydia. She and the children had removed to Longbourn at the report of Wickham's death.

"Think nothing of it," said Darcy. "We shall leave tomorrow after breakfast to collect Mrs. Tucker, and thence to Hertfordshire."

Georgiana stuttered, "Were you there, Colonel... when..." She could not finish.

Denny struggled over what to say. "Yes, I was there, but I did not see Major Wickham fall." He in good conscience could not tell the girl the whole truth. Wickham had awaited Napoleon's approaching Imperial Guard like a man in anticipation of his execution. When Denny found Wickham's body after the battle, he saw that a cannonball had practically cut his old friend in half. No, Denny would never share those visions. They were forever entombed along with Wickham in a grave at Waterloo. "He fought well, but so did many others we left behind us in Belgium."

"I understand that Richard was made a knight," Georgiana continued. "Do you receive any award?"

"No, Miss Darcy, save that my brevet promotion to colonel was made permanent. That is award enough for me."

"Why is that?"

Denny smiled. "I will now have money enough to marry, Miss Darcy." Georgiana blushed.

Darcy asked, "So you plan to remain in the army, Denny?"

"Yes, sir. I find the military life suits me."

"What is your next post?" asked Christopher.

"For now, I am to return to Horse Guards. But I think I will put in for a transfer to India next year."

"Why India?" asked Georgiana.

"A colonel's pay goes further there, and I hope to work towards promotion, Miss Darcy."

Elizabeth smiled. She could read between the lines better than most, and Colonel Denny's attentions to the Widow Wickham had been very marked. She wondered whether Lydia would like living in India.

Sir Richard and Anne finally entered the sitting room, walking in hand in hand. Elizabeth, Marianne, and Georgiana embraced the couple with cries of delight. It was some time before the pair could sit down upon a sofa.

"If you do not mind, Darcy," Sir Richard said, "I think there will be a change of plans."

"I thought there might. Kent or Derbyshire?"

"Rosings first—Lady Catherine deserves at least that." Sir Richard then grinned. "Besides, I need to survey my new properties now that harvest time grows near."

"Do you think you will enjoy farming, sir?" asked Denny.

He gave the younger man a stern look. "Denny, we are comrades now. You may call me…" he hesitated, and then with dramatic importance, "*Sir Richard.*"

A pause—then Fitzwilliam dissolved into laughter.

"Denny, if you call that fool anything but Fitz, I will personally cuff you," demanded an amused Christopher.

After a poke from Anne, Sir Richard stopped laughing. "I think I will like it well enough, Denny. I know I will fancy the accommodations." He started chuckling again when he noted that Anne was not amused. "What is it, my dear?" She simply gave him an arch look. "What?"

"Oh, do not be cross, Cousin," cried Georgiana. "Tell us of Richard's proposal!"

"You have hit upon the heart of the matter, Georgiana," Anne responded. "There has been no proposal!"

"What? Then how are you engaged?"

"You had a hand in that," Anne said with a look.

"Oh, the letters!" Georgiana blushed while Denny simply looked confused.

Anne nodded in confirmation. "Yes, we have compromised ourselves! We *wrote* to each other, Colonel Denny, and there is nothing for it but to marry! Which is all fine and good, but it would be nice actually to receive a *proposal*," she turned to her intended, "especially as Colonel Sir Richard Fitzwilliam acts as if Rosings Park is his already!" She gave Richard a *de Bourgh* glare.

Sir Richard looked thoughtfully at Anne for a moment and then away. "Hmm, we cannot have that." He began to stand.

"Richard?" Anne was afraid her teasing had gone too far and she had offended her beloved.

But abruptly, Sir Richard threw himself at her feet. On one knee, with one hand on his breast and the other raised to the heavens, he declared, "Sweetest, loveliest Anne! You are the light of my life, the song in my soul, the starch in my stockings—"

"The starch in your stockings?"

"Quiet, woman, you are ruining the moment. Where was I? Ah yes, I cannot live without you! Would you—could you—might you—consider taking pity on this poor fool? I offer all that I have—an old warhorse and a slightly used sabre. What treasure! All I own and my heart. Say yes and make me the happiest man in the world! Reject me, and call for the undertaker the next instant, for I shall surely die of a broken heart. My fate is in your hands, my lady."

He lowered his face into his hands for a moment before peeking up at her. He beheld a smirking Anne, trying not to giggle. He could not see the various looks of his audience, ranging from delight to amusement to astonishment. "Marry me, Annie?"

She smiled sweetly. "Of course! Before you inflict yourself on some other unfortunate lady."

Sir Richard sweetly kissed each of Anne's hands before retaking his seat next to her. "How was that, Georgiana?"

His cousin just shook her head as the others exploded into laughter.

The three colonels took their leave of each other before the Fitzwilliam family's London townhouse. Darcy had arranged for the house to be opened, for Sir Richard and Colonel Denny could not remain at Darcy House while Anne was in residence. Denny would be retrieved in the morning by the Darcy party when Anne and Mrs. Jenkinson were delivered for their journey to Kent with Richard.

"Good-bye, Denny. Mind the army for me," said Christopher. "I expect you will be a general 'ere long."

"Thank you, sir."

"Denny, I am Brandon to you."

"Brigadier," cried Denny, using Brandon's brevet title, "you will *always* be sir to me." He snapped off a salute, which Christopher returned.

Marianne embraced the younger man. "May you obtain your heart's desire, Colonel."

"All things in God's time," he replied with a grin. Denny estimated that Lydia would require only six months of mourning before she would allow him to make his intentions known.

Christopher and Sir Richard shook each other's hands. "Congratulations, Fitz. I know you will be happy."

"Thank you, Brandon. Give my love to that daughter of yours. Marianne, farewell."

She kissed his cheek. "Until the wedding, I suppose. I am so happy for you and Anne! Safe journey." She turned, and Brandon helped her back into the carriage.

Christopher turned back to the others, one foot in the carriage. "Good-bye, friends! Drive on, driver!"

As the carriage moved away, Marianne moved into her husband's arms, a place she planned to spend much time in the future—perhaps the rest of her life.

"I cannot help thinking of poor Sir John. Had it been you—oh, I cannot bear it! I shall speak of it no more!"

"Hush, m'love. Do not worry. I have put in my papers. I will fight no more forever."

"I was so proud of you yet frightened for you at the same time. I might be a coward, but I want you home in our bed, never to leave again."

He kissed her tenderly. "I wish to be nowhere else, my Marianne,"—he started to smile—"although it will be a crowded place soon, I trust. When is the baby due?"

"Around New Years. Maybe it will be a Christmas baby."

Christopher counted backwards. "After, I should think."

"Perhaps. Do you think Joy will like a baby brother?"

"You do not know it will be a boy."

"I was right about the other thing. You must trust me on this."

Christopher gave up with an amused shake of his head. After all, she might be right. "I have but one request. If the babe is a boy, his name must be John Richard."

She looked at his face with tears in her eyes. "Perfect—and Sir John and Caroline shall be his godparents."

As Christopher bent to kiss her again, he murmured, "Perfect."

There were no more sounds from the Brandon carriage as it rolled through the London night towards home and Joy.

Epilogue

THE EMPEROR STOOD ON the deck of the *Northumberland*, a seventy-four-gun, third-rate ship-of-the-line, one hand holding a stay, fighting off seasickness while surveying the horizon for his new realm. He was as rigid as stone; the only movement of his body was his eyes. Three months to the day had passed since he stepped upon the deck of the HMS *Bellerophon* off Rochefort and into the hands of his enemies.

The officer of the deck, the ship's second lieutenant, was at his station upon the quarterdeck, trying to keep his mind on his business. Yet, the young Englishman could not prevent his eyes from returning to the living statue. He knew all aboard had been ordered to refer to the ship's honored guest as "*Monsieur*" or "General," rather than some of the less-flattering names British tars had devised for the Destroyer of Mankind. However, the lieutenant could not think of the man as anything but the emperor.

The lieutenant wondered what the emperor was thinking. Once, this man was Emperor of the French, near-conqueror of Europe, the most dangerous and feared man in the world. Now, he was a powerless prisoner on his way to exile.

There would be no escape for him from this prison, the lieutenant reflected. Saint Helena was in the middle of the bloody South Atlantic Ocean.

To make sure that the emperor would spend his last days there, the lords of the Admiralty had decreed that a squadron of warships should keep station off the god-forsaken piece of rock until *Monsieur* Bonaparte was no more.

"LAND HO!" cried the lookout.

"WHERE AWAY?" returned the lieutenant.

"TWO POINTS OFF THE STARBOARD BOW!"

A half-dozen telescopes were clapped to a half-dozen eyes, but it was useless. From the deck, the island was still below the horizon. As he lowered his instrument, the lieutenant noticed that the statue had come to life. The emperor strained to see the isle, standing on tiptoe. The officer almost handed him the telescope but thought the better of it.

Turning to a midshipman, the lieutenant said, "Give the captain my compliments and report land two points off the starboard bow."

The youngster repeated the order and scurried below decks. Within minutes, the captain was on deck, placing his hat on his head and ignoring the salute, all the off-duty officers following in his wake.

By now, the emperor was completely still again.

"Where away?" the captain demanded.

The lieutenant pointed out the reported direction as others, mainly the emperor's entourage, emerged from below and began to fill the decks. Patiently, the captain peered through his telescope until the island was revealed. By now, those on deck could make out the dark spot on the horizon.

Turning to the midshipman, the captain said, "My compliments to the admiral and report that we have raised Saint Helena." The lad saluted and left.

In the minutes that followed, as the *Northumberland* sailed on, Saint Helena was shown to be the ugliest and most dismal rock conceivable, rising like an enormous black wart from the bowels of the deep. The emperor and all aboard watched in silence as the ship grew ever closer to the ends of the earth.

The End

BIBLIOGRAPHY, SOURCES, AND SUGGESTED READING

Austen, Jane, *Pride and Prejudice*
——, *Sense and Sensibility*
Coote, Stephen, *Napoleon and the Hundred Days*, 2005
Cornwell, Bernard, *Waterloo*, 1990
Heyer, Georgette, *An Infamous Army: A Novel of Wellington, Waterloo, Love and War*, 1937
Moore, Richard, *The Napoleonic Guide*, 1999–2009 www.napoleonguide.com
O'Brian, Patrick, *The Hundred Days*, 1998
Roberts, Andrew, *Napoleon & Wellington*, 2001
——, *Waterloo*, 2005
Schneider, John, *Napoleonic Literature, The Anglo-Allied Army Order of Battle*, 1996–2010 www.napoleonic-literature.com/Waterloo_OB/Allied.htm
——, *Napoleonic Literature, L'Armée du Nord Order of Battle*, 1996–2010 www.napoleonic-literature.com/Waterloo_OB/French.htm

READ ON FOR AN EXCERPT FROM

NOW AVAILABLE FROM
SOURCEBOOKS LANDMARK

Prologue

Oh, I wish I was in the land of cotton
Old times there are not forgotten
Look away! Look away! Look away! Dixie Land.

In Dixie Land where I was born in
Early on one frosty mornin'
Look away! Look away! Look away! Dixie Land.

Oh, I wish I was in Dixie!
Hooray! Hooray!
In Dixie Land I'll take my stand
To live and die in Dixie
Away, away, away down south in Dixie!

"Dixie" by Daniel Decatur Emmett, 1859

Vicksburg, Mississippi—May 22, 1863

THE DAY WAS SEVERAL hot, stifling hours old when the young, gray-clad captain of infantry once again peeked carefully over the ramparts of his position into the morning sun, telescope in hand. He saw nothing, but he was not deceived. Since the initial assault upon their location three days ago, the enemy had tirelessly moved men and materiel into position for another attack. The sounds of horses and cannon wheels had been constant since before daybreak. The heavily wooded hilly terrain was not only perfect for defense but also for hiding the maneuvers of their attacker.

"Them Yankee boys are gettin' ready to come a'visitin' again, Cap'n?" a voice whispered into his ear.

William Darcy, captain in the Texas Legion, Confederate States Army, turned his bright blue eyes to his sergeant beside him and wiped a dirty hand across his beard-covered chin before answering. "My compliments to the colonel, and report that the enemy is moving forward."

No sooner had the man offered the barest of salutes and moved away from the front lines than the woods opposite exploded with noise. Darcy's screams of warning were unnecessary as men ducked from the incoming cannon fire. Darcy lay at the bottom of the trench like the others, keeping his head as low as possible. On an impulse, the twenty-year-old officer pulled out the pocket watch his father had given him for his birthday two years before.

Ten o'clock exactly.

The cannonballs began to fall behind the lines towards Vicksburg itself. Darcy knew what that was about even before the cries of the enemy reached his ears. He pulled out his sword and stood in a low crouch.

"To the line, boys, to the line! The enemy is upon us! Give 'em hell!"

The bedraggled Texans, in various uniforms of Confederate gray, rushed to the ramparts, muskets in hand, screaming the Rebel Yell that had terrified more than one Union solider since Bull Run. Just in time, too, as the first of the men in blue were mere yards away. Darcy's view of the attackers disappeared behind a cloud of smoke as the muskets fired in a volley. The smoke cleared to show a score of figures in dirty blue scattered on the bare ground before the earthworks, but there were a hundred more advancing. The first line of defenders fell back to reload as the second line took their places.

"Fire at will!" Darcy yelled as he drew his Colt revolver. "Fire at will!"

Time lost all meaning as Darcy fired into the advancing horde again and again. The Texans knew that their position, straddling a rail line, was a key point in the defense of Vicksburg, and they fought desperately against the Union soldiers, who were just as desperate to take it. The din was deafening as gunfire, explosions, and screams blended into an unearthly sound.

Darcy had ducked down to reload his pistol for the third time when he noted that the noise had abated a bit. Creeping up, he saw through the smoke and haze that the Yankees were pulling back in good order. He ordered his men to cease firing and conserve their precious ammunition as he glanced at his watch again.

Ten fifteen.

Darcy and his company had been relieved about midday as fresh troops took up their position in the lunette[1]. They were resting as well as they could, with the occasional cannonball falling throughout the afternoon, when they were approached by a group of officers on horseback. The commander of the legion, Colonel Waul, spoke to them.

"Men, we've got some Yankees that have broken through at the redoubt. They're a stubborn bunch, an' I need some volunteers to help clear the vermin out. Are you with me?"

Darcy looked at his men. "Sir, how many do you need?"

"A score will do, Captain. We muster down the lane here." With that, the party rode off. Darcy rose to his feet and looked around. A good two

---

1 A fortification that has two projecting faces and two parallel flanks.

JACK CALDWELL

dozen men volunteered, and soon the detail moved off to the rendezvous point. They joined up with others and the plan was formed. By late afternoon, the force moved into position near the railroad redoubt.

Darcy could see men in blue hiding in the trenches or behind shelter. He knew this assault would be costly.

A shout went up, and the Texans charged. Darcy ran before his men, the Colt in his right hand and a sword in his left. The men to either side fired their muskets on the run and continued the charge, bayonets gleaming in the afternoon light. The enemy returned fire from their positions, but even as men fell around him, Darcy knew it was too little, too late. They were almost upon them. The Union soldiers began to fall back in some disorder. Darcy bared his teeth as he smelled the impending victory…

There was a mighty explosion, and Darcy experienced a feeling of flying before the world crashed into his face.

Will Darcy knew nothing, except that he hurt. Hurt all over. Hurt *bad*.

After a while, he was able to discern something besides the ever-present pain: a low murmuring in the background of his darkness. It took a moment before he realized that it was the sound of men groaning and crying. Darcy opened his eyes to behold a dark, uneven ceiling, lit by the light of lanterns.

He suddenly realized that he could only see out of one eye. In a panic, he raised a hand to his face and tried to sit up. A wave of agony crashed into him, and he could not prevent crying out as he fell back.

Darcy heard voices close by. "Doc—Doc—this one's wakin' up." A moment later a face came into his limited field of vision.

"Captain, how are you feeling?"

Like I'm about to die! his mind screamed. He peered closely at the man. About Darcy's own age, the young man had a broad, flushed face and light-colored hair. It was a face that usually would be happy, he considered. That it wasn't was a cause for concern.

"H... hurt," was all Darcy could manage.

"I should think you do," the unknown man said in a soft Georgia accent with a hint of a smile. The break in the man's serious mien was comforting.

Darcy waved a hand before his face. "E... eye?"

"Rest easy," the man said. "Your eyes are undamaged. You have a serious injury to your forehead, and the bandage must cover one eye. You're in a hospital, Captain, in a cave to protect y'all from the incoming artillery... Don't sit up!" he cried as Darcy moved. "Do you want to lose that leg?"

His patient lay still in fear.

The man grew grim. "Good thing you were insensible when your men brought you in. I had to do a bit of digging to get all the shrapnel out. You've lost quite a bit of blood, Captain. We must keep your leg still and clean, or the gangrene may set in. Do you understand?"

Darcy managed a nod, which only hurt like blazes. He determined he was speaking to a surgeon, as he could now make out the dried blood all over the man's apron.

"Good," the doctor grinned in return. "I must see to my other patients, but I shall stop by later. Rest, sir, and you'll be up and walking again."

As the doctor began to turn, Darcy fought to speak. "Th... thanks. D... Darcy."

The doctor turned in surprise. "I beg your pardon?"

Darcy gestured again. "D... Darcy."

"Ah," the man breathed in realization. "Captain Darcy, is it?"

Darcy nodded.

He smiled. "Charles Bingley, at your service."

Meryton, Ohio—June 20

"Beth! Beth, come back!"

The thirteen-year-old girl disregarded her mother's voice as she ran out the back door. Almost blinded by her tears, she managed to reach the large chestnut tree next to the barn without running into anything. The girl threw herself against the trunk, her body shuddering in sobs.

It was there her older sister found her, kneeling by the tree. Wordlessly, the blond girl gathered her sister into her arms, their hair blowing in the breeze.

"Beth—oh, Beth!" she tried to console the child.

"H… he can't be dead!" Beth Bennet sobbed. "Samuel can't be dead! He can't be, Jane!"

"Beth…" Jane began.

"He promised to come back. You… you heard him. He promised!"

Jane bit her lip as she continued to stroke Beth's curly brown hair, her own tears quietly streaming down her face. She could hear her mother and other sisters wailing in the house, an uproar that began a half-hour before as her father read the words of that hated telegram:

"We regret to inform you that…"

"Beth—oh, Beth!" was all Jane could manage. Her own distress was great. Samuel Bennet, the eldest of the Bennet children and the only son, proud corporal in the Ohio infantry, gone to save the Union as part of the mighty Army of the Potomac, had died of influenza in Maryland. Samuel was beloved by all of his family, but Beth was particularly fond of him. Jane might be Beth's confidante, but Samuel was her hero and could do no wrong. Jane could only hold her sister, allowing her to cry herself out.

Finally, as Beth's sobs subsided, Jane said, "Beth, we must return to the house and see to our parents and sisters. We cannot add to their distress. We must be strong, Beth."

"S… Samuel was always strong, Jane."

"Yes, he was. Now, it is our turn. Our family needs us." She took the girl's face in her hands. "It is what *he* would want."

Beth nodded. Their mother loved her only son almost as fiercely as Beth, and their father doted on him. *They* would be shattered, leaving the three younger sisters little comfort.

Jane got to her feet and helped Beth up. Hand in hand, they turned to return to the house. As they walked, Jane heard Beth mumble something and asked her about it.

"I said it is *their* fault, Jane," she spat.

"Whose fault?"

"Those damned Rebels!"

"Beth, please!" Jane cried. "Please don't talk like that in front of Mother or Mary! You know how they feel about coarse language."

"Very well, but I'll never forgive those evil slave-owning Rebels—never! It's their fault Samuel went away. Those evil, evil people! I hope God smites them. I hate them! I will hate them for the rest of my life!"

In Appreciation

My thanks go to Debbie Styne, Ellen Pickels, Mary Anne Mushatt, Sarah Hunt, Grace Regan, and Amy Robertson, who worked endless hours editing this work.

I could not have done it without all of you.

ABOUT THE AUTHOR

Jack Caldwell, a native of Louisiana living in the Midwest, is an author, amateur historian, professional economic developer, playwright, and, like many Cajuns, a darn good cook. Mr. Caldwell has been a history buff and a fan of Miss Austen for many years. He is the author of *Pemberley Ranch*. A devout convert to Roman Catholicism, he is married with three sons.

Darcy and Fitzwilliam

by Karen V. Wasylowski

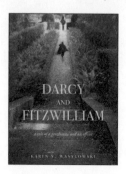

A tale of a gentleman and an officer

Fitzwilliam Darcy and Colonel Fitzwilliam couldn't be more different, and that goes for the way each one woos and pursues the woman of his dreams. Darcy is quiet and reserved, careful and dutiful, and his qualms and hesitations are going to torpedo his courtship of Elizabeth. Colonel Fitzwilliam is a military hero whose devil-may-care personality hides the torments within, until he finds himself in a passionate, whirlwind affair with a beautiful widow who won't hear of his honorable intentions.

Cousins, best friends, and sparring partners, Darcy and Fitzwilliam have always been there for each other. So it's no surprise when the only one who can help Darcy fix his botched marriage proposals is Fitzwilliam, and the only one who can pull Fitzwilliam out of an increasingly dangerous entanglement is Darcy...

Praise for Karen V. Wasylowski:

"Her work is page turning, humorous, maddening, and touching. This is a fine edition to the ever-growing library of Austenesque novels."—*The Calico Critic*

For a celebration of all things Jane Austen, visit:

www.austenfans.com